The RESTORER

THE SWORD OF LYRIC

1

SHARON HINCK

NAVPRESS®

BRINGING TRUTH TO LIFE

OUR GUARANTEE TO YOU

We believe so strongly in the message of our books that we are making this quality guarantee to you. If for any reason you are disappointed with the content of this book, return the title page to us with your name and address and we will refund to you the list price of the book. To help us serve you better, please briefly describe why you were disappointed. Mail your refund request to: NavPress, P.O. Box 35002, Colorado Springs, CO 80935.

NavPress
P.O. Box 35001
Colorado Springs, Colorado 80935

Published in association with the literary agency of The Steve Laube Agency, LLC, 5501 N. 7th. Ave., #502, Phoenix, AZ 85013.

ISBN-13: 978-1-60006-131-8
ISBN-10: 1-60006-131-1

Cover design by Kirk DouPonce, www.dogeareddesign.com
Photo of woman by Stephen Gardner, www.ShootPW.com
Author photo by Ritz Camera Proex Portraits

Creative Team: Jeff Gerke, Reagen Reed, Arvid Wallen, Kathy Guist

This novel is a work of fiction. Names, characters, places, and incidents are either the product of the author's imagination or are used fictitiously. Any resemblance to actual events, locales, organizations, or persons, living or dead, is entirely coincidental and beyond the intent of either the author or publisher.

Hinck, Sharon.
  The restorer : a novel / Sharon Hinck.
    p. cm. -- (The sword of lyric ; bk. 1)
  ISBN-13: 978-1-60006-131-8
  ISBN-10: 1-60006-131-1
  I. Title.
PS3608.I53R47 2007
813'.6--dc22
                              2006100494

Printed in the United States of America

1 2 3 4 5 6 7 8 9 10 / 10 09 08 07

to all wanderers and pilgrims

Acknowledgments

MORE THAN ANY OTHER BOOK I'VE developed, this project has been touched and blessed by many hands. My dearest thanks go to Ted, my first reader, first love, and first-rate soul mate; my children, Joel, Kaeti, Josh, and Jenni; and my lovely daughter-in-law, Jennelle, for their constant support and lively conversations about characters.

My women's small group Bible study—dear women who formed the model for Susan because of their heroic passion for God—prayed with me when I said, "I have this very strange story to tell, and I'm wondering if God might want it to be published." They are my heroes, along with our amazing church life group at St. Michael's.

The Restorer would not have been birthed without Word Servants Writer's group. Thank you for constant enthusiasm and savvy suggestions. I still remember your faces around the table in Margaret's office as I nervously brought you a new chapter.

Many professionals in the publishing world helped me in elements of the journey. I feel humble gratitude for Randy Ingermanson, who took me under his wing and enjoyed my constant confusion at my first writers conference; for Karen Hancock, who relentlessly turned my focus back to the One who is really in control; for Jan Dennis, who instantly saw the vision of the work and honored me with his willingness to have faith in something so unlikely; for Steve Laube (a.k.a. Agent Extraordinaire), who went above and beyond to secure a happy home for this project; for Jeff Gerke, who talked me into telling him about it and then fought to bring it to life; for Reagen Reed, a remarkable editor who made the process of refining an exhilarating joy; and for all the NavPress staff. No matter what other challenges they were facing, they always took time to show me that they cared about this project.

I've also been fed, nurtured, and educated through writer friends and colleagues from Mount Hermon Writers Conference, American Christian Fiction Writers, The Writer's View, Christian Authors Network, and Minnesota Christian Writers Guild. I've seen some of the dearest and best of the heart of Jesus amongst you, dear ones.

I give huge thanks to critique partners who followed chapter-by-chapter as I wrote, pointed at plausibility holes, circled commas, and never hesitated to say, "do over" when a scene needed honing. Sherri Sand, Cheryl Bader, Carol Oyanagi, Jill Nelson, and Kelli Standish gave particularly lavish time to this project. You are all insightful, wise, and wonderful.

Great appreciation goes to my earliest test readers, who offered helpful feedback, as well as an unflagging cheering section. Kristin Melendez, Sue Bosshardt, Becky McClain, Nancy and Sarah Muyskens, Deb Kellogg, Carl Olsen, Vicki and Jon Lorton, Marci Mohan, all the Word Servants, and many more. I'm so glad you will no longer have to pass around a tattered manuscript to your friends, with whom you want to share the book.

Special appreciation goes to my mom, Flossie Marxen, who

raved about each chapter and kept me writing fast by clamoring for more.

Also, many thanks to all the prayer supporters who stood in the gap when battles loomed. My "Book Buddies" are the true guardians of this series. If you'd like to join their number, visit www.sharonhinck.com and sign up at the "Contact Sharon" page.

My most sweet and tender gratitude goes to the One who called me on this journey and has been faithful to reveal Himself as my comforter, defender, and strong tower. Through Your Son Jesus, You have truly restored my soul.

Chapter One

THE ATTIC HIDEAWAY WAS ALL MARK'S idea. He meant to be helpful, and I admit he had good reason to be worried about me.

I couldn't seem to cope with the little things anymore—scrubbing jam off the kitchen counter for the millionth time, carrying decaying science projects out to the garbage, answering the constant questions from two teens and two grade-schoolers. Was I the only person in the house who knew where to find clean socks?

Self-help books told me to regroup—find time to feed my soul. But when I'd sit at the kitchen table with my journal, the children would fly toward me like metal filings to a magnet.

Mark had noticed how often I'd been snapping at the kids. More troubling than my short temper, a heavy fog had settled on me. It pressed down with growing weight and separated me from everyone else. I didn't have the energy to care anymore.

One day, in his typical determination to fix things, Mark pulled me toward our back hallway. "Susan, I have a plan."

He must not have heard my groan because he kept talking. "I can build some pull-down stairs into the attic. We'll clean it up, and you can have a place to get away once in a while."

Mark had the remodeling gleam in his eyes. He was a gladiator in that moment—about to charge into his favorite arena. Every project he took on resulted in lots of whacking and pounding until some wall or closet or tile surrendered to him. Then he would shake his drill over his head and roar in victory.

I sighed. "I guess it would be nice to have a space off-limits to the kids. I could leave my journal out and not find it doodled on with gel pens the next time I opened it."

Would a hideaway really end my cranky outbursts—the only times I seemed to feel any energy? I couldn't muster much faith that this attic room would cure the malaise swallowing me. But Mark never met a problem that couldn't be solved by a trip to the hardware store. So I surrendered to a weekend of Sheetrock dust, noise, and a very enthusiastic husband.

Mark's weekend undertaking took a month to complete, which was a better time ratio than most of his projects. A hint of anticipation stirred in me when he finished framing in the trapdoor. I'd never been in the attic before, because Mark dragged out our Christmas decorations each year. I climbed the new pull-down stairs and looked around. Mark had nailed ply-wood over the insulation and wired a light bulb with a dangling chain. He had salvaged an overstuffed chair from our basement and squished it through the opening. It sat in a pool of light under the dusty rafters, and a small table next to it completed the inviting refuge. A faint golden glow fought its way through the dirty windows on either end of the long attic, casting shadows on storage boxes and remnants of past remodeling projects.

A flicker of hope ignited in my tired heart. This was a place where I could find my way back from the dark vortex that was draining my joy. I backed down the steps.

Mark grinned at me, waiting for my response. Sawdust

stuck in clumps to his flannel shirt and wavy blond hair. Band-Aids covered several of his fingers. Tools of every shape and size filled the hallway.

For a moment, I felt a break in the thick cloud that enshrouded me. "Thank you." I hugged him with a bit of desperation. "It means a lot that you wanted to do this for me."

He squeezed back.

"Hey, Dad. This is cool. Can I see?" Jon ran past us and scampered up the narrow treads.

Mark released me, grabbed our nine-year-old, and swung him away from the steps. "Wait a minute. We're going to have a family meeting." Words to inspire terror in our children.

Even though it was Saturday, it took awhile to corral everyone. We finally chased the kids off the phone, away from the computer, and into the living room. As usual, my two teens fidgeted on the couch. I was into simplified decorating—mostly so I'd have fewer knickknacks to dust—but even with our bare wood floor and mission-style furniture, our small living room felt crowded with all six of us, especially because the kids got bigger every time I blinked.

"Mom, I have to be at Amanda's house in fifteen minutes." Karen checked her watch.

She slept in until one, and *now* she's in a hurry?

"Is this going to take long?" Jake's lanky frame sprawled over the arms of the couch. He cracked his knuckles and yawned.

I clenched my teeth and smiled. "As long as it takes."

"Jon took the good pillow!" Seven-year-old Anne pulled it out from under his perch on the floor.

He crashed backward and pulled the piano bench down with him. "Did you see that?" Jon yelled.

Mark took the pillow away from both of them and cleared

his throat. "Your mom's been stressed out lately, so I built her a space where she can be alone. But we need to have some rules." He smiled at me with the post-construction glow in his cheeks.

I let my heart melt for a second as I looked back at him. Rugged lines, warm smile, gentle and honest as the day is long. He was no longer the lean, melancholy youth I met in college. Marriage had agreed with him.

"Ouch!" Anne slammed her Barbie to the floor. "Jon poked me. Tell him to stop poking me."

Mark grabbed Jon's shoulders and slid him along the floor several yards.

Jake used the distraction to fiddle with his keys. "I'm gonna be late for work. Can't you have this meeting after I leave?"

"No!" I took a deep breath. "My new room is off-limits. *No one* is allowed up there. If an emergency happens, you can call through the door for me, but you can't come up. And no interrupting me unless it's a real emergency. Like someone bleeding. A lot."

"We got it." Jake slouched to his feet. "No blood, no interruptions. No problem. Gotta go."

The kids scattered, and Mark looked at me with a slightly bewildered expression.

Affection made my lips twitch. He could manage complex projects at work and oversee a large staff, but family meetings always left him dazed and confused. No wonder my own little neurons were drooping from the effort to keep up with the dizzying pace of our family life. That was probably why I was listless these days. I moved into the circle of Mark's arms. Our marriage was my biggest motivation to fight off this lethargy. The cloud was pulling me away from him, and that terrified me.

I felt a tug at my sweater.

"Mommy, don't you like us anymore?" Anne's face tilted up at me.

Ouch. Might as well wear a scarlet *W* on my shirt, for World's Worst Mom. "Sweetie, I love you all to pieces. But you know how sometimes you need a time-out when you get crabby? I need a place to have a time-out sometimes."

That must have made sense to Anne; she giggled and ran off.

If only my guilt would run off with her. I had a great family, a cozy home, and everything any sane person could wish for. But it seemed that each day the gray fog was growing thicker. My first thoughts in the morning centered on how soon I could get everyone off to school so I could go back to bed. I forced myself through laundry and car pools and uninspired suppers. It was all meaningless. And I felt piercing guilt for not being happy when I had so much reason to be.

Since Mark was home to run interference, it seemed like the perfect time to initiate my new retreat. I grabbed my Bible and journal and climbed the ladder into the attic, determined to dig out the spiritual secrets that would snap me out of this.

I ignored the decades of dust that smelled like wet wool in the eaves beyond my overhead lightbulb. In my imagination, I was at a luxurious retreat center instead of a cramped attic with beams that threatened to crack my skull if I straightened up in the wrong place. I curled up in my upholstered chair to read the story of Deborah. In an era when women's roles were narrowly defined, people came to sit at her feet and hear her words. In my world, I solved disputes about who got the good pillow or the longest french fry. She guided people in life-and-death matters. She even had a tree named for her. And when no one in Israel had the guts to defend the people, she shamed the leaders by offering to ride into battle herself.

I opened my journal and jotted down a few thoughts about the woman of God I wanted to become. My pencil sketched a tree with myself beneath it. The figure was a good likeness. Long thin form, long sallow face, long straight hair. In my mind's eye, I was still the sunny blonde of my childhood, but I forced myself to darken my hair in the drawing to represent the color it had actually become in adulthood—dull brown. I added a sign on the tree, *The Oak of Susan.*

As I thought of Deborah's story, I penciled a figure in armor approaching the tree.

A scraping sound under the eaves interrupted me. For a second, I thought I saw something move in the shadows.

I slammed my journal closed. "Jake, I told you no one is allowed up here." I stood, keeping my head bent to avoid the rafters as I walked out of my circle of light and deeper into the attic.

Boxes, odd sticks of furniture, and my grandma's old sewing mannequin cluttered the edges of the room. I didn't sew but could never bear to part with it, so its headless form remained wedged under the roofline. I looked behind it and around a stack of boxes but didn't see anyone.

Maybe I wasn't just going through middle-age angst. Maybe I was starting to see things. Coughing from the dust I'd stirred up, I retreated to my chair. I opened my Bible again and found my spot.

A metallic clunk reverberated far back in the shadows.

My skin prickled into high alert. "Mark, is that you?"

"Honey! I'm taking the kids to the park!" Mark's muffled yell floated from the hallway below.

With a nervous glance at the dark angles behind the mannequin, I scurried to the square opening in the floor.

Mark's beaming face tilted up from the hallway.

At first I thought he was smiling at me, but then I realized he was admiring the carpentry around the trapdoor.

"Are the kids down there with you?" I asked.

"Just Jon and Anne. Karen's at Amanda's house, remember? And Jake left for work right after our meeting. His car's gone. We'll probably stop for cheeseburgers on the way home. What would you like?"

"The usual. But Mark—"

"Love ya!" he hollered over his shoulder as he headed down the hall. Hangers rattled in the closet. At least the kids remembered to grab their jackets. Anne's high-pitched voice was chattering nonstop, as usual, and Mark's low laugh rumbled just before the front door closed. The house settled into heavy silence.

I dusted off my knees and looked back at my chair and the inviting circle of light.

"Those noises must have carried through the ductwork or something." The sound of my voice was reassuring, so I kept talking. "Let's not be crazy here. I have my attic retreat. Mark's taking care of the kids. I'm going to dig in and figure out what's been wrong with me lately."

As soon as I stopped speaking, I heard something new.

Voices.

The words were garbled, but the voices seemed to be arguing. Karen probably had forgotten to turn off the radio in her room. She did it all the time. But in the weird way sound travels in an empty house, the voices seemed to come from the boxes in the darkest end of the attic.

There was no way to concentrate on my devotions until I figured out where those sounds were coming from. I descended the pull-down ladder and did a quick walk-through of the house. No radios were playing, but I did find our emergency flashlight plugged into the wall by the washing machine. I grabbed it and clambered back into the attic.

Good grief. I finally had precious time and space to myself, and I was wasting it. On the other hand, there were quite a few old boxes stuffed under the eaves. It might be fun to see some of the treasures we had abandoned. I pulled out the mannequin, which wobbled precariously until I braced it against some other rafters. I slid out a cardboard box of tax records and discovered a plastic tub. The words "Dress Up" were scrawled across the lid in faded marker.

Fingers of nostalgia tickled me. That bin had once been a favorite of all the kids. Anne and Jon would probably still enjoy it if I hauled it down the stairs. Prying off the lid revealed assorted hats, capes, and sequined recital costumes. Near the bottom rested a collection of plastic weapons. For many years, Jake's career goal had been to become a knight in shining armor—until he learned that not many companies were hiring knights. The gray shield brought back memories of many battles enacted in our front yard. Sitting back on my heels, I hugged the shield to my chest and felt an ache of loss pierce me. What had happened to those whimsical days?

That was when I heard the whispers. I whipped my head around and scanned the whole attic. My hand tightened on the flashlight. *Keep breathing. This is ridiculous.* I was alone in the attic. Alone in the house. An overtired mom in a quiet neighborhood who probably needed a nap.

Or maybe I needed one of those antianxiety medicines they

advertised on television. A semi-hysterical giggle slipped from my throat.

"Stop it." I delivered the order in my best mom's-in-charge voice. Maybe I had accidentally bumped the kid's old spy walkie-talkies, and they were making the sounds. Humming to block out the whispers, I set the flashlight on the floor and dug deeper into the storage bin. I rummaged through masks, rabbit ears, and flannel superhero capes, and then lifted out a sword.

The flashlight bounced enough light off the rafters for me to see the tooth marks in the plastic hilt. The gray sheath was cracked in several places.

The weapon made me think of the Bible story I had been studying. "Wake up, Deborah! . . . Arise, O Barak," I quoted, pulling the sword from the sheath.

In that instant the air became thick with pressure. My breath caught in my lungs. My ears roared as forces surged together under the eaves. The attic crackled with threads of electricity. The rough plywood under my knees seemed to shift. Then everything exploded. Windows shattered. The lightbulb flickered and died. The room seemed to fill with dark smoke or dust.

Underneath and inside the chaos, I curled in around myself and squeezed my eyes shut as the energy grabbed and shook me. In spite of my instinctive jerk away, an invisible hand held me—as if I had gripped an electric fence and couldn't let go. Lightning ran through my nerves. Terror ignited every cell in my body. Then I was beyond awareness, part of the swirling darkness.

As abruptly as it seized me, the energy gave me one last shake and dropped me.

Chapter Two

COLD RAIN STUNG THE BACK OF my neck as I huddled on the ground.

Rain?

My mind was in shock, but I knew there wasn't supposed to be rain in the attic. Over the persistent ringing in my ears, metallic clangs beat a sharp, broken rhythm. The sound was familiar, and I tugged at the memory.

The noises in the attic. I'd been looking for the source when something happened. An electrical storm? Had we lost the roof? I opened my eyes with dread.

Black pools of water rippled on the tar road in front of me. Tall concrete buildings rose nearby in the dusky light. Crates and bundles edged the alley.

My head throbbed, and I blinked a few times. I didn't recognize these buildings. Where was my attic? How did I get here?

Rain dripped off my bangs to run down my face. The cold water cleared the cobwebs from my dazed mind, and my senses exploded back to life. The roaring faded from my ears, and I could hear each raindrop ricochet. The uneven clashing sounds grew louder.

Could a storm have carried me to an unfamiliar part of

town? Bewilderment gave way to panic. I needed to get help, but I couldn't convince my shaken muscles to move.

Suddenly, two men lurched into view at the far end of the alley, slashing at each other with swords.

Swords? I would have laughed if my head weren't throbbing. Were these actors rehearsing a scene? That was impossible. The community theater was miles from my house. While the two men circled each other, my eyes seemed able to take in visual details with an impossibly keen focus, even through the haze of rain.

One man lunged in with lightning speed, and the other blocked. Metal scraped as one sword pushed along the edge of the other before disengaging.

The taller man's long, brown hair flung rain in all directions as he whipped his head around and turned for a rapid parry. Every muscle of his face was tight with fury. His breath whistled through clenched teeth. He was a constant swirl of movement, unhindered by the loose gray sweatshirt and trousers he wore—both of them torn and dirty.

The shorter man's mop of tight curls hinted at reddish gold, even though matted with rain. He also wore something shapeless and solid colored. At least these actors had the sense not to wear their costumes if they had to practice out in the rain. The shorter man grinned. His teeth stood out brightly in the otherwise muted colors of the scene. Swords crossed and held, the men's bodies drawn together as they wrestled for control.

Though it shouldn't have been possible at this distance, I could hear each rapid breath and gasp from the men over the sound of the rain.

"It won't do any good, Tristan," the red-haired man said. "Kendra won't be coming back."

The words made no sense to me, but the taller man stumbled back, his face raw with pain. At first I thought he'd been hit, but he didn't seem to be wounded—just defeated. The men stared at each other, chests heaving with exertion. Then, with a suddenness that blurred the movements, the man called Tristan rushed forward with strike after strike and drove his opponent back. The shorter man slipped on the slick blacktop, and his guard faltered.

The sword thrust right through the torso of the redhead. His high-pitched wail echoed against the alley buildings. Somehow my vision was acute enough to see dark liquid on the blade as Tristan pulled his sword back.

These weren't actors.

A nightmare, maybe. Or gang members fighting over a dark corner of the city. But not actors.

Screams stuck in my throat. I couldn't draw breath to make the sound. My mouth opened and closed like Anne's goldfish, while my fingers clenched in reflexive terror around the sword hilt in my right hand. I looked down at where it lay, heavy and cold, across my knees. It was no longer plastic. Lifting it away from my body, I saw the luster of the metal and felt its impossible weight. My wrist shook from the effort to hold it with one hand.

When I looked up again, the victor had collapsed to his knee near the body of his opponent and was still breathing hard, bracing himself with his sword. Before my frozen mind could take in what was happening, he turned and looked right at me. His expression snapped instantly from exhaustion to alarm.

I willed to disappear. I prayed to melt into the puddles on the ground.

The man's focus dropped to the sword in front of me. His

eyes widened as they traveled back to my face. Using his sword for support, he pushed up off his knee. Dangerous purpose hardened his face as he stalked toward me.

My mental paralysis released me. I dropped my sword with a clatter and stumbled to my feet. *Run! Run, run, run!* my brain screamed. My confusion no longer mattered. In that moment, I stopped wondering where my attic was. I didn't care if I was dreaming or suffering a concussion from a rafter that hit my head in a storm. I couldn't sort out why there were actors, who turned out not to be actors, playing with swords in the rain.

All I knew was that one of them was well and truly dead, and I had to get away, or I might be next. My legs wobbled the way they do after the first long bike ride each spring. Then they remembered how to move, and I sprinted down the alley.

"Wait!" The man's shout only spurred me on. I ran hard—already I was half a block away and near the entrance of the alley. My heart pounded in rhythm with my feet thudding against the wet asphalt. I looked over my shoulder and saw him coming.

I didn't see the curb that made me stumble, and I didn't see the truck that hit its brakes too late. I saw only the man with the sword.

He yelled something, but I couldn't hear the words over the squeal of brakes.

Something slammed against me. Then everything disappeared.

Through the haze of pain, I sensed movement, but couldn't open my eyes to see where I was. Sounds seeped into my awareness in splinters.

"Bringing home souvenirs now, Tristan?" mocked a voice from a distance.

"Shut up and help me," said someone close to my ear. I felt myself being jostled and lowered, and heard a gasp.

"Who is she?"

"I don't know." The voice belonging to Tristan was no longer as close. "The Rhusican is dead. She saw it. Ran into a transport trying to get away. I don't think she's one of them."

"And you risk bringing her here? Have you lost what little mind you have? Why didn't you just leave her?"

There was something important I needed to remember. I had to pay attention. But the pain roared back in, and I moaned. The voices were dissolving.

"Kieran, find out what you can about her. I need to clean up. Just—find out. I've been wrong before. . . ." The words fractured into meaningless sounds, and all my senses went as black as my sight.

I coaxed a deep breath of air into my lungs and had the strange sense that it was the first breath I had taken in hours. As soon as my ribs expanded, pain exploded outward, and my mind overloaded trying to sort all the things that felt wrong. Every part of my body shrieked with hurt. Squinting my eyes open, I got an impression of lying on a couch or bed in a warmly lit room. I squeezed my eyes shut as another wave of pain rolled through me. My jaw clenched to hold back screams.

"It hurts!" I hissed to no one in particular.

"I know," a quiet voice answered. Someone took my

hand, and I held on with desperation, as if the hand could pull me out of the swirling misery. "It'll pass. Hold on."

I imagined I could feel bones knitting together within me. Itchy prickles made me squirm as torn flesh regenerated and internal wounds mended. I was about to whimper, "Make it stop," but then it grew easier to breathe. I was finally able to open my eyes again.

The man holding my hand was slim and wiry. Cropped black hair framed a face full of angles. He studied me with more curiosity than sympathy.

"What happened?" I asked when I managed to form words again.

"You lost an argument with a transport."

"Is this a hospital? Are you a doctor?"

"My name is Kieran. A friend brought you here." He eased his hand away from mine, as though embarrassed by his earlier compassion. On second look, my question seemed silly. He was no doctor. He had the rough-edged look of a suspect on *Crime Stoppers*, complete with dark, piercing eyes.

I pushed myself up to see the room. As I struggled to sit, my head sagged forward, and I couldn't suppress another groan. The pain was easing, but there was still a thrumming ache inside my skull.

Kieran poured something into a stoneware mug and held it out to me. "What do you remember?"

Turning the cool mug in my hands, I winced at the effort it took to think. The whole room looked odd . . . like a stage set or a museum exhibit of some obscure culture. There was light but no lamps. The gently curved walls seemed to give off a soft glow but without the fluorescent buzz I would have expected. In fact, the room was strangely empty of sound, like our house when a storm knocked out our power: no hum of a refrigerator or whir of an air conditioner.

I was sitting on a couch near a low table. Those few pieces of furniture triggered curiosity about the unfamiliar designs, but my first priority was remembering. I feared my memories would be as elusive as the fragments left when waking from a dream. I had to look at them sideways, gently tugging on the remembered threads to pull more images into focus.

"I remember running. Being scared. But why . . . ?" I frowned as I pieced together my thoughts. "I heard brakes squeal. A truck came out of nowhere. I was running. Looking back . . ." Suddenly, the fog lifted and memory returned. The murder in the alley.

"There was a man. . . . Where's your phone? Police . . . Call them!" The words tangled in my hurry to be understood.

I tried to stand as panic took over, but the dark-haired man pressed me back down.

"You don't understand." My urgency cast aside the remnants of pain. "Someone was stabbed. We have to call the police. He's still out there somewhere. He could kill someone else."

Why was he just staring at me? Didn't he understand? He may have provided first aid, but if he didn't let me call the police in the next two seconds, I was going to start screaming.

Kieran's eyes broke contact with mine, and he looked over my head and rubbed a hand over his mouth. "Don't worry; he's not still out there."

I stopped fighting to get up and turned my head to follow his gaze.

Standing in the doorway of the room behind me, only yards away, stood the man I would likely see in my nightmares for years.

His victim had called him "Tristan." His long hair was still wet, and he stood in bare feet and formless pants, with a towel around his neck. His eyes were weary. Hardly the look of a crazed murderer, but all my memory had surged back now. Those same eyes had burned with rage as he drove his sword through another man.

The mug fell from my hand and hit the floor with a thud. I dodged Kieran and bolted. Where was the exit? Tristan blocked one doorway, and I wanted to get as far from him as possible. There was another door across the room, and I tried to sprint toward it. My progress was more of a desperate, lurching stagger. I expected one of the men to grab me, but I made it to the door and fumbled with the unfamiliar latch. I glanced back.

The men weren't even looking at me. Tristan was glaring at his friend. "Great, Kieran. You're a real help."

Kieran shrugged, unconcerned. "Do you want me to get her?" He deliberately settled back down on the couch and propped up his feet.

"Never mind," Tristan growled. He grabbed a sweater off the top of a trunk and pulled it on.

I wiggled the bar that held the door shut. It had a little play but refused to slide and release the door. Finally, I gave up and pounded the door itself. I hit the hard surface again and again.

A heavy hand clamped onto my shoulder.

That's when I started screaming.

A large, warm palm closed over my mouth. I kept shouting for help, but the words came out as muffled shrieks.

"Don't be afraid. You're safe here." Tristan's voice rumbled near my ear.

Funny, I didn't feel particularly safe. Terror shot adrenaline through me, and I slammed one elbow backward while my free hand clawed at the fingers over my mouth. I managed enough leverage to crash my heel back, and I heard a grunt of pain behind me.

Instead of loosening his grip, Tristan shoved me forward against the door, knocking the wind out of me. "We just want to talk to you. Please." He released me abruptly and stepped back.

I spun to face him with the door against my back.

He held his hands up. I had another flash of visual detail and saw the ridges on the calluses above his palm and even the jagged edges of a broken blister at the base of one finger. He spoke slowly, gesturing as if he were trying to calm a family dog. "I won't hurt you. We just need to talk to you."

I tried the same tactic, forcing my voice to be soothing. "Sure. I'd love to talk to you. But right now, I need to go home." I spoke with exaggerated slowness. "Just open the door for me, and we can talk tomorrow."

Kieran snorted in amusement from the couch where he still sprawled. He linked his hands in his short black hair and leaned back to watch. Tristan turned to glare at him.

Breathing rapidly, I felt for the door catch behind my back but still couldn't loosen it.

"Tristan, let her go. If I'm right, we can talk to her later." Kieran's voice was bland with a hint of humor. I didn't see anything funny in the situation, but if he could convince his friend to open the door, I wasn't going to criticize.

Tristan moved toward me.

I squeaked and flinched sideways.

He ignored me and flipped up the long latch and pulled it

to the right. The door swung inward.

"Thanks!" I shouted over my shoulder as I ran out. No harm in being polite.

I'd find the closest phone or flag down a car. Most people carry cell phones. I'd tell the police what I'd seen and where to find Tristan. First I had to call Mark. He was probably worried sick about me. And what if the kids had still been at the park when that storm hit? What if . . . ?

My thoughts were racing, and I was a half block away from the door before I actually saw my surroundings. I stopped dead. From my throat came a whimpering sound I hadn't made since I was six years old — the day our neighbor's German shepherd lunged at me, barking and straining against its leash. That day, panic had glued me to the sidewalk.

Now I was frozen again — like a six-year-old overwhelmed by a terror way too big for me to face. I blinked several times — the only movement I could manage.

Stark concrete buildings squatted all around me like huge bubbles of gray spackle. Their edges were rounded, and they had no windows. The strange shapes reached only a story or two upward from the tar street, some butting against each other or layered like an adobe village. This didn't look at all like the tall buildings around the alley where I'd witnessed the murder. Rain continued to fall, a softer drizzle than earlier. The sky was a darker gray than I remembered from the alley, and there were no street-lights. There were also no cars or people. The silence was terrify-ing. Then I heard the swoosh of something traveling on the wet tar pavement. About a block away, a truck crossed the opening between two buildings. There was no engine noise, only a splash of water as it passed. The truck was even the wrong shape — long and sleek like a moray eel nosing out from the rocks.

This was not my town. This was no place I had ever been. It looked like a Play-Doh village Anne had once made for her Polly Pockets—lumpy, abstract caverns with arched doorways and no windows. The light was wrong, the shapes were off, and even the smells were confusing. Instead of the cut grass and wet dirt scent of my neighborhood, the air smelled like burnt marshmallows.

God, help me. I had slipped from mild depression into psychosis. Or I was lying in a coma somewhere, struggling to recover from the attic roof collapsing on my head. This could not be real.

Movement caught my eye. A lizard-shaped creature the size of a squirrel ran across the street and up the side of a curved building. It was muddy red in color and seemed to have wet fur all over its body.

A shudder ran through me. "Mark," I whispered, "where are you?" The thought of Mark—who always squashed the scary bugs in our house and defended me against relentless insurance agents or dishonest repairmen—did me in. I fell to my knees and covered my face. "Please find me. Please." I cried until my nose started running. Eventually, I had to stand up to fish into the pocket of my slacks for a tissue. It was the first time I noticed my clothes. My cardigan was torn and stained with blood and dirt. What was it Kieran had said? "You lost an argument with a transport." From the looks of the damage, I belonged in a hospital, not the rain-soaked streets of a deserted Play-Doh city. My limbs and ribs still felt bruised. The feeling of bones knitting together had been real—or as real as anything was at the moment.

The sky seemed darker, and something slithered behind a nearby building. Fine hairs on my arms prickled. Danger stirred out there among the amorphous buildings. I turned back. Tristan was leaning in his doorway watching me. Light pooled around him, accenting the furrows on his forehead. "You're welcome to stay here. We'll be safe for tonight."

I realized that he felt the danger, too. He might be an actor, a murderer, or a hallucination, but he was also afraid. Somehow that gave me the courage to walk toward him. He ducked back into the house, then stepped into the doorway with something wrapped in a cloth. He flipped back the fabric to reveal a sword.

"You dropped it in the alley. It's yours." Tristan held it out to me, hilt first. "Maybe it will help."

The blade had the sheen of liquid mercury. My right palm itched. I reached out tentatively, and my finger traced knots carved on the hilt. I flexed my hand, then clenched the grip and lifted the sword, standing taller, ignoring the way my muscles ached. Emotions had overloaded me until I'd gone numb, but now a new feeling stirred inside me, moving from my sword arm into the center of my being: determination.

I looked up. Tristan had seen the change in me. He nodded and stepped back so I could enter the house. He didn't smile. If anything, there was a deeper weariness in the slump of his shoulders. His eyes studied me and reflected back only sadness.

Chapter Three

"BETTER THE DEVIL YOU KNOW THAN the devil you don't," I said under my breath as I walked back into the large room.

"What?" Tristan threw me a startled look.

"Nothing. Just a saying." I was studying the room. Now that I was here by choice, I took the time to soak it all in.

The couch where I had regained consciousness had a wooden frame and a simple design. However, the wood was a rich honey color, with amazing whorls in the grain and smooth, rounded edges. Mark would be fascinated by the craftsmanship and warm finish. I once caught him touching his tongue to a small carved box at a craft fair to help him identify the unusual wood.

The couch frame held an earth-toned, fabric-covered futon that provided cushioning. There were a few rounded chairs scattered around the room, which also supported upholstery that looked removable.

The low table in front of the couch was made from the same unusual wood. Its long, oval shape rested on several fat round legs running along both sides. The floor was the same bare concrete as the outer walls — the stucco substance I kept thinking of as dried, rather dull Play-Doh.

Behind the couch stretched a large, bare area, which made the room look as though someone were in the process of moving in or out. Someone with sparse possessions. A side of the room had cubbies shaped into the wall, like arched lockers with no doors. One of the shallow caverns protected bulky bundles wrapped in fabric. A sword was propped against a small trunk nearby. The doorway where I had first seen Tristan after I woke was at the far end of the room.

Kieran was busy at a high table in the corner of the room to my right, although with the rounded shapes of all the walls, it wasn't actually a corner. Still, it seemed to be a separate area. If I had to make a guess based on what Kieran was doing, I would say it looked like some sort of kitchen. Steam was rising from a large bowl, and he sprinkled something over the top and set a lid on it.

A growling moan rose from outside the building. My pulse stuttered into a faster rhythm.

Tristan quickly swung the door shut and slid the latch across, rotating it to lock it into place.

"Right," said Kieran from the corner, "may as well have something hot to drink." He turned with a tray in his hands, saw my sword, and cocked an eyebrow.

With the weapon in my hand, I felt self-conscious and a bit silly. But I was strangely reluctant to put it down. Finally, I braced it against the wall near the other sword and returned to the table.

Tristan pulled up a chair, and the wood creaked as he settled into it with a sigh. I was about to perch on one end of the couch when I realized how dirty and wet I was.

Kieran set the tray on the low table and ladled hot liquid

into mugs. He glanced up. "Go on. Sit. We've seen worse."
He lifted a round, grainy loaf from the tray. "Hungry?"

I shook my head, but Tristan was already tearing off a piece
of the loaf. Kieran leaned across the table and handed me a mug.
The smell of cloves rose in warm and comforting steam around
my face. I wondered about the wisdom of drinking something
I didn't recognize, but if getting hit by a truck hadn't killed me,
this probably wouldn't either. And if these men had planned to
attack me, they could have done so by now.

I settled on the edge of the couch and sipped the hot liquid,
cradling the mug in both hands. It had a richer flavor than any
tea I'd tasted before, with a spicy bite that warmed me all the
way to my stomach, like wine. My spine relaxed back against
the couch.

"I suppose introductions are a good idea," Kieran said, flop-
ping onto the floor across the table from me, unconcerned about
the hard surface. His lanky form seemed all angles of knees and
elbows. "You've already met Tristan. I'm Kieran, as you know,
and you are . . . ?" He leaned back on his elbows casually, but
his eyes were sharp as they watched me.

"Susan Mitchell. I live on Ridgeview Drive." For a moment,
it felt natural and normal to introduce myself. Then my eyes
traveled around the odd room again. I set my mug down on
the table, and my voice grew smaller. "Do you know if we're far
from there?"

The two men looked at each other. Tristan lifted one shoulder and shook his head.

"I'm not sure," said Kieran, still studying me through
narrowed eyes. "But my guess is that you're a long way from
home."

My skin prickled with a warning of danger. Tristan was a

killer; so why did his dark friend frighten me even more? The magnitude of my isolation and confusion overwhelmed me. Tears stung my eyes, but I blinked them back.

Tristan shifted and then reached forward with his sword arm. "Well met, Susan-mid-shawl. You are welcome here."

I reached my own hand forward to shake his, but he grabbed my forearm in some kind of soldier's greeting and patted my shoulder with his free hand.

"Thank you," I said softly. "And it's just 'Susan.'"

Satisfied that he had cheered me, or at least fulfilled the requirements of hospitality, Tristan nodded, released me, and sank back into his chair.

I glanced over at Kieran. Even in the glow of the room, he managed to look as if he were lurking in shadows. Darker hair, darker eyes, and much darker mood than his friend.

He didn't offer his hand. He continued to scrutinize me, as if I were a moth pinned to a science fair display board.

I picked up my mug again and turned back toward Tristan. "Could you please tell me where we are?"

"This was my cousin's home before . . . well . . . back when my people lived here. I use it when I'm traveling through. It's about as safe as anywhere in the Gray Hills. We're only a day's ride from Braide Wood." He waited for me to give some sign of comprehension. When I just stared at him, he continued. "That's my home." The way he said the word *home* was rich with longing, fatigue, and pride.

"Have you been away long?" I floundered for the right questions to ask, still making no sense of what was happening.

"Tristan's a guardian," Kieran cut in, his voice cold. "He doesn't get home much. The Council keeps him too busy."

Tristan glared at his friend. "She saw me. If she's working

for the Council, we're already in trouble. There's no harm in answering her questions."

I decided to ignore Kieran and, instead, searched Tristan's face. "What I saw ... was it ... I mean, was that real? At first I thought you were an actor rehearsing a scene. I didn't realize ... I mean ..." My throat felt thick. In my mind, I could still see the man before me with rage in his eyes, gasping for breath and lunging forward, his sword skewering another man. The memory of blood on his sword made me queasy.

"He poisoned my wife." Raw anguish edged Tristan's words. "I've been tracking him for two seasons."

I remembered phrases from the sword fight—and a name: "Kendra."

Tristan looked at his feet and nodded, lost in his pain.

Kieran jumped up. "Tristan, get some rest. I'll talk to her." He helped the larger man to his feet with an odd tenderness. There was murmured conversation as Kieran grabbed some blankets from a cubby; then he and Tristan moved to the far end of the room and rolled out a pallet. I glanced over my shoulder and saw the light of the far wall dim and go out. Kieran pulled a flexible panel out from the curving wall to create a partition.

I settled back into the couch and sipped some more of the comforting drink. Breathing in the scent of cloves, I stared into my mug and tried to sort out what I knew.

I had been in my attic, but now I was someplace far from home. I didn't know how I had gotten here. I'd leave that question for later.

But I needed to know where I was. Maybe it was some sort of commune far on the outskirts of town. That was why it was such a deserted area. And maybe they were living in an abandoned movie set. That furry lizard was probably an animatronic prop. I was trying to use logic where logic didn't seem to apply. It hurt my brain. Once, when Mark and I were driving to the grocery store, we saw a blue van — identical to ours — just ahead of us on the freeway. "Look," I said. "It's us in the future!"

"No," said Mark, drumming his fingers on the steering wheel. "That's us in the past, because they've already been where we are going to be."

His reasoning made my head hurt the way it was hurting now. Maybe the issue of where or when could slide as well. I just didn't know enough. What *did* I know?

Tristan was a guardian (whatever that was) who would be in trouble with the Council (whatever that was) if they found out he killed a Rhusican (whatever that was). He had lost his wife, Kendra, and sought revenge. The memory of that revenge brought on another shudder. Still, Tristan had offered me a safe place to stay. Maybe if I got a good night's sleep, I'd have the energy to figure out what had happened to me.

And then there was Tristan's friend, Kieran.

Staring into my tea, lost in thought, I didn't realize Kieran had come back until he shoved the tray aside and sat directly in front of me on the edge of the low table. I looked up and jumped at the sight of his face so close to mine.

Cheekbones, lean angles, and very cold eyes faced me.

"What do you know about Kendra?" He was barely speaking above a whisper, but there was a biting menace in his voice.

I swallowed. "Nothing. I just heard the man say something. The man that Tristan was fighting. The one he . . ." I stopped.

"Killed." Kieran waved that away. "What did he say?"

"I don't know. Something about . . ." I looked down as I tried to remember the exact words. "It won't do any good. Kendra won't be coming back." I lifted my gaze.

Kieran's jaw tightened. His eyes were hard and remote. "And why were you there?"

"I don't know. I was in the attic. Mark built me a room, and I kept hearing noises. I looked in the bin of toys and pulled out a sword, and there was this roaring in my ears, and everything tilted. . . ." I hated the quaver in my voice, but I forced myself to continue. "I don't know what happened, but all of a sudden I was in an alley. When I looked up, Tristan was fighting. I saw . . ." I couldn't finish the sentence.

Glinting eyes narrowed and continued to stare at me.

"I was scared. I started running. Something hit me, and I woke up here. And . . . and I know this is a nightmare, and I really want to wake up now."

Kieran leaned forward. "Do you work for the Council?" he asked.

I pressed as far back into the couch as I could. He was trying to intimidate me and succeeding easily. I didn't like the feeling. Didn't he realize I'd been terrorized enough today? "I'm not on any councils," I stammered, wondering what to say to get him to back off. "Well, unless you count the band parent's booster club. But we just sell candy bars at the football games. They asked me to serve on a church council, but I'm not big on meetings. With the kids being so busy, I had to say no."

Kieran's left eyelid started twitching. "Stop babbling." He rubbed his temple, obviously annoyed. "Are you a Restorer? Tristan's ready to believe anything. But I'm not."

The icy suspicion in Kieran's face made me angry. I hadn't asked for any of this to happen. I was tired, cold, and wet, yet I'd been very accommodating. I wasn't yelling for the police. I was sipping tea and answering all his crazy questions.

"What do you want from me? What's a Restorer? What's a

guardian for that matter? What is this insane place anyway? It can't be real. *You* aren't real." Tears threatened again, but I didn't care anymore. I was tired of trying to be brave. "I want to go home."

Kieran ignored my questions and grabbed my chin, his fingers bruising my jaw. His eyes locked with mine, as if he were trying to see into my heart. "Are you the Restorer?"

I shoved his hand away and stood up. "I don't know what you're talking about." I walked to the kitchen, set my mug on the tall table, and began pacing the floor. Three paces. Turn. Three paces. Turn. "I'm a housewife and a mom. I got hit on the head, and I'm in a coma. But I want to wake up now. I need to wake up now. I have to find out if the kids are okay. And Mark—he was going to take them to the park. I have to get back to them. Now." I knew I was working myself up to hysteria, but I figured I'd earned it. "I don't want any more furry red lizards or Play-Doh buildings. And definitely no more swords." I looked up toward the coved ceiling. "God, let me go back. Please. I want to wake up. Whatever you're trying to tell me, it's not making sense. Let me wake up now."

Kieran grabbed my arm to stop my pacing, and guided me to a chair. "Who are you talking to?" His voice sounded strained, but I ignored him.

"God, please. I need you." My mutters and sniffles continued. Sure, I was sounding crazy, but since I probably *was* insane, it didn't seem worth fighting to stay calm anymore.

I shivered from the cold rain that had soaked my clothes—or from fear. Hard to say. My shoulders began to shake, and hysterical laughter bubbled from my lungs. "Restorers and guardians and swords. It just makes so much sense, doesn't it?" I gasped, holding my stomach. My giggles morphed into strangled sobs.

"It's not real. Go away. None of it's real."

Kieran's face moved in front of me again, but I couldn't focus.

"Susan." His voice was sharp.

I ignored him. I had heard of people who would disassociate when faced with incredible trauma. They'd just go away somewhere in their head. I wanted to go away.

Kieran held my wrist against the chair arm. "Susan, look at me."

At his words, I came back to the present, only to find the nightmare taking a new frightening turn. He knelt in front of me holding a knife.

I tried to pull away, but his grip was strong. He pushed the sleeve of my cardigan up and ran the knife quickly over the back of my arm, cutting deeply into the skin.

I cried out and jerked my arm, but couldn't free it. Searing pain overwhelmed my initial shock as blood coursed across my skin. My breath hissed through my clenched teeth, and I closed my eyes.

"Look at it." The steel in his voice brought my head up in panic. Would he slit my throat next? He saw my terror and softened his tone. "You have to see this. Look at your arm."

I glanced down. My breath caught. Kieran let go of me, but I didn't move. My fear of him gave way to a much deeper fear. Something very strange was happening.

Beneath the line of blood, the skin of my arm was visibly rejoining.

Stunned, I wiped away the blood with my other sleeve. I began to breathe again in trembling hiccups. Rubbing my arm, I looked up at Kieran, my mind a little more connected to reality—or at least *this* reality.

He met my questioning eyes and nodded, something close to sympathy in his expression. "It's true." He gave me a moment to take it in. "Restorers heal very fast. It makes them difficult to kill."

I didn't like the speculative way he studied me as he said that.

"And they always discover other gifts. Things beyond their natural strength."

I thought of the flashes of detailed sight I had already experienced, and the easy way I had heard Tristan's voice from half a block away. Pieces of this delusion could almost make sense—except that it was all impossible and insane.

Kieran seemed to make a decision to dial back his hostility. He pulled clothes from one of the bundles at the side of the room and handed me an armful. "Some of this should fit you. Put on something dry. Do you want anything more to drink?"

I shook my head and walked in a daze toward the open doorway of an inner room. Getting clean and dry suddenly sounded like the best plan in the world. As I pulled the door shut from within the wall, I thought of Mark. He would love these pocket doors and dividers. This room was only a little larger than an airplane bathroom, and as streamlined and effi-cient, with metallic walls layered over the plaster. I fiddled with a spigot over a shallow aluminum sink.

Whatever place this was had running water, at least—though it was only moderately warm. The plumbing was similar enough to home for me to figure out. The pants I had assumed were sweat pants turned out to be a shapeless drawstring design in a type of linen fabric. The woven sweater looked handknit, although the stitches didn't seem quite right. Soon, I padded back out into the large room, bundled in the warm, earth-toned clothes. Oversized woolen socks flopped as I walked.

Kieran had pulled the padding off a chair and unfolded it near the door. The near-empty central room apparently didn't include any convenient Murphy bed that pulled out of the wall. This was like camping out in our house before the moving van arrived. He tossed me a blanket. "You can have the couch." He stretched his lithe body out across the doorway.

Was he guarding the door to keep creatures out, or to keep me in? I was too tired to care.

"Could you get the light?" he asked.

I stood looking around the room, bewildered.

He sighed. "Never mind." He sprang up and slid a catch on the wall near the kitchen. The glow from the walls gradually dimmed.

By the time I had curled up on the couch cushion, the room was completely dark. I squeezed my eyes shut so I wouldn't have to see the blackness. A strange longing pulsed through me: I should have set my sword nearby. It was my last thought before I tumbled into exhausted sleep.

Chapter Four

I OFTEN WAKE UP FEELING COLD. Then I scootch closer to Mark and nestle my body in against him. He spoons around me and the warmth of his bulk eases me into wakefulness. Sometimes we chat about our upcoming day, and his breath tickles my ear when he talks. At some point in the conversation, we always agree we'd like to stay right where we are all day.

I smiled to myself and scooted over, but couldn't find Mark. Was this one of the days he had an early meeting at work? I went through my morning ritual of figuring out which day of the week it is. Yesterday we did chores in the morning and had a family meeting. The kids were going to the park. It must have been Saturday. That meant today was Sunday. The shower wasn't running. Where was Mark?

Stretching my arm out farther toward his side of the bed, I felt empty space. My eyes squinted open and I poked my head out from under the blanket. A pale pink glow enveloped the room. The walls were curved and seemed far away. I twisted my head to the side. No alarm clock, no stack of books. I turned the other way. No Mark. Just a low table. I pulled my head back under the blanket.

Oh, right. I'd been having a bizarre dream. Mark always loved to hear about my dreams. He claimed to never dream. I told him that was scientifically impossible—he just wasn't remembering them. But whatever the case, he always enjoyed hearing about mine. They were usually spy stories, involving long chases through empty buildings. But this was a new one. He would really enjoy this. I'd just sleep a little longer and finish the dream so I could tell him about it on the way to church.

"Let's go." A deep bark sounded much too close to my ear. "We have a long way to travel today."

I pulled the blanket down to my nose and peered out.

Tristan no longer looked tired. His golden-brown hair was wild and disheveled and framed an unshaven face. He was full of suppressed energy—like my neighbor's huge golden retriever waiting to be let off the leash to go bounding into the local pond.

I groaned and ducked back under the covers.

The blanket was yanked away, and a hand grabbed my shoulder to pull me upright.

My head fell back against the couch, and I groaned again. This apparition was not following dream etiquette. "I need to finish sleeping," I mumbled.

"We could just leave her," said a voice across the room behind me. "She's not your responsibility."

"Kieran, I'm a guardian." Tristan's words were firm.

The threat of being left behind in this nightmare was enough to propel me off the couch. I glared at the back of the room where Kieran was rolling up a bundle of clothes and stuffing it into a pack. "You are not real."

"Oh please, let's not go through that again," he said irritably. Kieran watched me shuffle to the washroom, my oversized socks flapping. He rolled his eyes. "Tristan, find her some boots."

I slid the washroom door closed behind me with a bang. It wasn't my fault I looked like a refugee from a hobo camp. My arm itched and I rubbed it absently. Then I rolled back the sleeve of the sweater. A thin white scar, barely visible, ran across the back of my forearm. *The Twilight Zone* music played through my mind, and I bit my lip.

It was going to take too much mental energy to keep denying everything. For now, for whatever reason, I was stuck in this dream. Maybe it would end sooner if I went along with it. That decided, I did what I could in the spartan washroom to prepare myself for the day.

There was a small reflecting surface on the back of the door. It didn't look exactly like a mirror, but could serve that purpose. I stared into it. At least I was still myself. My hair was a mess from sleeping on it wet. I splashed water on my hands and ran my fingers through the tangles. I wanted to braid it, but didn't have any rubber bands.

I looked more deeply into the reflection.

"Are you a Restorer?" I whispered, wondering what that might mean. All I saw was a pale woman with wide, confused eyes. Suddenly I saw details—strands of amber and brown in my irises, tiny veins that shouldn't be visible, pores in my skin.

I jumped back. I'd forgotten about the heightened senses I experienced yesterday. I closed my eyes and listened. Yes . . . deep voices murmured in the other room. They became clear enough to understand as I focused, almost like tuning a radio station.

"But why leave now? At least come home for a few days." That was Tristan.

"I don't need the complication. Besides, you'll do a great job with training her. You're a fine teacher."

Heavy feet stomped a few steps.

I slid the door open an inch to see what was happening.

Tristan stood nose to nose with his friend. "I am not taking on a student. Not after what happened."

"Get over it." Kieran turned away, his breathing uneven as he stuffed something down into a pack. "Guardians lose students. He won't be the last. What worries me is that you're wasting time with your Restorer myths. We have more important things to think about."

"She was sent. You said yourself that she has the signs."

"I don't deny she might be a Restorer." Kieran yanked hard at one of the ties on his pack. "What I'm saying is that I don't believe a Restorer can help us now."

"In every time of great need, a Restorer is sent to fight for the people and help the guardians," Tristan said in a sing-song voice, as if quoting a well-known creed. "The Restorer is empowered with gifts to defeat our enemies and turn the people's hearts back to the Verses."

Kieran snorted. "Then whoever sent her has a strange sense of humor. It's clear she doesn't know the Verses, she can't fight, and all she wants to do is go home. How is that going to help us?"

"Kieran, just help me find someone to take her in."

"I don't want to get involved in this. You are a very bad influence," Kieran said as he moved out of my line of sight.

I edged the door open farther to bring Kieran back in view.

"It's not like I'm asking you to train her," Tristan said. "A lot of good that would do anyway."

"No, you just want me along because you don't trust yourself not to get her killed. But you know where this will end."

Kieran's eyes narrowed as he stared at the larger man. "She won't only get herself killed, Tristan. She'll cause the deaths of others. Can you live with that?"

Tristan turned away and pressed his fists against the kitchen table. Kieran studied his friend for a minute, then stepped closer and put a hand on Tristan's shoulder. The dark man's next words were barely audible. "Fine. I'll help. Leave her here, and I'll get rid of her. Problem solved."

My sudden intake of breath sounded loud in the silence that accompanied Tristan's glare. They turned at the same time to see me in the doorway.

My stomach churned. I forced a smile, pretending I hadn't heard anything as I edged slowly along the wall, my eyes on the two men. Why had I thought I could trust them last night?

Kieran threw down his backpack with an oath.

Tristan cleared his throat and forced a smile that he probably meant to be reassuring. "Would you like something to drink? I'll find you some boots. Are you hungry?" His words trailed off.

I kept moving sideways toward the trunk until I could grab my sword. I'd forgotten how good it felt in my hand. My loafers were near the trunk, and I pulled them on over the thick socks with some effort—keeping one hand free to hold the sword. Both men watched me, wary but still.

"I'm leaving." I wedged my second foot into its shoe.

Tristan nodded. "We're almost ready—"

"Alone," I cut in. "I'll manage on my own." I had watched Tristan work the door last night, and this time I handled the procedure of rotating and sliding the latch. I pulled the door open.

Tristan frowned and started forward.

Kieran grabbed his arm and gave a small shake of his head. Then he smirked at me. "Safe travels."

Right. The sword in my hand gave me confidence, and I cleared my throat. "Stay away from me," I said loudly. Then I pulled the door shut behind me.

When I stepped outside, I expected the bright glare of sunlight. Instead, the sky was the same hazy gray as when I had first opened my eyes in the alley yesterday. I hurried a few steps forward, hoping to see a familiar landmark.

Nothing had changed. There wasn't one hint of home. No telephone poles, no traffic noises in the distance. No trees, birds, squirrels. Without the rain to blur my vision, I could distinguish some differences in the shapeless buildings. Some were tan. Others were light beige. A few were a deeper brown. The tar pavement was still damp, although there were fewer puddles now that the rain had stopped.

All right, I was still lost in some strange experimental housing project or a failed theme park. But it had to end somewhere. I just needed to find a street sign or a phone. And I needed to get far away from the scary guys with the sharp blades.

I jogged for several blocks, weaving between buildings, losing myself in the maze of small alleys. Worry kept me checking back over my shoulder, but the streets were always empty in all directions. Finally, the fear of pursuit began to ease, and I slowed to a walk.

I approached a building. The door was missing from the arching entryway, and I risked a few steps inside. It looked deserted. I couldn't see much because there were no windows, but I was pretty sure there was no phone. I stepped back outside and tried the next building. My nose wrinkled at the smell of mold and wet ash. Near the entry, I found a catch that looked like the one Kieran used to turn off the lights last night. I pushed it, pulled it, and managed to slide it to one side. At first nothing happened. Then a faint peach glow appeared on all the walls at the same time. I had a moment to see that it was another empty room before the lights flickered and cut out.

I hurried out, happy to be back in the open air of the street. Even outside, though, the air wasn't very fresh. The rain hadn't cleared the humidity. The sky seemed to hang low—heavy and cloying. I had to get away from these lumpy buildings and get a sense of where I was. I hurried down the street, wishing for a sheath for my sword. It didn't seem right to drag it along, scraping the ground. But the weapon was heavy, and my arm already ached from holding it out in front of me. I finally rested the flat against my shoulder and carried it like a hobo's staff.

I crossed several alleys and wider streets. There seemed to be taller buildings ahead, and I aimed for those.

Passing one curved building, I noticed a door that was intact. I touched its smooth wooden surface, and it swung inward with a sigh. Drawn inside, I searched for a light switch, wishing as I did that my flashlight had made it here with me. That would have been more useful to me than a sword. My hand fumbled over a lever, and again a moment passed before a glow spread across the walls like a blush. The growing illumination revealed a room similar to the one where I'd spent the night, with a broken chair resting on its side amid shards of stoneware. I stepped farther in to examine something piled in one of the curved cubbies. I pulled aside a tattered blanket and saw a box the size of my daughter's flute case underneath. It was empty.

Had it held a musical instrument? Letters? Jewelry? Someone lived here once. A wave of sadness hit me. Where was the person who once sat in that chair to relax after a hard day's work? Was the blanket a favorite of a child who long ago dragged it along everywhere? I turned the lights off as I left and closed the door gently behind me.

Movement at the end of the street caught my eye. One of the silent trucks glided by. I ran toward it, but it had disappeared by the time I reached the corner. Still, it gave me a plan. If I could wave down a truck, I might get some help.

I continued toward the taller buildings. These had more traditional boxy shapes. I ignored the gaping doorways and crossed several more streets. Then an alley to my right caught my eye.

My nerve endings chilled. I recognized this place. Concrete buildings rose on either side; crates and tattered bundles littered the space along each wall. I took a few more steps and waited, hoping to feel a crackle of electrical current. I searched the dingy sky, but there was no portal, no sign of the home from where I had dropped. Still, there was no doubt this was the place where I had first opened my eyes to see the sword fight. This was where my nightmare began.

I moved farther in to the spot where Tristan and the Rhusican had fought. Dark liquid stained the ground—blood or something else. Did the Rhusican have friends who came and claimed his body? Or did scavengers drag it away in the night?

I shivered and backed away. Something rustled in a pile of rubbish on one side of the alley, and I brought my sword forward. I edged past the sounds and knelt on the spot where I had regained consciousness the afternoon before. I hoped for a door or a whirling tunnel, a star gate or a transporter platform, but my examination of the ground revealed nothing. "I've watched way too much television," I said to the emptiness.

A distant swishing sound alerted me that another truck was approaching. Jumping up, I ran out to the street, waving my arms. Today the brakes started squealing in time to stop the sleek machine before it flattened me. I ran to the driver's side and peered through the clear plastic window, eager to meet someone who could help me.

There didn't seem to be anyone inside. I used my sleeve to clear away the film of dust and got my nose right up against the window. Nothing. The machine was automated. Now that I was no longer flapping in front of it, it began coasting forward again.

"Wait!" I pounded my hand against the side, where a door should be. But it pulled ahead and was gone.

The isolation and emptiness haunted me. Something very bad had happened in this place. There were so many streets, dozens and dozens of buildings. People had once lived here—gathered, worked, laughed, quarreled. Where were they? Why had they left? Why did empty trucks still circle mindlessly through the streets?

God, I'm in way over my head. Show me what to do. It didn't feel odd to pray inside a dream. I did it all the time. In fact, in my dreams, I often felt surges of faith and conviction that carried me through vivid sleeping adventures. Too bad I didn't have that kind of courage or passion in real life.

I wandered back into the alley, to my starting point on the small area of black tar pavement. If I were to have any hope of finding my way back, it would be from here. But I couldn't find any clue of how I had arrived. I held my sword out in front of me and waited. The overcast sky shimmered on the blade as it tilted. My arm tired and sank to my side.

I strained to hear sounds, but there was no rustling of leaves, no distant radios playing. This was the emptiest place I had ever been. Even on a family vacation through an old western ghost town, there had been tumbleweeds and jackrabbits and the sound of wind howling through broken windows. Here, there was street after street of silence and regret.

Suddenly a high-pitched voice floated far above me: ". . . more french fries than me . . ."

My daughter! "Anne!" I shouted up into the heavy, dull sky. "Anne! Can you hear me?" I waited, holding my breath.

Giggles floated far away. Then another fragment broke through: "Save some for Mom." Mark's voice.

Hope and yearning raced through my veins. "Mark! I'm here! Can you hear me?" My shouted words came out hoarse and strained. I listened again. Silence.

Fine. I would stay here. I'd stand here and shout until they heard me. Until whatever had brought me here put me back.

"Jon! Anne! MARK! Can you hear me? I'm here! Mark? Kids! Help!" There was no answer except the reverberation of my own desperate cries.

Then, in the pause between my calls, as I strained to hear a response, something scuffed by the entrance of the alley.

I spun around to face it, sword lifted.

Tristan strode into the alley. He stopped several yards away from me. "I wouldn't make so much noise. Most of the scavengers stay hidden until night, but this still isn't a safe place."

I glared at him and kept my sword raised.

He was wearing a bulky backpack with several rolls and bundles tied to it. His sword hilt jutted out the top of one side of his pack. He studied the anger and distrust in my face. "I don't know why you're here," he said, raking one hand through his hair. "You don't seem like an enemy, although I've been wrong before. But whatever you're doing here, I can't just leave you. And we don't have much time. If we don't catch an early transport, we won't get to Braide Wood before nightfall. It's not safe to travel close to dark—even there."

I shook my head. "I need to get home to my family. I heard something. They were here."

Tristan glanced around. "Where?"

"Not actually here . . . just their voices."

"People hear voices all the time when they pass through Shamgar," he said with gentle concern. "This isn't a safe place."

"Look, I don't really know you. And Kieran . . ." I scanned the street behind him. I wasn't about to let his scary friend make me conveniently disappear.

Tristan shook his head. "Kieran left. He has his own plans, and he delayed them long enough helping me. He won't be traveling with us." He shifted his pack with impatience. "I don't know what you thought you overheard, but he doesn't mean half of what he says. He's changed since . . . since Kendra. He wouldn't hurt you."

"Kendra?" I asked, puzzled.

"His sister. I thought he told you. Kieran's my brother-in-law." The pain was back in Tristan's eyes.

I took a step forward, lowering my sword. "I didn't know."

"We were friends from childhood and true brothers when I married Kendra." Tristan looked at the ground. "He would never say the words, but I know he blames me for what happened." He looked up at me, and in a blink, the remorse in his face disappeared and his eyes were alert.

"Don't move." He pulled a narrow dagger from the side of his boot.

"What?" I stumbled a few steps back.

Tristan swore under his breath and flicked the dagger in my direction. It landed near my feet with a thump and a hiss.

I sprang back.

Only a few feet away, a furry lizard was skewered to the pavement. It hissed once more, showing rows of sharp teeth before its head collapsed and its eyes closed.

I pointed and started hyperventilating. "That . . . what? . . . Ehyew!"

Tristan pulled his dagger out of the creature and kicked the carcass to the side of the alley. He wiped the blade on his pant leg and slid the dagger back into his boot sheath. "Kieran told me you have the signs of a Restorer," he said, as though nothing had happened. "He also told me not to trust you. But he worries too much. So friend or foe, you're coming with me."

"Keep your friends close but your enemies closer?"

Tristan laughed. "Now that sounds like something Kieran would say." Then his face sobered. "Susan, if I can help you to find your people one day, I will. But right now we have to leave." He was practically vibrating with impatience.

I knew I was out of options. There was no way I was going to stay by myself in this strange, empty town. But traveling alone with this rough escapee from a medieval novel didn't seem like a good idea either.

Of course, if he'd wanted to harm me, he could have done it by now. And he was mourning his wife, which made me feel a little safer. "Let's go." I shrugged, braced my sword over my shoulder again, and walked with him to the end of the alley.

"I brought some things for you." Tristan grabbed a bundle that was leaning against a building. He helped me ease into the unfamiliar shoulder straps and belts. When he reached out to take my sword and stow it with my other gear, I hesitated. My hand clenched on the grip; I had to coax my muscles to relinquish the weapon, but I didn't have time to analyze my reaction because he secured it in moments.

"We have to hurry." Tristan hitched up his own gear and loped down the street.

I followed behind at a stumbling jog, adjusting the pack that lurched from side to side on my shoulders. My pack felt as off balance as I did.

Chapter Five

TRISTAN DIDN'T SLOW DOWN UNTIL WE were well clear of the town, following a road with a slight incline. I paused to catch my breath and look back. From this vantage, I could see the lumpy homes as well as the taller structures that formed the town center. A ragged banner, interwoven with colors of dark gray and silver, hung limply from the tallest building.

The air was easier to breathe now. It was still heavy and humid, but the wet scent of leaf mold reminded me of spring, instead of decay. Rolling fields covered with gray-green moss surrounded the town. The horizon line blurred as the gray hills melded into gray sky. The landscape looked like a photo of Irish farmland with all the color leached out of it. Beyond the town, a series of ponds or bogs looked like pits of wet concrete.

Awe hummed in my heart, followed sharply by a new jolt of fear. What was this place? I thought if I got away from the empty structures, I'd be able to figure out where I was. Instead, I was even more confused. If this was some demented theme park, it was huge.

All I could do was let this hallucination spin itself out. I'd stay alert, learn whatever I could, and figure out how to get home.

Tristan turned back and saw me gawking. "Keep moving."

He reminded me of my brother: shaggy, gruff, quick to boss me around and throw exasperated glares my direction, rough in a way that disguised unexpected flares of kindness.

I hiked up my pack and followed him but didn't stop looking back.

I've never been good at navigation. My husband can be in a crowded shopping mall and instantly point to true north. I've been known to get lost in the basement of a friend's house—getting disoriented enough to forget where the stairs are. I need to look directly into the setting sun to know that I'm facing west. Even then, it rarely helps me figure out how to get where I'm going.

Trailing behind Tristan, I studied the sky, but it was uniformly overcast, with no hint of a sun. I didn't have a hope of figuring out which way we were heading. My brain was filling with questions to ask Tristan, but he was intent on covering ground, and it was all I could do to keep up.

My feet began to hurt, even though the tar road made for easy travel. We approached a small grove of trees with a shelter that looked like an adobe clamshell at the side of the road, and Tristan finally slowed. Another street intersected the one we had taken from town. Tristan looked up and down this new road with a frown. It was such a normal, impatient gesture that, for a moment, I felt right at home. We could be at a bus stop or a train station in my hometown, wondering if we had missed our connection.

As I looked more closely at one of the trees, the illusion of familiarity slipped away. The leaves stretched far overhead, huge and wide, like those of a rubber tree. There was no rough bark on the black trunk. Instead the entire surface was covered with a series of overlapping runnels of smooth, glossy sap.

I reached out to touch it.

Tristan jerked me back by the straps of my pack. "Don't touch that," he said. "In fact, don't touch anything."

I bit back an indignant response and eased the pack off my shoulders.

Tristan sighed and removed his pack as well. He flung himself down against the curved wall of the alcove. Made from the same rough gray plaster as the buildings in Shamgar, the open-sided half-dome provided protection from the elements.

Drizzle tickled my face. Great. More rain. I shoved my pack under the cover of the shelter and sat down near Tristan. He wasn't looking very friendly, but there was no one else to ask about this nightmare I had stumbled into.

I decided to start small. "What kind of tree is that?"

"What?" He looked at me as if he had forgotten me — or wished he could.

"The tree. What kind is it?"

"It's called a bitum. The sap is used to make roads. But you don't want to touch it. It's a sticky mess."

I stuck my head out into the rain to look up at the surrounding trees again.

Tristan gave a half smile. "Do you know what sap is?"

"Of course I do." I settled back under cover. "We have a maple tree in our backyard. Every spring the kids try to tap it, but we never get enough to make syrup. One year we went to a real sugar bush and watched them collect the sap and boil it down. That was the best maple syrup I ever tasted." My mouth watered at the memory.

"You eat the sap?" Tristan looked alarmed.

"It's nothing like those." I waved at the surrounding trees. "But speaking of eating . . ."

Tristan gave a reluctant grin. "You didn't get any breakfast, did you? I'm guessing we missed the early transport, so we may as well get comfortable." He dug in his pack and took out a semi-flat bowl that he set out in the rain. Then he pulled out a round loaf, tore it, and gave me half.

I broke off a small piece and nibbled it. It was hard and coarse but had a walnut flavor that reminded me of a specialty loaf from my favorite bakery. "Thanks." We chewed for a while, and I tried to organize my questions. "So why is the town back there deserted?"

His eyebrows pulled together in a frown, and he looked like he might not answer me. Then he swallowed his bread and stared out into the misty rain.

"For many years, the Gray Hills were home to a proud clan—the sons of Shamgar," he began, speaking in the stylized way that I used to tell fairy tales to my children. "They built a strong and beautiful city in the midst of the hills. The streets were filled with travelers, and music was heard in its square every day." He dropped out of his formal tone and grinned. "My grandmother's brother lived there, along with more distant cousins than I could keep track of. I remember visiting when I was young. It was crowded and noisy. At night everyone left their doors open so light spilled into the streets, and the town seemed to glow." He shifted his weight and cleared his throat.

"Where was I? Oh, right. The music." He looked out into the distance again. "And music was heard in its square every day. But the people of Shamgar forgot the Verses. They sought power and wealth from the gods of the hills. On the far side of the clay fields, much too close to Shamgar, live the people of

Hazor. They are a strong and cruel nation. For generations they grew in strength, fighting and conquering all the tribes around them. They never crossed into the Gray Hills because the People of the Verses were protected. But when Shamgar forgot the Songs, their protection was gone. One day a fierce army crossed the clay fields from Hazor and killed every guardian and every songkeeper, every weaver and builder, each councilmember and transtech, each mother and father. They carried off the children and all the wealth of the town. The city of the Gray Hills has been deserted ever since. And those who brave its empty streets can sometimes hear the hill gods laugh." Tristan's voice trailed off, but he continued to stare out past the gray horizon.

I shivered and hugged my upper arms.

Tristan turned to me and the spell was broken. "There's a cloak in your bag if you're cold."

Mute for the moment, I shook my head. He reached out into the rain for the shallow bowl and offered me the water it had collected. I took a sip and handed it back to him. He finished the rest and set the bowl back outside.

"I bet these hills are beautiful in the sunlight," I said, squinting past the drizzle.

Tristan stared at me blankly. "Sunlight?"

"Yeah, you know, 'The sun to govern the day and the moon to govern the night.'"

He still looked confused. Couldn't he at least make an effort to follow the conversation? "The big ball in the sky? Where our light comes from? It comes up in the morning and goes down at night. Well, not really. It just looks that way because the earth rotates. . . ."

Had I started speaking Swahili? Tristan's face didn't reflect an ounce of comprehension. The implication soaked in. "You don't know what I'm talking about, do you?"

Another shiver ran through me. If this place didn't have a sun, I was a lot farther from home than I wanted to believe. The bleak landscape glowered back at me. There had to be a sun somewhere out there to give this world light and heat, but it was shrouded by thick atmosphere — a constant blanket of gray.

None of the homes I'd seen in Shamgar had lamps. People had invented glowing walls that duplicated the muted illumination of the sky. Light didn't come from one source. It came from all around. It explained one of the things that had felt out of place to me. This was a world of few shadows. The tall bitum trees cast no shade.

"So how do you know which way is north? How do you draw your maps?" I asked.

Tristan edged away from me, looking uneasy at yet another odd question.

"How do you know which way you're going?"

He pointed back toward Shamgar. "Past the clay fields is Hazor. It borders all our lands along that side."

I arbitrarily decided Hazor was "north." It helped me to picture a map in my mind.

"The River Borders are that way, several days travel." He pointed the opposite direction. The Kahlareans live there, and we've fought several wars with them. There are rumors that —" He cut himself off, giving me a sharp look.

I ignored his flare of distrust, immersed in drawing a mental map. South. Hazor on the north, Kahlarea on the south.

Tristan pointed down the road in the direction I determined to be east. "Two other clans live that way, along the coast. Past that is the sea." He was beginning to warm up to this geography lesson. He signaled behind the alcove. "That's the direction we're heading. To Lyric, and from there to Ferntwine. After that we head toward the River Borders before reaching Braide Wood. That's my home." He stopped, checking to see if I was paying attention. "Past Braide Wood are the Morsal Plains—farmland. Far beyond that are two other clans that were part of the People of the Verses, but they left the Council."

I wanted to ask Tristan more questions, but I heard a distant sound. "It's coming." I jumped up.

Tristan tensed and reached for his sword. "What's coming?"

"Something with wheels on the road. Don't you hear it?"

Tristan stepped out into the rain and listened. After a few long moments, he grinned. "You're right. It's the transport." His smile faded into a suspicious frown. "How did you do that?"

"I heard it. How do your trucks run so quietly? I suppose you don't use combustion engines, because with an atmosphere like this, you want to avoid air pollution. Is it batteries?"

Tristan made a low sound in his throat and shook some of the rain off his cloak.

I squinted down the road. "How do you get power for your trucks and transports?"

He shifted his shoulders in irritation. "You should have asked Kieran. His father is a transtech. He can make anything move. He told me once that it's the power of opposites."

"Electromagnetic?" Best guess I could come up with, given my limited science knowledge.

"Skyler has an incredible mind," Tristan mused, ignoring my question. "He wasn't thrilled when his daughter wanted to marry a guardian. Kieran is just like him. He can take things apart and remember where every piece belongs. Should have been a transtech like his father, but—" Once again, Tristan clamped his mouth shut, as if he'd said too much.

Frustration made the muscles in my shoulders tighten. I was never going to figure this place out if he kept interrupting himself. The transport pulled up before I could think of a way to get him talking again.

Similar in style to the trucks I had already seen—but much larger—the vehicle was long, sleek, and silver. It looked like part of a bullet train, or a subway car, although it appeared to run on wheels. I crouched down to peek under the body.

Tristan hauled me back up by my pack again. "Would you pay attention?"

A curved door slid up into the roof of the transport, and Tristan stepped on and pulled me after him. The door slipped back down, and the machine pulled forward. I stumbled, sank into one of the metallic benches molded along both sides of the car, and settled my pack at my feet—again feeling a twinge of the familiar. With the long central aisle, this looked exactly like a subway car. I looked for posters advertising the latest play in town, or ads for a new cell-phone plan. But the inside of the transport was as stark and bare as its outer shell. There were no other passengers. The humid air smelled stuffy and uncirculated, and again I was reminded of burnt marshmallows.

Tristan braced himself against one of the dusty plastic windows. Alert eyes scanned the passing countryside.

I tried to gauge his level of patience. I was beginning to feel even more like an unwanted kid sister tagging along. "Tristan?"

"Hm?" He watched the road ahead.

"If this is not my world—and I'm getting a strong suspicion that it's not—why are you speaking English?"

He flopped down onto the seat across from me and winced. "Why am I speaking what?" He rubbed the back of his neck.

"You speak the same language as I do. How is that possible?"

"I speak the language of the Songs. We are the People of the Verses. What else would I speak?" Tristan was trying to help, but I was clearly giving him a headache.

I massaged my temples. My head wasn't feeling so great either. "But you can understand me. That shouldn't be possible."

"If that's what's bothering you, don't worry. I can't understand most of what you say." The corner of his mouth curved up. I couldn't help but smile back at him. Then his face grew earnest, and he leaned forward. "If you were sent to us, then Someone sent you. Doesn't it follow that the same One who brought you here would also equip you with what you need? I don't send a young guardian out on patrol without his weapons."

He stood again to stare out the window while I pondered what he'd said. Logical, but hardly comforting. I didn't feel "sent." I felt like an accident. Or a lunatic. Or the only sane person in a world full of lunatics.

The transport continued to surge forward—not quite freeway speed (at least, not the lead-footed way Mark drove) but still fast. I watched the deceptively ordinary scenery fly by. Meadows, trees, the road we were on, even some distant animals that looked like sheep—if I let my eyes go slightly out of focus, I could be on a road trip through Iowa. About twenty minutes rolled past; though without my watch, it was hard to tell. If I were ever yanked into a different world again, I would definitely bring a flashlight and a watch. When we slowed down, I peered through the windows. More questions spun through my mind. "So where are—"

Tristan swore under his breath and turned sharply away from the window. The color leached from his face.

"What's wrong?"

"It's Cameron. A councilmember. He's getting on at this stop."

The door slid up and revealed a group of people waiting to board. A plump young man with pimply skin jumped on first, pulling a cloth from his sleeve. He dusted off a section of bench. The next man to board entered the transport like a rock star with an entourage and sat down on the freshly dusted seat. As tall as Tristan, he had a designer face—every feature perfect. He carried the smug confidence of a man who had never lacked wealth, looks, or power. Black, shoulder-length hair was slicked back from his smooth features, and his rust-colored tunic was sleek and clean.

I brushed some dust from the baggy layers of my rough woven clothes. "Probably uses bitum sap on his hair," I muttered under my breath.

Tristan wasn't listening. He eased onto the bench next to me. Tension flexed through his limbs.

My palm itched, and I turned my pack slightly so my sword hilt was closer.

Two women and an older man, all carrying bundles, followed the others on board. Although not as polished in appearance as Cameron, the fabric of their tunics and pants was finely woven and clean. One woman spared a chilly smile for us, but quickly averted her gaze, as if our presence threatened her social standing. As they found places to sit, Cameron continued a conversation. "So then the Council voted to put a team of transtechs to work on it." His voice was resonant. He beamed at his audience as they laughed and murmured approving words.

A wave of distaste rolled over me. Fawning looked ugly on any world.

He leaned forward and lowered his voice, as if divulging a secret. "I'd say the guardians will be obsolete within five or six seasons."

Cameron glanced in our direction. "It looks like we have company," he said, showing too many teeth. "Tristan! I didn't see you there. This is a surprise."

My distrust deepened. He had noticed Tristan the second he boarded.

Cameron's brow wrinkled in mock puzzlement. "Aren't you assigned patrol in Morsal Plains this season?" He turned his gaze back to the young man by his side. "Someone has to keep the rizzids out of the grain fields."

The boy's high-pitched giggle turned his face red. The women chuckled, but the older man glanced at Tristan, then looked down.

"Cameron." Tristan greeted him with outward calm, though his teeth ground together audibly. "I didn't know the Council was in session."

"The work of serving the people never ends," Cameron said with a smirk. "At least for some of us. I guess guardians are entitled to more time off." He paused. When Tristan didn't rise to the bait, Cameron leaned back and crossed his arms, his gaze dark and speculative. "You might be interested to know, we've just had a very successful trade mission with the Hazorites of Corros Hills."

Tristan sat up straighter. "You can't be serious. There's no trade allowed with Hazor."

Cameron's eyes sparkled, but he put on a concerned expression. "Tristan, Tristan, you've been on patrol too long. I find it distressing that the guardians aren't kept better informed." Cameron turned to one of the women. "Remind me to bring this up at the next Council meeting." Then he targeted Tristan again. "I thought messengers were sent to all outposts . . . even as far as Morsal Plains." Cameron tapped one long finger against his pursed lips. "Oh, but that's right. You weren't at Morsal Plains, were you? Where have you been? Wait. Don't tell me. Out causing trouble with our allies again?"

"The Rhusicans are not our allies," Tristan spat out.

Cameron raised an eyebrow. Basking in his control of the situation, he turned to analyze me.

Dread chilled my blood. I inched back behind Tristan, willing myself to look insignificant. When he first boarded, I had hoped Cameron was a smarmy bureaucrat who wouldn't notice me, but now that hope fizzled. How could I diffuse his interest and avoid trouble? It would have helped if Tristan had explained more.

"And who is this?" Cameron gave me a smile full of self-importance. "I'm Cameron of Lyric, councilmember of the People."

Fine. Tristan may have left me twisting in the wind, but I'd had enough of cowering. I sat up straight and looked Cameron in the eyes. "I'm Susan from Ridgeview Drive."

Genuine confusion flickered across his face.

Ha. Figure that one out, Mr. High and Mighty.

Cameron's eyes narrowed and raked over me, pinning me, even as he spoke to Tristan. "She looks like she could be Hazorite. Have you been doing some trading of your own?"

Hazorite? Me? I waited for Tristan to come up with something plausible, but he was silent. Cameron continued to watch me.

I fought the urge to squirm. *Come on, Susan, think of something.* "I've been on a long journey and was lost," I said slowly.

"Tristan found me and has been helping me." That sounded safe. Sticking close to the truth seemed like a good idea.

Unfortunately, Cameron was becoming even more interested. And his interest was the last thing I wanted.

"Well, Susan of Ridgeview Drive, let me officially welcome you. As a councilmember, it is my responsibility to meet with all foreign guests. Tristan has delivered you into safe hands. You may journey with us to Lyric." He said it like a king bestowing a boon on a grateful subject. "I'm sure it's been an interesting experience traveling with Tristan. I know you'll enjoy telling me all about it. Tristan, you have our gratitude." Cameron was practically smacking his lips at the thought of the tasty secrets he planned to pry out of me.

Panic started as a flutter in my stomach and then tightened in my throat. I opened my mouth to argue.

Tristan put a hand on my arm. "Thank you, Cameron, but she's traveling to Braide Wood." His voice was firm.

"You know the law." Cameron's dark eyes flashed. "All foreign guests meet first with the Council. I'm sure she'll be more comfortable with us. When we stop at Lyric, I have several Council guards meeting us—so I can assure her . . . protection." There was a clear threat in his smooth words.

Could Tristan overpower a pack of Council guards? I figured I could take out the chubby youth and the women. Whatever it took, I was not going anywhere with Cameron.

"Normally I would never disagree with a councilmember." Tristan squeezed my arm in warning. "But she's very ill. I have to get her to the healers. I know she'll be eager to meet with the Council once it's safe, but we don't want her spreading a plague through Lyric."

I coughed a few times, trying to be helpful.

The entourage looked alarmed and edged farther down to their end of the car. Cameron frowned in irritation. "You're sick?"

I nodded, trying to look feeble.

"We have fine healers in Lyric." Cameron picked a piece of lint off his sleeve.

"Of course. But it would be wrong to endanger so many people—so many *important* people—by bringing this illness into the city." Tristan played his argument to the entourage, who nodded and muttered in agreement.

Cameron shot a quelling glare at his group then turned back to Tristan. "You're traveling too late to reach Braide Wood before nightfall."

"It's so kind of you to be concerned." Tristan smiled thinly. "But you know guardians. We have friends everywhere." His hand rested casually on his sword hilt. "Many friends."

Cameron leaned back, eyes hard.

Tristan kept his face bland. "No need to worry. I'm sure we'll find safe shelter." He sat back, closing the subject, then turned to me. "Are you all right?"

I was touched by his concern. "Yeah, I'm fine."

He frowned, and his heavy foot squashed down onto my loafer.

"Ow!" I winced, taking a second to catch on. "Oh . . . Owwww!" I continued a dramatic moan and doubled over. "The pain is returning." Based on the worried whispers coming from the other end of the transport, my overacting had been effective. But Cameron was glaring murder at Tristan. Glittering with stark hatred, his eyes promised that this conflict wasn't over.

The ice in my bones caused a shudder I didn't have to fake.

At the next stop, several more people got on, and Tristan

edged us farther into the corner, greeting one man and making murmured explanations to a few others that his companion was sick.

I didn't breathe normally until Cameron and his group left at Lyric. I craned my head up to see the city, but a large berm blocked my view down the road that met this station. Why didn't the transport go through the center of any towns? I wanted to see something besides Shamgar. Bitum trees and clumps of blue ferns framed several more clamshell-shaped shelters. A few children dashed around clusters of travelers who chatted and snacked, just like passengers at a crowded airport. The rain had stopped, and people wore a range of sweaters, tunics, and light layers for the cool but temperate climate. Because there were more people here, I suspected that Lyric must be a larger city. I wondered if it were as long a walk from the transport stop as Shamgar was from where we boarded. Where was the logic in that?

Several uniformed men moved forward to meet Cameron as he left the transport. He spoke to one of the guards and pointed to the window. The man stared at me, as if memorizing my face.

Prickles danced across my skin like spider legs, and I quickly ducked down.

Once the vehicle was moving again, I turned to Tristan. "As soon as we're someplace safe, I want you to teach me to use my sword. Cameron is a lot scarier than those furry lizard things."

Tristan didn't smile. "A sword is not the weapon to use against the Council. They're the chosen leaders. It's my job to serve them."

He was impossibly stingy with his explanations. I'd done a good job improvising so far, but I was tired of floundering through a foreign film with no subtitles. Whether this was a dream, a delusion, or an alternate reality, I needed more information.

Instead of saying more, Tristan turned a grim face toward the window.

I cleared my throat. "Are you in a lot of trouble?" I asked, trying to get him talking again.

He glanced at me, as if debating how to answer. "No worse than usual." He shut me out with a half grin.

Subdued, I sat back and listened to the whoosh of wheels rolling on wet tarmac. The strange gray landscape continued to fly past, each mile taking me farther from home. Hurtling forward into this world I couldn't understand, I'd never felt so alone. All I had for comfort was a sword I didn't know how to use and a cranky guardian who didn't trust me.

Chapter Six

AT THE NEXT STOP, ANOTHER TWENTY minutes later, Tristan nudged me. "It's Ferntwine. We're getting off here. Night's coming, and I need to get help."

I lugged my pack over one shoulder and followed him. This station was larger than Shamgar's, with several wooden benches stretched along the side of the road. We seemed to have moved into a new architectural style. No more adobe clamshells for shelters. Where Shamgar's buildings looked like they'd risen fully formed from the clay pits around the city, here the twining legs of the benches made the seats look as if they'd grown from the ground. The area held scattered groves of trees, and a bitum road wound into the woods and out of sight.

"Is Ferntwine a town?" A street sign would be helpful.

Tristan shook his head. "A clan, a town, a transport stop."

He led me to an empty seat. "Stay here," he ordered. "I'll be back soon." Tristan strode along the edge of the road toward a cluster of people who greeted him with enthusiasm. He returned their greetings with obvious affection and was soon in earnest conversation. Where did he get his energy?

Trying not to think about my own weariness, I stared down at my hands in my lap and focused my thoughts on Tristan's voice. Soon it became audible. I liked these heightened senses. This would be a great trick for eavesdropping on the kids when they were plotting mischief.

"Things are worse than I expected," Tristan was saying.

"The Council is feeling the threat on the River Borders," one of the women said. "That's why they're seeking alliances and weapons from Hazor."

"With Kahlarea building an army, all the more reason the Council should support the guardians," protested one of the men near Tristan.

A light female voice drifted into the discussion. "If the clans stay true to the Verses, they will never dissolve the guardians."

"It was Cameron who convinced the Council to let the Rhusicans live here. I can't believe they've allowed trade with Hazor. I wish Kieran had come back." Tristan sounded defeated.

Other voices around the station intruded, and I stopped straining to listen to him.

Political intrigue gave me a headache anyway, especially without anyone to explain the players to me.

Nearby, a family group drew my attention. A mother pulled two quarreling boys apart. She looked as harried as any suburban housewife at the mall, and the familiar scene threw my thoughts back to my real life. Where were my children? What were they doing right now? The ache of longing made me lower my head into my hands.

"It's always sad traveling alone, isn't it?" a sweet, clear voice piped up beside me.

I turned, startled.

A doll-faced girl with auburn ringlets sat next to me. She pulled a dried fruit the color of a pale apricot out of a cloth bag and nibbled it. Then she took out another and offered it to me, but I shook my head. She looked about the same age as my seven-year-old, Anne, but her green eyes were compassionate and wise. "You're far from home." It wasn't a question.

I nodded. "Yes, and I was just missing my children. I have a daughter about your age."

Her eyes grew sad and full of sympathy. "You are so alone here."

The pain inside me suddenly had a name: loneliness. It felt so good to have someone understand, to clarify it for me, even if it was just a little girl. "That's true. I don't belong here. It's . . . hard." Tears welled up, but I blinked them back.

"Away from everyone who loves you. No one to trust. It isn't fair."

I looked into her bright eyes. She was the first person I had met on this strange world who really understood what I was feeling. It was silly. She was only a child, but I found myself wanting to ask her all my questions about what had brought me here and what my purpose was.

Before I could speak, a rude hand yanked my upper arm and pulled me to my feet. "What are you doing?" Tristan hissed at me.

I tried to wrench free. "Nothing." Leave it to him to interrupt the first comforting conversation I'd had in this strange place.

He grabbed my pack and dragged it, along with me, toward his group of friends. "What did she say to you?"

How could I explain the maternal yearning that had stirred in me, or the soothing feeling of having someone sympathize? "Nothing. She's just a little girl."

He stopped short and glared at me. "She's a Rhusican." He

spat the words out, as if it burned his tongue to say them.

A queasy ball knotted in my stomach. "You mean, like . . . like the one who poisoned Kendra?"

"Poison is their only skill."

"It's a good thing I didn't eat anything." I glanced back over my shoulder, but the Rhusican was gone.

Tristan squeezed the bridge of his nose and was about to ask me something, but his friends bounded up to us and interrupted. A quick round of introductions was punctuated with laughter, snide comments about Tristan, and genuine friendliness that warmed me. The group made it clear that they insisted on changing their plans to travel with us to Braide Wood. In case we didn't make it before dark, there was safety in numbers.

A burly young man called Wade laughed and patted Tristan on the back with affection. "We can't just leave you two to risk it alone. Tristan's saved me more times than I can count."

"Which isn't saying much," said a young woman in the group, leading to another round of laughter.

Wade made a face at her and continued. "So I'm glad to help him for a change." His expression sobered, and he met Tristan's eyes. "You know I'm happy to face any danger for you."

Tristan looked uncomfortable. "Let's hope that isn't necessary tonight." He tried to make his words light.

I felt a quick spin of anxiety. He was expecting trouble.

The next leg of the journey began pleasantly enough. Our boisterous group boarded a smaller transport that barely contained us all. It pulled out onto an intersecting road that soon left the rolling plains and scattered groves behind and wound its way into thick forest. I wished the transport had lights, because the gray light coming through the windows was no longer as strong.

I gave up trying to see much out the window and concentrated on sorting out all of Tristan's friends.

Wade was a guardian, although he was much younger than Tristan. He had a short, scruffy beard and the loud, somewhat clumsy demeanor of a class clown. After he threatened to die of starvation on the spot, one of the women handed him a piece of bread. He bit into it and pretended to break a tooth. He laughed harder than anyone else at his own humor, but in this bleak and frightening world, I found myself enjoying his silliness. He reminded me of some of Jake's friends. They were full-grown men with jobs or college classes and adult responsibilities, yet the awkwardness of boyhood still clung to them in fragments, like eggshells they hadn't quite shaken off.

The young woman in the group, Linette, had the fragile bone structure of a sparrow, with long blonde hair pulled back into a narrow braid. From the teasing conversation that swirled around the transport, I learned that she was engaged to Dylan ("the most wonderful, handsome, sensitive man in the world"), who was a guardian on patrol along the River Borders. They had been separated for eleven long days.

"Are you a guardian, too?" I asked her.

She looked down shyly. "Oh, no. I'm just a songkeeper."

"Linette, don't say that," chided Bekkah. "Your gift is as valued as any other." Bekkah looked about my age, with thick chestnut hair cinched at the nape of her neck. She wore a dagger in her belt, and the hand resting on the hilt revealed broken nails and rough skin. She reminded me of a trail guide I'd met on a week-long canoe trip—competent and strong with little interest in the fluff of modern life. She ducked as the men started batting a knotted ball of fabric around the car, like kids on a school bus.

"Boys." Bekkah shook her head. Linette grinned, and I relaxed in the pleasure of being with other women and sharing affectionate humor.

"Bekkah is a guardian," Linette told me with admiration.

"I always loved being outside, running and climbing trees. My parents hoped I'd be a messenger, but that wasn't for me." Bekkah shrugged.

I pulled off one of my loafers as I listened. The woolen socks Tristan had loaned me were too thick, and the earlier walking had raised a blister on my heel, which had healed and returned several times throughout the morning. Now it was little more than a rough callous, but it itched like newly healed skin. I rubbed it absently and decided to ignore the whole unsettling phenomenon.

"It's a bit of a hike to Braide Wood. Do you have any boots with you?" Bekkah asked.

"No. I, uh, packed in a hurry."

She shifted into maternal mode. "Hm . . . I got these boots in Lyric yesterday and was saving my old ones for my sister, but they might fit you." She dug in her pack and pulled out some stained and scuffed boots with thick soles. She held one up to the foot I was rubbing. "Try them."

The boots were larger than my shoes, but with the thick socks they were a comfortable fit. Bekkah looked so pleased that I didn't put up even a polite resistance to the generous gift. I leaned down to stuff my loafers into my pack, and something hit me on the back of the head with the force of a tennis serve.

"Yow!" I popped my head back up. A fabric-covered ball

dropped to the floor. When I grabbed it, I could feel that it was filled with something like dried beans.

"Who threw it?" Bekkah growled at the men, making me wonder if she had children. She certainly had the stern-mom voice perfected.

Wade and Tristan looked everywhere but at Bekkah. Wade whistled nonchalantly. Davis, the oldest member of the group, leaned against the side of the transport fighting back laughter. He had been introduced to me as a builder and had been very quiet so far, but now his eyes sparkled. With close-cut silver hair receding back from his bald forehead, Davis looked old enough to be my father. He caught my eye and then glanced over to Kyle. The young transtech had been a bit aloof from the general conversations thus far. He hadn't laughed at Wade's jokes earlier, and I hadn't heard him join in the political conversation on the platform. Now Kyle's face turned red, and he looked like he wanted to sink into his bench.

Bekkah took the ball from my hand and tossed it up and down a few times. "Confess, you fiends! Who missed his catch?"

I giggled at the four wide-eyed and innocent male faces that turned toward her as one. No one spoke.

"Fine. Then I'm keeping it," Bekkah said in triumph.

"Hey wait a minute! That's mine! Not fair!" came the chorus of protests. She tossed the ball up once more, and Kyle leaped forward to bat it out of the air and over her head. Wade pounced on it with a roar. By the time the men untangled from the resulting pileup in the narrow aisle, the transport was slowing for the next stop.

After we climbed out of the transport, it didn't pull out to continue on its automated way. Instead, the quiet hum of the machine lowered in pitch and then shut down. The last run of the day? No one bothered explaining. Tristan and Davis were looking at the sky, deep in discussion.

"They're wondering if it would be better to camp in the transport for the night or try to make it through the forest," said Bekkah, who had stayed near my side. The sky's shade of gray was perhaps a bit deeper in color, but it was hard for me to guess how long we had until darkness descended. "Stopped transports attract scavengers at night, but they aren't sure how fast we can travel—whether we'll make it to Braide Wood before dark."

I could tell she was being tactful. They were debating how fast *I* could travel. Instead of a pesky kid sister tag-along, I began to feel like a serious hindrance. "If it's so dangerous, why didn't they run the road right up to Braide Wood?"

Her head snapped around, and she fixed me with a piercing stare. "What are you talking about?" She gave me the look I used on Jon when I overheard him utter an obscenity.

If someone would just give me a playbook, I wouldn't keep saying the wrong thing. "I'm sorry," I said, torn between cha-grin and frustration. "I guess I don't understand. But you have flashlights along, right?"

Bekkah recoiled, and her eyes widened. "Where exactly are you from?"

It seemed smarter not to answer that.

"Don't your people have Verses?" She gave an uneasy laugh. "What, do you just treat the night like it's day?"

"Not exactly, but—"

I broke off as Tristan called her. She gave me a last sharp look and walked over to him. Kyle and Linette had their heads together, deep in conversation, and Wade, who had jogged part way up a trail, was bounding back toward Tristan and Davis.

A wave of loneliness washed through me, leaving bitter

debris on my mood as it retreated. I didn't belong here. These were old friends with shared adventures in common. They knew how to navigate this world. But no one understood how lost I felt. No one cared.

"Let's go!" Tristan called.

I shook off the self-pity and shouldered my pack, determined to keep up. Tristan disappeared around the bend of the forest trail, followed closely by the others. Bekkah waited for me to fall in after them, and she took up the rear.

I took a deep breath, comforted by the piney smell of the air under the trees. Mark and I loved to take hiking trips in the woods a few hours' drive from our home. We spent happy afternoons clambering over rocks, stumbling over roots, and finding hidden waterfalls and cliffs. Some of these trees looked like the same tall cedar and spruce I admired on my hikes back home, and like the trees at home, they had cushioned the trail with a thick carpet of needles. But other trees were less familiar. Gnarled, honey-colored branches reached out at twisting angles from the trunks. The tang of pine in the air was colored with the scent of cinnamon.

Almost no underbrush grew in this part of the forest. I peered through the dense stands of tree trunks, trying to catch a glimpse of the small animals that I heard scurrying in the needle bedding, but the pace of the hike didn't allow for lingering.

Sometimes Mark and I had dragged the kids along on hikes. They always moaned about it but seemed to secretly enjoy the experience as much as we did. One thing they didn't like was my love of identifying every plant and wildflower. I always carried a field guide in my pack. When I would pause to pull it out, all four kids would groan in unison. Even Mark would scratch his head and suggest that we move on when I'd hold the guidebook up to a small blue blossom and ask him if it looked more like a Creeping Bellflower or Lobelia. I longed for a field guide now, and time to investigate all the unfamiliar plants along the trail, from the blue ferns clumped around the base of some trees to the tiny red flowers that flashed out from silver-green ground cover.

Our path grew steeper, but no one slowed down. I was breathing rapidly now and falling farther behind Kyle. After one challenging switchback, he glanced back and noticed how far behind I was. He called something ahead to Tristan, and the group stopped to wait for me to catch up. When I reached the top of the switchback, I doubled over, rested my hands on my bent knees, and struggled to breathe. Bekkah laid a hand on my back. "You're doing great." Then we were moving once more.

It wasn't long before Kyle was looking back again. This time he didn't hide the annoyance on his face. I tried to walk faster, but the pack was cutting into my shoulder, and my legs burned. We had maintained our grueling pace for nearly an hour. My feet were heavy and sore, as if someone had velcroed weights around my ankles and lit matches against the raw skin of my heels. They no longer cleared all the roots jutting out along the path. I stumbled and caught myself over and over. Once, I tripped and fell to my hands and knees. Though Bekkah was beside me in an instant, helping me up, the path wasn't wide enough for us to travel side by side as it wound upward between tree trunks. I trudged on alone.

Was this how my kids felt when we took them out on long hikes? I just wanted it to be done. I was tempted to whine, "Are we there yet?" but stopped myself. I was still breathing hard and could feel my pulse pounding in my head whenever I paused.

Up ahead of us, Kyle frowned at the sky. It was definitely growing darker now.

A low, moaning growl sounded from deep among the trees. I stopped short. "Did you hear that?"

Bekkah stood still, listening. "I don't hear anything. How are you doing?"

I shook my head.

"Stay here." She leapt up the path, feet barely touching the rocks as she passed Kyle. His back disappeared up the trail.

Great. Just walk away and leave me. I've been ripped away from my family. I'm completely alone. I'm in a dangerous place—and there's no one to help. I'm alone.

Then it occurred to me that perhaps it was wiser to go on alone anyway. I didn't really know any of these people. How could I trust them? They could be leading me into danger. They didn't care about me.

God, what should I do? Are you ever going to give me a clue?

No, He didn't care about me either.

I had a vague sense that I wasn't thinking clearly, but couldn't seem to stop myself. I slid the pack off my back and let it fall to the path.

It felt so much better to be alone.

And I needed to go back. I didn't belong here.

I began moving slowly down the path the way we had come.

Yes, that was better. I had to go home. A mental fog welled up and clouded my thoughts, pulling me along.

The hike had been too hard. Too hard. I didn't belong. I was so alone.

From far away Bekkah called. Her words became indistinct as my thoughts became louder.

Away from everyone who loves you. No one to trust. It isn't fair, breathed a sweet voice into my thoughts. Yes. It wasn't fair.

My feet kept moving, although I wasn't aware of a trail anymore. Something compelled me to move forward. *Alone. Alone. Alone.* The soft crunch of the pine needles underfoot spoke to me with each step, grinding my spirit into the ground.

Then something stopped me. I squinted through the fog around me. Someone blocked my way. I put my head down and kept walking, but hands pushed against my shoulders, stopping me again.

"What's she doing?" A voice interrupted my thoughts, annoying me.

"I don't know. She keeps talking to herself."

"What's she saying?"

"'Alone.' Tristan, do you know what she's talking about?"

I had to get away. I flung off the arms that were trying to hold me back and began walking again. Cold mist surrounded me. Nothing mattered but my need to get away.

"Linette, come quick!" There was panic in Tristan's voice. I recognized it from a distance, then pushed the thought aside as unimportant. "She was talking to a Rhusican at the transport stop. I think she's been poisoned." Then his voice faded completely.

Chapter Seven

THE NEXT SEVERAL HOURS WERE AMONG the most miserable of my life. At first I felt nothing but the compulsion to get away. I tried to move, but someone held me back. I lashed out and felt myself fall. Then something pinned my limbs. I thrashed against it for a while, but eventually stopped caring. All I saw in my mind were clear green eyes and auburn ringlets and the sweet face of the little girl at the transport station. Her voice was compelling and soothing at the same time. I fell into her words. *You don't belong here. It's so sad. You are all alone—no one to trust.* My mouth formed the words to agree with her. I let myself slide downward into a space far from conscious thought.

Then from outside the cocooning haze around me came a melody in a minor key.

> *The eyes of the One*
> *Are always on His people;*
> *His arms surround us,*
> *And we are not alone.*

He does not forget us
In the night when scavengers howl;
He does not leave us
In our sorrow.

He makes Himself known
To the People of the Song;
His arms hold us up,
And we are not alone.

The voice was breathy and wavering, but insistent. I had been sliding—sliding inexorably downward into emptiness. The mist promised peace. Now something held me back.

Let me go. Let me go deeper into the aloneness. It's where I belong.

Wrapped in gray fog, I stood at the edge of a dark abyss. One more step forward and I would be at peace.

But the new voice kept pulling me back. It hurt. My soul was being stretched and torn.

"Let me go!" I screamed in frustration. I was remotely aware of my body struggling—kicking, scratching, writhing.

The mist cleared for a time. Linette's pale face hovered above me, her lips moving, her eyes fixed on mine with a burning intensity. My screams drowned out her words. I was on the ground beside the rocky trail, and large arms wrapped around me from behind. I couldn't break free. Worried faces surrounded me. I saw them briefly before the mist began to take me again. A hand clamped over my mouth. As soon as my screams were muffled, I could hear Linette's song. This time other voices joined her.

The eyes of the One
Are always on His people;
His arms surround us,
And we are not alone.

The horrible, wrenching tug-of-war continued. At one point I came out of the mist long enough to see Tristan's face. "Susan, don't go. Stay with us." He was using the commanding tone of a guardian, but there was pleading in his voice as well.

Night had fallen, and there were no stars overhead. Distant tree branches were barely visible in pale artificial light. I couldn't see where the light was coming from, but I sensed that we were off to the side of the trail. The hand that had been over my mouth was gone.

I tried to speak. My throat was dry, and my tongue felt thick and clumsy. I coughed and tried again. "My sword," I rasped.

Tristan's face disappeared for a moment, and then he took my hand. He pressed the hilt of my sword into my palm and wrapped my fingers around it.

I stayed aware for longer and longer periods. Linette never stopped singing. One melody wove into the next, sometimes joined by a chorus of voices.

Finally, exhausted, hurting, I was dragged far back from the edge of the void where I had hovered. I smelled the pine air again. I heard a heart beating and realized my head was resting on someone's chest. I looked up and saw it was Davis who was holding me. His relieved smile deepened the creases around his mouth, and he smoothed my damp hair back from my face. I was drenched in sweat.

Kneeling on the ground next to me, Linette held my left hand in both of hers. She had the eager and relieved flush of an athlete who had won a race. "Susan, sing with me."

I tried to follow her simple chorus, but my mind was too tired to keep up with the words.

She stopped and thought for a moment. "You don't know our Songs, but your people must have Verses. Sing one of your Verses."

I tried to explain that I didn't know any Verses, but it took too much effort. My right hand flexed around the hilt of my sword, and a memory surfaced.

"O Lord, you have searched me and you know me," I whispered. "You hem me in—behind and before; you have laid your hand upon me." It hurt to speak, and a fit of coughing interrupted, but the words continued to flow. "Such knowledge is too wonderful for me, too lofty for me to attain. Where can I go from your Spirit? Where can I flee from your presence? If I go up to the heavens, you are there; if I make my bed in the depths, you are there. If I rise on the wings of the dawn, if I settle on the far side of the sea . . ." I must have learned this psalm back in fifth-grade Sunday school. We had a teacher who gave us stickers if we learned our memory work each week. I loved those stickers.

I didn't know how the words were returning to me now, but Linette stared at me with an expression of awe. "Even there your hand will guide me, your right hand will hold me fast," I finished.

I was too weak to move, but my mind was beginning to piece together what had happened. Tristan said I'd been poisoned. When he warned me about the Rhusicans, I had assumed their poison was in food or drink. But poison was an accurate word for the thoughts that had gripped my mind. Relief and gratitude mixed with a horrible dread as I remembered the place of emptiness that had seemed so inviting. "O Lord, you have searched me and you know me," I began again. I turned my head and could see several flat, glowing light panels scattered around us on the ground. Tristan had set up camp, in spite of the taboos about traveling at night. Even as I realized what he had done, a low growl moaned from somewhere behind us.

I stirred, working to lift my sword, but it was too heavy. I couldn't even raise my head.

Linette lifted a worried gaze to the darkness between the surrounding trees, but then she quickly focused on me again. Her hands framed my face. "No. You can't help them. Tristan and Wade have fought bears before. Keep singing."

I wouldn't have called it singing. My voice croaked out hesitant phrases, and every time I stopped, the sounds in the woods became more frightening. I heard a strangled yell and several shouts. There was a great deal of thrashing and deep roaring growls. I stared up into the night sky, wishing for the sight of moonlight or even a few stars. My limbs shook.

Davis bent his head forward. "If I make my bed in the depths, you are there," he repeated after me. His deep voice rumbled in his chest; I drew strength from it and began the psalm again. Soon Linette and Davis were both chanting the words with me, and Linette began to form a melody. Abruptly, she broke off, worry etching her face as Tristan strode into view.

"We killed it," he said quickly.

She released my hand and sank back with a sigh of relief. Now that she was no longer singing, exhaustion hollowed her eyes in the faint light from the strange panels.

"How is she?" Tristan rubbed his sword with a wad of cloth and slid it into a leather scabbard with practiced ease.

"I'm fine," I croaked.

He looked down at me, startled. Then he turned to Linette.

"I think she'll be all right," she said with a smile. Then her face sobered. "Is anyone hurt?"

Tristan nodded. "I know you're tired, but Bekkah could use your help. Wade got clawed pretty bad."

Linette stood up slowly, rubbing her back. "Will you stay with her?"

"All right. Kyle is on watch. And if you get a chance, convince Bekkah to let you take a look at her. She took some hits—but you know Bekkah." He shook his head.

I could hear Linette and Bekkah's murmuring voices nearby and worried about Wade. I wanted to help, but weak from battling the poison, I could only lay there trembling.

Tristan disappeared for a time and came back with a blanket that he tucked around me. My head lolled to one side.

"Would you like me to take her?" he asked Davis in a low voice.

"No, I'm fine. Let's not move her right now. But you can get me a pack to lean against. These bones are getting too old for sleeping on the ground."

Davis's voice vibrated under my cheek as I rested against his chest. My eyelids were sinking closed, but I felt a moment of panic at the fatigue that was claiming me. If I closed my eyes, would I slip back toward the dark chasm that had almost pulled me in? Then Davis rested his hand on my forehead. He and Tristan continued to talk, and in the reassurance of their murmured conversation, I sighed into sleep.

Chapter Eight

IN THE PALLID LIGHT OF MORNING, Tristan roused everyone and gathered us together by the side of the trail. We were a haggard group. To my right, Tristan sat cross-legged. His clothes were even more torn and dirty than before. Next to him, Wade leaned back on one elbow, cradling his other arm, which was wrapped with knotted strips of cloth. Blood seeped through the layers of fabric, but he continued to crack jokes. Bekkah had a bruise deepening on her jawline, and the stiff way she moved hinted at injuries that weren't visible. She avoided looking at me. Linette's eyes were red-rimmed in her pale face. Her thin body slumped with fatigue, but she gave me a soft smile. When she shivered in the cool morning air, Kyle wrapped a cloak around her shoulders. He glared at me from across the circle, and I looked away.

Davis sat to my left and leaned over to pat my shoulder, seeming to read my dreary thoughts. "We'll all feel better with a little food in our bellies."

In the center of the circle were several flat trivets that glowed with light and warmth. Tristan's wooden water bowl sat on top of them; wisps of steam began to rise from some kind of stew within it. Bekkah passed pieces of dry bread around the group, and everyone began dipping their bread into the stew.

The thick broth had the earthy flavor of mushrooms and root vegetables and made me long for coffee and Cheerios. I couldn't muster much appetite, but I forced myself to eat, determined to build up my strength.

The sheer relief of having survived the night had passed, and now I faced another emotion: shame. Humiliation clung to me from the dark place I had tried to reach. I was embarrassed by how easily the lies had pulled me in. As I looked around the circle, I felt a terrible guilt at the trouble I had caused. Instead of reaching the safety of Braide Wood, Linette looked ready to drop, Bekkah's silent misery was obvious, and Wade could have been killed. I looked over at the young man. What if his arm didn't heal?

I wanted to apologize, but saying "I'm sorry" seemed absurdly trivial. So I stayed silent. I couldn't even help when everyone got up to break camp. I wanted to pitch in, to prove I could be something other than a hindrance, but I didn't know what to do. Finally, I just found my pack, tightened its ties, and hoisted it onto my back. The effort made me dizzy, and I put my hand against a tree for support.

Linette approached me. "It's not too much farther," she said, her voice low and hoarse. "Don't forget your Songs. You'll need their strength." She watched me for a moment, like a doctor diagnosing a patient. "There might be echoes. Let me know if the voices come back, all right?"

Kyle walked over and heard her last question. He put an arm around Linette's shoulders, leading her away. "You've done enough already," he told her gently. There was no gentleness in the look he gave me over his shoulder. I wanted to shrivel and melt into the ground.

Bekkah led the group out and everyone fell in, leaving Tristan and me to follow. Before starting up the trail, I made one attempt to ease my guilt. Tristan was crouched, busy weaving a belt through loops in his scabbard, preparing to wear his sword rather than carry it in his pack. I cleared my throat, and he looked up.

"Tristan, I'm sorry." My voice broke, and I couldn't meet his eyes.

He stood up, wrapped the belt around his waist, and cinched it. He adjusted the scabbard. "You're not what I was expecting in a Restorer."

I waited, hoping for some glimpse of understanding or forgiveness in his face.

His grim expression didn't change as he studied me. "I'm glad you came back from the voices," he said at last. "Now move."

I headed up the trail and thought about Kendra. Tristan said the Rhusican from the sword fight had poisoned her. Had Tristan been with her when she was lured away by the voices? Had he fought through long hours trying to pull her back, with no success? Did he resent me for surviving when his wife had not? I wouldn't blame him.

These emotions felt familiar. They tapped into my daily disappointment for all the ways I didn't measure up, for all the hurting people I wasn't able to help. My own children faced struggles that I wanted to solve. Yet all too often I was helpless and inadequate.

God, I hate letting people down. I felt a twinge of the despair that had almost destroyed me last night. What was it Linette said? *Don't forget your Songs. You'll need their strength.*

An old melody popped into my head. It was from the

liturgy we sang at my childhood church. As I hummed it, some of the words came back to me.

> Create in me a clean heart, O God;
> And renew a right spirit within me.
> Cast me not away from thy presence;
> And take not thy holy spirit from me.
> Restore unto me the joy of thy salvation.

My voice caught.

Restore me, I prayed in silence.

We reached a long ridgeline, and the path leveled. Up the trail, Bekkah was setting a slow pace. She moved with a limp, and Davis stayed near, occasionally pointing something out to her along the trail. Wade followed, holding his arm to keep it from jarring. Linette and Kyle hiked close behind Wade. From the hard set of Kyle's shoulders, I could tell he was still angry. I paused to catch my breath before following.

Tristan stomped along the trail not far behind me.

My mind drifted to his pain. He took his role as protector of his people seriously. Yet his own wife had been killed, and the very Council he served seemed to be forsaking everything he worked for.

Restore them, Lord. It was all I knew how to pray at that moment, but it was enough.

The trail continued to be studded with large rocks and roots, so I kept my gaze down, especially as we now edged along a steep cliff on our right side. Focused on my footing, I was startled when Tristan clapped a hand onto my shoulder.

"Look." His voice was as warm and happy as I had heard it so far. From our vantage I could see a scattering of homes.

Braide Wood made me think of a mountain retreat center where our family had once vacationed. The buildings looked like log cabins chinked with bitum. The simple architecture formed around the trees in a way that made the homes seem a part of the forest.

"It's beautiful," I said, making Tristan smile. "I thought it would look more like Shamgar."

"Shamgar is close to the clay fields. Why would we drag clay way up here for our homes?" He pointed to the right. "See the house between the two tallest trees? That's my family's home." Encouraged, we all picked up our pace to weave our way down the switchbacks and into the valley.

Bekkah shouted a "halloo" as we drew closer, and we stirred up plenty of excitement with our entrance into the village. Our company scattered, greeting friends, but I followed Tristan as he kept moving straight to his home. He paused to look over his shoulder. "Wade! With me."

Wade pulled himself away from a conversation with a few girls his age and joined us. As we approached the house, the door flew open and a white-haired woman who looked to be in her sixties ran out, moving like a young girl. She grabbed Tristan's face in her two wrinkled hands and pulled him close. She rested her forehead against his.

"Thank the One," she murmured. Then she planted a quick kiss on his brow and released him. When she stepped back, her tone changed.

"You couldn't send word in two seasons? Do you have any idea how worried we've been? And how did you get here so early in the day? Tell me you didn't spend the night in the transport."

I grinned. Some things transcended cultures.

Tristan pulled me forward. "This is Susan. I found her in Shamgar, but she's not from the Gray Hills. Susan, this is my mother, Tara."

Should I shake hands? Curtsey?

Tara grabbed me in a bear hug. "Well met, Susan. Come in, come in." She guided me toward the door.

Tristan pulled me away. "We'll come back soon. I have a lot to talk to you about. But first we have to go to the healers."

Wade, Tara, and I all protested in unison.

Tristan glared at me. "Do you think Cameron will ignore you? He has people who report to him even from as far as our village. I have to take you there to be 'healed' before you spread plague throughout Braide Wood. And Wade needs care."

I was embarrassed to realize I had forgotten all about Cameron and my convenient fake illness.

Tara cupped my face in her hands, thumbs massaging the lymph nodes in my neck. "You don't feel feverish."

Tristan pulled me away. "I needed an excuse to bring her here."

His mother sighed. "I'm guessing you haven't stayed out of trouble. All right, just a moment." She popped into the house and came out with a gourd-shaped canteen that she handed to Wade. He took a long swallow and passed it to me. I sipped tentatively; the tart liquid rushed over my tongue, reviving me with an earthy sweetness like papaya and a bite like pineapple. While I was drinking the tangy juice, Tara lifted up a small bouquet of wildflowers to Tristan, which he tucked into his belt near his sword.

She rested one hand on his cheek, and they exchanged a private look that was heavy with sadness. He nodded in understanding and turned.

I had missed something, but didn't have time to think about it as Tristan hurried us down a path and back out of the village.

It was a short walk—maybe ten more minutes—before we reached a clearing with a small waterfall splashing from a cliff. A lodge-type building stood near the falls, surrounded by several smaller buildings. I guessed we had arrived at the healers'.

Good thing it wasn't any farther, because Wade was looking pale. "This isn't a very convenient location for medical help," I observed. "How do really sick people manage the walk?"

Tristan ignored me, so Wade answered for him. "Most towns have their own healers. This is a place for long-term or special care."

Tristan squared his shoulders and led us up the boardwalk ramp and through the door of the large lodge. We entered an open common room. Several people, who I guessed were patients, sat near windows and looked out at the trees. Tristan scanned the room and seemed relieved when he spotted an older man in a green tunic that looked like a uniform. Tristan walked over to greet him, leaving Wade and me standing in the center of the room.

Tristan made urgent explanations in a low voice, gesturing with his hands and pointing back at us. The healer rolled his eyes and shook his head, but finally nodded and signaled to us. We followed him down a hall and into a small room.

He looked at me first. "I hear you have a very contagious illness." He frowned at me, making his bushy eyebrows meld into one furry line.

I looked uncertainly at Tristan.

The healer burst into laughter. "Here." He poured me a drink from a row of pitchers and bottles on a shelf along the wall.

I sniffed. It smelled like harmless clove tea. I tasted it and looked up.

"Amazing what cures we're able to work these days." The man threw us a wicked grin. "She's completely better. Another triumph for the healers. Of course, we'll want to keep her in Braide Wood for several days to be sure it doesn't return." He winked at Wade. "I cannot allow her to visit any large cities while there's any chance of this plague returning. Can't be too careful."

Then his mood sobered, and he turned to Tristan. "I know you have other things to take care of. You go ahead. They'll be fine here."

Tristan thanked him and ducked out of the room. The healer made "tsking" sounds as he unwrapped the stained and dirty cloth tied around Wade's arm. I looked away, not wanting to see how deep the claw wounds were. The healer said he needed to get some more supplies and left us. Wade twisted his arm, trying to see how bad it looked.

I'd never been good with my kids' skinned knees, or even loose teeth. Now I worked hard to look everywhere in the room but at Wade. The sweetly pungent smell of blood and growing infection hit my nose, and I felt a wave of dizziness. "I'm going to look around," I said to a point on the wall several feet from Wade's head. I turned without waiting for a response. He chuckled behind me.

In the hall I took a deep, cleansing breath and wrinkled my nose. Sour smells floated from other open doorways, and I decided to look for the exit. I'd rather wait outside.

True to my ability to get lost anywhere, I found myself wandering down a long wing in a different part of the lodge from the lobby we had first entered. Here, rows of small windows revealed tiny, empty rooms. I continued to the end of the quiet hall, turned a corner, and pulled back quickly.

Tristan was in the next hallway, staring through one of the windows into a room. His palm was flattened against the clear plastic, and his expression was bleak. I peeked around the corner again. Now he rested his forehead against the frame. His hand closed into a fist and his face twisted. Unwilling to intrude, I watched in silence as a young woman in the green tunic of the healers emerged from the room and slid the pocket door closed behind her. Tristan straightened and exchanged a few words with her. She shook her head, and his shoulders sagged. They walked down the hall away from me, still talking.

What was Tristan so upset about? Apparently not all the rooms on this quiet wing were deserted. Compelling curiosity drew me toward the room as soon as Tristan was out of sight. I tiptoed up the hall and peered into the window. A woman sat in a chair in the small room. On a tiny table, small flowers drooped over the lip of a stoneware mug. Tara had pressed that bouquet into Tristan's hands. This must be someone that Tara knew.

The chair was near a window that faced out on the forest, but was angled so I was able to see the woman's face. She had been beautiful once. I could see it in the bone structure of her youthful face and her exotic black hair. But there were deep circles under her eyes, and above her loose tunic, her collarbones protruded. Her hands moved aimlessly, picking at the edge of a blanket that covered her lap. She looked alone and forgotten in this empty part of the lodge. As I watched her, memories surfaced of visits to a local nursing home with my church Ladies' Guild each month. The loneliness of the patients always stirred me, and their gratitude for our brief visit humbled and saddened me. Aged or ill, people needed to feel connected. Following an impulse, I eased the door open and entered the room.

The woman didn't respond. Her blue-gray eyes remained vacant and unfocused.

I knelt in front of her. "Hello," I said softly. "My name is Susan."

She continued to stare, unmoving except for her fingers. They were no longer holding the blanket, but kept pulling and moving in strange patterns. She appeared to be crocheting an invisible scarf, or weaving a non-existent tapestry. Then her lips moved. She mouthed some words.

"What is it?" I leaned closer. "What do you need?" I waited, trying to make out what she was communicating.

"Faster," she said in a voice barely above a breath.

"Faster?" I repeated, but she didn't seem to hear me.

"Not enough. More. Faster. Do more. Do more. It's not enough."

I wanted to take her hands—stop their bizarre and random movements—but was afraid to upset her. As she spoke, my own pulse began to quicken. Yes. Hurry. Whatever I was here to do, I needed to do it faster. I shook my head, confused at the sudden urgency. I pushed it down with an effort.

"It's all right," I soothed. "You don't have to do anything." Did her hands slow down a bit, or was I imagining it?

The door of the room slid open with a bang. "What are you doing? You can't be in here!" The young woman in uniform I had seen in the hallway earlier glared at me.

And behind her stood Tristan. The rage on his face was an exact match of the expression he had worn in the moments before he killed the Rhusican. But this time he was looking at me.

Chapter Nine

THE YOUNG WOMAN HEALER GRABBED MY arm and pulled me from the room.

"I'm sorry," I said, my eyes on Tristan. "She just looked so sad and alone. I thought a visit might help." I tried hard to ignore his clenched jaw.

The woman shook her head in disbelief. "No one is allowed in these rooms. It's too dangerous."

"Dangerous?"

"Yes. We've seen cases spread, especially to close friends and family. That's why we no longer allow visits." She glanced at Tristan.

He didn't notice. He was too intent on glaring at me. "She's a stranger," he snarled. "She didn't know. I'll make sure she finds her way out. Right now."

Tristan grabbed my upper arm with a fierceness that would leave bruises and dragged me down the hallway. "What were you doing?" he ground out. "No, don't say anything." He cut off my attempted explanation. He wouldn't say another word until we were on the wooden walkway outside the front of the building. He hauled me forward.

I dug in my heels. "Where's Wade?"

"He needs to stay overnight. He's fine." Tristan walked faster, still gripping my arm.

I stumbled trying to keep up. If he didn't calm down, he'd soon be dragging me in the dirt. "What's the matter? I don't—"

"Quiet!" His teeth clamped together. In moments we were down the trail and out of sight of the buildings.

As confused as I'd been by this world, I'd come to trust Tristan. After all, he'd saved me from the lizard back in Shamgar and from Cameron in Lyric. But what did I really know about him—or his culture? In the face of his fury, my meager trust dissolved, and I became acutely aware of being alone with him. My stomach muscles clenched, and I tried again to pull my arm free. A few YMCA self-defense classes wouldn't do me any good if he—

Tristan stopped, grabbed my other arm as well, and threw me against a tree with a force that knocked the wind out of me. His eyes were wild, and he was breathing hard. Bruised and terrified, I struggled for breath.

"Tell me the truth. What were you doing?" he roared, his face inches from mine.

My mouth opened, but no sounds came out. I swallowed and tried again. "What do you mean?"

His anger grew. Releasing me, he pulled his sword from its scabbard. Before I could take another breath, the sharp point was poised directly over my heart.

I froze. "Tristan, please. I wasn't doing anything. I just wanted to help." *Please, God, don't let him kill me.*

"What did you say to Kendra?" he shouted.

His words slammed into me. "That was *Kendra?*"

Tristan must have noticed the shock on my face because

his rage dialed back one notch. But he didn't withdraw his weapon.

I was careful not to breathe too deeply. "Tristan, I thought Kendra was dead. You said she was poisoned, and I thought . . . I didn't know who the woman in the room was. Please believe me. I'm—I'm so sorry." What else could I say? I poured every ounce of earnestness into the apology.

He stared at me for a long moment. Finally, he pulled the sword back and then thrust it into the ground with a groan of frustration.

My knees buckled, and my back scraped against the tree trunk as I slid down to sit on the bare dirt. Black spots peppered the edge of my vision, and I dropped my head forward onto my knees, sucking in oxygen.

Great. Tristan wanted to believe I had been sent to help restore his people. And all I had done so far was cause more harm. I concentrated on breathing until my pulse rate slowed and the black spots faded away. I was finally able to raise my head.

Tristan sat on a rock across the path, watching me. The rage was gone; he looked confused, embarrassed, and bone weary. He said nothing.

I wrestled with some confusion of my own. "What did I do? I don't want to keep making mistakes. Please tell me what just happened."

He looked down and nodded. "You really don't understand anything, do you?"

I bristled. I was tempted to point out that I'd been adjusting to a world with technology, politics, and geography that was almost totally foreign to me, not to mention my own heightened senses and the ability to heal so quickly that the bruises he had just given me were gone almost before they could form. I thought I was doing a pretty good job of coping. But this didn't seem to be the time to bring that up.

"What was I supposed to think?" he continued. "The first time I leave you alone, I find you talking to a Rhusican. Then you keep us from reaching home before nightfall. Then I find you in Kendra's room." He leaned forward, meeting my eyes. "I won't let anyone hurt her again."

"I didn't know who she was," I replied, meeting his gaze without flinching. "She looked lonely, and I thought I'd talk to her. Besides . . ." I wondered how to describe the compulsion that guided me to her door. "I felt like I was supposed to see her."

Tristan's eyes went cold. "Stay away from her."

I held up my hands. "I will. I'm sorry."

He picked up a twig from the ground and pulled strips of bark from it, twisting it in his hands.

"How did it happen?" I asked quietly.

He was silent for a full minute. Then he sighed, keeping his focus on the stick he was systematically shredding. "Kendra and I had a disagreement. She saw the danger our people were in and wanted me to defy the Council."

I could see it was costing him to relive this story, so I stayed tactfully silent.

"I guess I was being a little stubborn. I said some things I didn't mean, and she was furious. She hiked to Blue Knoll to visit a friend. That's where she met the Rhusican. He must have begun to poison her then." He snapped the stick and threw down the pieces.

"At first I didn't notice. She came home and seemed fine. The next day she went to Blue Knoll again. I offered to go with her, but she knew I was busy training some of the young guardians and getting ready for patrol. She said she didn't need me along. I should have gone with her. I didn't know whom she was talking to. But I should have noticed the changes." Tristan's voice cracked, and he stopped for a moment. He stared at the path between us and swallowed. "She kept visiting Blue Knoll every day. I was so busy that I didn't bother to ask her about it. You know what it does. The poison. She began to go away inside herself. By the time I saw what was happening and got her to the healers, she was gone."

Frustration churned in me. "How can they allow Rhusicans in your towns? Don't they see what's happened?"

"When they first came, the Council met with some of them. The Rhusicans offered an alliance. In no time the Council had welcomed them to live right among us—in our villages. It's against everything the Songs tell us, but," Tristan shrugged, "the Council figures we need every alliance we can get."

"Yes, but once people started being poisoned, why didn't they make them leave?"

"The Council claims it has nothing to do with the Rhusicans. Not everyone who talks with them is harmed. They choose their prey carefully. So the Council says it's just some new illness that damages the minds of those who are infected. Some of the healers are agreeing."

"That's garbage! I felt it." A shiver rippled through me. "I *know* the words got inside and twisted me. Why didn't they sing the Verses—like Linette did for me?"

"We tried. It was too late. The poison had been at work in her for days. She won't be coming back."

"But . . ." I looked at Tristan's face and decided not to push it.

Despair colored his voice. "They won't even let me get close to her. They think it's too dangerous. She won't be coming back." Those words seemed familiar. Where had I heard them before? The thought slipped away as Tristan pushed himself to his feet. He held a hand out to me. I gripped it and let him pull me up.

We looked at each other uneasily.

"Susan, I never should have drawn my sword against you. I don't know if you are a helpless fool or a Restorer, but either way . . ." He trailed off and shifted his weight.

It wasn't much of an apology. I sighed. "It's all right. I understand." *Well, sort of.*

"At least the healer gave us an excuse to keep you away from Lyric for a while. It should give us enough time to figure out what you are doing here and what we need to do next. Let's go home."

I was relieved to follow him down the short trail to Braide Wood, but my mind kept straying back to the poor woman sitting alone in a room—her mind tormented with lies.

Tara had prepared a large midday meal for us. When we entered her home, I sighed with pleasure at the padded chairs, the table filled with food, and Tara's genuine warmth. For the first time in days, I stopped feeling bombarded by hidden dangers, intrigues, and speculative distrust. Tara showed me to their washroom and gave me some fresh clothes that were a much better fit. I scrubbed my skin until it was red, wanting to rub off the slimy feeling of the Rhusican's poison in my mind, along with the grime of traveling and camping.

As I joined Tara and Tristan around the large table that dominated the common room, my stomach growled. I was actually hungry. Despite the shock of being in an incomprehensible place, my mind had begun to accept this situation as a new kind of normal. Even with the danger I had been facing from fanged lizards, mind poison, and a sword-toting guardian with a temper, I began to relax.

Tara passed me a bowl of thick, creamy soup. There were a variety of vegetables swimming in it, including some that I couldn't identify. The warm steam rising from the bowl made my eyes water. There was a platter of small loaves, and Tristan and Tara each took one and tore pieces off to dip in their soup. I followed their example. The soup was delicious and peppery, and after several bites, my tongue tingled. I reached for the stoneware mug of water in front me to cool my mouth, but was soon digging in for more.

"I sent Dustin to let your father know you're here," Tara said quietly to Tristan. "He'll get word to everyone else to meet here tonight. In the meantime, you look like you could use some rest. How can I help?"

Tara's patience amazed me. If I were Tristan's mother, I'd be drilling him for information like a KGB interrogator. Instead, she fed him soup. My eyes darted around the room, still trying to absorb everything, sorting out the familiar from the strange.

"I didn't get much sleep last night." Tristan looked at me thoughtfully for a moment. "If you could talk with Susan and keep her out of sight for now, maybe I'll get cleaned up and get some rest."

"My pleasure." Tara smiled at me.

Tristan rolled his eyes. "You say that now, but wait until you hear how many questions she asks."

Tara's laughter was rich and deep. "I'm sure she's no worse than you and your sisters were as children. And I survived that."

When the meal was finished and Tristan had left the room, Tara and I settled onto two well-padded chairs with mugs of steaming tea. She smiled with genuine warmth. "Tristan said you live a long way from here. Do you have family back home?"

"My husband, Mark, and four children: Jake, Karen, Jon, and Anne." The sound of each name pierced me like the sound of the bell they tolled at church on New Year's Eve to honor each person from the congregation who had died that year.

No. They weren't dead, and neither was I. Somehow I'd find my way back. I bit my lip. "Tell me about your family."

She beamed. "Payton and I have been blessed with three children. Tristan is the oldest. Talia is our second. She and her husband, Gareth, live here with us. My youngest daughter and her husband live in Lyric." She couldn't hide her disapproval as she added the last statement. Then she brightened. "Gareth and Talia have two children, Aubrey and Dustin. You wouldn't believe how much fun it is to be a grandmother."

I thought of my gangly teenagers and laughed. "I'm not ready to find out." I sipped some of the tea. "Have you lived in Braide Wood all your life?"

"Of course." She looked at me as if it were an odd question, then got up and walked into the kitchen area off the great room to ladle more tea into her mug. "Would you like more clavo?"

I brought my cup over to her, and she filled it from the bowl resting on glowing tiles.

"What are these?" I asked.

"Heat trivets." She tilted her head. "Where exactly *are* you from?"

I hesitated, unsure how to answer.

"Never mind. What else do you want to know?"

Soon she was explaining every unfamiliar object I spotted throughout her cooking area. Tara answered my questions with so much patience that I began to have doubts that Tristan was really her son. I could see that some of my questions startled her, and some came close to causing offense, but she stayed calm and continued to clarify everything she could.

In some ways the people here reminded me of an Amish community I had once visited. Here, as there, large extended families remained in tight circles. Respect for traditions and the Verses was of prime importance, while exploration, individuality, and change were minimized. Removed and somewhat isolated from the outside world, the clan necessarily gave priority to growing and preserving food. Skills in building and crafts were highly valued. There was little clutter, and most items were multifunctional. There were no distracting noises from radios, television, cell phones, or faxes.

But there *was* technology. I was confused by the juxtaposition of capabilities beyond anything I was familiar with, odd gaps in technology, and an emphasis on avoiding unnecessary progress. Convenience and luxury didn't rule here because the people of this world seemed to recognize that there were other things of more value.

When I asked Tara about talking to someone from a distance, or sending a letter, she smiled.

"How can the words be given to someone apart from the speaker? How can you judge the truth and the character of the words if you can't observe the truth and the character of the one who brings them?"

Once again I didn't know how to answer.

We had made our way back to the chairs, and the last of the tea in my mug had grown cold when I finally broached the subject I was most uneasy about. "Tell me about the Restorers."

"In every time of great need, a Restorer is sent to fight for the people and help the guardians. The Restorer is empowered with gifts to defeat our enemies and turn the people's hearts back to the Verses," she recited.

"Yes, I've heard that. But I don't understand. How do you recognize that someone is the Restorer? Where have the other Restorers come from? What happened to them?"

She looked at me for a long moment. "What do your people understand about the One?" She seemed to be choosing her words carefully.

I let my breath out through pursed lips. This would be a sensitive conversation if I were safe at home sharing muffins with a neighbor in my living room. In this world it could be potentially deadly. "The One?"

"The One who made our world." Tara waited, gaze intent.

"The Creator. He gives life to all people." I spoke slowly, feeling my way. "We rejected Him, and brought death and suffering into the world. But He's not only holy and powerful. He's also full of love. So He chose one special nation and spoke to them. He gave them His promise that . . ."

"A Deliverer will come!" Tara exclaimed. She sat forward on her chair in excitement. "Susan, that is the heart of our Verses. But I don't understand. How can your people know this?"

I was sorting through possible answers when the door crashed open.

"Grandma! Look what I found!"

"I found them first!"

Young voices tumbled into the room, followed soon

after by their bodies, which never stopped moving. Tara's arms opened and two mop tops charged at her and wrapped dusty arms around her neck. When they untangled themselves, they opened grimy fists to show her some shiny orange berries.

"Susan, meet Dustin and Aubrey," Tara said.

Two heads turned owl-like in my direction, wide eyes blinking.

"Little ones, this is our guest, Susan. Tristan brought her to visit."

"Where did Tristan go? Can we play with him? Please?" Dustin and Aubrey had the same uncanny skill as my own children. Their two small voices could make the room seem filled with people.

Tristan came in from the hallway, scratching his head and yawning. "I guess nap time is over?"

"Grandma made you take a nap?" Aubrey asked, running toward him. Dustin joined her, and they tackled Tristan in a pileup of giggles.

The scene reminded me forcibly of my own family. Mark always tussled with the kids when they were little. They'd charge into him as soon as he stepped through the door after work, resulting in a scramble of arms and legs just like this one. My heart clenched. Was Mark looking for me? Were the police searching our neighborhood? Once, I'd gotten home late from a church meeting on a snowy night to find he'd been pacing the house, filled with bottled-up anxiety ready to explode. He must be a wreck by now. I'd been gone two nights already.

Mark, don't give up. I'm going to find a way back.

"Dustin," Tara called. He climbed off Tristan and pulled himself away from the fun. "Did you find everyone I asked you to talk to?"

"Yes," he said and began counting them off on his fingers. "Grandpa and Mother and Father and Bekkah and Lukyan. Grandpa and Father are coming in from the fields early. Mother said to tell you she'd be home in time to help with supper." His head kept turning to where Aubrey was sitting atop Tristan's stomach.

Tara captured his chin. "What about Skyler?"

"He said he has other things to do. Can I go now?" Tara released him, and Dustin made a running dive onto Tristan, causing a huge bellow and another volley of giggles.

"I wish Skyler would come," Tara said with a sigh.

"Who is he?" The name sounded familiar, but I couldn't remember where I had heard it.

"Kendra and Kieran's father. He has the keenest mind of anyone in Braide Wood. We could use his help." She eased herself from her chair. "Well, time to get supper ready." Tara rolled her shoulders with a bit of stiffness, then headed across the room on light feet. She pulled Aubrey and Dustin off Tristan and shooed them down the hallway to get cleaned up. "Aubrey," she called after them, "get some more work done on your three-pegging. Dustin, your mother wants you to finish your carving before Feast day."

Tristan lumbered to his feet and looked down. Orange berries were smeared across the front of his shirt. He wiped at them with his sleeve and shrugged. Pulling up the chair Tara had just vacated, he studied me for a moment. "You look better."

"It helped to talk with your mother." I still felt like a small token in a strange board game, but at least now I knew some of the rules.

"I want to explain something." He paused. "I have to tell them what I know. This is my home. I won't lie for you here."

I stiffened. "I don't want you to lie." Then I remembered he had already lied to Cameron. And he'd remained vague with his friends—introducing me as a lost traveler. Now he was planning to say a lot more about what he knew or suspected.

I felt new worry wrinkles bunching on my forehead.

"I want to be sure you understand." He cleared his throat and looked away. "Things could get—difficult."

Right. Because up until now, things had been so easy.

Chapter Ten

THE EVENING BEGAN CALMLY ENOUGH. I suppose that should have been a warning of what was to come. Sort of like March coming in like a lamb.

Talia arrived first and rushed through the door, tossing a pack into the corner. She crossed the room to give her brother a quick hug, but then pulled back to look at him. "Tristan, what have you gotten yourself into this time?" She was tall, with the toned muscles of an athlete and a profile as sharp as her movements. Her brown hair prickled out of a thick braid.

Tristan turned her around to see me. "This is Susan. Our guest."

I smiled.

Talia didn't. She gave me a brief nod, then turned on her heel to join Tara in the kitchen. Her husband, Gareth, arrived next. His straight blond hair was a contrast to the rest of Tristan's family, and he was only about my height. He had been tending the grain crops all day with Talia and with Tristan's father, Payton. When Payton came in, he looked dusty and tired but lit up at the sight of his son. They shared the same stubborn jaw line and long tousled hair. I imagined that in twenty or thirty years, Tristan would look a lot like his father did now.

Bekkah had spent time with friends all afternoon and seemed to be in a good mood when she showed up. In spite of her obvious eagerness to find out more about Tristan's plans, she still avoided looking at me. After only a day, she'd won my respect. My heart shrank, knowing I hadn't earned hers. Back home, she was the kind of woman I would have loved to call friend.

Chilled, I moved toward the corner of the room. This was far worse than the Christmas dinner Mark's company hosted each year. There, I struggled to keep names straight, worried about saying the wrong thing, and fumbled my way through painful cocktail conversation with strangers, but at least Mark stood by my side. And none of his coworkers wore daggers or swords.

Tara must have sensed how overwhelmed I felt. She left the kitchen alcove and came to stand near me just as the front door opened again. A white-maned man hobbled into the room, shoulders stooped. "That's Lukyan. Now we're all here," she told me quietly.

"Is he another relative?" I asked.

"He's the eldest songkeeper of Braide Wood. Everyone values his counsel." She left my side to hurry forward and greet him. He straightened and touched Tara's forehead gently, as if in blessing.

I was delighted to see Linette slip into the house behind him and close the door. Lukyan leaned on her arm as she helped him to a comfortable chair. When Linette glanced around the room and spotted me, she smiled warmly. Her sweet acceptance eased some of my alone-in-a-crowd awkwardness.

Talia and Gareth set out platters of food, and everyone gathered around the large common room table. I slipped into a chair beside Tara.

Tara rested her hand on Payton's arm. "Skyler didn't want to come," she said, resigned sadness in her voice.

He patted her hand. "You tried. We've done what we can."

Tara turned and saw me listening. "Skyler keeps to himself, but I keep hoping. He never forgave the village."

"For what?" I tuned out the conversations farther down the table to focus on my hostess.

"He married a woman from Hazor. She renounced her citizenship, but it still took people a long time to accept her." Tara tore her bread into little pieces, letting the crumbs pile up on her plate. "She died giving birth to Kendra, when Kieran was four. It destroyed Skyler. And now . . ." She sighed and pushed the crumbs around.

Now Kendra had been taken from him as well. How often did Skyler hike to the healer's lodge and watch through a window as his daughter wasted away? Did he blame Tristan? Such loss would make anyone bitter.

Conversation rose and fell around the table, reminding me again of Mark's office parties. Animated discussion about people and events I knew nothing about, inside jokes, and stray awkward glances my direction all sealed my feeling of isolation.

Finally, the food was eaten and voices stilled.

Tara had informed me earlier that after the evening meal came the traditional time of reciting Verses. At the time I had looked forward to hearing more of the revered Songs. Payton began speaking with familiar ease, followed by some passages that the group spoke in unison. Other members around the table added their own recitations, but after a few minutes, my eyes glazed over. They spoke long lists of names, family trees, and brief histories that meant nothing to me. Maybe it was meaningful for them because some of those named were their great-grandparents, and the villages, rivers, and plains that were mentioned were familiar landmarks, but my foreign mind wandered.

When the Verses for the day were completed, Dustin and Aubrey were tucked in bed, and the table was cleared. Tristan leaned forward on his elbows and looked at his family and friends. Tension built in the room, and the curiosity that had been suppressed for social niceties demanded to be assuaged.

He began his story of finding me in the alley in Shamgar. I watched the people around the table as they listened intently, eyes on Tristan. When he told them my guess that I'd come from a different world, I waited for shock and disbelief to flare in their faces, but they all simply nodded.

Okay. Alternate universes didn't faze them. My tight muscles relaxed, and I sat back into my chair. We had passed the hurdle that frightened me the most.

Then Tristan explained that I didn't know *how* I arrived in the alley in Shamgar. Frowns formed on several faces. When he told them I had been crushed by a transport and healed—wounds, broken bones, and bruises—in only a short time, they looked at each other uneasily. When he reported that I'd been poisoned by a Rhusican and recovered, Tristan's parents gasped, and his sister Talia pushed away from the table to pace. Agitation around the table built, like wind gusts on the leading edge of a storm.

My shoulders began to knot again. When Tristan shared his theory that I was a Restorer, the room exploded.

"You idiot! Do you have any idea what the Council will do when they find out?" Talia yelled at her brother. "What possessed you to bring her here?"

"You should send her to Cauldron Pass and let her fight." Bekkah shouted her down.

"Just because that's where Mikkel fought doesn't mean she's supposed to have the same role," Tara said softly.

Gareth waved his arms and spoke over her. "Talia's right."

All the voices overlapped. Tristan pulled his hand through his hair in frustration.

I looked at the angry faces around the table and measured the distance to the door.

"How do we know she isn't an agent of the Rhusicans, or a Hazorite spy?" Talia's shrill tone rose above the others.

I opened my mouth to protest, but Tristan spoke first, momentarily silencing the others. "Even Kieran thinks she's a Restorer. He's not easy to fool."

Payton and Tara murmured in agreement.

"But she could have clouded your minds," Gareth said. "It could all be a trick."

Talia nodded. "That's why she came back from the voices—she's really one of them."

Terrific. Visions of Salem witch trials danced in my head.

"I've lived to see three Restorers." Lukyan's voice quavered, but all eyes immediately fixed on him. "Oren, Ilias, and Mikkel. They were all guardians first. They came from our people. They weren't strangers." He didn't seem to be upset by that, just musing aloud.

"No, she isn't the kind of Restorer we're used to. But her people have Verses." Linette's high, clear voice cut through the murmurs. She smiled at me.

"Yes." Tara folded her arms. "I don't know what her purpose will be here, but she knows the One."

"Easy to claim," Bekkah muttered.

Linette seemed undisturbed. "Would you share some of your Verses?" she asked me shyly.

Eight pairs of eyes turned in my direction: rheumy blue eyes, clouded with age; cold brown eyes, reserved and uncertain; worried eyes; suspicious eyes.

God, where do I start?

I thought of the Songs shared after supper. What did I know that was similar? The second-grade Sunday school class I taught recited the first part of the Christmas story in the pageant last year. I had those verses memorized.

"And it came to pass in those days, that there went out a decree from Caesar Augustus, that all the world should be taxed. (And this taxing was first made when Cyrenius was governor of Syria.)" Whew. That was a mouthful. I looked around the table and saw that I had their attention. They didn't recognize the names, of course, but I could see from the nodding heads that the formula was familiar to them. Trouble was, I couldn't remember the rest.

"Um . . . Joseph and Mary had to be taxed, so they went to Bethlehem, but she was about to have a baby, and there was no place for them to stay. They ended up in a stable, and that's where the baby was born." My palms were sweating, and I rubbed them together and pressed them into my lap.

Talia looked over at Gareth and rolled her eyes. Lukyan tilted his head and squinted. Bekkah shook her head and looked away.

I had to do better. They wanted the real verses.

God, I need some help here. Help me remember.

I closed my eyes. An image emerged of little cartoon figures standing around a small but brave evergreen with its trunk wrapped in a blue blanket. *A Charlie Brown Christmas.* My kids watched it every year. I smiled to think of them all—even Jake—gathered around the TV with mugs of hot cocoa and blankets, the lights from our Christmas tree counterpointing the glow of the screen. In my mind, I could hear the voice of Linus as he recited the Christmas story. I took a breath and started again.

"And there were in the same country shepherds abiding in the field, keeping watch over their flock by night. And, lo, the angel of the Lord came upon them, and the glory of the Lord shone round about them: and they were sore afraid."

The words were flowing now.

"And the angel said unto them, Fear not: for, behold, I bring you good tidings of great joy, which shall be to all people. For unto you is born this day in the city of David a Saviour, which is Christ the Lord. And this shall be a sign unto you; Ye shall find the babe wrapped in swaddling clothes, lying in a manger. And suddenly there was with the angel a multitude of the heavenly host praising God, and saying, Glory to God in the highest, and on earth peace, good will toward men." I stopped. It was all I could recite from memory.

The room was silent. Lukyan's head nodded, his eyes unfocused, as if he were lost in a dream.

"Who was that Savior? One of your people's Restorers?" Tara asked, her tone reverent.

I shook my head. "No. These are our Verses that tell about the one you call Deliverer. In my world the Deliverer has come."

I expected another outburst of questions, but there was a holy stillness around the room.

Most of the faces turned toward Lukyan, waiting for his response.

The old man rested his fingertips on the table, lightly tapping them, like a seismic measuring device. Then he flattened his palms against the wood surface and sat up straighter. He looked into my face, and his soft smile caused a starburst of lines around his eyes.

"You want to know if she is a Restorer. I can't answer that. Her deeds will reveal that in the days to come. But you also feared she was a danger to our people. That fear I can answer." He turned to Tristan with a slight frown. "Don't doubt what your heart revealed to you."

Lukyan pushed against the table to help himself stand. "In the name of the One who sent you, we welcome you to make your home among us. May He guide your steps and preserve us all from darkness."

"So shall it be," the group murmured in unison. I looked around the table. Tara and Linette smiled broadly. Bekkah looked thoughtful.

My throat thickened. "Thank you." I wished I could think of a blessing to offer back to them, but nothing came to me. I sank farther back into my chair, feeling drained.

"So now what?" Gareth asked Tristan.

"All the other Restorers were guardians, so I assume she should start training," Tristan said with a shrug.

"I can take on a student," Bekkah said.

"I could think of no one better." He gave her a grateful smile.

"My Morsal Plains rotation begins tomorrow, but when that's finished, I'll work with her." Bekkah sized me up, assessing my strength. I wished I had kept up with my exercise classes at the YMCA. She didn't look impressed.

"I'll send word to your captain," Tristan said, "and see if I can get you off before season end. In the meantime I'll start her training. But we'll have to keep her out of sight. Spread the word she's still recovering from the plague. I'd like to keep her away from Lyric as long as possible."

"And keep yourself from Lyric as well." Payton smiled, but worry lines tightened around his eyes.

Perhaps having my future discussed and decided by committee should have bothered me. But after the past few incomprehensible days, it felt wonderful to let go of the responsibility to figure anything out. I listened to voices flowing around me and didn't bother to follow the discussions.

"Speaking of Lyric," Gareth said loudly, "what are we going to do about the Council?"

Everyone froze. It was the sudden silence that caught my attention.

Talia swatted her husband's arm and whispered something in his ear. Tristan turned from his conversation with Bekkah and looked at Gareth, and then at me.

"I think Susan has had enough to deal with today." Tristan met Payton's eyes.

"You're right." Payton nodded and spoke up quickly. "Talia, would you show Susan where she can sleep tonight?"

Talia sniffed and pushed her chair back.

I looked over at Tristan, ready to argue.

"Susan, go get some rest. We have things to discuss that you don't need to know about right now."

My earlier feelings of warmth and acceptance drained away as I rose to follow Talia. They'd relegated me to the level of Dustin and Aubrey—a child who shouldn't be kept up past her bedtime. It became clear to me that they may have accepted my presence in their home, but they didn't really trust me.

Talia showed me to a pallet in a back room and left without a word. I curled up and felt loneliness lower down on me like a suffocating blanket. I saw again the horrible gray mist that the Rhusican poison had stirred in my mind yesterday.

"Lord, give me words to fight this," I whispered.

A memory surfaced of Jon standing near the refrigerator with a fistful of homework papers. His nine-year-old voice had rattled off words in one long stream. "Psalm 16:11, 'You have made known to me the path of life; you will fill me with joy in your presence, with eternal pleasures at your right hand.'" He had paused a moment to catch his breath. "Mom, when do we get those presents?"

"Presents?" I had asked him, confused.

"Yeah, you know: 'You will fill me with joy in your presents.' When do we get them?" I had laughed, hugged him, and grabbed a pen from the counter to sign his school worksheet.

The memory drifted away.

"You will fill me with joy in your presence."

I felt so lost. Was I really still in His presence? I didn't belong in this world. Had I slipped through some cosmic tear into a place where He couldn't find me anymore? If He were really here, wouldn't He have noticed by now that something was wrong? Wouldn't He have taken me home to where I belonged?

Are you here, Lord?

Silence. I waited to feel a touch of reassurance in my heart, but there was nothing. I sighed and rolled over. I thought about stretching my hearing and listening in on the conversation in the main room, but I decided I didn't really want to know any more about the dangers and intrigues that filled this world. I had enough fear to deal with already.

Chapter Eleven

EACH MORNING, I FELT A LITTLE less confusion in my first moments of wakefulness. Now I expected to feel the coarse fabric of a pallet under my cheek, and smell the rich aroma of steeping clavo. I no longer felt alarm when my reaching hand couldn't find Mark's flannel-clad body next to me, but each morning, the grief of his absence hurt me all over again.

Close to two weeks had passed, and my days were settling into a routine. I tried to help out around Tara and Payton's home, but my attempts to assist with cooking ruined so much food that Talia finally banished me from the heat trivets. She unbent long enough to try to teach me three-peg, a complex weaving technique using a small handloom. I was a disaster. Each time I thought I had completed a small section, I'd discover my fingers were firmly knotted into the design. At least it made little Aubrey laugh. She and Dustin were a great comfort to me with the giggles and chaos they stirred up everywhere they went and their ready acceptance of me into their home. But they also rekindled the ache I felt in missing my family. It was a good thing that my days were so full; otherwise I would have crumbled under the pain.

My mornings were devoted to guardian training. After

the first week, Tristan decided Wade's arm was well enough to handle some basic sparring and recruited him to work with me. Each day, Tristan would meet with us and supervise drills for a while. Then he'd tell Wade what to work on with me and disappear to take care of the guardian business he had set aside for two seasons. I dragged my sword along with me everywhere because it seemed to give me courage. But Tristan insisted I wasn't ready to train with it yet.

Painfully eager to please, Wade seemed almost to burst with pride at being able to perform a special service for Tristan. His boyish humor kept me from giving in to total frustration as I tried to develop skills I had never needed at the grocery store or at church potlucks. I soon realized it would take decades to achieve the lethal proficiency of the guardians. I didn't plan to be here that long. However, since no one seemed to know what else to do with me, I resigned myself to pointless training.

"That wasn't bad," Wade said as he rolled to his feet. This morning he was teaching me how to pivot to the side and flip him in an attack from behind.

"Only because you helped."

He grinned. "So try it again, and this time I won't make it so easy."

"After a break?" I dusted my hands off on my pant legs, caught the canteen that Wade tossed me, and guzzled some water. "Wade, don't your people have any better weapons than swords and knives? You've got all kinds of other technology."

He grabbed the canteen from me and took a few steps back. "What are you saying?" His voice had lost its usual warmth.

"Nothing. I just wondered if there was something I'd be better at, that's all."

"I don't know what you mean. The Songs tell us to fight

with our swords and the power of the Verses. Anything else is forbidden." He stuck out his chin, daring me to argue.

"Okay. Sorry. I didn't understand." I seemed to be saying that a lot in the past few weeks. "Never mind. Show me that move again."

After enduring a few hours of sparring, elementary weapons training, and basic survival lore, I was rewarded with my favorite part of the day.

Wade and I hiked over the ridge to a plateau curving around one of the edges of Braide Wood. In the high pastures, the clan kept a large herd of lehkan. These creatures looked like elk and stood about as tall; but unlike elk, they grew long, llama-soft coats. I was tempted to see them as cuddly pets, but guardians rode the male lehkan into battle, and the animals were trained to use their fierce antlers as weapons. I was given a limpid-eyed doe to prevent me from impaling myself on antlers.

To my surprise, I really took to riding and outgrew my initial clumsiness after a few days. The slim leather saddle reminded me of an English riding saddle, although I didn't need to learn to post the trot, since lehkan either walked or ran. The lehkan were guided with leg commands, leaving the warrior's arms free for weapons. Holding my seat at a walk wasn't too difficult. Even at a canter they had a rolling gait that I could handle in the saddle—as long as I ignored the incredible speed at which the turf flew past us. Unfortunately, the lehkan had a tendency to spring, deer-like, in any direction when startled. For the first several days I was grateful for my ability to heal quickly, as I was catapulted to the ground over and over. As I kept working with my doe, Mara, each day, I learned to feel the coiling of muscles that signaled she was about to spring, and I spent more time in the saddle than on the ground.

Learning to ride gave me the added benefit of being able to explore more of the area around Braide Wood. I looked forward to those midday rides and conversations with Wade. He knew each family in Braide Wood clan and filled me in on the interconnections and histories of the people who lived here. He also explained more to me about Tristan's role. He was a captain responsible for about one hundred guardians. In times of war he would lead the Braide Wood clan guardians, which included several nearby communities besides our village. His contingent also included a few men and women from Rendor, Lyric, Blue Knoll, and other clans. Tristan sent out messengers and gathered the oral reports from the handful of Braide Wood guardians on border patrol, as well as supervised ongoing training.

Wade also tried to explain the complex system that governed the assignments of guardians. The Council had developed a plan to centralize control by assigning some guardians to serve under captains from different clans. That was why Bekkah, who was from Braide Wood, wasn't under Tristan's captaincy, but served under the leadership of the Rendor head guardian and sent reports to him on her patrol of the border near Morsal Plains. I supposed that the theory was sound. There was less chance for infighting between the various clans of the People of the Verses. Still, based on the little I knew of the Council, the thought of them dividing and controlling all the guardians made me uneasy.

I pushed the thought aside as we rode over a low ridge and saw the plateau stretched below us. Paddocks nestled against a rock wall along one side of the plateau, and nearby, a few long lodges provided shelter for guardians on rotating assignment from other clans. Tristan was drilling a group of about twenty riders on lehkan. It took my breath away to watch them wheel around in formation and thunder across the plateau.

As we sat astride our own mounts, watching from a safe distance, Wade shifted in his saddle. I could see how he ached to be part of that group of riders, and I realized what a sacrifice he was making by taking on the job of babysitting a stranger.

"Tristan told me Bekkah will be back from her patrol soon," I said.

He nodded, then looked at me sideways. "It's been an honor to assist you." He rubbed his short beard. "But I've never spent time training someone before. I don't think it's my best skill."

I hid a smile. "Wade, I'm grateful for your help. It's not your fault I'm not guardian material."

A blue beetle flew toward his mount's face, and Wade leaned forward to swat it away while his lehkan sidestepped. "So tell me some more about the guardians in your world." Most of the clan had little curiosity about where I came from and how my culture was different. Wade was one of the few who genuinely enjoyed hearing about my world—and it gave me a chance to keep a grip on my connection to it.

In my early days in Braide Wood, I wondered if my purpose would include bringing them some advance in technology or industry from my world that would remove the threat of the Hazorites or defeat the armies across the River Borders. I decided quickly that I was no Connecticut Yankee. I didn't know how to create gunpowder, factories, or telegraphs, and they had no interest in those things, even if I did.

We continued to chat while we watched Tristan and his lehkan cavalry enact a mock battle. As I watched, I remembered something about the conversation I overheard between Tristan and Kieran.

"Wade, when Tristan found me, he was worried about taking on a student to train. Kieran said he lost one. What was he talking about?"

Wade's genial expression disappeared. "That's not for me to tell you. But whatever anyone else says, it was *not* Tristan's mistake." He wheeled his lehkan around and started back to the paddock. "The boy's death was his own fault."

The glimpse of icy indifference in the easygoing young guardian unsettled me. I let him go on alone and stayed astride Mara to continue watching Tristan drill his troops. He was a strong leader, and I understood how he'd inspired fierce loyalty and admiration in Wade. I sighed. Under different circumstances I would have enjoyed watching the group of rugged warriors as they trained. Tristan and his guardians evoked Arthurian legends and romantic epics. But I would have traded the whole plateau full of sword-wielding hunks for my power-tool-toting, suburban husband. Mark was mine. We belonged to the same world.

There was an otherness to the people here. Even Tristan and his family treated me with a wary reverence because of the Restorer myths, and their attitude constantly reminded me that this wasn't my world.

I nudged Mara into a springing leap away from the ridge. I was going mad from missing Mark and my children. "Mark, I'm going to find a way back to you." I threw the promise toward the sky, the words falling behind as Mara galloped across the hill, racing the inevitable afternoon rain shower. *Lord, are you listening? I need to get back to my family.*

After a quick lunch with Tara, I hurried to Linette's home. She had offered to teach me the Verses, and during the rainy hours each afternoon, I met with her to listen, learn, sing, and sometimes pray together.

Today her eyes sparkled when she opened her door. "We aren't staying here," she said, wrapping a cloak around herself and bouncing with excitement. "Follow me."

I had to move fast to keep up with her along the well-worn path that wound around several homes to a small cabin under a tree. Drizzle misted us as we arrived, but it seemed to do little to dampen Linette's high spirits. She tapped on the door, shaking moisture off her cloak. "I know you've been worried about why you're here. There's someone who can help." Linette dropped her voice. "He sometimes hears directly from the One." We heard a thin call of welcome from inside, and she slid the door open and pulled me in out of the rain.

Lukyan wore the shapeless tunic and trousers customary in the village, but he was also wrapped in a woven blanket that bunched around his thin shoulders. He sat near a large clay pot full of blue ferns, his hands resting tranquilly in his lap. Linette beamed like a little child, delighted in giving me a gift. "Lukyan has offered to meet with you today." She ducked back out into the rain before I had a chance to respond, and Lukyan gestured to another chair, inviting me to draw it closer.

I hadn't seen him since the meeting at Tristan's home my first night in Braide Wood. "Thank you again for welcoming me at the meeting. They didn't trust me until you did that."

He smiled. "I could see that you were sent. What that means for our people, I cannot know right now. But Linette has told me that you struggle with that question." He stopped smiling and his eyes softened with compassion. "Tell me what is on your heart," he invited gently. His skin was like fragile parchment stretched over bone. Yet despite the frail appearance of his aging body, strength of spirit radiated from him, drawing me in. Here was a man who had walked with the One for many years.

I sensed from the core of my being that I could trust him, and I felt grateful that Linette had brought me here. Where could I begin? "I don't know what everyone expects from me," I blurted out at last. "They want a Restorer, but I'm just a soccer mom. I can't do anything for them. I can't help the guardians; I can't turn people back to the Verses. I don't know what I'm doing here." Now that I'd started, more words tumbled out. I told him about the pain I felt being wrenched away from my family. I admitted my fear that God had forgotten me or lost me. I confessed my confusion about this world, and my doubts about finding any purpose I could serve. And as I unraveled and examined them, one by one, all those emotions loosened their grip on me.

Lukyan listened with his whole body, leaning forward, nodding. He understood. He cared. He accepted.

After I had rambled on at length, the torrent of words slowed. I sat back with a sigh. The sound of light rain dripping from the eaves soothed me.

"Are you willing to walk any road that the One chooses for you?" Lukyan asked in a voice as soft as the rain.

"I'm willing to go where He sends me," I said with conviction. "If He can use me for His purpose, there is nothing that would make me happier. I just want to know how *long* I'll be here. If He would only tell me when I'll be back with Mark and my children, then I could accept this." The hint of a whine slipped into my voice.

Lukyan smiled. "To not know is then part of the gift you offer Him. It is where your obedience is tested."

My shoulders slumped. He was right. Back home, I kept begging God to use me, to show me His purpose. But there were no answers that satisfied me. I suddenly saw how much of my service came with an "if." I'll support my husband if I feel loved and cherished. I'll raise my children if I can feel fulfillment and respect. I'll reach out to a friend if I can see results. And yes, I'll even go through trials bravely — if I understand the purpose and value of them. Could I ever learn to walk a road that was not of my choosing, without even an explanation from God?

"How much do you trust His love?" Lukyan asked.

My eyes prickled, and I rubbed my nose, holding back the urge to dissolve into tears. "I don't know," I finally answered, my voice breaking. "I thought I knew, but . . . I've been learning how tiny my faith is."

Age tremors shook Lukyan's hands as he reached forward and took my hand in his. "Holy One of Susan's world and ours, we come before You today in all our smallness," he prayed. "Open our hearts to You. Let us see Your love so we can walk forward without fear." Then he stopped. We sat in a holy silence.

Tingles danced along my spine with the hint of the presence of One who is beyond all understanding. I expected Lukyan to say more, but he just rested, waiting. Soft splashes sounded outside as water dripped from pine boughs into waiting puddles. I closed my eyes and felt time slow down. The tightness around my temples eased as my breathing grew deeper and softer. The restless questions in my mind stopped hammering. For this one moment, I felt peace. It soaked deeply into my marrow, strengthening me. I don't know how much time passed, but I finally opened my eyes. Lukyan released my hands, and I looked at him with awe. I couldn't speak—it would have desecrated the experience we had just shared. He nodded to me in understanding, and I left in a silent daze.

I wandered among the trees, processing all the things I'd seen in myself and the precious gift of reassurance I felt. I dawdled on the path back toward Payton and Tara's home. Wade had said he'd help me with my sword training before supper, so I stopped in to grab my pack. It held the wooden training swords that we used, along with my own real sword. Approaching the cabin where Wade lived with his family, I saw him sitting on a bench with Linette, engaged in conversation with someone I didn't recognize. They appeared to be having an intense discussion.

I hesitated to interrupt, but I was eager to thank Linette for taking me to meet with Lukyan. And Wade was expecting me. So I brushed aside my shyness and walked toward them.

Wade never took his eyes off the man he was talking with, and Linette seemed to be staring at something in the distance. I tried to remember if the man standing in front of them was one of Wade's relatives. I had seen many of the Braide Wood clan, but there were still faces that were unfamiliar to me. This man looked older than Wade and Linette, with tightly curled red-blond hair framing a rounded face that made me think of a Raphael painting. The stranger ignored me. Wade was nodding sadly as the man spoke. "Of course they can't expect you to do well in battle," he said, his voice dripping with sympathy. "You'll never have the skill of Tristan or the others."

Tiny hairs on my arms stood up. I expected Linette to interrupt and disagree, but her face remained passive, eyes vacant. I had seen that empty expression one other time—on a frail woman in a small room at the healers' lodge.

"Linette!" I shouted.

She didn't respond, but the man standing in front of her did. He turned and looked into my face.

I sucked in a sharp breath that stuck in my chest. The straps of my pack slipped out of my hand, and it dropped to the ground.

The man's irises were a vibrant aqua streaked with flickering verdigris. The variations of color made his eyes seem to twirl.

They drew me in, even as a cold, invisible hand gripped my throat. I was repulsed as recognition flared in my mind. This place of mental fog was painfully familiar. I tore my eyes away and looked down. The pommel of my sword poked out of the top of my pack. In a burst of panic, I grabbed the hilt, pulling the sword free and holding it in front of me.

The man's placid face changed. Suddenly the light in his eyes captured me with hypnotic power, and the muscles around his grinning mouth pulled back, contorting his appearance. This was no Raphael angel. This was a gothic gargoyle. "We know you . . ." he said in a singsong voice.

"In the name of the One—get away from them!" I meant to shout, but the words came out as a choked cry.

To my horror he began to laugh. Instead of one voice I heard several—deep sneering laughter overlaid with high wailing cackles.

My sword shook. I wanted to throw it down and run, but I forced myself to step between the creature and my friends.

> *The eyes of the One*
> *Are always on His people;*
> *His arms surround us,*
> *And we are not alone.*

I quoted the song that Linette used to bring me back from the Rhusican poison. I wanted to sing the words, but could barely force sound out of my tight throat.

The laughter stopped. A growl of ugly and mindless rage rose from the man's throat. Then, in the space between two heartbeats, he sprang forward—clawed hands reaching for my neck.

I thrust my sword out by pure reflex and squeezed my eyes shut.

Someone wailed, and overpowering weight pushed against my arms. Somehow my hands kept their grip on the sword even as the hilt pressed back against them, forcing me to the ground. I heard someone screaming as I fell, and smelled the stench of blood and something sour as bile. I turned my head toward the wholesome scent of wet dirt. Something was crushing my ribs. Moisture seeped into my clothes. Under my ear the ground trembled as footsteps ran in my direction.

"Get off her!" Bekkah was shouting. Mercifully, someone pulled the weight away. As it rolled off of me, I opened my eyes a slit.

"Susan! Can you hear me?" Bekkah's worried face floated over me. Why was she here? She was supposed to be on patrol at the outpost by Morsal Plains.

"Is she alive?" Another voice sounded nearby—Kyle, the young transtech who'd traveled with us on the trip from Ferntwine.

My throat had been so twisted by fear that it took a moment to get the words out. "I'm fine," I said at last, my voice hoarse.

"Don't move," Bekkah ordered in her guardian voice. She turned and issued commands to someone else.

I ignored her and eased myself up onto one elbow. Looking down, I saw that the liquid seeping through my clothes was blood. I was covered in it. I waited for the shock to wear off and the pain to flare, telling me where I was injured. But nothing happened. Nothing hurt. Finally, I realized the blood wasn't mine. Somehow that was even worse. My stomach twisted.

"Get it off me. Get it off me." I pulled the wet tunic away from my skin.

"Susan, I told you not to move." Bekkah was white. Although she spoke with deliberate calm, the muscles around her eyes were tense with worry.

I pushed myself farther up. "I'm not hurt."

Wade and Linette were still sitting on the bench, looking confused, but no longer in the Rhusican's thrall. A few neighbors had come out of their homes and stood nearby. Wade's little sister peeked out of the door of her home before someone pulled her back inside.

I turned to my other side and looked past Bekkah.

The Rhusican's body rested on the ground with my sword wedged into its chest. The young guardian kneeling by it looked at Bekkah. "He's dead." The guardian's voice was impassive, but the glance he sent my way held alarm.

I edged myself away. "Bekkah, help me up."

She started to argue with me.

I grabbed her arm. "Please. I'm going to be sick."

A glint of humor flickered in her eyes as she let me pull myself up. With an arm around my waist, she guided me quickly into Wade's home and to their washroom.

I waved her away and stumbled into the small room. I doubled over, retching. As soon as it stopped, I pulled the bloody tunic over my head and dropped it on the floor, kicking it toward the corner of the small room. The sour smell started me gagging again. It was several minutes before I was able to splash my face with cold water, wrap myself in a blanket from the washroom shelf, and wobble back out to the common room.

Bekkah chased Wade's little sister from the room and sized me up. "Are you injured?"

"I don't think so." I hoped she wasn't going to comment on my weak stomach.

"Good. Please sit down."

I was happy to collapse into a chair. My knees were shaking, and I felt dizzy.

Bekkah signaled to someone near the door. Kyle walked in, his expression as hostile as it had been the morning after our group had been attacked by the bear. "Kyle is here as a witness," Bekkah said in a crisp, detached tone.

Realization began to sink in. If this were a crime drama, she'd be reading me my rights. I didn't know how to respond. Had I really killed someone? Could I have a nightmare within a delusion? I moaned.

"Susan," she tried again, "I'm going to ask you some questions. Answer truthfully. Kyle is here to verify what you tell me. Do you understand?"

I nodded, numb.

"All right." Bekkah took a deep breath. "What happened?"

As simply as I could, I explained everything—although I didn't mention how the Rhusican had claimed to know me. I told her how it had seemed to fix me with its eyes, how its face had contorted, and how it had leaped at me. When I explained that I closed my eyes and threw my sword up in front of me, Bekkah's stern frown relaxed for a moment, and she rubbed her hand over her mouth. Embarrassment warmed my face as I realized she was trying not to laugh.

Bekkah turned to Kyle. "What did you see?"

He might not have liked me very much, but he quickly corroborated my story. I was thankful he had been nearby and seen the man throw himself at me. Bekkah asked Kyle a few questions, but I stopped paying attention.

"Susan?"

I jumped. Bekkah was looking at me as if she had called my name several times already. I had drifted away.

"It's shock," she said, resting a gentle hand on my shoulder. "It's normal. You'll be fine." She turned to talk to someone else, and a short while later, Wade's young sister pressed a warm mug of clavo into my hands.

I held it to my lips, but my hands were shaking, so I gave it back.

"Can I talk to her?" Wade's voice came from somewhere in the room. Bekkah stepped away, and Wade crouched down in front of my chair. "Susan, are you all right? I'm so sorry. I was . . . it was . . ." He stammered to a halt.

"I know. Believe me, I know. Are *you* all right?" I searched his eyes for signs of poison. His round face was beautifully normal—alert and dirt-streaked. The relief made me want to cry. "Is Linette safe?"

"She's fine. Her family took her home. She woke up the instant you impaled the man." He grinned.

I grimaced at the admiration in his voice. "Um, Wade, I think I want to skip our sword training this afternoon, okay?"

He laughed. Then he took my hands in his and sobered. "How can I thank you for what you did?" I started to shake my head, but he jumped up, heedless of my response. "Wait. I have an idea. Stay here." He jogged out of the room and was back in a moment, whistling to himself. He tossed me a pair of what looked like leather gloves.

I examined them, confused. The fingers had been cut out of them, and they were longer than any gloves I'd seen before.

"Gauntlets," he explained. "They'll protect your hands and help your grip next time you decide to chop someone up."

My stomach lurched. I think I remembered to thank him for his gift before I stumbled back to the washroom.

Chapter Twelve

BEKKAH TOOK ME BACK TO TRISTAN'S home and explained everything to Tara when I couldn't string two coherent sentences together. Tara tucked me into bed with plenty of warm blankets, and Bekkah said she'd wait for Tristan so she could give him a full report. I was dozing when he got home. I woke for a few minutes to the sound of an angry guardian bellowing and thrashing around in the common room. Bekkah and Tara must have convinced him that things were under control because I was mercifully left to sleep.

At some point in the night, I woke up screaming, covered in cold sweat. I had been drowning in blood, with horrible multitoned laughter echoing off the walls. Tara knelt near my pallet. She hugged me the way I hug Anne when she falls off the swings. She rocked me, murmuring soothing words. "You did what you had to do. Shh. It'll be all right." I finally fell back asleep.

My mouth tasted sour when I woke up, and emptiness gnawed my stomach. I pulled on several layers of warm clothes and hurried out to the common room for some hot clavo. I sank into a chair with a sigh, but jumped when Tristan stomped into the room and dropped an armful of supplies onto the table.

"Just what did you think you were doing?" he growled.

His irritation rolled right off of me. The tone was too familiar. It was the same tone I used when Jon ran out into the street chasing his soccer ball and forgot to check for traffic.

"I'm fine, Tristan," I said, guessing it wouldn't help. I was right.

"Why didn't you call for help? What made you think you could take on a Rhusican? And do you realize what would have happened if Kyle hadn't seen him attack you? You'd be tried for murder!" He was working up a head of steam.

I let him get it out of his system while I sipped my tea. When he stopped for a breath, I answered quietly. "Look, there wasn't time. I didn't plan it. I was just there. It happened."

He ran his hands through his hair and flopped down at the table. "*And* you didn't clean your sword. You just left it there."

I looked around for my pack and sword. They were propped against the wall in the usual place, and I was relieved to see someone had cleaned the sword for me.

Tristan scolded awhile longer, but I could tell his heart wasn't in it. He got himself some tea and patted my shoulder as he walked past me. "Next time, keep your eyes open." Though he turned his head away, I caught a glimpse of his grudging grin.

Cradling a warm mug of clavo and resting my feet on a nearby chair, I basked in the relief of being alive. Linette and Wade, two people I cared about, were safe, and I had a part in that. Not a bad day's work for a suburban housewife from Ridgeview Drive.

After breakfast Tristan walked with me to meet Wade. As we followed the well-worn path through the village, he filled me in on a few things. No one knew who the Rhusican was or where he had come from. No one had noticed him before I came across him talking to Wade and Linette. Most of the clan were busy out near the fields, preparing for harvest, but Kyle had broken his test-gauge—a tool for checking the moisture level of the grain—so had come back early. Bekkah had popped into the village for a brief visit to restock supplies for the outpost.

"We have a new problem." Tristan watched me, as if unsure I was ready to hear more. "The Council sent a messenger yesterday to request that you report to Lyric. I thought we'd have more time. We're going to start harvest in a few days, and I hoped they'd let you stay until after the Feast. The healer might be willing to say you are still contagious, but we may have to move you."

My stomach tightened and the post-trauma euphoria evaporated. I needed to find a way home, and the people in Braide Wood were the only allies I had. I didn't want to go anywhere near Lyric, Cameron, or the Council.

The next day, Tristan gave Wade a day off and decided to work with me himself. Bekkah had reported my combat technique of closing my eyes in panic, and I think he felt honor bound to break me of that habit himself. This was why I was never good at sports in school. Whenever a ball headed in my direction—baseball, kickball, or basketball—it seemed a logical impulse to close my eyes and duck. It wasn't a great approach to sports and, apparently, was also frowned upon in swordplay.

We were warming up with long staffs in a forest clearing some distance out of the village when I heard the sound of someone approaching through the woods. I stepped back and held up my hand.

Tristan froze, alert. A moment later a thin figure in a

mottled sweater sauntered into the clearing, a pack hanging from one shoulder.

"Kieran! I didn't know you were back." Tristan's smile lit his face with warmth.

I gripped my staff with both hands, feeling wary.

"Just got in. Don't let me interrupt." He ignored me and settled down on a log. He was even leaner than when I had seen him in Shamgar. Tristan watched him with one eyebrow raised. When neither of us moved, Kieran tilted his head toward Tristan. "Go on." Then he rummaged in his bag, feigning disinterest. Tristan shook his head, but turned back to me and picked up the lesson.

At first it was a struggle for me to focus, but once we were back into sparring, I tuned out the audience. I managed to block several swings, able to anticipate Tristan's sweeping attacks. But as I countered one overhead blow, struggling to push his staff away, he swung around and under, knocking my feet out from under me. My back hit the packed earth with a whomp that rattled my teeth. I looked up at the pine branches framing the sallow sky and stayed down, waiting to catch my breath.

Tristan walked over and offered his hand, hauling me back to my feet. I glanced over at Kieran. Bony elbows rested on jutting knees. His chin balanced on his fists. His gaze shifted from Tristan to me and back again. Then his eyes narrowed.

Tristan tossed me a gourd full of tart orberry juice. "Take a break. Kieran and I have a few things to discuss." The two men headed deeper into the forest to talk, disappearing from sight.

"You're babying her," Kieran said when they halted some distance away.

"You came all the way back to Braide Wood to tell me how to train first-years?"

Even Tristan didn't realize how keen my hearing was becoming. I felt no compunction about eavesdropping. Not after I'd heard Kieran offer to get rid of me back in Shamgar.

"You're not doing her any favors," Kieran continued. I heard a twig being snapped and shredded, and guessed it was Tristan. He didn't like being nagged. "She spars like she's dancing. When she's down, she waits. She trusts you not to press an advantage. When she attacks, she holds back. She's just going through the motions. You're wasting your time."

"Fine." Tristan's deep voice answered. "You work with her."

"You know that isn't possible."

"Oh, it's possible. You just can't be bothered." Tristan's voice rose with real anger. "You don't want anything to interfere with your schemes. It's all about protecting yourself, never mind what happens to anyone else. Why did you even come back?" There was silence for a long moment.

I held my breath. Why was Tristan deliberately baiting his friend? For all his slouching nonchalance, Kieran was dangerous. Even I could see that.

When he answered, Kieran sounded faintly amused instead of angry. "Fine. I'll make a trade. I'll work with her while I'm here. I can only stay a few days, though, and I'll be living out at the caves. I don't want anyone knowing I'm around." Tristan started to say something, but Kieran cut him off.

"In exchange I want your promise." Kieran's voice dropped, and I closed my eyes, straining to hear. "If, after I work with her, I decide it's a waste of time, then you forget all these myths and come with me to Hazor."

I heard Tristan's angry exclamation, and I struggled to hear more, but my head was beginning to throb with the effort, and I couldn't keep the voices focused anymore. Whatever

Kieran was up to, he was dealing with enemies. From everything Tristan had told me about Hazor, Kieran's involvement with them meant treason at worst, or forbidden alliances at best.

Their voices grew audible again, along with approaching footsteps.

"Come on," Kieran wheedled. "You've been trying for years to prove to me that the Verses are true. Now's your chance to convince me."

Terrific. Tristan would take that as a challenge he couldn't refuse. My wariness of Kieran deepened into anger. He was a master manipulator.

The men entered the clearing. "Let me talk to Skyler," Tristan was asking.

"No." Kieran's jaw was tight. "Don't let anyone know you saw me." Kieran grabbed his pack and walked over to me. "I'm not here." His glare was hard with warning. "You haven't seen me."

"I wish," I muttered under my breath.

When Kieran continued to stare me down, I ducked my head and busied myself retying my boots.

"Don't worry. She won't say anything." I looked up to see Tristan rest a hand on Kieran's back.

Kieran turned to his friend, and his expression softened. "Is Kendra any better?"

"They don't think she'll last much longer." Tristan's voice was thick. "You should go see her."

"I can't. Not now."

So Kieran wouldn't even visit his father or his dying sister. His secret agendas were all that mattered to him. How could Tristan trust him so much?

"I'll bring you some supplies." Tristan offered his hand.

They clasped forearms, and Kieran met Tristan's eyes. "Watch your back." He shouldered his bag and disappeared among the trees.

Tristan pulled out the blunt practice swords. "Let's get to work."

With a groan I pushed myself back onto my feet.

At supper that night, Tristan waited until Dustin was showing off his woodcarvings to the family to pull me aside.

"I took supplies out to Kieran this afternoon. He's agreed to help with your sword training. It'll be a good chance to work with someone else. When Bekkah finishes her patrol at Morsal Plains, she'll take you on as her student. But the more experience you can get, the better."

He was talking too much. The longer he tried to convince me that this was a good idea, the more my stomach muscles tightened. Besides, I was getting tired of all the effort to become some sort of guardian, when what I really needed to do was find a way home.

"I'll show you where the caves are tomorrow, first light." He was still talking. "And remember to keep your guard high enough to protect your head when you parry a lateral swing."

"Enough!" I covered my ears and groaned.

The next day, when we were within sight of the caves, Tristan left me with a pep talk and a few tips. Then he hurried off to meet with two new first-years that were arriving from nearby Blue

Knoll. I trudged the rest of the way to the rock-studded clearing alone. A good night's sleep had left me with more optimism. Tristan was right; it would be good practice for me to spar with someone else. And Kieran wasn't even a guardian. He had a much slighter frame than Tristan or Wade, so I wouldn't have to compensate as much for my smaller size. How bad could it be?

I didn't spot him at first. He was sitting tailor-style on a boulder, his back to me. Ragged traveling clothes bound up with crisscrossed straps of fabric matched the mottled grays and greens of his surroundings. He was whittling a piece of wood.

"Let's get on with it," he said without turning.

His hearing must be as good as mine, I thought uneasily. He sprang off the boulder and faced me.

I untied my cloak and shrugged out of my long, narrow daypack. "Fine, I'll warm up." I did a few stretches and pulled a band of fabric from my pack to tie my hair back in a tight ponytail.

Kieran rolled his eyes. He walked over to the cave entrance and disappeared inside.

I swung my arm around a few times to loosen my shoulder. I was crouched on the ground digging the practice swords from the pack when Kieran emerged from the cave. He held a sword in his right hand, while his left grasped the scabbard. He pulled the sword out in a smooth, practiced motion, tossing the scabbard aside.

My mouth went dry. "Um, Tristan didn't tell me you had guardian training."

He shrugged. "Oh, I picked up a few things here and there. We won't need those." He tilted his head toward the wooden training weapons. "Draw your sword."

Tristan and I never sparred with live blades. I carried my real sword everywhere because it was the one thing I had brought from home, and it gave me courage. It was a security blanket to me, not a weapon. Yes, I'd used it against the Rhusican, but that was purely by accident.

I opened my mouth to inform him that I wasn't that far along in my training. Real swords didn't strike me as a good idea. But Kieran's eyes were challenging me, and I thought of the deal he had suggested to Tristan. I hoped Tristan hadn't taken the dare, but even so, I wanted to make my teacher proud.

"Fine." My fingers felt cold and clumsy as I fumbled to untie the straps that held my sword to the side of the pack. I tried to hurry but made a worse mess of the knots. Suddenly I felt something harshly cold against my neck. I turned my head in slow motion and looked up the length of a very sharp blade.

"Lovely." Kieran's voice dripped sarcasm. "I'm sure any enemy would have too much honor to attack you until you're ready. That must be why you're completely unprotected and paying no attention whatsoever." He glared at me for a long punishing moment. Then he eased the sword back an inch. "Lesson one. Stay on guard." Reaching past me, he flicked the tip of his sword and easily sliced the ties on my pack.

I scrambled to pull my sword free and backed away into the center of the clearing.

We faced off, and Kieran wasted no time. He attacked, and I barely blocked in time, stumbling back a few steps as I did. Instead of explaining and demonstrating strikes and parries, Kieran immediately pressed his advantage.

My heart lurched into a faster rhythm as I reacted out of instinct, throwing my sword up and retreating again. Within seconds Kieran's sword slipped through my feeble defense and sliced across my right shoulder. I grabbed at the wound with my free hand, my sword hanging down, my eyes wide with shock.

"Don't drop your guard!" He struck again.

I dodged to the side, but still felt a scrape across my ribs as his sword made contact. I swung my blade up, keeping my weight low and my knees bent. My mind raced. I tried to remember what Tristan and Wade had taught me. Tristan was a technician. He treated sword work as an art form. Kieran apparently belonged to the school of "whatever works." We circled each other.

"Come at me." Kieran beckoned with his free hand.

My cuts stung, even as they healed. I clenched my jaw and took a wild swing.

He deflected it easily. "You can do better than that." Kieran was taunting me now. "Aim for me, not for my sword."

In ten minutes sweat was stinging my eyes. My arm trembled, and I switched to a two-handed hold on the sword's grip. It felt heavier with each minute that passed. My clothes were stained with blood from a dozen small cuts. My breath was coming in gasps, as if I had run a mile uphill.

Kieran's face was expressionless, and he gave me no time to recover. He wasn't teaching me. He was brutalizing me. As he moved forward to swing again, I stepped back and lowered my sword.

"Wait," I panted. "I can't . . ."

Kieran lowered his sword and stepped closer. "You mean you surrender?"

I nodded. "Yes, yes. I surrender, all right?"

"Sorry, that's not an option," Kieran replied in clipped syllables. The hilt of his sword slammed against the side of my head from out of nowhere. The ground sprang up to crash against my face and sparkles of gray dissolved into black.

A picture faded into place around me like a hologram. A woman sat under a bare light bulb, in a dusty attic, writing in a journal. I floated closer and could see words, but the letters drifted off the pages and swirled around the rafters of the room before I could read them. The woman looked so tired and sad. I wanted to help her. I reached out and tried to say something to her, but there was dirt in my mouth.

I spat it out, but still felt as if I were choking. I opened my eyes. Why was there a pinecone so close to my nose? The attic had transformed back into hard dirt, and I was sprawled on the ground. Why did it feel as if someone were tapping a rock against my temple over and over? I moaned at the pain throbbing in my skull and curled in around myself. The ache began to ease as my head healed, and I pushed myself up to sit, still confused.

"Find your weapon first," said a quiet voice behind me.

I looked around quickly, causing sparks to dance in front of my eyes again. Kieran sat on a tree stump, chin in his hand, looking bored. "Your first priority is to find your sword. Then check your surroundings. And watch your back." He spoke like a college professor lecturing on themes in English literature.

I glared at him, but reached for my sword. "What kind of training is this? I thought you were supposed to help me." I spat out dirt in between the words and rubbed grit off the side of my face. As I stumbled to my feet, using the sword for support, I kept my eyes on Kieran.

He rose to his feet as well, and his face showed no remorse. "When you go into battle, there's no time to rest. No surrender. Kill or be killed. Nothing else matters. Do you understand?"

"Yes, I understand," I snarled.

"Do you?" He moved closer. In the second it took me to

consider stepping back, he grabbed my arm, twisted my sword free, and tossed it away. He gripped my upper arms and pulled me close. His face was inches from mine. "Do you really understand? This is no polite competition. If you let your guard down, you *will* die. And so will others."

I glared back up at him, angry at the pummeling he had given me, and equally angry at the mindset he was trying to force on me. I thrust my arms up to break his hold and managed a snap kick that drove him back. Some of Wade's training had stuck with me. I dove for my sword and came up with it in front of me, crouching to face Kieran.

He reached behind the stump and pulled out his own sword. His grin was feral. He was enjoying this.

In that moment I hated him. I wanted to hurt him the way he had hurt me. No, worse. I wanted to run him through. The rage was an uncontrollable creature inhabiting my body like a hissing poisonous lizard. Feeling red-hot evil charge through me pulled me up short. I kept my sword up but stepped back out of my crouch. "I can't do this. Don't make me do this. I don't want this hate."

"It's the price you pay to stay alive." Kieran advanced slowly, his eyes fixed on mine.

"What if it's not worth the price?" I asked in a hoarse whisper. I looked at the sword in my hands and threw it down.

Kieran was beside me in a second. He grabbed my hair and jerked my head back. His sword was cold against my throat.

But my fear of him, and my rage, had all boiled away. I felt charred and empty. "If you plan to experiment on what it takes to kill a Restorer, just get it over with," I said wearily.

He shoved me aside with an oath.

I sank to my knees and hid my face in my hands. *God, why*

have you left me here? What am I supposed to do? I'm in way over my head. Kieran had tried to rouse my killer instincts. In his own warped way, he was probably trying to be helpful. But all he'd done was reveal my despair. I couldn't do this. Whatever was needed, I didn't have it in me.

As I confronted my inadequacies again, a breath of peace brushed against my thoughts. An inaudible voice whispered to my heart.

I have used the small. I work through the weak.

When I lifted my head, Kieran was sitting on the large boulder at the edge of the clearing, staring off into the distance. The forest was quiet, but I imagined I could still hear the echo of our swords clashing and Kieran's sneering words floating around the clearing. I had a wicked thought that I could flick a boot knife from where I was sitting, and he'd never be able to react in time. Disgusted, I shook that temptation out of my head and stood up. I walked over to the boulder and followed Kieran's gaze. Through a cleft between two cliffs, we could just glimpse the roofs of the Braide Wood village far below us.

His tension and dark edges had softened. He seemed wistful as he stared down at his home, as if he wanted to help his people but had cut himself off from them all for some unknown reason. I sank down onto the rock beside him.

"Don't give them false hopes," Kieran said without looking at me.

"Would you rather give them no hope?"

"I'd rather they know the truth." His voice was raw.

"That they are alone, weak, with nothing to rely on but empty Verses?"

He looked at me in surprise.

Deep behind my insecurity and inadequacy grew a small

seed of stubborn faith. It was from this place that I had those dreams of great adventures that Mark loved to hear about, and from that strong spirit, I spoke with courage to the people in those dreams. From that same place, conviction welled up in me now. "Kieran, I know that's what you believe. You've lost so much and you want to blame the One. He had the power to change things, and He didn't. But you are *not* alone. He travels every dark road with you. And He hasn't forgotten His people. He hasn't forgotten you." The power in those words came from beyond me.

Kieran's eyes widened, and he stood up, backing away from me.

I had a glimpse of how fulfilling it was for Linette to sing Verses that held the power of the One. These weren't my own words, and I saw them hit home. It was enough for now. The moment passed, and I took a slow breath. "I guess you'll win your bet with Tristan."

"What?" Kieran still looked a little dazed.

"You told him that if you decided I was hopeless, he'd have to give up on his plans."

He shook his head, dark hair brushing his temples. "Oh, you're definitely hopeless with a sword. Tristan already knew that. But there are other kinds of strength. I think we'd better keep all our options open."

His acceptance, half-hearted as it was, warmed me. "But you're still going to Hazor?"

He stiffened at the mention of the enemy, and his momentary open mood vanished. I could almost hear steel transport doors dropping closed as he looked at me with stony eyes. He didn't answer my question.

I should have paid attention to the sudden chill, but I was

feeling too confident. "Kieran, why don't you stay and help the guardians?" Surely he was meant to be with his clan to help them face the danger that Tristan believed was coming. "Don't you care about Braide Wood? Tristan needs all the help he can get right now."

Kieran continued to ignore me. He slid a dagger from the sheath on his boot and buffed it on his sleeve. "What did you hear about me going to Hazor?" He peered down the blade to assess its edge.

"I heard you talking with Tristan. Don't you realize how much it took for him to ask for your help?"

Mark believed that if you threw enough power tools at a problem, you would always find a solution. I've always believed the same about words. If I kept talking long enough, I'd be able to convince Kieran to trust the Verses and stand with Tristan. I had felt the exhilarating power of words reaching him just moments ago. I could make it happen again.

Kieran pulled a small stone from his pocket and began honing his dagger blade with smooth strokes. He didn't seem to be listening. With a foot on the boulder, he braced one arm on his thigh, eyed the edge of the blade, and then polished it again on his sleeve.

I kept talking — trying to conjure up a feeling of power in my words as I argued against whatever schemes would take him to Hazor.

"Susan," he interrupted me in mid-sentence. "Do you trust me?"

I looked up at him, hopeful that my arguments had gotten through, but I couldn't read his guarded expression. "Tristan does. He cares about you — so yeah, I trust you."

"Fine," he said in a measured tone. "Because I'm going to

tell you something that I want you to believe."

I nodded, watching him stroke his dagger slowly against his whetstone again.

His next words were matter of fact. "I am *not* your ally. I could slit your throat and feel nothing."

I went very still. My eyes widened, and I stopped breathing.

No hint of uncertainty moved on the hard lines of his face. His eyes were as empty as the gray overcast sky. "And that is exactly what I'll do if you tell anyone about my trips to Hazor — or if you ever spy on me again."

Chapter Thirteen

I JUMPED UP, PUTTING THE BOULDER between us. As I absorbed his words, I waited for panic to grab me — or anger.

Instead, something odd happened. Looking at Kieran's cold, angular face, I saw another face floating in front of him. This visage was a younger version of him, one with softer lines. The expression reflected deep pain and yearning. It was as if I was seeing him through someone else's eyes.

I blinked and the vision disappeared. Yet the impression stayed with me, stirring an odd mix of calm and sorrow. "You don't need to be afraid." I heard myself saying, wondering where those words came from. "No one knows you're here in Braide Wood, and I won't tell anyone what I know." I found myself walking around the boulder to stand in front of him. Taking the dagger from his unresisting hand, I held it out between us, balanced across my palm.

"It cuts both ways, Kieran." I still didn't fully understand what I was saying, but the words flowed from a compassion that grew so strong it made me ache. "You've made yourself believe that you don't feel anything. Or that you only feel hate. That's a lie. And it's hurting you. You care about Tristan. You care about Kendra, your father, your whole village."

Kieran shook his head.

I wasn't finished. "You can hold everyone off with this." I grasped the handle of his dagger. "Except One. Keep shutting Him out, and you're only driving this into your own heart." I offered the hilt to Kieran.

He snatched it and slid it into his boot sheath with force. "Doesn't worry me." His words were clipped. "I don't have a heart anymore."

"Right," I scoffed. "You helped Tristan find the man who poisoned Kendra. You helped me when I found myself in Shamgar and feared I was insane. You came back to Braide Wood to check on the people you care about. I'm sorry, but you're as human as the rest of us." As I said the words, I realized they were true.

Kieran exhaled with a huff and sat on the boulder, resting his forehead against his fists.

A last impulse stirred in me. I rested one hand on his head, the way I did when praying a blessing for my children at bedtime. "You don't need to be afraid." Those were the last words I felt compelled to speak—as if they came from somewhere else. With that the powerful sense of seeing with other eyes and speaking with another's voice faded away.

I sank down next to Kieran on the boulder, feeling shaken. Glancing over at him, I waited for my fear and anger toward him to return. But I couldn't forget what I knew from the vision. I couldn't shake off the truth of the words I had spoken. I wouldn't see him in the same way ever again.

"That wasn't only you, was it?" Kieran looked at me sideways, head still in his hands.

"Oh, no." I gave him a rueful grin. "I guess it's one of those Restorer things."

Kieran sighed and buried his face in his hands again, so his next words were muffled. "This is *not* what the last Restorer was like."

I wanted to ask him about the other Restorer, but felt an inner nudging to stop talking. For once I paid attention and sat quietly watching a blue, feathered moth flutter in a random path around an overhanging branch. When it disappeared among the trees, I stood up. I walked into the clearing and retrieved my sword. Wiping the dust off with my sleeve, I went to stow it in my pack. Without the ties to hold it in place, it threatened to cut a hole in the bottom of the pack as soon as I loaded the bag and lifted it.

Kieran collected his sword and scabbard and returned them to the cave. When he came back out, he watched me struggle with my pack. He shook his head and went back into the cave.

Watching him out of the corner of my eye, I felt a flicker of annoyance at his exasperation. After all, he was the one who had cut the ties I had used to secure my sword until now.

When he came out, he carried something in his hand. "Here. With war coming, you'd better learn to wear your sword."

I took the leather belt that he offered me and turned it in my hands, confused.

"It's a baldric." He sounded irritated. "It crosses from shoulder to hip, and your sword fits here." He dropped the wide leather across my shoulder and showed me how to position my sword at my hip, the belt and straps holding the hilt secure. "You should really get a sheath for it, but at least you can carry it now."

I was collecting quite an assortment of borrowed gear. Bekkah's old boots gave me support for all the steep trails around Braide Wood. Wade's gauntlets rested in the bottom of my pack. And now Kieran's belt held my sword in place, so I could keep it close. "Thank you," I said, strangely touched.

I wanted to ask him what he planned to do next. I wanted to ask if the words I had spoken had made a difference to him. I wanted to encourage him to hike the trail down to the village with me. But I had spoken what I was meant to speak. It was time to go.

I picked up my pack and looked around the clearing. I couldn't spot the trailhead and didn't remember from which direction I had approached.

Kieran saw me search the edge of the clearing in confusion and gave me a shove in the right direction. "Watch your back," he said automatically.

I waved and headed down the trail.

At the outskirts of the village, the trail intersected the footpath that led deeper into the woods toward the healers' lodge. Tristan often used his midday break to walk there and stand outside the window of Kendra's room, searching for any sign of hope. It was still early, and I decided to head that way. Maybe I'd softened Kieran enough for Tristan to convince him to help.

I found the guardian sitting on the steps in front of the lodge, shoulders drooping, furrows cutting into his forehead as he stared at the woods. When he noticed me, his eyes widened.

I glanced down at my torn and bloody clothes.

Tristan spotted the baldric. "That's Kieran's. What happened? Duel to the death?" He was only half joking and looked worried.

"A gift." I shrugged, not wanting to explain more than that. "But I don't think I'll be training with him anymore."

Tristan raised his eyebrows, but didn't ask me any more questions. His gaze shifted out into the woods again, and his sadness settled back over him like a cloak.

"How's Kendra today?"

"The same. She's wasting away."

"There's got to be something we can do."

He shook his head. "It won't do any good. She won't be coming back."

Those words. A chill grabbed me with the suddenness of an ice cream headache. "Tristan! Listen to yourself. I remember where I heard those words before. *He* said them. The Rhusican you killed."

Tristan looked up at me, confused.

"Don't you get it? They lie. They lie all the time. He convinced you there's no hope, but it's a lie. He planted that poison in your mind right before you killed him. I remember him saying it. But I didn't know who he was then. Come on!"

I grabbed his arm and tugged, urging him to his feet. He didn't move fast enough for me as I hurried him into the lodge. "Take me to her room."

Doubt and hope battled across his face. If this were my first day in Braide Wood, he would have ignored me. But since then, I had shared Verses with his family, trained with the guardians, and killed a Rhusican who had threatened his friends.

He didn't respond quickly, but at last he nodded. "This way." He led me down a hallway. When we reached her room, a young attendant approached us, blocking our way.

"We need to see Kendra," I said with certainty. I don't know if it was the sword at my side or the blood and dirt on my clothes, but something made her step out of the way. I slid the door open.

Kendra looked the way I remembered her: gaunt, empty, beautiful. Someone had braided her long black hair today. Her eyes were still vacant, and her hands were still moving in a desperate pattern.

I knelt in front of her chair. Tristan hovered in the doorway, fear and longing in his face. He was putting a lot of trust in me.

Lord, don't let me get in Your way. "Come here," I said to Tristan. He put a lot of value in obeying the rules, and he had been told to stay out of Kendra's room. It took tremendous effort for him to walk forward.

As I watched him, I had a flash of insight. "Tristan, we need to free you from your poison first. Tell me a verse about the One. About how He can do anything."

He just shook his head. His gaze never left Kendra as hopelessness took hold of his heart again.

I rested my hand on my sword hilt. This time I wasn't even surprised when a verse came to my mind—a song our youth leader composed for Vacation Bible School. Jon and Anne had marched around the house last summer singing it until I was sick of hearing it.

"Therefore the redeemed of the Lord shall return, and come with singing unto Zion; and everlasting joy shall be upon their head," I sang, feeling my way along the melody. "Tristan, sing it with me." He glanced up at me, and I held his gaze and sang again. He began to mouth the words as he learned them. Finally he sang them with me in a gravelly voice that sounded more glorious to me than any Italian tenor ever could.

I could actually see the despair wash from his face. He shook himself and blinked, as if waking up from a nap. I saw it in his face a second before he said it.

"She can return." Tristan's voice was as strong as when he ordered his guardians in lehkan maneuvers. His eyes lit up. "What should we do?"

I wanted to have him send someone for Lukyan or Linette. I didn't want to take this risk. I was terrified of letting him down. But I had learned a little more about obedience in recent days. I was meant to be here. "Talk to the One."

He dropped to his knees near Kendra, resting a hand on her shoulder. His lips moved in silence, and he kept his eyes open, watching Kendra's face.

"Kendra," I coaxed, "please come back. I know you feel lost in the mist, but you aren't alone. We're here." I prayed for guidance and reached out to take her hands, stopping their frantic weavings. Her body stiffened as I held her hands still.

I can't do this, God. Help me.

"Be still, and know that I am God." The words sprang to my mind, and I chanted them softly. I felt the strength of the One flow into me as I repeated the words. Soon another verse came to mind: "I am the Lord that healeth thee." I gave it a simple melody, and the words floated in the air around us.

Kendra began to tremble.

I held on and kept singing.

"Hurry!" she shouted. Her voice sounded rough from lack of use. She jerked in her chair, falling to the side. Tristan caught her and held her close.

"They're coming!" she screamed. "Faster! You have to do more! It's not enough."

The power and urgency of her words hit me like a physical force, and I sat back on my heels, my heart pounding. Tristan put his hand over her mouth to muffle her screams.

I took a deep breath, feeling determination flow into me along with the air. Grabbing Kendra's hands again, I looked into her clouded eyes. "The man who gave you these lies is dead. His words have no power. He's gone. His lies have no more power over you."

A glimmer of awareness flared in her eyes before she began to thrash and fight.

I kept reciting every Verse from this world and mine that I could remember. I sang songs about peace and trust, about healing and redemption.

She was so thin and weak that it was easy for Tristan to hold her and keep her from hurting herself. Last week I had seen Tristan free a lehkan fawn from a bramble of thorns. The animal had struggled and bucked, sides heaving and eyes rolling. Tristan used his bulk to hold it down, talking in a calm, soothing voice as he cut away branches with his boot knife. When it was finally free, the fawn stood before him, trembling and scratched. But it didn't flinch when he held out his hand to stroke the soft fur of its neck.

He used the same voice now, cradling his wife in his arms and murmuring words with his face pressed against hers. He hadn't been able to touch her for so long. Now it was as if he wanted to soak her right in through his skin. When exhaustion finally ended her flailing and screaming, Tristan took his hand from her mouth and turned her sideways in his arms so she could look up into his eyes.

Her face brightened in recognition. "Tristan?" Then she disappeared back into herself.

We continued to pray and sing and call to her. I felt like we were diving to rescue a drowning woman. We could drag her to the surface briefly, but then she would sink out of our reach again and again.

At one point I looked up and saw the bushy-browed healer that I met on my first visit here. He stepped into the room, anxious staff hovering behind him.

I glared at him. If he tried to stop us now, he was in for a fight.

He watched Tristan and Kendra for a moment, and saw one of Kendra's brief moments of coherence. He nodded to me and backed out of the room, shooing several attendants away from the entry. He slid the door closed.

I released my grip on my sword hilt. I hadn't even realized I had reached for it.

Perhaps my own night of battling with the mist and lies helped me fight this. Perhaps it was one of those mysterious "Restorer powers" I was still in the process of discovering. Perhaps it was because the Rhusican who poisoned Kendra was dead. Whatever the reason, after more than an hour of fighting, Kendra began to improve rapidly.

After she had been lucid for a long time, I took my gaze from Kendra and looked at Tristan. His eyes scanned every inch of her face in wonder, moisture glistening on his cheeks.

I eased away, and neither of them noticed. I stood in the doorway and watched for a little longer, but Tristan didn't need any more help. Slipping from the room, I closed the door behind me.

In the hallway I leaned against the wall and found that my legs refused to support me, so I sank down to the ground, hugged my knees, and let the tears come.

A hand on my shoulder startled me. The old healer handed me a cup of something steaming and sweet, and I accepted it gratefully.

He lowered himself, joints creaking, to sit beside me on the floor. "Were you injured?" His eyebrows joined into one bushy line as he frowned in concern.

I glanced down at the blood on my clothes. I'd forgotten what I must look like. My sword work with Kieran seemed days ago. "No, I'm fine. I was just doing some training this morning. It's not as bad as it looks."

He waggled his brows. "You guardians keep us in business."

I wondered if I should explain that I wasn't really a guardian, but decided it wasn't worth the effort. Whatever potion the healer had given me to drink, I felt stronger with each sip. "I think she's going to be okay now. Will you let Tristan take her home?"

"Let me check on her. If there is no physical problem we need to keep an eye on, I think home would be the best place for her to be." He paused for a moment. "How did you do that?"

"I'm not really sure." I shrugged. "I don't think *I* did."

He nodded slowly, studying me. "We have other people here that we haven't been able to help. Perhaps later . . . ?" He left the question unfinished.

I nodded. "Yes. If I can. Later." I was too weary to think beyond today. But maybe I would find others I could help in coming days. Maybe that was my purpose here.

And then can I go back to my family, Father? They need me, too.

About an hour later we emerged from the lodge. Tristan supported Kendra as she wobbled down the steps. I looked up at the sky, amazed that it was still light. I had expected to emerge into the darkness of late night. I felt so tired; it was hard to believe it was still the same day. Kendra's gait was slow and uncertain, and Tristan finally scooped her into his arms and carried her along the trail. I followed behind, wishing I could curl up on a bed of pine needles under one of the trees to sleep.

The joy and wonder at Payton and Tara's home when Tristan arrived with Kendra in his arms was beautiful to watch. But I felt like I was seeing it from a distance. Fatigue left me disconnected. I could only summon enough energy to nod or shrug in answer to the questions and excitement. Tristan stayed glued to Kendra until she convinced him she would like to rest for a while. He carried her to their room, and even then he sat by her side while she slept.

Just before nightfall he slipped away to the caves to tell Kieran what had happened and to take him more supplies. When he arrived back home, he told me he had found the cave deserted. Kieran was gone, along with all his gear.

That night, as I prayed for my family (Mark, Jake, Karen, Jon, and Anne), and my new family (Tristan, Kendra, Tara, Payton, little Dustin and Aubrey, and even Talia and Gareth), I added Kieran's name to the list.

Chapter Fourteen

I WOKE THE NEXT MORNING BEFORE first light, probably because I had collapsed into exhausted sleep right after supper the night before. I stretched and yawned. My mouth lifted at the corners when I thought about Kendra's eyes as she emerged from the effects of the mind poison. Tristan's face had reflected the adoration in his wife's eyes, and the thought of their rescued love warmed me. Then my smile wilted. I missed Mark so much. Thinking of Tristan and Kendra, wrapped in each other's arms in their room down the hallway, made my own arms ache with emptiness. I wanted to feel only happiness for them, but I couldn't fight back the envy that surged into my thoughts.

Pulling on my clothes, I decided to go for a walk before the village stirred.

I remembered to belt on my sword, though the hilt resting against my hip kept snagging my cloak. The sky was still dark gray, but there was enough light to see the trail. A short climb up the path would take me to an overlook that gave a view of Morsal Plains for several miles out.

As I walked, I inhaled a deep breath of morning air, then stopped. Something was wrong. There was a chemical scent in the air that was foreign and disturbing. It reminded me of the mess I had created once by accidentally mixing bathroom cleaners. I ran back to the house to tell Tristan but then paused, uncertain. I didn't want to disturb him. What if the smell was something normal to this world? I didn't want to look like an idiot. I was finally beginning to fit in.

I sniffed the air again and shivered. That could not be normal.

Inside the house, I tapped on Tristan and Kendra's door. It slid open in a few seconds, revealing a tousled but alert guardian with a boot knife in his hand.

"What?" He rubbed sleep from his eyes when he saw me.

"Something's wrong."

He cast a worried look back at Kendra, but she was sleeping peacefully.

"No. It's outside. Please hurry."

He met me outside in less than a minute.

"Do you smell that?" I asked him.

He took a deep breath and looked at me, puzzled. "No. What do you smell?"

I tried to explain, but he didn't know what ammonia was, or any of the other chemicals from my world that I used to describe it.

"Let's check the overlook." Tristan jogged up the path, which was growing clearer in the dawning light. I followed him, huffing and puffing. No one in this community would ever get heart disease with all the hiking and running they did. When we reached the ridgeline, Tristan scanned in all directions.

I looked out toward Morsal Plains and grabbed his arm. "What are those?"

Bulbous silver machines crawled through the fields. They

looked like metallic beetles moving among the grain. Tristan squinted in the direction I was pointing but couldn't see them. Stretching my heightened vision, I did my best to describe the scene.

"Sounds like minitrans. But that doesn't make any sense. They're used in cities to move cargo, and they're usually larger than what you're describing. We don't have any here. What are they doing?"

I focused my gaze and was gradually able to see more and more detail. Some of the minitrans were spreading out through the fields, but many had stopped. A thin telescoping rod stretched up and out of each one . . . maybe ten feet into the air. Liquid sprayed out of the rod and coated the grain in all directions.

"Tristan, you don't use irrigation systems, do you?" He frowned at me in confusion, and I rephrased. "Do you ever need to spray water on the fields?"

"It rains every day. Why would we do that?"

"Well, something is being sprayed on the fields. That's not normal, is it?"

Tristan grabbed a palm-sized device from his belt and held it over his head. He squeezed it, producing a sharp, ringing tone that grew steadily in volume. It reminded me of the smoke alarm that I set off every time I baked cookies back home, only this sound wasn't as shrill. It had a clearer, sweeter pitch, but there was no doubt that it was an alarm. I covered my ears as the sound grew. Everyone for miles would have heard that.

Tristan released the signaler and hooked it back onto his belt. "We'll take the lehkan. They're faster, even though the trail is rough. Let's go."

I never aspired to join a branch of the military, but if I ever had, I would have wanted a captain like Tristan. By the time we reached the paddock and saddled our lehkan, there were people milling everywhere. Tristan noticed Payton and called out to him.

"Something is happening down at Morsal Plains. I'll send a messenger back when we know more."

Payton nodded his understanding and began herding some of the villagers out of the way of the guardians.

Tristan snapped orders to several of his men, who carried them out without question or hesitation. Having someone in charge blunted the edge of the swelling panic. He didn't bother with explanations as he signaled to several of the guardians to ride with us. I saw Wade in the confusion, and he gave me an eager grin.

"Stay close to me," Tristan ordered as he urged his mount forward.

I followed him at a full gallop across the plateau until we had to slow our pace at the forest trail leading down toward Morsal Plains. The route was steep and twisting, and our lehkan slid and skittered their way along the switchbacks. When we reached the bottom, we charged full out again across an open field and up a hill. From the crest we would see all the rich farm-land of the Morsal Plains stretched before us.

To the right was the craggy mountain range that formed a barrier between Braide Wood and Hazor. Behind us, the steep slopes we had scrambled down were stippled in shades of green from the thick forest of Braide Wood. As we reached the top of the hill, the fumes hit us. An acrid chemical haze stung our eyes. The lehkan balked and tried to bolt back in the direction from which we had come. Unwilling to waste time fighting the wild-eyed beasts, we dismounted.

The whole valley was filling with a yellow cloud. We watched as one of the minitrans rolled into an unoccupied field near us and stopped. Up close, I could see they were no larger than an oversized canister vacuum cleaner, but were self-propelled. Where had they come from?

As the telescoping rod of the closest minitran shot into the air, Tristan ran toward the machine. Before he reached it, mist sprayed out—covering huge areas in all directions. Tristan tried to reach the rod, but as the liquid hit his clothes, it burned through in places, leaving angry welts on his skin. He grimaced in pain.

I ran forward and grabbed him, pulling him back. Some of the mist hit my skin and scorched it like a splatter of hot bacon grease. The grain hissed as it shriveled and collapsed from the chemical burn. Once Tristan and I were back out of range, I checked the blisters on our arms. Mine healed quickly. His didn't.

Tristan coughed from the smoke and fumes, but squinted into the fog, searching for a way to stop the machines. Another metallic beetle rolled past, ready to spew out venom.

I pulled the hood of my cloak over my head, drew my sword, and charged at it, sending a quick and silent thanks to Wade. His gauntlets gave my hands some protection. I reached the nearest minitran right as it started spraying. Pain seared my skin wherever it was exposed.

I'll heal. I'll heal. Ignore it.

I swung my sword against the extending rod, jarring my arm. I swung again and again. It took several tries, but I managed to break it off at the base.

The chemicals in the machine's belly spilled out the hole where the rod had extended, but at least it didn't throw more mist into the air. The ground under the minitran fizzed and boiled, but some areas of grain were spared.

I ran toward another of the machines, ignoring the fiery damage that the mist was doing to my skin. Each machine I could destroy was another acre of grain spared. My eyes burned, and my ribs ached from coughing. My skin blistered even faster than it could heal. Too bad Kieran wasn't here to see me now. I had no trouble feeling enough anger and hatred to keep my sword swinging. These hideous, bulging weapons were destroying the lifeblood of Braide Wood. But no amount of anger could keep me going indefinitely. Finally the coughing took over, and I couldn't stagger forward any more.

Strong hands pulled me back. Tristan. He had tied a strip of cloth over the lower half of his face, but was still coughing as well.

"Susan, fall back!"

"No, we have to—"

"We tried. Too many guardians have been burned. I had to order them back. You did what you could. Fall back."

My eyes watered from the mist, and I kept them squeezed to a narrow slit as Tristan guided me back up the hill. Still, I kept looking back to watch the progress of the attack. Each automated machine dispensed its spray and then shut down, remaining like a scab in the center of the ruined field. Apparently the unmanned weapons were one-use only.

Wade strode forward to meet us. "Why didn't the outpost sound an alarm? Who's on patrol right now?"

Tristan set his jaw. His red-rimmed eyes burned with a fear he tried to hide. "Bekkah is staying at the outpost. I've got to find a way around this to get to her."

"I'm coming." I struggled to breathe between coughing fits.

He nodded and scanned the valley, looking for a way to

reach the outpost. Through the yellow fumes, I could see the crude shelter where guardians camped while monitoring this usually peaceful plot of land. The building was only a mile off, but we couldn't reach it through the fields without being doused in chemicals and burned alive. We'd have to circle around, skirting the edge of the rocky cliffs to the north.

"Do you see a way to the shelter?" Tristan squinted against the smoke and the painful blisters on his face.

"Yes, but it's a long way around. Can we use the lehkan?"

Tristan nodded, and we stumbled back to our mounts. They fidgeted on the hill out of range of the smoke, pawing the ground, ears flicking forward and back. One of the first-years held their reins, murmuring calming words. Tristan issued orders to his men even as he mounted. He sent some northeast to where the forest poured down from Braide Wood and met the rocky Hazor mountains—the direction the minitrans seemed to have come from. Others were commanded to circle the far southern borders of the fields, on alert for enemies. Someone had set these monsters loose. He assigned a few to help the wounded back to the village.

Tristan and I rode around the north edge of the fields, close to the looming darkness of the cliffs. The tears running down my face weren't only caused by the chemicals. The beautiful farmland was already blackened and scarred as the weapons did their work. There was no way to stop them. I could have screamed with frustration. These fields had been ready for harvest. This was food for the people of Braide Wood and the surrounding area for the next full season. Worse yet, this destruction would affect more than one season's crop. The chemicals continued to hiss as the foul mess soaked into the ground. The clan wouldn't be able to farm here for years. The very earth was being murdered.

I turned away from the ruined fields and set my focus determinedly on Tristan's back. He must have had the right words to soothe his great, antlered lehkan, because somehow he steered him along the rim of the destruction. My doe, Mara, followed with only occasional skitters in random directions.

My anxiety grew as we rode. As far as I knew, Bekkah was alone at the outpost. *God, please let her be safe.* She was smart and tough. She would have found a way to survive the chemical attack. I thought of her ready smile when we first met in the transport—teasing the men, resting her hand comfortably on her dagger hilt, telling me how she'd always wanted to be a guardian. As we drew close to the outpost, we noticed black charred markings on some of the trees and even on the ground. When we reached the shelter, Tristan leapt off his mount and ran forward. It took me longer to dismount, but I hurried to join him. Someone lay face down on the ground several yards from the open door of the shelter. Full, chestnut hair gathered at the nape of her neck. Bekkah. The side of her face was blistered from the poison mist. She must have passed out from the fumes.

I rolled her over before Tristan could stop me and then stumbled back with a gasp. A deep, charred wound marked her chest. She wasn't unconscious. She was dead.

"No," I choked out. I fell to my knees next to her body.

Tristan dragged me to my feet. "Long-range weapons," he said, pulling me toward the shelter. He scanned the area around us as we ran. "Do you understand? Do you know what those are?"

I understood all too well what long-range weapons were. I didn't know what kinds were used in this world, but if that's what had killed Bekkah, they were clearly as deadly as any in my own world. I ran faster.

As we stumbled into the shelter, we confronted another surprise.

A young man with cropped black hair and foreign-looking clothes stood against the back wall of the room. Tristan drew his sword with a cry and stepped forward until the tip of the weapon hovered inches from the boy's chest. The boy flinched, but didn't try to run.

"Tristan!" I was still having trouble breathing. "He's not armed!" I tugged on Tristan's sword arm, but it was like trying to move a gnarled branch of one of the broad trees that grew in the village.

He didn't budge. At least he stopped short of running the boy through. "Who are you?" he demanded.

The boy swallowed and looked almost cross-eyed as he stared down Tristan's sword.

"Speak!" Tristan roared.

The boy jumped, glancing at me and back at Tristan. He pulled himself up as tall as his slight form would stretch. "I am a messenger of the sovereign kingdom of Hazor. Your land has been claimed. I have been sent to deliver terms." He used a formal singsong tone. Even in his fear the words were spoken with a hint of pride that rekindled the rage of the guardian standing in front of him.

Tristan's sword arm lifted.

The boy's eyes widened. "If you kill me, you won't learn everything you need to know," he squeaked, no longer using a formal cadence.

Tristan eased his sword back . . . barely. Tension coiled in his body, but he took a deep breath and gestured toward the door. "Did you kill her?" he asked in a low, tight voice.

The young man's mouth dropped open in shock. "No! I'm

just the messenger. They brought me here after—" He glanced out the window that overlooked the fields, where the last stages of the devastating automated attack were unfolding. He steeled himself and looked back at Tristan. "Let me deliver my message before you kill me. Otherwise they'll have to send another."

I could read in his face that he expected to die, and I shook my head in disbelief. "Are your people still out there?"

He seemed confused by my question, but shook his head.

While we questioned him, Bekkah's body remained sprawled in the dirt. "I'm not leaving her out there," I told Tristan.

"He's probably lying. Stay where you are."

I looked pointedly at the backs of my hands, where all the blisters had disappeared. Even if someone were still out there shooting, I had a good chance of healing from anything they threw at me. "I'll be fine."

Tristan took his eyes off the boy long enough to glare at me with genuine anger.

It dawned on me that he wasn't used to having guardians question his orders. This probably wasn't a good time for me to start promoting democratic principles. I nodded and sank onto the cot at the side of the room, determined to keep my mouth shut and pay attention.

"So, *messenger*," Tristan said venomously, his eyes back on the boy. "What are these 'terms' you're supposed to deliver?"

The young man hesitated a moment, and I couldn't help but feel sorry for him. He looked younger than my son Jake. What kind of army would leave an unarmed boy alone in the territory of a provoked enemy, just to deliver its message?

"May I know whom I am addressing?" the youth asked. Before Tristan could respond to the gall of that question, he quickly added, "My orders are to deliver the message to the leaders of Braide Wood."

Tristan lowered his sword and took a step closer to tower over the boy. "I am Tristan, captain of the guardians of Braide Wood." Tristan's eyes burned red, his face was raw and blistered, and his voice shook with anger. He was a powerful and frightening warrior, yet the boy met Tristan's eyes with a nod of resignation.

I could read the youth's face as easily as those of my own children. He had been left here to deliver his message and die. Because he fully expected death, he wouldn't give in to fear.

"Hazor has claimed these lands." His voice reminded me of Councilmember Cameron issuing boastful predictions in the transport. "We have destroyed the plains to show you our might. Next we will destroy Braide Wood. Not one log will remain above another. Not one life will be spared." The youth couldn't keep looking at Tristan. He stared at a point past the guardian's left ear and took a deep breath. "Unless, within the time of twenty days, Braide Wood delivers tribute to Zarek, king of Hazor, in Sidian."

The Hazorites had to be crazy. First they hauled machines over the mountains separating Morsal Plains from this end of Hazor. Then they destroyed all the fertile land for miles. It would be of no use to them now either. What possible purpose did this serve? Then they left a scrawny kid near the body of a murdered guardian, ordering him to deliver an ultimatum. And what tribute could they possibly expect from a community that never possessed much to begin with and now would be driven to near starvation? I stared at the boy, stunned by the insanity of all of this.

Tristan, however, had taken a step back and was no longer vibrating with suppressed rage. He seemed to be making sense of the message. "What tribute is requested?" he asked in a formal tone that indicated this was a ritual exchange of words.

"The tribute *demanded*," the messenger said, "is for you to give over each Braide Wood child of fewer than twelve years to Sidian as a surety. Deliver them before nightfall of the twentieth day, and they will live and Braide Wood will be unharmed."

"What?" I gasped. Neither man looked at me.

"If the tribute is not met, they will die along with every other soul in Braide Wood."

Like a recording that had run to the end of its tape, the boy's voice slowed and dropped as he finished. He looked at the floor and then closed his eyes. I wondered if he was praying, and if so, to whom. His thin body tensed, but he didn't move as he waited for Tristan to run him through. For a moment I wasn't sure what would happen next.

Tristan apparently had no indecision. He sheathed his sword and ignored the boy, turning to me. "Since they've sent terms, the Hazorites won't be out there anymore. Tie him up. We'll take him back to the village. I'll get Bekkah." Tristan grabbed a blanket from the end of the cot where I was sitting and left the shelter.

The messenger opened his eyes and looked at me in confusion.

My earlier pity for this young man had faded after hearing his ultimatum. I untangled a rope from a sack of grain in the corner of the room and walked over to him. "Hold out your hands." I wrapped the rope around his wrists. His arms shook.

When I was sure the knots would hold, I lifted my gaze from them to his face.

The mask of resignation and determined courage had dropped away. He was terrified.

I wanted to hate him because Bekkah's body was being wrapped in a blanket right outside the door, and his people were the ones who killed her. I wanted to blame him because he stood and watched at this window while hideous machines destroyed Morsal Plains. I wanted to scream at him for repeating the threats and demands of his king.

But he was a skinny kid who should have been climbing trees or playing ball games with friends, not playing the pawn in an insane war. He was watching my face and must have seen it softening. "Please," he whispered.

Did he think he could talk me into letting him go? I may have felt some compassion for him, but I wasn't crazy.

"Please. You have a sword." He was trembling. "Kill me now. By all the gods of my people and yours, don't let him take me." He dropped to his knees. "Hurry!" He looked up at me, then glanced toward the doorway.

I crouched down in front of him, shaking my head. I needed to calm him. The ride back up to the village would be hard enough without a hysterical prisoner to cope with. "What's your name?"

He looked startled. "Nolan."

"Nolan, my name is Susan. I'm not going to kill you. I really don't like killing people." It would be nice to reassure him that no one would hurt him, but I didn't know if I could promise that. I didn't know what would happen to any of us in the near future.

"Give me your knife. I'll do it myself."

"Why are you so eager to die?"

He stared at me as if I were making a sick joke. "I know what the barbarians of the Wood do with their prisoners. Please, if you have any mercy, let me die now. I've given you the message. You don't need me anymore." His thin chest was moving up and down rapidly, his panic growing.

I had to get him calmed down. I reached out a hand to touch his shoulder, and he flinched, expecting me to strike him. My stomach twisted at the unfamiliar feeling of being feared. I couldn't stand any more of this.

I stood up, planning to go outside for Tristan.

Before I reached the doorway, he strode back through. "We need to ride back and send word to the Council. Can you manage him?" He looked at the boy, who was still huddled on the floor.

I clenched my jaw and nodded.

"On your feet," he snapped at our prisoner.

Outside, I saw the blanket-wrapped body strapped across Tristan's lehkan and felt a wave of vertigo. I battled back the nausea and misery that hit me at the sight of Bekkah's form bundled like a sack of grain. There wasn't time for my grief right now. I climbed onto Mara.

Tristan emerged from the shelter, hauling Nolan by the arm. He boosted him up to sit behind me. The boy gripped one side of the saddle with his tied hands, and I hoped he'd be able to stay on. Tristan swung up into his saddle and eased his animal forward. With the cargo we carried, we couldn't gallop, but the large creatures covered ground quickly even at a walk. We retraced our path to the eastern hill overlooking the fields, where several of the guardians waited for Tristan. He paused to receive reports from his men. They sent curious looks at the boy behind me, but with military protocol, they waited for Tristan to explain Nolan's presence. When he didn't, they hurried away to carry out their orders.

I sat still in the saddle and looked out at the plains. I couldn't stomach the destruction and quickly focused on the strong, tall stalks of grain on the few acres that had been spared. If the poisonous fumes didn't destroy them, there would be at least a little food to glean.

Something cold touched my face, and I tilted it upward. The afternoon rainfall was beginning. Clean water sprinkled down onto the valley and stopped the spread of the yellow cloud. The sight was the only shred of hope I could cling to as we nudged our lehkans toward the more gradual southern trail up to the plateau and back to Braide Wood.

Chapter Fifteen

WHEN WE RODE THROUGH THE LEHKAN pastures, Tristan didn't stop at the paddock, but continued on the trail into the village. I'd never seen anyone ride on the footpaths into this part of the forest, and from the stares we received, the villagers hadn't either. They trailed behind us, watchful, tense.

Tristan rode right up to a home near the center of the village. He dismounted and carefully lifted down the bundle from his lehkan. The door to the house flew open, and Bekkah's sister and several other family members ran out. Cradling Bekkah's body, Tristan walked past them into the house. A woman inside wailed.

I let my own tears fall. Bekkah was one of the first women I met in this world. Within minutes of meeting me, she had given me her old boots, the boots she was saving for her sister. She encouraged me along the steep and unfamiliar trail to Braide Wood. During the meeting at Tristan's home, in spite of a brief flare of mistrust, she had volunteered to train me. She would have been my teacher, and she had already been my friend. I wiped at my tears with my sleeve, but the chemicals on my clothes only brought more tears as they burned my eyes.

Tristan came back out and signaled to me. I dismounted,

leaving Nolan alone on Mara. The boy's thin body slumped, and he kept his focus down. He was trying to become invisible.

Whispers traveled among the gathered crowd, but they stayed at a respectful distance. Tristan spoke quietly, his face a mask of duty. "Susan, will you take care of Kendra for me? Make sure she's all right? I'll check back when I can."

It was evidence of his growing respect for me that he was asking me instead of ordering me. I knew that in the midst of this crisis, he wanted to be home with her, but his responsibilities didn't allow him that luxury. "Of course I'll stay with her. She'll be all right. I'll see you later."

He nodded his thanks and hauled our prisoner away.

I hurried down the path to his home.

Confusion and stunned disbelief spread through the village in overlapping ripples as more details of the attack spread. Healers were busy helping the guardians who had been burned fighting the minitrans and their acid spray. Songkeepers gathered and invited families to prayer. Friends visited at Bekkah's home to comfort her family. In a community this small her death hit every person in some way.

When I arrived at their house, I told Tara, Talia, and Kendra what I had seen and assured them that Tristan was safe. I didn't tell anyone about the message from Hazor. I wasn't sure what Tristan wanted to be public knowledge. Payton and Gareth had gone out with other men from the village to see how much grain could be salvaged. They'd hiked down the steep path through the woods to the field while we had been riding up the south hills to the lehkan plateau, so we'd missed them. I stayed at home talking quietly with Kendra and trying to keep Dustin and Aubrey content indoors. I was reassured to see that Kendra really was fine. She was horribly thin from the weeks of being trapped by the poison, but Tara was already focusing all her energy on feeding her daughter-in-law, and I was sure Kendra would regain her strength.

Tara coped with her anxiety about the attack by baking batch after batch of round bread loaves, until Talia pointed out that it might be wiser to save the grain. Then Tara shifted her energy to washing the chemical residue from my cloak. There were several gaps where the fabric had burned through, and I feared Tara's vigorous scrubbing would add more holes.

Talia slipped out often throughout the day to gather news. She heard that Tristan had sent a messenger to the Braide Wood Council chief, who was currently in Lyric. He was also meeting with other village leaders. The reports on the condition of the fields continued to be bleak. The lehkan patrols followed tracks through the mountains showing the path the Hazorites had taken in mounting their attack, but the enemy was long gone now. They had apparently lugged the machines over the mountains on their backs, since the minitrans couldn't traverse the rocky terrain. They'd set them loose to cause their damage, but the enemy soldiers disappeared back to Hazor long before Tristan and his troops arrived. The healers were struggling to find a way to treat the blistering burns of the men who had come in contact with the chemicals. One guardian had gone blind, and they feared it would be permanent.

I taught Aubrey and Dustin how to play "Pick-Up-Sticks"—a new game to them. Once they were busy with that in the corner, Kendra and I poured mugs of juice and sat down to talk.

By unspoken consent, we deliberately confined our conversation to topics other than the day's tragedy. Kendra was curious about where I had come from and even laughed a few times as I described my early days in this world. In turn I asked her how she was feeling and what she remembered about the past two seasons.

"The last thing I remember was Tristan planning to leave for a patrol on the River Borders. He was sure an attack was coming from Kahlarea and had given his evidence to the Council, but they wouldn't listen. I was furious that he was going ahead with his patrol when he knew about the danger. Did they ever attack?"

"I don't think anything happened on the River Borders." I sipped my juice, mouth puckering with the sour tang of orberries, and tucked my legs up underneath me. "I know Linette's fiancé is patrolling there this season, but I haven't heard about any problems. Tristan's been more worried about Hazor. When we were in the transport traveling here, Cameron told Tristan he had been trading with Hazor. He also said something about the guardians being obsolete soon."

"Did Cameron say what they had been trading?"

"I don't remember. I'm sorry. None of it made much sense to me at the time. I was going to ask Kieran when we met to spar yesterday, but—"

"Kieran? He's here?"

I bit my lip and shook my head. "I'm sorry, I shouldn't have said anything."

Kendra's whole body had tensed. "Tell me where he is."

I met her eyes. "I don't know. He stopped here to meet Tristan and get supplies, but when Tristan went to talk to him last night, he had disappeared. I really don't know where he is right now." That, at least, was true.

Kendra's face fell. "How did he seem?"

I wasn't at all sure how to answer her. "Like he doesn't want to have hope, but he can't keep from trying to make a difference in spite of himself."

Kendra tucked a strand of black hair behind her ear and smiled. "Sounds like you've gotten to know him pretty well."

"He's not thrilled with the theory that I might be a Restorer. He seems to think that's just going to cause more problems."

"The last Restorer saved our people. But the cost was high." Kendra's expression became wistful. "Mikkel was an incredible guardian. He knew that Kahlarea planned to invade through the pass by the Cauldrons. He begged the Council for support, but they didn't believe him. Finally, he gathered a handful of other guardians who were willing to ride with him to defend the pass. When the attack came, Mikkel himself killed two hundred enemy soldiers. Even after he was badly wounded, he kept fighting with a power beyond anything the guardians had ever seen. They held off the enemy and drove them back across the River Borders. But most of the men who rode with Mikkel died. Kieran and I were still young when it happened, but we had a cousin who fought beside the Restorer. He died at the Cauldrons."

"What happened to Mikkel?" I asked, not sure I wanted to know.

"He died the next day. Too many wounds. Too much damage. His body couldn't heal anymore."

I squeezed my mug. "No wonder Kieran doesn't want to rely on a Restorer. He told Tristan that I'm only going to get a lot of other people hurt."

"Kieran always has to do things his own way. I guess I'm more like him than I realized. If I hadn't gotten so angry at Tristan for ignoring my advice, I wouldn't have run off to Blue Knoll." Kendra's shoulders sagged.

I recognized in her the same shame and regret that had battered me after I was trapped by the Rhusican poison. "Kendra, I understand," I said. "I was poisoned, too."

Her eyes widened, but she waited for me to say more.

"When I came back, I hated the fact that I had hurt other people by giving in to it."

"Yes," she said. "That's exactly it. And Tristan told me about tracking the man who did this to me. If the Council finds out . . ."

I interrupted her, cutting off the dangerous line of thought. "The important thing is that you're better. It will help him so much to have you back."

Kendra looked at her hands in her lap. She had been rubbing them absently. Now she clenched her fingers together to still their movements. "Susan, do you ever fight with your husband?"

I laughed. "Way too often—and about some pretty silly things. I was baking cookies one night a few weeks ago, and Mark told me that if I'd line the rows up diagonally on the sheet, I'd fit more on. I told him I liked my straight rows and we kept arguing like it was some important issue." Pain twisted behind my ribs. Would I ever get to have silly arguments with Mark again? But even while it triggered an ache, I was glad to talk about Mark. It helped remind me that he still existed somewhere in the world where I belonged. Soon Kendra and I were sharing more stories and laughing about the foibles of husbands. It was as if we could hold back the day's tragedy if we talked about normal things. Any distraction from grief and fear was welcome. Maybe it was a form of denial, but I needed the reprieve.

It was close to dark when Tristan came home. He opened the door and shoved Nolan inside. Ignoring the boy, Kendra jumped up and threw herself into Tristan's arms. He buried his face in her hair then pulled back to rest his forehead against hers. Both men reeked of sweat and the acrid chemical smoke that permeated their clothes. Nolan's wrists were still tied and he kept his gaze down. His lip was cracked and caked with dried blood, and his face was puffy and swollen.

I shot Tristan a questioning look.

He untangled himself from Kendra's embrace. "I decided to bring him here for the night. Some of the guardians I asked to watch him were a little . . . overzealous. I need to talk to him, and he'll be safe here."

"Maybe so, but how safe will we be?" Talia asked her brother, striding into the room and glaring at the boy. She glanced over to the corner of the room. Dustin and Aubrey had dozed off after their game and were curled around each other like puppies. I thought about the Hazorite demand that these children be handed over to Zarek in Sidian and shuddered.

"Susan can take care of him," Tristan said.

Terrific. As far as I was concerned, guarding an adolescent hostage wasn't in my job description. But then, none of this was. Tristan whispered something to Kendra, and she smiled. He touched her face again. "I'll be right back." Then he gestured to me to follow him. When we stepped outside, I could barely see the trees a few feet from the house. Night was falling fast.

Tristan dragged a hand across his forehead. "We need to find out everything we can about how strong Hazor is and what their plans are. Did the boy say anything to you earlier?"

"He begged me to kill him. He seemed terrified about being brought back here."

Tristan grunted. "Good. We can use that. Keep him scared and find out what you can."

"I . . . I don't think I can handle that," I said, my stomach clenching at the memory of Nolan's fear earlier that day.

"I'm not asking you to torture him. Just try to get him talking."

"What's going to happen now? Will the Council gather an army to come and help defend Braide Wood? And why did Hazor ask for something so crazy?"

Tristan's face was indistinct in the darkness, but I heard him sigh. "If Hazor is as strong as I fear, there may not be a choice. It's common for them to take children when they conquer a land. That way they know the nation won't retaliate. A war would put our own children at risk. Their strategy gives them more control over the countries they absorb." His foot scraped against the hard-packed earth as he shifted his weight. "By the way . . . I didn't get a chance to thank you for raising the alarm this morning—"

"It didn't help."

"—and for bringing Kendra back. I . . . I'd lost hope. She's everything to me. I owe you my life."

I could hear the effort it took him to voice his feelings, and a glow of pleasure and gratitude swept over me. "I'm just glad I could help. Now go inside and clean up. We all need some supper."

The meal was quiet. Everyone cast uneasy glances at Nolan, whom I had convinced Tristan to let me untie. I tried to get the boy to try some soup and bread, but he just gave me a sullen glower, probably suspecting that I was trying to drug or poison him. After the meal Dustin and Aubrey dutifully chanted the

Verses they were learning, with a few corrections from Gareth and Talia. I covertly watched Nolan as the children's clear voices filled the room. He seemed to be listening, though he was careful to keep his gaze averted from everyone.

Tristan made a point of gathering up all the weapons before heading to bed. He showed me a closet with no windows, where I could lock Nolan in for the night when I was done talking to him. After steering everyone to the back rooms, he slapped his boot knife into my palm. "Keep this handy."

Nolan huddled in his chair at the end of the table. He didn't look like much of a threat, but I nodded and tucked the dagger into my belt.

"I'll be close by if you need help with anything," Tristan added loudly. Nolan flinched. Then Tristan left me alone in the common room with our prisoner.

I was tired, but the boy had to be exhausted. The Hazorites must have risen hours before dawn in order to launch their attack at first light.

I walked over to the kitchen and brought a pitcher and mug to the table. "Have some water," I offered, pouring.

He ignored me, staring at his hands in his lap, but he licked his cracked lips.

I sat down at the table near him. "Nolan, look at me." I waited until he complied before continuing. "You can watch me drink some first so you'll know it's safe." I drank a few swallows and pushed the cup over to him.

He glanced up at me through his dark cropped bangs, and after a long pause, he reached for the mug. His hands shook as he held it to his lips and drained it.

Great. And Tristan wanted me to keep him scared. I wanted to send the poor kid home to his parents for a good night's sleep.

"So, Nolan, I'm not from around here. Something puzzles me. Why did they leave you behind to deliver the message? Isn't that kind of dangerous for someone so young?" I poured him some more water from the pitcher.

He shrugged but didn't answer.

I had to grin. With two teenagers at home, I had lots of experience with the silent treatment.

Reaching for the mug, he looked up and saw me grinning. His eyes widened, and his hand shook so much that some of the water splashed onto the table. He set the mug down, and his eyes darted around the room. He was looking for exits.

I shook my head and leaned forward. Time to pull up everything I'd ever learned about intimidation from watching TV spy dramas over the years. "There's nowhere for you to go. I know you're mad that I wouldn't kill you. I'm sorry. Maybe it would have been easier for you. But Tristan . . ." I tilted my head toward the back rooms. "Well, Tristan wants you alive. I don't know why. But I think it'd be better for you if you just talk to me and don't make me call him away from his bed."

"What do you want?" he asked in a small voice.

"I just want to talk. I'm curious about your customs. Answer a few questions for me, and I'll do my best to keep Tristan away from you. Deal?"

He blinked at me in confusion.

"A deal. A bargain. Is it a bargain?" I asked again.

He made a noncommittal sound in his throat and slouched back into this chair, staring at the table.

I felt another wave of familiarity. This reminded me of many kitchen table conversations with my teens. Unfortunately, taking away the car keys wasn't going to help in this situation. I slapped my hand down on the tabletop and pushed my chair back as I stood up. "Fine. I'll just go call Tristan. I'm tired anyway. Since you'd rather talk to him, I can get some sleep."

"No!" he said.

I stood, waiting.

"They left me because my life isn't important," he blurted out, answering my earlier question. "I'm not strong enough for the army, so they made me a messenger. That was my job. I went where I was needed, so they didn't waste the life of someone useful."

I slid back into my chair, careful not to let him see the pity I was feeling. "And why does Hazor want Braide Wood?"

"Why not? Hazor is growing. Hazor can take any nation it wants, so it will."

"And this is just a start?"

"Maybe. Probably. The hill gods have told us that Hazor will rule the entire world." There was no small hint of a boast in his voice.

"So you worship the hill gods?" I knew this line of questioning wasn't getting to the military information Tristan wanted, but I was curious.

"Of course. It's why we're a strong nation. We serve them. They give us power."

"Here in Braide Wood, we serve only one God."

"We know." His lip curled. "It's not really a fair battle, is it? Your one god against all of ours? Your swords and knives against our weapons?"

"Tell me about your weapons," I said, jumping at the opening he gave me. "What did they use to kill Bekkah?" Anger edged my voice, and this time I didn't have to fake it.

"I wasn't there then. They brought me in afterward."

"But you know the weapons the army carried. You've seen them."

He nodded slowly. "Syncbeams. Focused heat weapons. Easy to carry. Works at a long distance if you have good enough aim. I guess it doesn't matter if I talk about them. They've been selling them out of Corros Hills."

"What?" That made no sense.

He looked at me with obvious pity for my stupidity. "Your Council paid a huge tribute for some."

"But why would Hazor sell their sync-things to an enemy nation?"

"Syncbeams."

"Whatever. But why would they sell them to our Council?"

Nolan shifted in the chair but didn't answer.

I was baffled. Cameron's conversation in the transport began to make more sense. The trade delegation had been procuring weapons—weapons that were forbidden by the Verses. But why would Hazor barter away their advanced technology? Unless . . . "They don't really work?"

"Oh, they work," Nolan said.

I kept thinking. The Council in Lyric was worried about an attack from Kahlarea. Lyric tries to build an alliance with Hazor. Hazor bleeds them for tribute in exchange for weapons. . . . "But Hazor only trades the old models," I said, catching on. "They have newer and more powerful syncbeams . . . and probably defenses against the old ones."

"Of course," the boy answered, looking at me as if I were a bit slow.

I carried the pitcher of water back to the kitchen to give me time to process this information. If Hazor planned to keep expanding, Kahlarea would be a target one day, too. By supplying the Council with weapons, Hazor hoped that the People of the Verses would weaken Kahlarea in war. Then, after Hazor moved through the clans, Kahlarea would be ripe for attack as well. I grabbed a cloth, soaked it in cold water, and wrung it out.

"But then why today's attack? It would interfere with Hazor's master plan if the People of the Verses mount a retaliation now."

Nolan shrugged. "Your people won't fight. Zarek is too strong. And with the Braide Wood children in Hazor . . ."

I nodded. "Less chance of a random invasion later."

When I walked back to the table, Nolan watched me warily. Dark bruises were beginning to show up on his face, especially around one eye.

I held his chin and gently blotted the dried blood at the side of his mouth. "What did Tristan's men do to you?"

He gave me another look as if he thought I were the village idiot and didn't bother answering.

Folding the cloth, I pressed it over the worst bruise on the side of his face. "Hold it there. It'll bring down the swelling a little." I sat down again and wished for the millionth time that I were home in my own world. Nolan was a messenger for the enemy Hazorites, but he was also a boy. Somewhere his mother worried about him. If I were back home, I'd know how to reach out to him. I'd been a volunteer tutor at Jake and Karen's high school, and even did a little career counseling. None of that was particularly helpful right now. I didn't get the feeling Nolan had many career options. He'd been sent with the ultimatum because he was considered dispensable. The thought of someone treating my son that way broke my heart. Whatever Tristan said, I had to offer this boy at least a little truth and encouragement.

"Nolan, this might be hard for you to understand, but the

One doesn't believe anyone is useless. Big or small, strong or weak, every single person has value." I stared into his eyes. "He cares about you."

The young messenger looked at me for a long moment and rubbed his raw wrists.

Would the power of the words reach him? It was hard to see if they were sinking in. He sagged with weariness.

"You need some sleep. Come on." I walked him over to the closet Tristan had shown me earlier. I felt badly locking him up, but I wasn't going to be able to stay awake much longer to guard him. I grabbed a pallet from one of the common room chairs and tossed it over the wood floor in the tiny room. Doubled over, it just fit.

Nolan stepped inside and sank to the floor in the corner, hugging his knees.

I slid the door closed and threw the latch, rattling the door once to test it. The lock seemed secure. The thought of waking up in the morning to find our prisoner gone was enough to keep me from heading down the hall to my room. Instead, I grabbed another pallet and stretched it out on the floor in front of the closet door. I lay down, and the dagger in my belt dug into my side. I was so tired, I barely had the energy to roll over and find a more comfortable position before falling asleep.

Chapter Sixteen

"SUSAN, WHAT ARE YOU DOING?" TARA'S whisper woke me early the next morning.

I stretched and smiled up at her. "Tristan wanted me to keep the boy out of trouble." I pressed my ear against the closet door but didn't hear anything. "Do you think he can breathe in there?"

Tara didn't look any happier at having a prisoner locked in her closet than I was at being given guard duty. "Yes, there's a big gap along the bottom of the door. Would you like some clavo?"

"If you're making some." It was our ritual morning exchange.

She smiled. "Yes, I'm making some. Why don't you go and get cleaned up. I'll keep an eye on the closet until you get back."

I gave her a grateful hug.

When I returned, I unlatched the closet to check on Nolan. He was curled on the floor, his face a motley mix of purple and blue bruises. The sliding of the door jarred him out of an exhausted sleep. He pushed himself up groggily, squinting against the light. The instant he remembered where he was, he pressed himself back into the corner of the closet like a trapped animal. I offered him my hand, but he ignored it.

"Did he give you any trouble?" Tristan's voice was loud in the quiet of the morning. Predictably, Nolan tensed at the sound and started breathing faster.

I stepped away from the closet door, pulling Tristan away with me. "No, he was very helpful."

Tara brought us each a mug of clavo, and we sat at the table. Tristan glanced at the open closet door.

I shook my head. "Let him be for now. I think he feels safer in there."

Tristan raised an eyebrow. "What exactly did you do to him?"

"Nothing!"

Tara brought us a bread loaf, and we dug into breakfast. When Talia's husband, Gareth, appeared a few minutes later, Tristan asked him to guard Nolan for a while so we could talk.

"And see if you can get him to eat something," I added. Tristan and I suited up with weapons and gear. I returned Tristan's boot knife to him and slid my sword into my baldric. From force of habit, I grabbed my pack, and we headed outside.

The air still smelled a little odd, but I took a moment to soak in the sight of trees in the pale morning light. They were comfortingly normal after the nightmare of yesterday. My eyes felt seared by the sights they'd seen, far more than from the foul smoke that had burned them. We hiked to the clearing where Wade and I had worked on my sword training. It was far enough away from the homes in the village that Tristan and I could talk in privacy.

I filled him in on everything I had learned from Nolan, along with my guesses about what Hazor was planning. "Tristan, how are we going to convince the Council to keep to the Verses? They can't trust in an alliance with Hazor. This attack has to show them that."

Tristan massaged the back of his neck. "I can't believe

Cameron is getting away with this. Most of the other members of the Council would never go against the Verses this way. I just don't know—" His head snapped up, and he froze.

I wished I'd developed his habit of being constantly on alert. With my enhanced senses, I was usually the first to hear someone approaching, but today I was tired and had been focused on our conversation. I didn't notice the crashing sound in the underbrush until it was almost on us.

Tristan tossed aside his pack and drew his sword. A few seconds later I realized this was the kind of reflex he had tried to instill in me through our training. Obviously I needed more practice. I dropped my pack but didn't have time to draw my sword before a burly shape charged into the clearing.

For a second I thought it was a bear. Then I blinked and realized it was just Wade.

"Tristan. Run!" Wade panted, wide-eyed with panic. "Council guards are on their way. They've taken the Records. You've got to get out of here."

"The Records?" Even as he asked Wade for information, Tristan was a blur of efficient movement. He sheathed his sword, shouldered his pack, strode toward mine, and tossed it to me.

"They're taking them to Lyric," Wade said.

"What?" Tristan hesitated, then shook off his shock and disbelief. "Pine Caves. Bring supplies if you can," he said. "And Wade? Thank you."

Wade nodded and turned to leave. Tristan grabbed my arm to steer me toward the trail, but the crashing sound came again—louder this time. And from all directions. Men poured into the clearing. It seemed like dozens—although when I later had a chance to count, there were only five.

I dropped my pack and tugged at my sword hilt to free

it, but Tristan squeezed my arm and gave a small shake of his head.

One of the men marched straight toward us. He was tall, with black hair slicked back from his forehead and the sleek type of tunic and trousers I had seen on Cameron and his entourage. However, he and his men also wore vests of thick leather, shin guards, and gauntlets. Their belts bristled with swords and knives.

"This is the one. Take her," the man ordered.

Tristan pulled me behind him. "Case, what is this about?"

Tristan knew the man, and was staying calm. That was a good sign, wasn't it?

"The Council sent a messenger four days ago requiring her to report to Lyric." The Council guard's voice was cold and condescending. Wade had once explained to me that some guardians went on to work as the elite Council Guard, protecting and serving the Council directly. At the time, I'd thought of them as a type of Secret Service, but seeing these men put me more in mind of secret police. My throat tightened, and I found it hard to swallow.

Tristan kept his tall frame relaxed and his voice casual. "Well, yes, but the healer felt there was still—"

"I spoke to the healer, Tristan," Case interrupted with a sneer.

I shivered. The bushy-browed old man at the healers' lodge had cheerfully lied for us. What had these Council guards done to him?

Case stepped closer, his hand resting on his sword hilt. "The Council wants to talk to her *now*." He gave a staccato nod of his head.

Two men grabbed my arms from behind and pulled me away from Tristan.

I looked at him in panic.

He was still staying deliberately relaxed. "All right. If it's that urgent, we'll be happy to make the trip." He shrugged. Then he picked up my pack and handed it to one of the guards who had a manacle grip on my arm.

"Not you, Tristan. We're only here for her." Case watched Tristan closely. "You've been reassigned. The Council is sending another captain in to deal with the mess here. Dylan is missing, so they want you to search the River Borders near Cauldron Falls. They'll expect your report in five days." The two guards pulled me farther from Tristan.

The tension in Tristan's body grew. His fingers flexed.

I glanced at Wade. He was also watching Tristan. I waited for the signal. Any second now Tristan would draw his sword, and I wanted to be ready to help in the fight.

Instead, Tristan slowly lifted his hands—away from his weapons—and looked at Case. "Tell them I'll be there."

Case glared back at him, as if disappointed that they wouldn't cross swords.

Tristan walked over to me, careful not to make any sudden moves. "Susan." He looked in my eyes.

Shock crept up from the damp forest floor and into my nerve endings. Tristan wasn't going to fight. He was going to let them take me. The betrayal knocked the wind out of me.

"Go with them. You'll be all right." His voice was firm and unapologetic.

I nodded that I understood, but couldn't speak. If I opened my mouth, I'd start begging him not to let them take me. So I stayed silent and held still while one of the men disarmed me and secured my sword to his own belt. Having my sword out of reach made me miserable. The pack of Council guards suddenly seemed larger and even more frightening.

"Let's go." Case jerked his head and two of his guards pulled me with them toward the trail.

I heard Tristan's voice disappearing behind me. "Case, you have honor, but not everyone on the Council does. Keep her safe. Please."

I couldn't hear if Case answered him or not. I was pulled along the path that ascended to the ridgeline above the village. At the top I looked down on the familiar log homes. Would I see them again? I hadn't had a chance to ask Tristan to protect Nolan from his men. I didn't get to thank Tara for all she had done for me. My heart sank as I wondered how the village would cope without Tristan's leadership. The Council had to be crazy to pull him out and send him to Cauldron Falls. What had Case said? Someone was missing . . . Dylan. I suddenly made the connection. Dylan was Linette's fiancé. He had been patrolling on the River Borders.

God, no, I prayed silently. *Don't let anything happen to him. Or to Tristan. Or to Aubrey and Dustin. Or to any of Braide Wood. Please, Father. Please help us all.*

We strode down the trail toward the transport, making the trip in what I was sure was record time. I tried to remember landmarks from my journey to Braide Wood a few weeks ago. Now that I was heading downhill and not fighting Rhusican poison, the hike didn't seem as long. The Council guards weren't harsh or cruel to me, but it might have been easier to cope if they were. I could have channeled all my fear into anger. Instead, they were aloof and all business.

I tried to strike up a conversation with one of the young

guards who stayed close to me on the trail, but he rebuffed my efforts coldly.

With no one to talk to, my mind was free to spin in anxious circles. What would happen to me in Lyric? I knew that Cameron was corrupt, but how much power did he have? Was there anyone on the Council I could trust? The trees blurred as they moved past me, each one becoming a tally mark for a different problem:

Tristan—if he obeyed his new orders and went to Cauldron Falls, would he find Dylan? Would he survive? And if he didn't, who would help me get away from the Council?

Dylan—had Kahlarea begun an attack by Cauldron Falls? Who would be with Linette while she waited for word on her dearly loved guardian?

Morsal Plains—how would Braide Wood eat next season? How would they answer Hazor's demands? Would the other clans help defend Braide Wood?

Kieran—he had been heading into Hazor. Did he find out about the attack? Had he been captured or killed? Or was he being pragmatic and working for the side that had all the power?

Nolan—would the guardians at Braide Wood execute him for his part in the attack? Would he ever have a chance to grow up or believe his life had value?

Mark and our children—how were they managing without me? What did they think when they returned from the park and found I had disappeared?

I was distracted from my spinning hamster-wheel of worries by a sound in the woods behind us. I strained to hear over our own footsteps. A soft rustling sounded again, and I was sure something was following us. The Council guard didn't seem to hear anything.

When we arrived at the Braide Wood station, there was a transport waiting—door open, engine silent. Case pulled out a device and slid a few dials. The transport powered up. Interesting. Council guards must have a lot of pull if they could redirect transports or hold one just for us.

Before the first guard stepped into the machine, a whistle floated up from the trail behind us. All the men turned and several drew swords.

Wade appeared from around a clump of trees and bounded down the path. He flashed a good-natured grin. "Well, this is great timing! I need to go to Lyric on guardian business." He headed toward the open transport door.

Case stepped forward and held his sword out across the doorway, thumping the flat against Wade's ample stomach. "This is taken. Wait for the next one, boy."

Wade hesitated for a moment, sizing up the contingent and all their weapons. "No problem. I'll be on the one right behind you." He winked in my direction.

I gave him a grateful smile before one of the guards shoved me toward the door.

The other men boarded and the transport door closed. The sound of steel sliding downward made me think of a door clanging shut on a jail cell. I'd never been arrested before. I never even had an overdue library book.

I looked at the grim faces of the men on the bench across from me, and Case's unrelenting demeanor. To him I was just a hazardous parcel to be delivered, and nothing was going to get in the way of his execution of that duty. Outside the window Wade's familiar figure faded into the distance. I felt as if I were shrinking in size as well.

God, give me courage.

Chapter Seventeen

THE TRANSPORT ROLLED QUICKLY ALONG THE forest road and toward open land. We arrived at Ferntwine, where Tristan had recruited his friends to help us on the journey to Braide Wood. Had that really been only a few weeks ago? So much had happened since then, yet here I was, once again frightened and lost, once again in the company of strangers whose intentions I did not fully understand. I could picture Bekkah and Wade exchanging friendly banter on the platform, and could hear Linette's musical laugh as Davis told a story. Even Kyle's scowl would be familiar and welcome to me today, but when I peered out the window, the platform was deserted.

The transport didn't stop at Ferntwine, but turned onto the road toward Lyric. Dread grew in my heart with each mile we traveled. The trip seemed way too fast, and I began to feel cold. One of the guards had my pack, and I wanted to ask if I could retrieve my cloak that was stuffed inside it. I glanced at their grim faces and was afraid to ask. Instead, I sat quietly and tried to make myself small.

I stared at my feet and started doing multiplication tables in my head, determined to fight my fear. I realized I was staring down at Bekkah's boots. She had worn these on patrols as she guarded and defended her people. I could never fill her shoes, but I could honor her memory. She wouldn't want me to cower. The thought strengthened me, and I sat up straighter. Focused on keeping up my courage, I didn't even notice when the transport stopped. The closest guard grabbed my arm and herded me out onto the road. As I tried to get my bearings, my hand moved by reflex to rest on my sword hilt. The reminder that it was gone made my heart sink, but I squared my shoulders and walked forward.

The men surrounding me were tall, frustrating my attempts to see much of the Lyric station. It wasn't until we stepped out of the tall grove of bitum trees that I had my first glimpse of the city.

I stopped short, awed. "It's amazing."

The rear guard stumbled into me and shoved me forward with annoyance. "Quiet! Keep moving."

Spread out in front of us, a smooth white wall seemed to glow in the gray daylight. The structure was several stories tall and stretched out in a scalloping pattern for the length of dozens of city blocks before curving to surround the city. Within the confines of the wall, numerous tall towers reached skyward. Those soon disappeared from sight as we drew closer and the wall towered above us. Case led us to a tunnel that formed the entrance into the city. We passed through an archway that was built with huge blocks of stone that looked like rose quartz and amethyst. The pink and purple crystal reflected light and made the road under our feet ripple with colors. The curved ceiling of the tunnel was at least two stories above our heads, and as we stepped farther in, the sound of the world behind us grew muffled. Then I became aware of a dull roar growing before us, drawing us forward and reminding me of walking through an arena tunnel into a stadium for a football game. As we came out into the open, the hum exploded into a variety of individual noises.

We emerged in an open square crowded with people, voices, and activity. Again I stopped without meaning to—desperate to absorb what I was seeing. The lines of the buildings were gothic in their vertical stretch toward the sky, but the style couldn't be more different. The shapes were clean and almost stark in their simplicity and lack of ornamentation. The stone structures were white, some with embedded transparent quartz. Most edges were rounded, with the tops of the towers scalloped like the surrounding wall. I wanted to stand still, entranced, and enjoy the limited view I had of those upper reaches of the city.

The guards to either side of me grabbed my arms in exasperation and hurried me through the crowds. I only caught stray impressions of grandeur, color, and the high energy of a modern city. In just moments we stepped into a narrow alley between two tall buildings, and the noise of the crowds was muted.

I figured the next few minutes would give me some clues about my status here. They might be taking me to a comfortable inn where I could stay in between meetings with councilmembers. Or they might take me right to some bureaucratic building where I could give a report of my visitor status. I tried not to think beyond those two options, but when they led me through a back door that looked like it was part of a loading dock and into a dark hall, my nervousness grew. As we proceeded down a flight of stairs into the bowels of the building, my stomach began to twist with dread. When they shoved me into a bare concrete room and slammed a steel door closed behind me, I decided I had collected enough clues. "Guess I'm *persona non grata*," I muttered.

There was no light, other than a hint of illumination that slithered under the door, but there was nothing to see either. I could pace about three steps in each direction. A ceiling disappeared out of sight over my head. I was cold, but they had taken my pack, so I didn't have my cloak. Panic crawled toward me like the fingers of light under the door.

"Get a grip, Susan." I felt the edges of the door, searched for a latch or handle, and even pushed my weight against it for good measure. Nothing. I strained to hear and realized I could still make out the heavy boots of the men going up a stairway. I kept focused on that sound and heard a door open. Voices murmured, and I closed my eyes, stretching my ability to hear farther than I ever had before.

". . . Records?" a resonant voice asked.

The answering murmur was probably Case.

"Good," the first voice said. "I'm still waiting for the copy from Blue Knoll. Then I'll have them all. Once I make a few changes, the Council will have no more silly objections."

I recognized the first voice now. Cameron. His booming campaign-speech tone made it possible for me to hear him from this distance. I grasped for each word, knowing it might be important. Case was asking something, but his words were unclear.

"Oh, the Rhusicans can help me with that." Cameron laughed. "It doesn't take much to nudge aside a memory. You've got the woman?" He paused, listening to Case's reply. "No, I don't want anyone else on the Council to know she's here right now. What did you find out?" More mumbled sounds.

My head throbbed with the effort of listening. Then, like a thread snapping, I lost the focused hold I had on the voices. Silence wrapped around me again. I sank to the stone floor and buried my aching head in my arms.

I didn't have long to wait before I heard boots in the hallway. I jumped to my feet before the door slid open.

Case jerked his head toward the hall. "This way."

I wondered what he'd do if I refused to move. Then I decided I didn't really want to know. I would save my resistance for when it really counted. As we walked through the dark hall to a narrow stairway, he stayed inches behind me. I glanced around but couldn't find any potential escape route, so I trudged up the stairs, through a door, and into a more brightly lit corridor. Case shot an uneasy glance down the hallway and hurried me to the first door on the left. It occurred to me that the other doors might mark the offices of councilmembers. Cameron had said he didn't want anyone to know about me. I opened my mouth to shout for help, but Case was too quick. He clamped a hand over my mouth, silencing me, and shoved me into the room. Once we were inside, he locked the door and stood guard in front of it.

I stumbled to a stop in the middle of the room.

Cameron sat behind a huge desk to my right. The top was polished black stone, and on it sat several gadgets I didn't recognize, along with my emptied pack and all its contents. My sword, Kieran's baldric, the cloak Tristan had found for me in Shamgar, Wade's gauntlets, and a few stray items of clothing Tara had given me were spread out across the desk.

My fingers tensed at the sight of my sword. The thought of Cameron pawing through my belongings filled me with disgust, and I lifted my outraged gaze to the man behind the desk.

Cameron's dark eyes gleamed, and his lip curled in amusement. His black hair was slicked back the way I remembered it from the transport. The tall collar of his tunic flared around his neck, like a cobra's hood. Behind him, a window gave me an enticing glimpse of a Lyric courtyard. Dragging my eyes away, I looked around the room, trying to get my bearings. There were two doors on the wall opposite from where I had entered. A cubby of shelves between them held pitchers and mugs. Gaudy tapestries embellished the wall behind me. There were no other chairs in the room, and I realized that my feet hurt and I was thirsty.

"You certainly took a long time to accept my offer of hospitality," Cameron said. "Someone with less patience than I might have become . . . annoyed."

I shifted my weight, determined to hide my fear and take the offensive. "Cameron, there are more important things to worry about than dragging me here for a visit."

His eyes narrowed. "My title is chief councilmember of Lyric. But since you're a foreigner I will forgive your lack of protocol." He stood and walked over to the built-in shelves and poured something into a mug. He handed it to me and smirked. "Now, tell me about these important things that are going on."

I lifted the mug to my mouth and inhaled the familiar fragrance of clove, but a subtle, bitter tone to the scent stirred a warning in me. I was learning to pay attention to all my heightened senses, so I handed the mug back to him.

He shrugged and set it aside, then leaned against the edge of his desk, watching me.

I wanted to urge him to let me talk to the Council, so I could plead for help for Braide Wood. But I felt entangled and confused by the few fragments of information I knew. Anything I said could become a trap for the people I cared about, so I held my tongue.

"I'm pleased to see that you've recovered from the plague," Cameron said in a bland voice.

My face heated. Tristan had used that flimsy trick to keep me out of this very situation.

Cameron had known right away it was lie, of course, but he'd avoided a direct confrontation with Tristan and allowed us a long line. Now he was reeling it in. "Some things are worth waiting for," he said, as if reading my mind. "What did you think of Braide Wood?" He crossed his arms and settled back against the stone desktop.

"It's a wonderful village," I said, pulling myself up taller. "And the clan hasn't forgotten the Verses like some people have."

Another flash of amusement crossed Cameron's face. "And you want to protect them. So we have that in common. It's my place as a councilmember to protect our people."

My fear of Braide Wood being leveled by Hazor made me forget caution. "Then send an army to Morsal Plains!" The words burst out of me.

"Is that what Tristan wants?"

"It's what's right! It doesn't matter who wants what. They need help."

Cameron raised one eyebrow. "And what is Tristan planning to do next?"

"How should I know? He's probably heading for Cauldron Falls where your stupid Council sent him—when his clan needs him instead." Giving vent to my anger wasn't wise, but it was the only emotion that seemed to hold back my fear.

Cameron ignored my show of temper. "So you met Tristan in Shamgar?" He steered the conversation back to where he wanted it. "Was he alone there?"

My mouth went dry. The image of Tristan killing the Rhusican flashed into my brain. I forced it from my thoughts, as if afraid Cameron could see right into my mind. When I didn't answer, he stood up. I took a step backward without meaning to.

"I've heard some interesting rumors about what you've been doing in Braide Wood," he said in a deceptively casual tone.

I swallowed and again fought to keep memories from my mind: killing a Rhusican, training with the guardians, arguing with Kieran about Hazor, healing from blistering burns, gathering information from Nolan. Even though I understood so little of what was going on, I suddenly realized I knew too much. Facts it was much better that he not know.

Cameron stepped closer.

I stood my ground. When I first met him on the transport, he was menacing as a man secure in his strength and position. Now I saw something else in Cameron. He was insatiable for power; like Shakespeare's Cassius, he had "a lean and hungry look; He thinks too much: such men are dangerous."

I longed for the hilt of a sword in my hand. "I have nothing to say to you."

His smile grew for a slow second. Then he backhanded me across the face.

I stumbled back, eyes stinging from shock more than pain. Out of reflex I brought my fists up in front of me as I recovered and turned toward him.

He nodded to Case, who stepped away from the door to yank my arms back and hold me painfully still. Cameron walked around me, his voice purring from outside my line of sight. "Oh, you're very wrong about that. You have a lot to say. I just need to be more convincing."

The dread I had been fighting off rushed back with a vengeance, but I didn't want to give him the satisfaction of seeing my fear. "I'm not telling you anything."

He leaned closer and his breath brushed against my face as he spoke in my ear. "I was hoping you'd say that."

Chapter Eighteen

CAMERON DROPPED ALL PRETENSE OF BEING a benevolent politician.

I stopped pretending he would let me answer a few questions and walk out the door. I fought against Case, struggling so hard that I came close to dislocating my shoulder. But he weighed twice as much as I did and had three times my strength.

Cameron opened one of the two doors flanking the shelves, and Case wrestled me forward into an inner room. The object in the middle of the floor reminded me more of a dentist's chair than a medieval torture device, but in my mind, they were one and the same.

God, give me the power of Samson. Give me the courage of Daniel. I bucked against the arms holding me, waiting for a surge of strength. If I could just get to my sword.

But no wave of might or courage welled up in me. I wasn't Samson. I wasn't Daniel. I was just Susan. Weak and terrified, I was being hauled into the room and forced onto a reclining chair that felt like a medical table.

A woman with curling auburn hair reaching midway down her back stood in the room. She stared out a high, narrow window and ignored the sounds of struggle behind her.

I tried once again to break free, but Case held me down, and Cameron fastened straps across my torso, arms, and legs.

Now. Now would be the moment that Restorer power would flow through me, and I would jump up and grab my sword. I strained against the straps, fully expecting them to snap.

Case left the room, closing the door behind him. Cameron retrieved something from a nearby table. Maybe this would be the moment Wade would burst through the door to rescue me. Or Tristan. Something had to happen soon. God wouldn't leave me here, would He?

From deep within my memories, I heard Lukyan's quavering voice asking again, *Are you willing to walk any road that the One chooses for you?*

"No!" I cried, not realizing I had spoken the word aloud.

Cameron's lips quirked upward. He pushed the sleeve of my woven sweater up past my elbow and adjusted the straps so he could twist my inner arm to face upward. For a moment he looked like a lab technician preparing to draw blood. Instead of readying a needle, however, he pulled the backing off of something that looked like a large Band-Aid and pressed it along the skin over the veins in my arm.

"It would have been simpler if you had taken the drink I gave you," Cameron said. "But this is just as effective. As amusing as it would be to continue batting words around with you, I really don't have the time to waste. This will help you be a little more . . . forthcoming." A tingling burn burrowed deep into my arm as a chemical soaked through my skin and entered my veins.

I bit my lip, fighting back a shriek of pain. A heavy pressure began to contract my lower chest. My ribs seemed to cave inward, and I realized it was taking effort to expand them enough to breath. I broke into a cold sweat and felt my heart begin to flutter. Black fog collected at the edges of my vision, and the light shrank until there was only a pinpoint. I couldn't breathe.

"It's taking effect too quickly," said a woman's expressionless voice. "Odd."

Cameron ripped the patch from my skin. He tore it and replaced a piece. I heard the woman step closer, and Cameron say, "It's not supposed to destroy her heart. I don't want her dead yet."

My heart was still pounding, but the strange flutters had stopped. The black fog was drawing back, although the pain in my chest was so fierce I wished for the fog to return, to swallow me up and make this room disappear.

The woman moved into my range of vision. She had a smooth, flawless face framed by auburn curls. Her eyes were a piercing green, and she leaned over to look into mine. "Yessss." She drew the word out. "We know her. This is the one."

I closed my eyes. Terror chased around my veins along with whatever drug they were giving me. I knew what she was, too. A Rhusican. "The Lord is my shepherd. . . ." I could only mouth the words. What came next? I couldn't remember, so I tried something else. "Our Father, who art in heaven . . ." Laughter ricocheted inside my head, and I couldn't focus. I opened my eyes and saw the ceiling. It looked like it was pulling away from me. Or maybe I was falling.

"Susan, tell me where you came from before you met Tristan in Shamgar." Cameron pulled up a chair and watched me with clinical detachment. His voice was arrogantly reasonable, as if I were a petulant child and he were being generous in his patience.

"The attic," I said through teeth clenched against the pain. "I was just moving some things around. There was lightning, and I woke up in an alley."

I can't say anything about seeing Tristan kill the Rhusican. It would get him into more trouble.

"So it was him," Cameron said, exchanging a look with the woman. I realized with horror that I had spoken my thoughts aloud.

God, no! You have to stop this! Where are You?

"Was Tristan alone?" Cameron asked.

"Kieran was with him. But he went to Hazor. He's gone." Pain compressed in my chest again, as though a great weight threatened to crush me. Threads of agony spread through my shoulder and down my left arm. I wanted to scream but couldn't take in enough breath. Tears were running down my face into my ears. My mind seemed split in two very unequal parts. One tiny part kept shouting to stop the flow of words and watched from a great distance as the person in the chair kept talking. I was aware enough to know the damage I was doing, but unable to stop. And all the time there was the searing pain.

Question by question Cameron probed for any hidden pocket of knowledge he thought would be of use to him. The drugs made me voice all my thoughts and emotions. At times I was alert enough to notice things around me. The natural tendency of my mind to veer off into tangents was causing Cameron a great deal of annoyance. Mark always teased me about the way my mind worked—joking that I had "jumped the tracks" again when he would lose my train of thought in a conversation. The drugs wore off enough at one point for me to recognize the frustration this trait caused Cameron. I felt a moment of satisfaction.

"I don't care how sorry you feel for the Hazorite messenger. Tell me more about the weapons," Cameron demanded in irritation. The Rhusican woman showed no impatience. She listened to every word, her eyes seeming to twirl as they watched me.

I looked toward the high, narrow window across the room. Somewhere outside there was fresh air and trees and sanity. I longed for a glimpse out that window—anything to pull me away from this. But then Cameron placed another strip on my forearm; the devastating pain returned to my chest, and I lost awareness.

The next time I was conscious of being in my body again, Cameron was still asking questions. I had lost track of what I'd told him, where I was, and why I had been fighting so hard not to talk.

"But why did Tristan take you to Braide Wood?"

The room was spinning, and I couldn't take a breath to form words this time.

A stinging slap burned my cheek, and Cameron's face came back into focus. "Why do you matter to him?" he asked again.

"Restorer," I mumbled, barely able to speak.

"What?"

I tried to lift my head up. "He thinks I'm a Restorer," I gasped. My head fell back against the chair's padded surface.

Stunned silence filled the room. I sighed in relief. The badgering questions had stopped for a moment. That was all that mattered. Blood pulsed in my ears—a swishing rhythm that gradually slowed. Cameron tore the chemical-laced bandage from my arm.

"That's why the drugs nearly killed her," said the Rhusican woman. "She absorbed them too quickly."

Cameron pushed his chair back and moved across the room.

When he returned, a sharp pain cut across my arm.

I jerked against the restraining straps and lifted my head to see what he was doing. Blood ran down my arm where Cameron had sliced it. The wound healed rapidly, and I let my head fall back, closing my eyes again as Cameron wiped the blood from my arm to examine it more closely. Couldn't these people figure out a better way to identify a Restorer?

As the drugs began to clear from my brain, I struggled to remember what had just happened. Questions. So many questions. What had he just asked me about? What had I said?

When the answer came to me, the knowledge grabbed and twisted my stomach. What had I done? Cameron's plans required getting the Council to reject the Verses. The Restorer's role was to bring the people's hearts back to the Verses. I had let him know exactly how much of an enemy I was to his schemes. Worse than that, he now knew he could inflict all the damage he wanted on me, and I would keep healing. I opened my eyes.

Cameron watched me, waiting. "You know, they say Mikkel was stabbed fifty times with Kahlarean swords before his wounds stopped healing." His voice was smooth, musing. "I was never sure if I believed the stories."

Apprehension washed through me more quickly than his drugs had earlier. I read his intentions even before a slow smile curved across his face. Raw terror gripped me by the throat.

"Wait," the Rhusican woman said, stepping closer. "Let me finish first." Looking into my eyes, she smiled gently. "It's fortunate you have us for friends now." Her tone was so soothing that I felt my tension soften in spite of myself. "You've betrayed your old friends, you know."

Shame flooded me as I realized how much damaging information I had shared.

"Kieran will kill you if he ever finds you. And what do you think Tristan's family will do when they learn you are the one who told the Council that he's a murderer? The people of Braide Wood will despise you when he's banished because of you."

I tried to fight the despair that was growing in my heart, but everything she said was true.

"Of course, you're a murderer, too," she breathed. Her soft tone betrayed an edge of malice.

I longed to feel my sword in my hand again. I'd run her through. Her and every one of her kind. My breathing quickened. Then I realized the rage building in me wasn't mine. It was hers. I had killed one of her fellow poisoners and had protected a man who had killed another. She hated me. I forced myself to take a deep breath. She couldn't plant this hatred inside of me.

God, help me fight this!

I must have said the words out loud, because she smiled. "Your god isn't here. He pulled you away from your family and left you alone in this world. The same way he abandoned Bekkah when Hazor attacked the outpost. And the way he left Mikkel alone to fight hundreds of Kahlareans and die."

I was alone. Even the people who had befriended me would despise me now. I was a worthless pawn dropped into this world for no purpose except to cause more heartache and then die.

"Do you think if your god could hear you, he would have let us take you? Wouldn't he have stopped the pain? He didn't rescue you. He gave you to us." Gray fog swirled in my mind, and I saw myself walking along the edge of a dark abyss. I recognized it. I had been here before. This same despair had called to me when I hiked to Braide Wood with Tristan and his friends. The knowledge helped me step back from the edge.

"God is our refuge and strength, an ever-present help in

trouble," I recited softly.

The woman ignored my words and nodded to Cameron. "You can have her now."

"God is our refuge and strength . . . ever-present . . . ever-present . . ." I breathed again. I didn't feel strong or invulnerable. But at least the gray fog in my heart wasn't consuming me.

Cameron walked the woman to the door and called to Case. "Bring me her sword."

The three of them hovered in the doorway. Case handed Cameron my sword, but glanced over at me and frowned. The Rhusican woman touched Case's shoulder and murmured something. He straightened, the expression of hardened resolve back in place. The woman turned to smile in my direction. Then she left with Case.

Cameron closed the door and faced me.

I prayed in a whisper. "God is our refuge and strength, an ever-present help in trouble. Therefore we will not fear, though the earth give way." More verses were returning to my memory. I couldn't stir up a feeling of confidence in the words, but I clung to them anyway. The confusion caused by the drugs had worn off enough to make me all too aware of what was coming. I wrenched against the restraints but couldn't break free. My clothes were damp with sweat, and I began to shiver.

Cameron stepped closer, admiring the sword in his hands. My sword.

"I'm here to help your people," I said. "You don't want to do this."

His smile grew wider, and he threw back his head and laughed. "You're very wrong." He lifted the sword.

I closed my eyes. At that same moment, I heard a

disturbance in the outer office, followed by a thud. I opened my eyes and saw Cameron's back as he turned. He slid aside a small panel in the door and hissed an oath at whatever he saw in the outer office. Then he dropped my sword onto a side table and quickly pulled away the straps that held me.

He was letting me go? I drew a difficult, shallow breath and tried to move, but my numb limbs couldn't respond.

From outside a heavy fist pounded the door.

Cameron glanced around the room, nodded to himself, and slid the door open. "Who let you in to a chief councilmember's office? You're interrupting an important interview."

A man stepped into the doorway. I recognized the formal tunic of a councilmember before my efforts to get up triggered another burst of pain from the drugs that were still in my system. Welcome darkness closed down my senses, but just before everything went black, I saw the face of the man in the doorway. That's when I knew the drugs were still confusing my mind. The man looked exactly like Mark.

Chapter Nineteen

I FELT MARK'S ARMS AROUND ME and burrowed my nose into his neck. I loved the unique male scent of his skin touched with a hint of Ivory soap. I sighed and curled up in his arms, sliding my head down to rest on his chest. "I have the strangest dream to tell you about."

His deep chuckle rumbled under my cheek. One of my arms was pinned under me, and I shifted so I could slide it around him for a hug. My chest ached deep inside, like it had the winter I had a bad case of bronchitis. Maybe I was coming down with a cold. My hand rubbed along Mark's arm, and instead of the flannel of his plaid pajamas, I touched the nubby fabric of raw silk. What on earth was he wearing? I opened my eyes a slit.

We weren't in our bed at home. We were on a couch made of honey-colored wood. And Mark wasn't in pajamas. He was in a formal, rust-colored tunic and woven black pants. I popped my head up to talk to him face to face, banging my head against his chin in the process.

"Ow," he complained, unwrapping one of the arms he had around me to rub his jaw.

"Where are we?" I asked, fully awake now. The walls glowed with light, and the room felt warm and cozy, but unfamiliar.

"Still in Lyric. But now that you're awake, I'll take you home."

So I wasn't out of the nightmare yet. But Mark was here now. Everything would be all right. I soaked in every detail of his face. A few silver strands highlighted his wavy blond hair. Now that I had spent several weeks in this strange otherworld, his conservative haircut looked too short to me. He had the perfectly formed nose of a Greek statue, and I often teased him about his classic profile—sometimes making him blush in embarrassment. The jaw he was rubbing had strong lines that hinted at his stubborn streak. But his silver-blue eyes were soft and warm as they met mine.

Tears pooled in my eyes, and I squeezed him hard, afraid he'd disappear. "Mark, how did you get here? How did you find me?"

He hesitated and looked away.

I eased off his lap to sit beside him on the couch, bracing myself. If Mark looked this uncomfortable, I knew I wouldn't like what he had to say.

"When we got home from the park, I went up in the attic, and you were gone." He still didn't look at me. Standing, he straightened his tunic and paced a few steps. "I saw you had opened a portal."

I frowned in confusion. "But wasn't the roof of the house gone? There was a storm. Lightning and wind and glass breaking."

"No." His forehead wrinkled. "Everything was fine. Maybe it just felt like a storm when you went through. You didn't have the stones lined up the right way, so it probably wasn't a very smooth passage."

I've never taken criticism well from Mark, so I immediately

geared up into defensive mode. "What do you mean I didn't line the stones up right? I didn't do anything with . . ." My voice trailed off as I realized what he had said.

He walked over to a window and rested a hand along the frame, looking outside. His shoulders were tense.

I could read his back as easily as his face. "Mark," I said slowly, "how did you know about the portal? How did you know how to come through? Where to find me?"

He kept looking out the window.

He might want time to search for the best answer, but I didn't have the patience for that. "Mark, talk to me. Please."

He cleared his throat. "It's the portal I used when I left this world," he said at last.

I wanted to laugh, but I could only stare at him.

He turned and looked at me, anxiety and apology blending on his face.

"What?" I asked, nearly breathless with shock.

He walked back to sit beside me and took my hand in his. "I've been here before, Susan. It's where I grew up."

I snatched my hand away and pulled back, looking at him in horror. This was the man I had pledged my life to. I woke every morning to nestle in his arms and talk about our coming day. We had shared every part of our lives, every insecurity, every dream. And all along he wasn't who I thought he was. Together we were raising four children. True to form, my mind veered off onto that important tangent.

"Mark! Where are the kids? If you came here . . . who's taking care of them? And how did you explain when I disappeared for weeks?"

"I took them over to your mom's for the afternoon," he said, as if he had arranged a movie date for us. He reached for my hand again but thought better of it and tried to calm me with his voice alone. "You've only been gone from the attic a few hours. And I'm taking you back now. Time works differently here. They'll never know you were gone."

I ignored his last statement, still sorting out what I wanted to feel right now. "You lied to me. All these years, it's been a lie. Who are you?"

I had felt hurt when Kieran threatened to slit my throat. I had felt abandoned when Tristan let the Council guards drag me off to Lyric. But the betrayal I felt now was ten times worse. A hundred times worse. How ironic. All the past weeks in this strange world, I had longed to have Mark with me. I had felt I could handle anything if only I could be with him. Now he was here, and my hurt and loneliness were sharper than any I had known before. The man sitting beside me was a stranger.

Mark grabbed my shoulders before I could pull away. "No!" His normally calm voice was harsh with emotion. "Susan, nothing has been a lie. I promise you. I was in your world for two years before I met you. After I found you, I knew I would never come back here. I made my choice."

"What were you doing in 'my' world?" I was amazed at how level I could keep my voice. I was pressing all my feelings into a tight ball of mistrust and anger.

"The eldest songkeeper sent me through the portal to keep me safe. It's a long story. Susan, stop looking at me like that."

I wrenched myself away and stood up, looking for my pack. It was propped against the side of the room, and I rummaged in it, suiting up with my gauntlets, baldric, and sword.

"What are you doing? Honey, calm down. It's all right. I'm taking you home."

"I don't even know who you are. And I can't go back now."

I paused and looked up from my pack. "I'm grateful you got me away from Cameron. Did you kill him?"

Mark stiffened in shock. "What are you talking about? I wouldn't kill a councilmember."

"Then how did you get me away from him?" I demanded.

"He said he was finished interviewing you and that you'd had a bad reaction to a drug patch and passed out." Mark seemed genuinely bewildered. "I told him the rest of the Council should have been informed that you were in Lyric. He said he was about to let them know, but he had concerns about you because you weren't very . . . rational." I ground my teeth together, but let Mark finish talking. "I told him you were my wife, not a foreigner, and that he didn't have any right to question you. He didn't argue. Since you had fainted, I carried you to my rooms here."

"I didn't faint." I pulled on my gauntlets and tugged the ties with my teeth. "It was the drugs. They did something to my heart."

"Susan, you're wrong." Mark meant his words to be soothing, but his tone sounded belittling to me. "Cameron handles foreign security. He sometimes uses harmless drugs when he interviews people, but it's nothing the Council hasn't approved. I'm sure you misunderstood."

I was breathing hard now. "You *know* Cameron? And you didn't kill him for what he did to me?" I adjusted the baldric across my shoulders, settling my sword at my hip.

Mark looked alarmed as he watched me. "Susan, it's all over now. I'm taking you home."

"He *tortured* me, Mark." In spite of my best intentions, my voice broke as I remembered the misery Cameron had caused—the horror of being trapped and in the grip of physical pain that wouldn't stop, the mental anguish of betraying my friends, the layers of suggestions the Rhusican woman had tried to plant in my mind. "He was working with a Rhusican."

Mark looked confused.

We had a pattern in our marriage. A problem would arise, and I'd be the one to get upset. The issue could be Karen dating an angst-ridden musician, or Mark's business threatening lay-offs, or Anne's spat with a neighbor. Mark's consistent approach of staying calm and detached would infuriate me and boost my level of emotion even higher. Often, when the crisis was past, I could appreciate the stability he brought to our relationship with his unruffled way of facing problems. Not this time.

"What's a Rhusican?" Mark walked toward me cautiously.

I glared at him. "They poison people. They're causing all kinds of damage to the People of the Verses. And Cameron is using that somehow. And he—" My words choked off.

Mark moved toward me, and before I could resist, he gathered me in a hug. "I'm sorry. I'm so sorry that you were hurt. I'm sorry I couldn't tell you where I came from before. But it's over now. It's okay. I'm taking you back."

I wanted to rest in his arms and cry on his shoulder. The temptation was so strong that I had to force myself to look him straight in the eye before I could give in to it. "I'm not going home."

"Don't be silly. It's not safe for you here. You said it yourself. You've been hurt. We need to get you home."

"Silly?" My voice rose an octave. "Do you want to know why I reacted so badly to Cameron's drugs? The Rhusican figured it out. It's because I'm a Restorer."

Now it was Mark's turn to pull back in horror. He didn't let go of me, but he held me at arm's length. His voice shook.

"What?"

"You heard me." I wrenched out of his grip. "Fine. Everyone has to see proof." I ran my finger sharply down the edge of the sword at my hip, and held it out to him. Blood dripped from the gash.

Mark grabbed my hand in a reflex born of tending to four accident-prone children. He pulled a cloth from his pocket and held it against my finger.

I tugged my hand away and held it up. The cut had disappeared.

The evidence hit him like a right jab to the solar plexus. He sank down onto the couch, shaking his head. "No. It can't be true."

A hint of a sneer stole into my answer. "I guess things aren't always what they seem."

Mark flinched at the accusation in my words. The guilt and pain on his face cut through some of my anger. "Susan, please come with me. You don't understand. We have to get you away from here."

"In every time of great need, a Restorer is sent to fight for the people and help the guardians. The Restorer is empowered with gifts to defeat our enemies and turn the people's hearts back to the Verses," I recited.

His eyes widened for a moment, and then his shoulders slumped. "And do you know what happened to the last Restorer?" he asked with a tremor in his voice. His words dropped to a desperate whisper. "Susan, I can't lose you, too." My normally steady and composed husband looked shaken to the core.

I was still furious with him but felt myself in the odd position of wanting to comfort him at the same time. In our marriage seesaw, when he became increasingly placid, I grew more agitated. This time the balance tilted the other direction. I rarely saw him this upset, and my emotions dialed back in response. "Mark, if the One sent me here," I said, slipping into the terminology of this world, "there has to be a reason." I tasted bitterness as I realized how little I believed that anymore. When I most needed strength and protection, it had come too late. But I couldn't look at that disillusionment right now. It would paralyze me. "We have to figure out how to save Braide Wood. How long have you been here?"

"A few days. I searched everywhere near the portal entrance outside Lyric, but no one had seen you."

"I didn't arrive in Lyric. I was in Shamgar."

"Shamgar?" Mark squeezed the bridge of his nose. "I didn't know the stones could work that way. So the alignment sent you to a different . . ." He interrupted himself as he noticed my stony glare and seemed to realize this wasn't the time for an analytical discussion. "Shamgar's not a friendly place. How did you get out of there alive?"

I pulled up a chair and sat down across from him. "Tristan found me." I wondered where Tristan was now and what would happen to him when Cameron tried to charge him with murdering a Rhusican "guest."

"Tristan of the Wood?" Mark's eyes brightened with interest. "How is he? I was practically still a kid when I left, but we all looked up to him. He must be an old man by now."

"Only if you're calling us old," I said, confused.

"Oh, I forgot. Time passes differently here. It takes getting used to. So how is he?"

"He's the head guardian of Braide Wood. His wife was poisoned, and when I met him . . ." I paused. I wasn't sure how much I wanted to share with Mark. The realization that I didn't trust him anymore made me feel that the whole universe had tilted off center. I changed the subject. "So you've been here a few days already?"

His eyes saw too much. Sadness rested like a weight on his shoulders, but he focused on my question. "Yes. An old friend and mentor from the Rendor Council delegation gave me these rooms to use. I finally found people who had seen you. I heard you were in Braide Wood, but would soon come to Lyric at the invitation of the Council. So I waited here, but you didn't come."

The conversation was beginning to feel more natural. We were slipping into our comfortable habit of catching up on each other's day. But I still felt disoriented seeing Mark in this world—realizing I never really knew him.

He watched my face. "Susan, I couldn't tell you about my past. But it doesn't change anything. I love you. You're my wife. Please don't shut me out."

Maybe it was an insinuation of Rhusican anger in my subconscious. Maybe it was my hurt that God hadn't spared me from horrible and senseless pain. Maybe it was the realization that the portal was all Mark's fault. Whatever the reason, I refused to sink into the warm love he was offering. I stiffened. "We'll talk about it later. I can't deal with what I'm feeling right now. There's too much to do. Why are you dressed like that? Are you on the Council?"

"I was when I left a few years ago—a few years for this world, twenty-two years for ours. I was only an apprentice for Rendor. They've restored my status, even though I didn't plan to be here long." His eyes traveled over me, hesitated on my sword, and then studied my face.

I wondered what he saw. My weeks in this world had changed me.

The corners of his eyes creased with concern. "You really mean to stay?"

"Just until I know the children of Braide Wood are safe and the Council gets rid of the Rhusicans. I'm a Restorer, Mark. I have to help."

He lowered his head into his hands, and I could barely hear his next words. "So this is my punishment for deserting my people. I couldn't leave you to come back here. And now I'll lose you anyway."

Mark was never a pessimist. His fatalism now frightened me. "Mark, did every Restorer die in battle?"

"Not all of them. But they were guardians. They were warriors. What chance will you have?"

"Thanks so much for the encouragement."

Mark sighed and met my eyes. I could almost read the thoughts as they played across his face. I saw the moment he made his decision.

"You need to do this." It wasn't a question, but I nodded anyway. He reached out and took both my hands in his. "Will you let me help?"

This was the Mark I knew. He could come home to find me in hysterics because the muffler fell off the car, the dishwasher flooded the floor, the kids had gotten poison ivy, and I was supposed to organize a church bake sale. Calmly, resolutely, he would step into the midst of chaos with those magic words: "How can I help?" Then he'd call the mechanic, help me mop the floor, run to the drugstore for calamine lotion, and convince me I'd survive the day.

I felt a rush of warmth and nodded.

"But I have one question for you," he said. "Are you staying to help the People, or because you want to get back at Cameron for what he did to you?"

"I want to save Braide Wood from Hazor. I want to stop the Rhusicans from poisoning anyone else." And if in the process I could destroy Cameron, so much the better. But I kept that thought to myself.

Mark's eyes were bleak as he watched me, but he nodded. "You'd better fill me in on everything that's happened these last few weeks. I've heard some things here in Lyric, but I've been out of touch for a long time."

We heard a discreet tap at the common room door.

My heart began pounding, and my hand clenched on my sword's grip.

Mark jumped up. "Don't worry. You're safe here." He nodded his head toward a door at the far side of the room. "Go get something to eat. I'll take care of this, and then we can make our plans."

I was happy to hurry out of the room. I poured myself some water from a stoneware pitcher as I stood in the small kitchen, working to slow my breathing. While I drank and rummaged around for something to eat, I kept my hearing focused on Mark.

"Councilmember Markkel?" a young woman's voice asked.

"Yes. Come in."

"The Council is calling a special session for the second day following the Feast. All councilmembers and clan representatives are requested to meet in the Lyric Hall at first light. Matters include Hazorite demands on Braide Wood, new problems on the Kahlarean border, a resolution to change our defense policy, and the murder of several visitors to our land." The young voice rattled off the list of information, oblivious to content. She was clearly in a hurry to move on and carry her message to the next councilmember.

Mark thanked the girl and closed the door behind her.

I stepped back into the room, nibbling a piece of fruit. "When is the Feast day?" I asked.

"You heard?" He raised his eyebrows. Then he sighed. "Of course you did."

"How much time do we have? When is the Feast day?"

"Tomorrow. The Council will meet the second day after that. That gives us three days."

"I don't suppose you could use your portal stones to make time slow down for a while?"

It was a feeble attempt at humor, but Mark grinned. He walked over to me but stopped short of touching me, still uncertain of my mood. "Sorry, it doesn't work that way. But I have a better idea. Come on." He reached out his hand.

I reminded myself that I was still furious with him and that I didn't plan to forgive him anytime soon. We needed to work together right now to get through this crisis, but I wasn't going to let myself lean on him. I couldn't count on anyone but myself. With that thought resolved in my mind, I took his hand and let a small grin answer his. In spite of myself, a current of warmth moved from his hand and curled around my heart.

Chapter Twenty

MARK KEPT HOLD OF MY HAND as he grabbed our cloaks and hurried me out of his rooms, down a hallway, and out into the fresh air. The overcast sky was the particular shade of gray that indicated there were only a few hours until nightfall. The streets were still wet from the afternoon rain.

I dodged puddles as I followed him. "Hey, slow down. Your legs are longer, so I have to travel two miles for every one of yours."

It was a long-standing argument. Mark grinned and shook his head, though he did slow down. "Distance isn't relative." He gave his standard answer.

"But apparently time is. And I never really believed that before." I slowed even more. The tall buildings on either side of us were unremarkable. I wanted to go back to the city entrance and see the magnificent gate and tunnel again.

"Time has always been relative. Remember how long your ninth month of pregnancy always was? And how fast the baby years went? Time distorts."

"Maybe. Mark, if I've been here a couple weeks, but only an hour or so has passed in our world; since you were in our world for over twenty years, then hundreds of years should have passed here. That can't be right. You still know people here."

Mark shrugged. "The time distortion is fluid. Time passes more quickly in the world that you are in than in the one where you aren't. When I was home, time here passed slowly. While you were here, time in our world barely moved. That's all I've been able to figure out so far."

My head was starting to hurt, so I dropped the subject.

Mark pulled me down an alley. This area was far from the town's center. There were few people around and the streets were quiet. We rounded a corner, and the scalloped white wall appeared in front of us.

I caught my breath again at its beauty.

Mark didn't notice my fascination, but led me to a small pocket door in one of the curves of the wall. He slid a latch, and we stepped through.

We were on the far side of Lyric, away from the road to the station. Miles of rolling gray-green hills stretched out before us. This was the kind of landscape that tugged at my heart, making me wish I were a foal in the spring. I wanted to kick up my hooves and gallop over one ridge after another just to see what was behind the next hill. I took a deep breath of the moist air and glanced at Mark.

He was watching my reaction. His face softened in a shy half smile. "This is one of my favorite places in Lyric. I never thought I'd see it again. I wanted to show it to you. And we can talk here without being interrupted."

I gave him an answering smile, but it faded quickly. Each time I softened toward him, I felt a painful ache in my heart. Not a physical pain, like the dull soreness I still noticed in my chest, but it was every bit as real. If each tiny step toward healing our relationship would hurt this much, I didn't know if I could do it. "Are you sure the Council isn't watching us? Are you sure they won't come and drag me away again?"

Mark looked confused. "I'm *part* of the Council. They won't hurt you."

Right. That's probably what Tristan thought, too. If Cameron was any representation, I didn't have a whole lot of faith in the People's ruling Council. I slipped my hand out of his to brush hair back from my face and walked ahead of him toward a small grove of trees.

They were the gnarled honey-colored kind that smelled of cinnamon, with branches as smooth as polished driftwood. I could see where Mark got his love of woodworking. He grew up with some amazing varieties of trees. By the time I reached the woods, I was short of breath. The weakness was an unfamiliar feeling. With each passing day in this world, I had grown stronger. Even the bumps and bruises of learning to fight and ride had left no lasting stiffness by the following morning. In fact, I was becoming very spoiled. When I got home, it would be a huge adjustment having sore muscles that took a few days to recover, or bruises that didn't heal within moments. I had grown used to my Restorer strength. This strange wobbliness in my limbs now was unnerving.

Mark was right behind me. He put an arm around me and asked, "Are you okay?"

I didn't push him away. "I think so." I tried to take a deep breath. "Must be something those drugs did to me."

Mark threw his cloak down over the damp moss. We sat down side by side, resting our backs against a large tree trunk. For a moment we were back in the North Woods on a hike. I'd pull out my field guide and Mark would groan. He'd see a hawk, get out his camera, fiddle with the settings, and the hawk would fly away, leaving only a memory in our minds. Then we'd laugh and continue on our hike, reminding each other of the hot tub back at the lodge when our bodies started aching.

"You better start at the beginning," Mark said.

"First I want to know about the portal."

Mark shifted and glanced away, but I tucked in my chin and glared. He let his breath out with a sigh. "Three stones. I kept them because—well—I just couldn't throw them away. But I knew I'd never go back again. I hid them. One was in the old mannequin and one was behind the insulation under the eaves. One was in an old box of tax records. I kept them separated so there was no way they could accidentally create a portal. I don't know how you did it."

I got defensive again. "I kept hearing sounds—voices. I moved some things around trying to find where the sounds came from. It just happened."

Mark looked somber. "That kind of supports the notion that you were called here." He didn't look any happier about his theory than I was.

"What about the notion that this is all your fault? That you shouldn't have left dangerous stones that could jerk me into this world just sitting around? What if the kids had gone up in the attic?"

"No one ever went up there. I'd almost forgotten about them. I didn't even know if they would still work. It's been so many years." Mark could almost compete with me when it came to being defensive. He stopped himself and looked me squarely in the face. "I'm sorry. It's all my fault, and I wish I had destroyed them years ago." He waited for a moment. We both had a lot of practice at apologizing after all our years of marriage. "Will you forgive me?" he asked in an almost formal tone.

I wasn't planning on restoration this quickly. I wasn't ready to even think about his dishonesty with me all these years, much less forgive it. But I decided I could let go of this one grievance. Keeping the portal stones had led to a lot of trouble, but he had had no way to know what would happen.

"I forgive you," I said, looking away. He would know my forgiveness was limited and reluctant. I didn't want to see the disappointment in his face.

"Your turn," he said. "Tell me everything."

I did. I told him how it felt to wake up in a strange world and immediately see Tristan battling the Rhusican. I recounted the frightening emptiness of Shamgar, Kieran's suspicion of me, Tristan's offer of help. I explained about my sword and how it came through the portal transformed and somehow gave me inner strength. I told him about everyone I had met that day on the transport: Cameron, the Rhusican girl, Bekkah, Linette, Wade, and the others. When I tried to describe the poison that overwhelmed me on the trail to Braide Wood, I faltered.

Mark took my hand.

I let him hold it, but I couldn't look at him. I hurried on with my story. I spoke of Tara's welcome, how Tristan's family took me in, and how Lukyan gave me his official approval as the eldest songkeeper. I hadn't realized how much had happened to me in a few short weeks until I tried to itemize each event and every new relationship. I sneaked glances at Mark as I talked, measuring his reactions. When I told him about my guardian training, he looked dumbfounded.

"My sword work isn't too great, but I love riding the lehkan."

He smiled and shook his head. "That's incredible. I never could get the hang of riding those things."

As I told him about my prayer time with Lukyan, and the

peace I felt after confronting the need to obey God's call, his face grew somber. He squeezed my hand, but I don't think he realized it. Lukyan had asked me if I was willing to walk any road the One chose. It hurt me to think about that question. Right now I was infuriated at the road the One had led me on. I felt confused and bereft. Peace and confidence had been crushed out of me in Cameron's inner office. Then my hope had been shredded by the discovery of Mark's twenty years of deceit.

When I told him about the Rhusican that had gripped Wade's and Linette's mind, and how I confronted it, my husband let go of my hand and stood up. He paced in agitation as I described its attack and my panicked but lethal defense. He looked at me as if seeing a stranger.

I was glad he was getting a taste of the foreignness I felt when I looked at him. Maybe we were both different people now.

I told him about Kieran's brief return to Braide Wood and the way I'd felt the One speak through me to him.

"But I don't think I talked him out of having dealings with Hazor," I said wistfully. "One more way I've failed."

Mark stopped pacing and sat down again. "You can't know that. Maybe what you said to him changed his mind. Maybe he went off somewhere else but plans to help Tristan when he can."

I gave him a grateful look, and then brightened as I told him about helping Kendra break free after two seasons in the thrall of Rhusican mind poison.

"I've never met her," Mark said, "but I saw Kendra once from a distance. She was with Tristan at a Feast day celebration. My friends and I all had crushes on her after that."

I had to smile at the picture of Mark as a teen, mooning over Kendra's exotic beauty.

"So what were you and Linette able to figure out about these Rhusicans?" he asked.

I could see he was beginning to understand the danger building in his former homeland and the urgency to do something. "We know that the best way to fight their influence is with the Verses. The Rhusicans don't work in the same way every time, so that makes it hard to know what to expect. The man who poisoned Kendra talked with her day after day, and when the suggestions took hold, she went so far into herself that she nearly died. I only spoke a few words with the Rhusican girl, but later the impressions she planted clouded my thinking entirely. Tristan just had one small thought he didn't realize was implanted by the Rhusican he killed. It kept him from trying to bring Kendra back, but it didn't affect him in any other way that we could tell. And the Rhusican talking to Wade and Linette seemed to have some sort of hold over them, but it snapped the instant he died. Tristan also told me that the Rhusicans interact with lots of people without any problems. I can't figure out what their agenda is . . . other than just causing general misery." I was sorting the clues like different colored patches of fabric for a quilt, trying to arrange them in a pattern that made sense. In spite of myself, I was enjoying organizing the pieces with Mark's help. We had always been good at giving each other new angles on a problem.

"And the Rhusican woman you said was working with Cameron?" Mark asked.

I flinched and shook my head. My heart started racing just remembering. I couldn't relive that.

Mark reached over and brushed the hair back from my face, then let his hand rest against my cheek. I met his eyes. Worry, love, and compassion looked back at me. "It's okay," he said softly.

"I . . . I can't. I can't talk about it right now." It was my turn to get up and pace. I continued my narrative, filling Mark in on the attack on Morsal Plains, Bekkah's death, the information I had learned from Nolan, and the Council guards coming to drag me to Lyric and send Tristan off to Cauldron Falls.

Mark looked back toward the city wall, deep in thought.

I felt another twinge of pain in my chest—more of a nerve memory than actual pain—and sank back to sit beside Mark, resting my head on my knees and trying to take deep breaths. "So now what?" I mumbled into my knees. "Should we go back to Braide Wood? I want to see how everyone is."

"Tomorrow is the Feast, so we can't do anything then. But after that, we have a day before the Council meets." Mark was thinking out loud. "Do you think you could sense if someone's mind has been taken over by a Rhusican?"

"I don't know. Maybe. With some people it's obvious. Other times I get a sense of something hidden, but don't really know what it is. Why?"

"There is no way the Council would be going against the Verses like this—allowing the Rhusicans to live here, buying long-range weapons that the Verses prohibit, trading with Hazor—unless their minds are being affected. If we visited the chief councilmember of each clan, maybe you could see what's been done to their minds. Maybe you can even heal them."

"Restore them," I said, looking up.

Mark's face blanched.

Why did that term upset him so much? He grew up in this world. He knew of the Restorers as great heroes of his people.

"But there is something else going on," Mark said. "Tell me again about what happened when the Council guards came to Braide Wood."

I frowned in concentration. "Wade ran into the clearing to warn us. He said the Council guards were coming and we needed to run."

"Slow down," Mark said. "Anything might be important. What else did he say?"

"He said they had taken the records, and Tristan seemed upset, but everything happened so fast—"

"The Records? Are you sure? Where were they taking them?"

"To Cameron, I think. Yeah . . . when I was locked up, I heard Cameron talking to Case about how he had them all now. He was just waiting for one from Blue Knoll."

All the color washed from Mark's face.

"Mark, what's wrong? What's the big deal about some records?"

"Susan, you know how important the Verses are to the people here? How they are passed on to the children, and reviewed every day and at every Feast? It's the way God chose to reveal Himself to them."

I nodded. I had figured that out. The Verses gave them a code to live by, but also important truth about the One's love for them and His plan to send a Deliverer.

"Well, even with great care, there is a danger of things being forgotten, or small words being changed as the Songs are taught year after year. So each clan was given a Record."

"A book?"

"No, it's a recording. More like . . . a CD of the One's voice. The permanent, perfect Verses. Once a year, the songkeepers of each clan play the Records for their tribe."

I was processing this, still not understanding why Mark was more upset about this than anything I had told him so far.

"It's like" — Mark struggled to find a parallel from our world that I would understand — "the Torah, the Holy Grail. No. It's like the ark of the covenant. It's the One's very presence. What is Cameron going to do with them? He wouldn't dare destroy them. Even with Rhusicans helping him, he couldn't get away with that."

Cameron's plot began to make sense to me. "Mark, he wants to change the Records. I heard him. What did he mean? What will he try to change?"

"Cameron has always wanted us to stop relying on Verses and guardians and instead trade for high-tech weapons." Mark rubbed his hand over his jaw. "He's never had support before now. I'll bet he wants to alter the Verses that say the People should let the One defend them. He'll twist things to say they can make alliances with other nations — use foreign weapons." There was growing anger in his voice as he guessed at Cameron's agenda.

"Is it possible?"

"I don't know. If he has a transtech to help him and overlays small parts . . . maybe." Mark's jaw clenched. He jumped to his feet, pulled me up, and started striding back to Lyric. "You don't have to worry about getting revenge on Cameron. I'll kill him myself."

I stopped short and tugged my hand away, planting my fists on my hips. "Wait a minute."

Mark paused to look at me, but shifted from foot to foot.

"I told you that Cameron had threatened me, tortured me, and probably would have killed me if he'd had more time. And you wanted me to forget about it and go home. Now you figure out he's going to erase a few tapes, and suddenly you're ready to kill him? Where do I rate with you?"

Mark froze. "Susan, I didn't realize everything that happened to you." He started to reach toward me, but drew his hand back as if he wasn't sure what to do with it. "It's not that I didn't care about you. I just didn't understand how bad things were. And the Records . . . do you realize what it means? If the People start picking which parts to keep and which parts to throw away, they won't have any truth left."

I nodded, still feeling a little hurt that defending the One stirred so much more passion in Mark than defending me. "Okay. But you're the one who told me we couldn't just go around killing councilmembers. If we're both arrested for murder, we won't be able to visit all the clan leaders or speak to the Council."

"But we have to do something. We can't let Cameron change the Records."

I thought for a minute and then grinned. "So we go get the Records back. Tonight. Before he can change them."

Mark's eyes began to sparkle, and he grabbed me into a bear hug. "Operation 'Records Recovery.'" He pressed his face against my hair.

I felt a rush of warmth toward him. This time, letting myself feel closer to him didn't hurt quite as much.

Chapter Twenty-One

"YOU SHOULD HAVE LEFT THE SWORD back at my rooms," Mark whispered, annoyed because he had banged into me in the dark and bruised his leg.

"Shh. I told you I'm not going anywhere without it. Someone's down at the end of the hall. Get back."

We pulled back around the corner. "How can you see anything? It's pitch black down there."

"My mom fed me lots of carrots." I didn't bother looking back at him in the dim corridor, but I knew he was rolling his eyes. "Okay, it's clear now. Hurry!"

We entered the dark hall and found the door to Cameron's office. Sweat broke out on my temples. There was no way I could step back into that room. "I'll stand guard."

Mark didn't argue. He pulled a gadget from his belt and used it to disable the magnetic lock on the door. Leave it to Mark to find a source for tech-toys after only a few days on this side of the portal. As he slipped inside, I wondered what the equivalent of a hardware store was like in Lyric. After he closed the door behind him, he must have palmed the lever for the room's lightwalls, because a glow appeared from under the door.

I winced at the obvious sign of our presence and drew my

sword in case anyone else was prowling the corridors. Time dragged, and I jumped when I heard Mark at the door behind me. He had shut down the lightwalls, and he locked the door behind him.

"Nothing," he whispered. "I searched everywhere."

I thought of the back stairs that Case had used. "Let's try downstairs." It took me a moment to get my bearings and find the unmarked door that led down to the cell where I had been kept.

"I never knew this was down here," Mark said, leading the way down the stairs. His footsteps sounded heavy on the metal treads.

"Mark, keep it quiet." I stayed on the balls of my feet, somewhat smugly demonstrating my ability to move silently, but my sword banged against a railing. The clash echoed against the concrete and steel walls of the basement. To his credit, Mark didn't comment. We paused, and I stretched my hearing to scan for anyone nearby. "Okay. Let's go." I started feeling my way forward and banged my head against something protruding from the wall. "Ow! Why didn't we bring a light?"

"Hold on." A soft light began to glow in Mark's hand.

I squinted at the object in his palm. It had a surface similar to a small heat trivet, but this was in the shape of a cube. "Hey, I haven't seen anything like that here before."

"You spent all your time in Braide Wood. They aren't exactly the high-tech capital of the world. Now, if you'd been at Rendor . . ."

"Where's that?"

"Near the River Borders. It's my clan. Um, Susan, could we discuss it later?"

It annoyed me when Mark was practical. But he was right.

It was dangerous to linger down here. I scowled at his back but followed him as he moved cautiously down the narrow hall, pausing now and then to test doors. The scrape of each door he pushed open echoed hollowly and sent nervous chills up my spine.

After some time we entered an open warehouse area the size of a twelve-car garage. In the pale light of the cube, it looked to be completely empty. Occasional drips of water interrupted the silence, and over the musty smell of the room, I noticed burnt-marshmallow scents again.

Mark sniffed. "Someone needs to get a transtech down here. One of the lightwalls is fried," he whispered.

"If there are lightwalls down here, why don't we turn them on?"

He made a dismissive sound. "We don't want to attract attention."

"Well excuse me if I'm not up on my breaking-and-entering skills. And you didn't seem to mind using the lightwalls when you were in Cameron's office."

Mark ignored my grumbling and headed toward an opening on the other side of the large room. He ducked ahead of me into the new hallway and disappeared from sight. The rasp of a footfall sounded in the empty space. I paused to look behind us. Was that an echo of Mark's last scraping step, or was someone else near?

Suddenly I heard a scuffle break out somewhere ahead, and a sound like a boxing glove making contact with a practice bag.

I drew my sword and ran into the hallway. It turned ninety degrees to the right a few yards ahead, the angle outlined clearly by the glow of Mark's light cube, which rested abandoned on the ground.

Where was he? My heart raced, and I tiptoed toward the edge of the circle of light thrown by the cube. Hugging the wall, I peered around the corner. I advanced a few uncertain steps into the darkness of the long corridor. "Mark?"

A large shape barreled out of a doorway at me. A sword flashed.

My pulse jumped again, and I swung my blade to block. Our swords connected with a ringing clash that bounced off the bare walls. As I strained to hold him back, the artificial light caught his face.

"Wade?" I asked, stunned.

"Susan?" He looked as confused as I felt.

I pulled my sword back to disengage. "What are you doing here?"

"I'm rescuing you. It took forever to get another transport, and I've been searching Lyric all afternoon. I finally tracked you to the basement of this building. I checked, but the Braide Wood Council chief didn't know anything about a troop of guards coming to get you. Susan, something funny's going on."

"Tell me about it. Where's Mark?" I stepped around Wade to scan the hall beyond.

"Who?"

"My husband. He was right in front of me." I started forward, sword still at the ready.

Wade grabbed my arm. In the eerie glow of the light cube, I could see him biting his lip. "Tall guy? Wearing a councilmember tunic?"

"Wade, what did you do?" I ran deeper into the corridor and stumbled over a body. Dropping to my knees, I felt for a pulse. Mark groaned, and my fingers found a big goose egg on the back of his skull.

Wade followed me, lifting up the light cube. "Susan, I'm sorry. I thought he was one of the men holding you here. I already ran into one Council guard farther down that hall and had to knock him out. What's going on?"

"It's a long story. Help me get him up."

We propped Mark against the wall, and he touched the back of his head gingerly and blinked a few times. "What happened?"

"Wade thought you were a councilmember and ambushed you."

"I *am* a councilmember." Mark turned to snarl at Wade. "What do you have against councilmembers?"

"I came here to rescue her," Wade declared staunchly.

"What?"

"Guys, can we sort this out later? We have to find the Records."

Mark staggered to his feet. He used the wall for support and glared at Wade.

"Wade," I said, quickly stepping between them, "keep watch while we search. I'll explain everything later." I paused to give him a warm pat on the shoulder. "Thanks for coming to find me." It really did do wonders for my morale to see his eager, friendly face.

Mark recovered his light cube, and we continued down the hall. "What did he hit me with?" he complained, touching the back of his head again. "And how come you were so much happier to see him than you were to see me?" His headache must have been fierce, because Mark is almost never cranky.

"Honey, we need to focus here. Wade said he knocked out a Council guard down this way. What do you want to bet he was guarding the Records for Cameron?"

We ducked into several side rooms. A few had odd supplies stacked in them—crates of woven fabric, panels of the smooth material used on heat trivets, even a large pot made of rough Shamgar clay and filled with dark stones. We spent frustrating minutes rummaging.

"Mark," I murmured, as we tiptoed down the hall to the next door, "aren't the clans going to raise a huge fuss about Cameron's Council guards taking their copies of the Records by force?"

"Of course. When the Council meets after the Feast, you can count on every chief councilmember demanding their Records back and protesting what Cameron did. I don't know what excuse he'll give, but he'll probably pretend to back down and return them. By then it will be too late. He'll have changed them. Hold this."

Mark thrust the light cube at me. He had discovered a door that was locked, and he needed his hands free to retrieve the gadget from his belt and work the electronic latch. He frowned, intent on his task, and tilted his head in concentration, the way he did when he helped Karen with algebra homework.

Maybe he really was still the Mark I had known and loved for so many years. Lots of people had secrets in their past. Of course that past didn't usually involve an alternate universe, portal stones, and foreign clans.

"Susan, wake up." Mark snapped his fingers in front of my nose.

I blinked and followed him through the now open door.

This small room was lined with arched cubbies built into the walls. Mark grabbed the light cube and twisted something at its base. The light grew to fill the room. We could see that most of the storage alcoves were empty, but a reflection glinted from one of the cubbies. Inside stood a silver cylinder, about two feet high. The metal had the same luster as my sword.

My hand caressed the hilt resting securely against my hip. I walked closer and saw that the cylinder was actually a stack of several round blocks. I reached to take them.

Mark grabbed my shoulders and pulled me back. "Don't touch them," he said softly. He knelt, eyes riveted to the cylinder, and dialed back his light cube to a soft glow. Reverence radiated from him.

Any thought that he didn't still have ties to this world fled my mind. But instead of allowing it to add fuel to my anger and distrust, I treasured this glimpse of a part of his life I had never known before. What had it meant for him to leave the world where he had grown up and never to have come back before now? What had he missed—besides the rolling hills and glowing towers of Lyric? What homesickness had he felt over the years?

He was mouthing words, probably praying.

I waited, listening for any sounds outside.

At last he stood up and scanned the room. He found a blanket that had been tossed against the wall and carefully wrapped it around the stack of Records, cradling them in his arms, taking care not to touch them.

We found Wade faithfully keeping watch at the entrance into the large warehouse. Mark was so focused on his burden that he barely gave the young man a glance. I paused to thank Wade and arrange to meet with him after the Feast celebrations.

"Are you sure you're all right?" Wade asked.

"Yes. Everything is fine. But I'm glad you're here. We're going to need help." He looked gratified and lumbered back into the darkness toward whatever entrance he had used in his search for me.

Slowly and silently, Mark and I retraced our steps through the basement, up the stairs, and down the dark corridor of the Council offices. A connecting courtyard led to the large building that housed Mark's borrowed rooms. In no time we were home behind a locked door, with the Records on Mark's table, still respectfully covered with a blanket.

"We did it!" I said. The adrenaline rush made me giddy.

Mark looked away from the Records and seemed to notice me for the first time since he had opened the door to their hiding place. "I love the way your nose wrinkles when you smile," he stated with a grin.

"It does not."

"Yes, it does." He walked toward me. "And you get one little dimple right . . . there." His finger touched the side of my lips. He was flirting with me. My predictable, comfortable, reliable husband of twenty years was flirting with me. An unfamiliar councilmember who'd had an eighteen-year history on this world before I ever knew him was flirting with me. Which man was he, really?

I stepped back, flustered.

He smiled slowly and closed the distance between us again. His head bent toward me.

In the second before his lips could find mine, I thought of how much he had hidden from me for our entire marriage. I jerked my head away and ignored the disappointment in his face. "So now what?" I gestured to the Records.

"I'm going to check each of them to be sure Cameron hasn't tampered with them. You get some sleep." He was sounding cranky again.

"Are you sure you don't want any help?"

"Just go to bed." He sighed. "Tomorrow's the Feast day, and you'll want to be rested."

I wanted to ask him what the Feast day involved, how he planned to examine the Records, and how this would affect our strategy of meeting with each clan's councilmembers. But he had turned away, and I was too tired to listen to his answers anyway. I washed up and found my way to his bedroom. As soon as I eased myself down onto the pallet, I was confronted again with everything that had happened that day.

Tristan had let Case take me. He hadn't put up so much as a token resistance. He was the head guardian of Braide Wood, but he didn't even *try* to protect me.

Cameron had broken me—broken more than my attempts to hide information from him. I'd never experienced physical pain like that before. It had changed something inside me. The whole universe felt different now.

And Mark . . . Mark had let me believe I knew him all these years when I really didn't. Worst of all, God had let it all happen. The Rhusican woman's words thrummed like a low chord in my brain. *He didn't rescue you. He gave you to us.* I curled into a tight ball and let tears run down my face in silence.

I didn't pray for my family in this world or any other. I didn't bring any verses to mind to ponder as I fell asleep. It didn't seem worth the bother.

Chapter Twenty-Two

I MUST HAVE SLEPT, BECAUSE I was startled when Mark's hand touched my shoulder.

"Susan. Wake up. It's Feast day." The eagerness in his voice reminded me of our kids on Christmas morning. He offered me a mug of clavo.

I groaned in gratitude and propped myself up, reaching for it. As I sipped, I studied Mark.

He must have been up all night. His eyes were bleary, but there was a suppressed energy in him that I hadn't seen since his favorite hardware store discounted all their table saws.

"What did you find out?"

"They haven't been changed. I listened to key sections of each clan's Records. May the One forgive me." He looked worried.

Touching something as sacred as the ark of the covenant had to be unsettling. "I'm sure He understands. He knows your heart."

Mark gave me a grateful smile. "It was wonderful to hear them again." His voice was wistful. How had he managed to cut off the first half of his life and leave it behind when he came to my world?

He pulled the mug from my hands. "Come on, sleepyhead.

It's almost first light, and we want to get to the tower before it's too crowded."

Although I was intrigued to see the rituals of the season-end Feast, I wondered if it would be wiser to stay here and have a day to rest. There was still a bruised ache in my chest that puzzled me. Even sitting up in bed made me light-headed. But the clavo helped, and I managed to get up, dress, and eat a little breakfast.

Mark wore his formal Council uniform again. I grabbed the cleanest of the "tramping in the woods" clothes from my pack.

Mark suggested I wear my cloak and keep the hood pulled up to hide my face. "There'll be so many people, no one will notice another stranger in the crowd. But until we begin meeting with councilmembers tomorrow, it might be best for you to keep a low profile."

Sound advice. I couldn't handle one more surprise or confrontation right now.

When we left the building, we found the streets full of people. They all moved in silence and in the same direction. In the pale glow of first light, they were as dim as shadows. Joining the procession gave me an eerie feeling, and I was grateful when Mark put an arm around my shoulders.

As we neared the huge central square, near the main entrance tunnel of Lyric, I heard a growing sound. Slowly my ear sorted the soft hum into the sound of thousands of voices barely raised above a whisper, singing a low melody, overlapping in a fugue. The quiet round was more moving than if it had risen at full volume.

Called by the One,
Draw near.

Maker and Protector,
He is here!

The phrases repeated and pulled us forward toward the tall tower. Open doors led into the tower from all directions. Men and women flowed inward, heads bowed, lips moving in the quiet call to worship.

Mark and I passed under the closest archway into the huge round hall within the tower. I caught my breath. Colored light glowed within crystal-lined walls. Above us the tower stretched for hundreds of feet toward vaulting skylights, with no other floors or balconies.

"Mark," I whispered, tugging his sleeve so he'd lean down, "why all this empty space?" In this very functional and practical world, the extravagance and luxury were a startling contrast.

Mark put his mouth so close to my ear that his words tickled. "It's to leave room for the One. This is where we welcome Him."

Goose bumps rose on my skin, and I looked up again—half expecting to see a burning flame or swirling cloud. However, the space remained empty of anything that could be seen. It overwhelmed me to realize that even though thousands of people filled the floor of the tower, there was hundreds of times as much open space above us.

Once, on a backpacking trip to the mountains, I stood at the base of a rugged, snow-covered peak. Looking up, I knew in the marrow of my bones that the One who created these mountains was much bigger than I'd ever understood before. That day I was comforted by my smallness. The weight of the world—even of my failures—didn't rest on me.

Today a tingle crept along my spine. All at once, the huge

tower over our heads was full—full of a presence that I suddenly wanted to hide from.

There was no way to go back. More people had filled in behind us, and we were surrounded on all sides.

Mark kept an arm around me, and the edges of my hood blocked my face as I continued to absorb the murmuring music and watch the gathering people.

God, how can you make me feel so hungry and so full at the same time? And why do I want to run toward you when I also want to run away?

Slowly, a round dais in the center of the tower began to rise, revealing a group of perhaps twenty people wearing long robes in the white-gray color of first light. They all faced outward in a circle with their faces raised to the vaulted space above us. The dais began to turn slowly.

For a moment I had the disorienting feeling that the floor beneath me was spiraling in the opposite direction. When I looked down at my feet, the illusion vanished.

The singing faded and a weighty silence rested over all of us. When I looked back toward the dais, I recognized a blonde, sparrow-boned figure. Linette stood on the round stage as one of the songkeepers representing Braide Wood.

We were quite a distance away, but I let my eyes stretch their focus and saw her face clearly. Dark rings marred the pale skin under her eyes. She had to be frantic, waiting for word from her missing fiancé, Dylan. Yet her gaze focused upward into the full empty space with passion and trust.

Instrumentalists that encircled the stage began to play resonate wooden wind instruments, leather-covered drums, and stringed circles that they plucked like a lap-harp to release a mellow sound like a classical guitar. The songkeepers proclaimed a worship song that swirled upward into the far reaches of the tower. Linette's face rotated out of sight for a time, but I thought I could make out the clear, high pitch of her voice.

> *Cover us,*
> *For we cannot hide;*
> *We turned from You,*
> *Yet You abide.*
> *Cover us*
> *To blot out our wrong;*
> *Only in Your mercy*
> *Can we be strong.*

The chorale was a haunting and plaintive plea, and the song-keepers repeated it several times. Then, as they reached the last line again, a low crescendo rumbled in from a group of drums that had the deep resonance of timpani.

The last word, *strong*, seemed to make the floor beneath us vibrate, and the musicians began a driving martial hymn, joined by the voices of the whole assembly. The sudden roar of thousands singing at full volume shook the walls.

> *Awesome in majesty, perfect in power,*
> *One to deliver us, He is our tower.*
> *Enemies circle us, darkness descending;*
> *He is the Morning Light, love without ending.*

Even over the crowd, Mark's familiar baritone rumbled beside me, and I looked back up into the huge tower's space, my eyes blurring with tears.

> *Lord of the Verses that teach us Your way,*

Guardian of seasons and Chief of each day,
Looking with mercy on each need we bring,
You give us strength through the Songs as we sing.

But You didn't! My heart cried out to God in silence as the voices continued to thunder around me. *You didn't give me strength. I was already sad and empty, confused by my life. And then you brought me here. I was so afraid and alone. I thought You would make me strong and give me a purpose. I was willing to serve You if You wanted to use me here. You did use me . . . a little bit. But now . . . What did I do wrong? Why did You abandon me?*

The hymn ended and one of the songkeepers began to recite a long section of the Verses. From time to time he would say, "The Verses of Life," and the crowd would respond, "One without end." Mark joined in each time, following the liturgical pattern easily.

I tried to absorb the words and find comfort in them, but they felt alien and obscure.

When another piece of music began, the mood shifted throughout the tower. The sense of reverence and majesty was still evident on all the faces around me, but there was a growing warmth and tenderness as well. Some people raised a hand, as if gently touching the invisible presence of the One hovering above. Others sank to their knees. Arms encircled loved ones, bodies swayed with blissful, uplifted faces.

The weight of the presence over and around us pressed me to my knees, and I buried my face in my hands, tears splashing between my fingers onto the floor.

Mark's hand rested gently on my shoulder, though in my mind, it wasn't *his* hand, but Another's.

I thought You wanted me to restore people. I wept, unable to speak, hardly able to breathe with the breaking of my heart. *Now I'm more weak than I've ever been. I'm hollow. There's nothing left that I can do for You. There's nothing left in me but doubt and pain. How will I ever trust You again?*

Soft as the sound of the wooden flute that came from the circle of musicians, a word sang into my heart.

Surrender.

I stiffened. I thought of Hazor's demands and Cameron's plots. *Is that what I am to You, Lord? An enemy to conquer?*

Surrender. The word whispered through my being again. Images flooded my mind: floating on the surface of a lake in the warmth of an August afternoon, letting the water carry me; flying down a snow-covered hill on a toboggan, giving up control and squealing with joy; a gold band slipping onto my finger, along with the golden weight of a lifetime covenant; life-shattering awe as my body surrendered to straining muscles and pushed a new baby into the world.

Surrender, breathed a still voice that could have roared and made the tower around me crumble. Not a demand, but a precious offer: *Stop trying to glue together all the broken pieces. Stop trying to understand all the reasons. Stop pushing Me away when I want to bring you healing. Surrender.*

My shoulders shook with sobs as I felt that voice inside me. "Yes," I whispered. And the hunger and fullness, yearning and completeness, brokenness and wholeness all blended and poured through me. Somewhere around me there were thousands of other worshipers. But I was absolutely alone in the presence of the One. And He loved me. There wasn't a single thing I could do to make myself useful to Him. But He didn't want my usefulness. He just wanted to love me.

I don't know how many more songs were sung at the

gathering. After what could have been hours or minutes, Mark knelt beside me and rested his face against my hair. "Are you okay?" he asked softly.

I nodded, not able to speak, but reached out and squeezed his hand.

He helped me to my feet, and I realized that people were slowly dispersing. The songkeepers' dais had lowered back to the floor of the tower, but the musicians continued to play a gentle hymn. Throughout the huge tower floor, there were quiet groups of people. Some chatted with friends, reluctant to leave. Others still knelt in prayer, oblivious to those around them.

I looked up at Mark. His face reflected the same kind of tenderness, compassion, and yearning that I had felt pouring through me as I knelt on the floor. I gave him a watery smile and threw my arms around him, nestling my face against his chest and getting his tunic damp with tears. He held me with a fierceness that conveyed both relief and desperation.

I savored the feeling of being where I belonged, and we both sighed at the same moment.

As I relaxed against him, inspiration hit me with a jolt. "Mark!" I threw my head back to look at him, the top of my head barely missing his jaw.

"Hm?" He looked content and not at all ready to be jarred onto my next train of thought.

"We need to find Linette. She was up there with the song-keepers. She could help us tomorrow." I squirmed out of arms that were reluctant to let go of me and headed toward the center of the tower. I had to detour around a few clusters of people, but the space was clearing out. It was easy for me to spot Linette as we reached the musician's area.

The young songkeeper was engaged in an intense conversation with another woman. She leaned forward, giving comfort and encouragement in her quiet voice.

I waited until the woman left before I stepped forward. "Linette?"

She turned, and her face lit up when she recognized my features under the hood. "Susan!" We hugged, and I introduced her to Mark. She studied him, puzzled. "You were a Rendor Council apprentice a few years ago, weren't you? I met you once before my commissioning here in Lyric. I heard you were sent to the lost clans. It must have been rough. You look so much older." Then she put a hand over her mouth, embarrassed by her lack of tact, and started apologizing.

Mark laughed. "I am older. I've lived about twenty-two years on Susan's world." He turned to me, eager to try explaining the time distortion again. "Linette met me when we were both about eighteen. Now she's twenty and I'm forty."

I didn't want to hear it. I didn't need the headache. "Linette," I cut in, "has there been any word about Dylan yet?"

Her shoulders drooped as she shook her head. "Tristan will find him." The confidence in her voice sounded forced.

"I'm sure he will." I gave her another hug. "You keep working on that song you're writing for Dylan. Are you finished here? Can you come with us to talk? We could use your help."

"They don't need me until the afternoon gathering. I'm happy to help."

We went back to Mark's rooms, waiting to talk until we were behind closed doors. He sighed with relief as he saw the table that still held the fabric-covered tower of Records. "I asked Jorgen to keep my presence here a secret. No one should know we're using these rooms, but it still worries me to leave these unprotected," he whispered to me.

We pulled up chairs around the table, and I told Linette our suspicion that the Rhusicans were controlling some of the Council. She and I had talked about how their poison worked several times after I killed the Rhusican outside of Wade's home. The mental threads seemed to seep into any inner doubt or weakness and take root. Then they grew and twined around all other thoughts, choking them. We were both uncomfortable with this topic. If the evil were just something imposed in the mind, it would be easier to confront. But the darkness it stirred couldn't fully be blamed on an outside force. The poison expanded on an evil that was already present, which neither of us liked to admit.

Mark grew impatient with our hypothesizing and told Linette about our plan to visit the chief councilmember of each clan before the special session. Mark also told her about Cameron's efforts to steal and corrupt the Records. He wanted to return each clan's Records to their chief councilmember, but only after we were sure the delegates weren't being influenced by Rhusican poison.

"Markkel, you need to return the Records to the song-keepers," Linette said, an edge to her soft voice. "Almost all the eldest songkeepers are in Lyric today. Send word to them. Or I can tell them."

"But how do we know we can trust them?" he asked.

Linette jerked as if she'd been slapped. "Well, they'll do a better job of protecting the Records than any councilmember will."

"But the Council controls the guardians," Mark said. "They can keep the Records secure."

Linette leaned forward. "It was the Council Guard that stole them in the first place."

Mark shook his head. "They weren't sent by the Council. Those were Cameron's own men." Mark's and Linette's voices were growing louder.

"Time out," I interrupted. "Before we do anything else, I need Linette's help with something."

She stopped glaring at Mark long enough to turn to me. Mark opened his mouth to continue their argument.

I held up my hand. "Hold on. Linette, you and I have both helped people who have been under the influence of poison, and we've both been trapped by it ourselves. Do you think you can recognize when someone has been affected by it?"

She tilted her head and thought for a moment. "Well, I didn't notice it in you when we started the walk to Braide Wood. But I wasn't looking for signs of it either. I think there might be a way to test, though." Her words came more quickly as she developed her ideas. "There are key parts of the Verses that summarize truth. I would guess that if someone is poisoned with lies, speaking the Verses would either make them uncomfortable and bring it to the surface, or help lead them to freedom from the poison. Eldest Songkeeper Lukyan sang through all the key Verses with me after you killed the Rhusican, to be sure no poison hid in me."

I had been thinking along the same lines. "It's not like the right words are a magic formula, but Verses and Songs of truth stirred something in me when you sang, and they helped pull me back. And I saw the same thing happen with Kendra. Let's give it a try."

Linette fingered the end of her long braid. "You want to go get someone you think has been poisoned?"

"No, I want us to test someone here." I looked at Mark. I'd trusted him for twenty years, only to discover deep secrets that shook the foundation of my love for him. I wasn't about to move forward until I'd done all I could to ensure that there were no hidden motives or Rhusican suggestions steering him.

His mouth opened and then closed again, hurt feelings narrowing his eyes. He stood up, chair scraping along the floor.

It looked as if my distrust might propel him out the door.

"I'm sorry," I said softly. "You don't know what it's like . . . what the Rhusicans can do. At least I hope you don't. What if one of them spoke with you, and you don't remember it? I have to know whom I can trust. I want to trust you." Maybe that statement would take some of the sting out of my suggestion.

"Fine." He sat back down, jaw set. He turned his back to me and nodded toward Linette. "Go ahead."

Linette shook off her own irritation with Mark and reached out her hands to him. Mark frowned at her, but grudgingly placed his hands in hers. She focused deeply into his eyes, and he looked down, uncomfortable.

"Markkel," she said in her breathy soprano, "it's all right." She waited for him to meet her eyes and then began.

"Awesome in majesty," she quoted and paused.

"Is the One eternal," Mark answered without hesitation.

"Perfect in His might and power," Linette said.

"The only truth and only source," he recited back.

"He made all that is and loves all He made"

"His works are beyond our understanding."

They continued speaking the Verses back and forth, and I watched, fascinated, as the anger seeped out of Mark's muscles. His spine softened, and he began to settle more deeply into his chair. I'd always known that words have power, but in this world, that power seemed much more immediate and tangible.

"In every time of great need, a Restorer is sent."

I started as I recognized the words Linette was speaking.

"To fight for the people and help the guardians," Mark responded in a voice hoarse and strained.

"The Restorer is empowered with gifts to defeat our enemies." Linette's eyes were compassionate.

I wondered again what troubled Mark so much about the Restorers.

Linette appeared to know. She nodded to him, responding to something they both seemed to understand.

"And turn the people's hearts back to the Verses," he said, a muscle along his jaw twitching.

Linette paused for a moment, studying Mark's eyes. She glanced over at me and then looked back at Mark.

I saw the pain on his face, but didn't understand it. "Linette, what's wrong?"

She shook her head, straightened her back, and moved on to the next Verse. "We wait in the darkness for the One who brings light."

"The Deliverer will come, and with His coming, all darkness will be defeated." They continued through their creed.

I sat back, feeling excluded. Linette had begun teaching me some of the Verses, and most of these words were familiar to me now. But I didn't share the intense devotion I saw in Mark and Linette. This was like air to breathe for them.

When Linette finished, she let go of Mark's hands. His eyes glistened, and he swiped at them with a few fingers, turning away.

Impatient for answers and worried about Mark, I grabbed

Linette's arm. "Well?"

She smiled, but spoke to Mark instead of me. "There's no foreign poison in you. But you need to talk to Susan. You won't have peace until you do." She turned to me with soft eyes. "I'll meet you here tomorrow, and we'll visit the councilmembers together. Right now you need to talk to your husband." She gave another sympathetic look at Mark and slipped from the room.

She hadn't said anything more about the stack of Records on the table. Mark must have won her trust in a powerful way if she was willing to leave with them still in his care.

"Mark?" He rubbed the back of his neck but didn't speak. "Please, Mark. No more surprises. What do you need to tell me?"

He looked past me toward the door, misery apparent on every line of his strong features. "It's about why I left this world. And why I don't want you to be a Restorer."

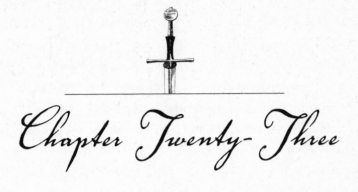

Chapter Twenty-Three

I TASTED BLOOD AND REALIZED I was biting my lip. "Okay. Tell me." I braced myself. How many more secrets did I still have to face? I was getting weary of this.

Mark traced a pattern in the wood grain of the table. Then he reached out to toy with the edge of the fabric over the Records. He seemed to draw strength from it and began to talk, though he still avoided my eyes. "You've heard about the last Restorer."

I nodded.

He didn't notice. "Mikkel was a great warrior, and when the People were about to be destroyed by Kahlarea, Mikkel raised up an army and guarded Cauldron Pass."

I knew this history lesson already and wanted to hurry him along, but I let him find his own pace.

"He did exactly what he was supposed to do." There was pain and a hint of anger in Mark's voice. "But he died."

"He gave his life for his people," I said. "Maybe that *was* his purpose."

Mark stopped playing with the piece of fabric, and his eyes burned into mine. "Mikkel was my father. I was only five when he was killed. Everyone in Rendor—everyone from all the clans—celebrated the great hero of our people. But I lost my father."

Shock ran through me, followed by deep compassion. "Oh, Mark." I pulled my chair closer to his and put my arm around him, resting my head against his. "I'm so sorry."

He exhaled heavily. "Our clan cared for us. They looked out for my mother and me. Then, when I was about twelve, a song-keeper in Rendor told the clan leaders that he had had a vision. He said Mikkel's son would provide a greater Restoration than his father. It was bad enough feeling that my father could never be my own . . . that he belonged to history. But now everyone expected me to add my story to his in the Verses."

"Wait." I hated to interrupt him, but I was confused. "I thought the Records aren't supposed to change. How could his story be added to the Verses?"

Mark rubbed the back of his neck. "The Verses are living. The oral history is added to by each generation. Those chronicles are sacred too, but they aren't finished yet. The Records are the first Verses. Those that the One gave in a particularly direct way. Kind of like"—he struggled for a comparison— "like the Ten Commandments—written by the finger of God."

I nodded. "Or in this case, spoken. So your father's story and this prophecy about you became the next chapter of the Verses?"

His eyes clouded. "Everyone looked at me differently. I was Mikkel's only son. They expected something that I didn't know how to give."

I'd been bewildered when confronted with the possibility of having the gifts of a Restorer. The thought of a young boy facing that pressure broke my heart. "Did you have any of the signs?" I asked.

"No. But that didn't discourage them. My father didn't have the Restorer signs until a year before the battle. That's when he began to hear and see things no one else could, and heal from injuries. I thought it was all wonderful—my father with special powers from the One—until later."

I reached for his hand and held it as he continued.

"To make matters worse, we learned that Kahlarea had heard about the prophecy. They sent assassins to kill me. I was about fourteen the first time. The Rendor guardians caught them before they could enter the village. Then, a few years later, they tried again. They came in the night. They knew exactly which home we lived in, but they didn't know I was visiting my cousins that night. They slipped into the house and killed the only person they found. My mother." Mark's head leaned more heavily against mine.

I shifted so that he could rest his head on my shoulder. I stroked his hair and drew a shuddering breath, fighting back tears. What could I say to comfort him? When I met him in my world, Mark only told me his parents had died. He rarely talked about his family. Now I began to understand the weight he had carried all these years.

"The head guardian of Rendor decided I should train because it was expected—all the Restorers in the past came from the guardians. I didn't have any calling to be a guardian, but I started the training anyway. I was miserable. The Rendor Council chief saw what was happening and convinced the village to let me become an apprentice councilmember instead. He mentored me, and I spent two years in Lyric learning to serve the People and the Verses. Then Kahlarea tried again." Mark's eyes looked across the room, but he was focusing on something I couldn't see.

"They sent two assassins right into Lyric. They almost succeeded that time." A shudder ran through him, and his gaze dropped to the floor. "I couldn't let other people die for me again. I went to the eldest songkeeper of Lyric, and he showed me the portal entrance and gave me the three stones. I was supposed to leave this world for a while, until the danger was past, and then return to 'save the people.' But I stayed. I made a new life. I met you. I didn't want to be a Restorer, and I never came back."

"Mikkel's son will provide a greater Restoration," I repeated. "Mark, your portal brought me here. You *did* provide the next Restorer."

He lifted his head and looked into my eyes. "Yes, but it's *you*. May the One help me; I don't want to watch you die." His voice broke.

The last of my doubts about him dissolved. Even though he had kept so much truth about himself hidden from me for the past two decades, his love for me had always been real. I hugged him and prayed for the right words. "Mark, we can't run from the path the One calls us to." I rested my forehead against his. "You've told me that so many times when the kids were driving me crazy. It's not about succeeding. It's about obedience. You told me that even if I can't see the results, I need to trust that God will use my efforts—just do what He asks me to for that moment."

"But I don't understand how he plans to use us," Mark interrupted. "Things are so much worse here today than when I left only a few years ago. The People are in greater danger than in my father's day. Hazor is demanding tribute, the Council is wavering, you've told me the Rhusicans have weaseled their way into villages and into people's minds, and Cameron nearly succeeded in defiling the Records."

"But he didn't succeed. And Hazor won't succeed. And we'll find a way to get rid of the Rhusicans. Mark, remember the promises. When enemies surround us, He is our tower."

Mark took a deep breath. "You're right. We'll just handle one problem at a time. But Susan?"

"Hm?" I asked, sinking down to rest my head on his shoulder.

"Promise me you'll be careful."

"Of course. Mark?"

"Uh-huh."

"I thought this was the big end-of-the-season Feast day."

"It is."

"So when do we get to eat?" I felt Mark's shoulders shaking even before I heard his deep laugh.

"All right." He grinned. "Let me show you Lyric on my favorite day of the season."

By unspoken agreement we put aside discussions of war, politics, religious apostasy, and mental poison—and ventured out into the city. Even travelers skipping into other universes need to eat.

All the normal businesses were closed, and people filled the streets and courtyards, especially near the huge city entrance. Mark was patient as I looked my fill at the crystal-lined tunnel and the huge open square surrounded by towers. I had already seen the Council office building and the central tower that was used for worship. Mark began pointing out other places to me.

"And down that alley was the door we would sneak through to watch the guardians train. My friends and I would sneak up a back stairway and hide on an overhanging ledge whenever we heard they were holding sword competitions."

I was charmed at the stories he told me about his teen

years in Lyric. Mark was the person I knew best in the world, but now I discovered new layers of the experiences that had formed him.

Then he showed me a courtyard full of trees, blue ferns, and glowing pathways. "This is where I used to come when I wanted to spend time with a girl," he said.

I felt an odd pang of jealousy and slapped his arm with the back of my hand. "Hey, let's walk down memory lane some other time. We're supposed to be finding food, remember?"

The corner of his mouth twitched. He was enjoying teasing me. "All right. This way."

Restaurants weren't common on this world, even in the large city of Lyric. But on Feast day, many people offered favorite family recipes to the influx of guests from the surrounding clans. Mark led me several blocks down a side street. We ducked into the storefront of a Lyric transtech. It was the kind of store Mark would have loved browsing on a normal day. There were shelves full of sleek items with levers I couldn't even guess at the purpose of. But today the owners were serving spicy wedges of meat on a skewer. Mark pulled some thin metallic squares from his pocket and slid two of them across the counter to the transtech.

I waited until we were back outside to start asking questions. "What was that? Is that money? How did you get some? Why don't they use it in Braide Wood?"

Mark handed me my food. Some sauce dripped onto my hand, and I paused to lick it off. "Mm. This is better than barbequed ribs!"

"He's got the best recipe for roasted lehkan in town," Mark said.

I gaped at him, horrified. People ate the spirited creatures I loved to ride?

His eyes gave him away first, as they began to sparkle. Then he burst into laughter. "I'm kidding. It's caradoc, a kind of mutton. They raise the animals on the Corros Fields. And the chips I gave him are magnetic power cells. They're used in the heat trivets, light walls, and other tools. It's a common currency in Lyric and Rendor."

"I've never seen them before." I was finding the food a lot more interesting. I slid a piece of the caradoc off the wooden skewer and bit into it. The meat was tender, and I recognized some of the spices from one of the soups Tara made frequently. My mouth tingled.

Mark laughed. "It could only happen in Braide Wood. I can't believe you've been here for over two weeks, and you've never seen a magchip."

It was odd that I'd never even thought about currency during my time here so far. The people of Braide Wood had shared their hospitality freely with me and used a barter system within their village. In contrast, the large city of Lyric was beginning to feel too similar to my world.

We savored every bite of the meat, strolling down quiet side streets where most of the shops were closed. We could hear the noise of large crowds in the main square only a few blocks away, but now that I'd satisfied my curiosity, I wasn't eager to continue back in that direction. I stopped to peer in the window of a fabric store. Although most of the colors were muted and earth-toned, they were rich with beautiful woven textures. I sighed with pleasure at a display of three-peg designs, and wished the store were open for business. I turned to ask Mark if we could come back sometime.

He was studying me with the same appreciation I had been showing for the fabrics.

I looked into his eyes and felt my breath catch in a moment of uncertainty. Mark and I had become so comfortable with each other after nearly twenty years of marriage. We finished each other's sentences and could practically read each other's thoughts. Of course many of those sentences and thoughts in recent years had centered on Jake's college applications, Karen's play practices, whether our old blue van could hold out for one more year, and whether Mark should remodel the bathroom.

Today I was transported back to our first months of marriage: so much to learn about each other, depths to explore, wounds that we could help heal in each other. It felt like we were starting over again — confronting new battles to be fought side by side. Yearning blossomed deep inside me, and I suddenly wanted more than gentle hugs and the grasp of his hand. All these weeks away from him, every inch of my skin had longed for his touch. Now he was here, and I'd been holding him at a safe distance. "Mark, I think I've seen enough of Lyric. Let's go back to your rooms."

"Are you sure?" His gaze moved restlessly, skimming my forehead, my cheeks, my lips.

Was I sure? I had thought I'd never forgive him for the secrets he'd kept from me. But after my encounter with the One that morning, I no longer wanted to press down the warmth that grew when I looked at him. I nodded and saw the crinkles deepen around his eyes as he smiled.

I licked my lips and tasted the peppery caradoc sauce.

Mark stepped closer and pushed back the hood of my cloak, burying his hands in my hair. When he bent down to kiss me, I expected the comfortable warmth I always felt when we kissed good-bye before he left for work. Instead, his intensity startled me, and my body felt like it had been recharged with new magchips.

"Definitely electromagnetic," I murmured when we paused to breathe.

"What?"

"I've been wondering what the power source is on this world."

Mark gave me a lazy smile and pulled me even closer. "I didn't know you were so interested in technology," he said. "I could have told you. It's magnetic attraction."

Chapter Twenty-four

WE SPENT THE RAINY HOURS OF the early afternoon back in Mark's rooms, rediscovering the familiar in each other and exploring the differences that were so new to us. We were dozing in a tangle of interlocking limbs when we heard a clear tone ring though the air outside.

I sat up quickly, alarmed. It sounded a little bit like Tristan's signaler, and brought back memories of the attack on Morsal Plains.

"Just the call to the second gathering," Mark murmured, pulling me within range for a kiss.

"They didn't do that this morning." I brushed strands of hair back from my eyes.

"Everyone knows when first light is. They don't need a call for that."

"Mark, didn't it drive you crazy living here? Why don't they all just get watches?" I knew this world never developed sundials because there was no visible sun. They also didn't divide time in tight neat hours the way I was used to.

"Actually," Mark rolled onto his back and stretched, "I found all the clocks and alarms and timers in our world a lot harder to cope with."

I was delighted he said "our world." Sometimes, watching him here in Lyric, I wondered which place he felt the most allegiance toward, and whether he would really want to return to "our world." I could understand the pull of this place. I was already half in love with Braide Wood. But the thought of my children kept my attachment to this world firmly fixed as short term. I hoped Mark would feel the same way after more time here. I pushed that worry aside along with the blanket over us and raced Mark to the washroom.

A short time later, we strolled back down the streets toward the tower, fingers interlocked, because we didn't want to break the new connection we felt. The streets were wet again from the daily wash of rain. The sounds of stray drops falling from the eaves and the splash of occasional pools of water under our feet complemented the voices around us, as people gathered from every part of the city.

The mood this afternoon was very different from the somber procession of the morning. I got the impression that we weren't the only people who had experienced an encounter with the One or a healing of relationships today. Glancing sideways at Mark, I was glad to see some of the fatigue and worry had eased from his face. A pale line of stubble shadowed his jaw, and his wavy hair was more tousled than usual. He had never looked better.

As we walked, we heard bursts of laughter and animated conversation. When we reached the central square, people began to join in a song. But this call to worship was as lively as a tarantella, and musicians were clustered near each door into the tower, urging the tempo forward. I would have loved to stop and study the instruments. Some of the drums were similar to Irish bodhráns, and the wooden flutes might have come from my world. But there were other instruments more difficult to identify, and the flow of people didn't allow me to linger.

This afternoon Feast gathering was a time of pure celebration: Verses, prayers, and songs. The air sparkled with hope. While the dais in the center rotated slowly again, those of us on the main floor began to circle in a counter direction. Soon it seemed everyone's hand was linked into a chain with others, forming circles within circles, dancing simple steps and weaving patterns.

I joined in, unconcerned about what my feet were doing, pulled along by the energy and freedom of letting every part of my spirit and body rejoice. I tried to absorb every second of joy and store it deep within me, like fuel, to give me strength for the days ahead.

The gathering ended too soon. The overhead windows revealed a darkening sky. After a powerful benediction from the eldest songkeeper, and an exhortation to remember the Verses and follow them each day, men and women hurried out into the square and toward their homes on the outer rings of the city.

When we arrived back at Mark's rooms in the building near the Council offices, we found Wade already waiting for us outside. We welcomed him in, although Mark was less excited to see him than I was. He rubbed the sore spot on the back of his head as he gestured Wade ahead of us into the room.

Wade eyed the fabric-covered stack of Records on the table uneasily. "Is it really them?" he asked me.

I nodded. "We got them back before Cameron could change them." I left Mark to explain more to Wade while I went into the kitchen and heated water for clavo. I kept my hearing focused on their conversation. They seemed to be getting along, so Mark must have forgiven Wade's ambush in the Council office basement, even though the bump on the back of his head was still tender.

Mark and Wade had never met before Mark left this world, but they had grown up in the same generation, so they soon discovered common acquaintances. By the time the clavo was ready, Linette had arrived as well. She brought several miniature bread loaves, which she placed on the low table near the couch. I added a plate of fruit from Mark's kitchen. Wade grabbed a couple chairs from around the taller table where the Records rested. He dragged them near the couch, eager to keep some distance between him and the covered stack he still eyed warily now and then. Linette also glanced over at the table, with something between reverence and hunger in her gaze.

When Mark and I sat down on the couch, our closest hands reached for each other's reflexively.

Linette smiled at us. "You had a chance to talk?" she asked shyly.

I nodded and thanked her again for her help. Then we dove into the food and our planning with equal eagerness.

We each shared pieces of information. Wade was very curious about Mark's experience. He was familiar with the vision that had led to the assassination attempts and was fascinated by how much older Markkel was now. Wade had also continued to do some digging into my arrest, and had confirmed that it was not a sanctioned Council action. Cameron must be feeling very sure of his power in the Council to have acted on his own that way.

As we developed our strategy, I kept feeling there were pieces missing in our understanding of the threats to the People. There was a rapid shift going on in the Council, and I didn't understand the agenda of the Rhusicans or Cameron. When Wade and Linette began talking about Tristan's trip to Cauldron Falls to hunt for Dylan, I remembered something that had seemed odd to me.

"Tristan isn't the head guardian of all the clans, right?" I interrupted.

Wade answered with defensive pride. "He's head guardian of Braide Wood. That's an important clan."

"Yes, but there are lots of other head guardians, right? And more powerful clans?" Wade nodded, not sure what I was getting at.

"When Cameron was questioning me . . ." My throat tightened, and I had to swallow before I could continue. Mark squeezed my hand in silent support. "He kept asking me questions about Tristan. He seemed obsessed with him—what his plans were. And in the transport, I saw him watching Tristan. There was rage on his face. I know Cameron is trying to disband the guardians, but why does he hate Tristan so much?"

Wade and Linette looked at each other. Linette turned to Mark. "I forgot it happened in the year after you left. You wouldn't have heard about it."

"What?" Mark and I both asked.

Wade rubbed at his beard, but when it was obvious we weren't going to let the subject drop, he shifted in his chair and cleared this throat. "Tristan was training a group of young guardians. I was there. It was my second year, and I was going to be commissioned soon. We had a group of new trainees that were about as green as early-season grain. They didn't know the first thing about how to patrol, but Tristan was taking us out to the Gray Hills, near Shamgar. He is the best guardian I've ever met," Wade added staunchly.

"I know," I said. "But please tell us what happened."

"One of the first-years was leading a small patrol. He disobeyed Tristan's orders and headed too far out. I think he was showing off. He was like that—never following orders." Wade paused again. "It wasn't Tristan's fault. The trainee was out too far from base camp."

I was getting frustrated waiting for him to get to the point. I leaned forward, ready to say something, but Mark gave a small shake of his head. I sat back and waited.

Wade took a deep breath and spoke quickly as if the words hurt to say. "The first-year was bitten by a rizzid, and his team panicked. They sent a runner back to the camp, but Tristan was in the middle of a climb with some of the other first-years." Wade looked away. "He decided not to leave until he got them all down. The runner kept begging him to come—said it was a bad bite. I guess Tristan figured the first-year's team would know what to do, but by the time he got there, it was too late. The boy was dead." Wade's face was somber as he relived the experience. He met my eyes. "It was Cameron's son who died."

My world tilted again. Nothing would ever change my opinion of Cameron as a power-hungry snake. But to lose your son . . . A tiny seed of understanding sprouted in the very hard ground of my feelings.

"Cameron blamed Tristan," Wade continued, crossing his beefy arms. "Tried to get him thrown out of the guardians. But the Council cleared him. Still, Tristan stopped working with first-years after that." Wade sat back, angry at having said anything that tarnished the image of his hero.

"Back when they found me in Shamgar, Tristan told Kieran he couldn't take on a student." My fingers traced the thin scar on my arm. "Kieran told him to get over it."

"Tristan isn't one to get over things," Linette said softly.

"And he's blindly doing whatever the Council tells him to, even though he sees that the Council is moving the wrong direction," I said. "He's motivated by guilt."

"Not just guilt," Mark argued. "The Verses appointed the Council to lead the people. He's doing the right thing in obeying them."

"I still think he belongs with his clan," I insisted.

"Susan, it's not your decision to make. And he hasn't been all that loyal to the Council either. You told me he was in Shamgar tracking the Rhusican that poisoned Kendra. That wasn't where he was assigned. And he had no authority to kill the man either."

"The Rhusican had a sword, too. It was probably self-defense." I knew I was making excuses. Tristan admitted that he'd been tracking the Rhusican for two seasons. But I couldn't agree that it was wrong for him to do it. "Besides, I killed one, too, in Braide Wood."

"I know." Mark rolled his shoulders and winced. "The Council is going to want to try you for that."

"Bekkah cleared me," I said.

"Yes, but Bekkah is dead."

I hadn't thought of that.

"Markkel," Linette interrupted, "you know that Wade and I will speak for her. And Kyle saw it happen."

Great. Kyle had never hidden his disdain for me. I was sure he'd have wonderful things to say to the Council about me.

Linette seemed to sense my qualms. "The Council will listen to reason."

"Unless they listen to Cameron," Wade said darkly.

Now Mark wasn't the only one with tense shoulders. My stomach knotted, and I wished I hadn't eaten a second bread loaf.

Mark squeezed my hand. "We just have to make sure they don't."

We agreed to spend the next day visiting the chief councilmember of each of the ten clans, except for Cameron. We already knew where he stood. If our meetings went well, we would be ready for the official Council session the next day. Cameron would undoubtedly make his accusations against Tristan using the information I had provided. We knew, from what the Rhusican woman told me, that Cameron would urge the Council to banish Tristan. Cameron would also do everything he could to discredit me. And that didn't even begin to address the issues of Rhusicans and Hazor. If I couldn't get the Council to trust me or accept me as the Restorer, they wouldn't listen to anything I had to say. I nibbled the edge of a fingernail.

"We'll all be there with you," Mark said, sensing my growing anxiety.

"Wade, where are you supposed to be after the Feast? Will it be a problem if you stay to help us?" I didn't share Mark's respect for the Council, but I didn't want anyone else getting in trouble because of me.

"Tristan assigned me to look out for you. So I'm officially exactly where I'm supposed to be," Wade said with a smirk. Then his grin faded. "I'm just sorry I didn't get here sooner. Tristan thought he could trust Case. If he had known . . ."

I cut him off, not wanting to go down that road again. "I know. It's okay." It wasn't, but given time, I'd get over it. Tristan needed loyalty from me, not blame. And Wade didn't need to feel guilt.

Mark released my hand and leaned forward, studying Wade. "How long have you been a guardian?"

"Almost two years now. I did my first-year training under the head guardian of Corros Fields, but advanced training with Tristan."

"Have you ever served in Rendor?"

Wade shook his head, puzzled.

Mark looked at Linette. "Would you please check him for poison?"

Wade pushed his chair back, frowning at all of us in confusion.

"Please trust us in this," Mark said. "I'll explain later."

I wasn't sure what Mark's questions were all about, but I supposed his suggestion was a wise precaution. "Just let Linette lead you through some Verses," I told Wade. "I'll help her. It'll be good practice for us for tomorrow."

Wade wasn't thrilled with the idea, but shrugged and nodded. Linette drew her chair closer to him and took his hands. I got up to stand beside her and focused my gaze on Wade's face. They began reciting the Verses and Wade relaxed as he spoke the familiar words with Linette. I smiled and studied his face. His cheeks weren't as lean as many of the other guardians, and his uneven beard hinted at how young he still was. His eyes were guileless. I thought of a Saint Bernard pup with oversized paws, eager, loyal, and a bit clumsy. Although, there was nothing clumsy about him when we sparred. He didn't have Tristan's finesse or Kieran's reckless skill with a blade, but he was still a well-trained guardian and light years beyond my abilities.

Something shifted in Wade's face. I rubbed my eyes. No, it wasn't his expression that had changed. Instead, a tiny pinwheel swirled deep in the pupils of his eyes. As my eyes enhanced their focus, I saw a miniature of Wade's face, mouth wide with fear. Outside his home in Braide Wood, the Rhusican had told Wade that he would never be as good as the other guardians.

He needed to hear one of the Verses that would speak to that doubt. I was frustrated by my limited knowledge of their sacred words, until I thought of a plaque hanging over my desk at home. I touched Linette's shoulder and stepped forward, kneeling in front of Wade.

"Wade, would you say this verse from my own people? 'I can do everything through him who gives me strength.' Say it with me."

Drops of sweat appeared on his temples, and he gripped the arms of the chair. Linette began singing a quiet melody about the might of the One. Wade spoke the words after me in a raspy whisper and then repeated them with more confidence. I was fascinated. Watching the inner struggle, I breathed in relief at the moment that the strange vision in his eyes disappeared. He sagged back into the chair, looking at us, bewildered.

"You mean they had me? They were controlling me?" He was horrified.

"No," I hurried to reassure him. "It was just a little suggestion he planted in you, but it's gone now. They try to add strength to our own doubts. You'll be fine." I looked at Linette. "I saw something that time. I could see the lie that was tormenting him like a tiny picture deep in his eyes. I hope that happens again tomorrow."

Linette beamed. "Another Restorer gift to help us."

Determination and a sense of purpose rose up in me, giving me new strength. I smiled too, until I looked back at Mark.

His jaw was clenched. I could read his thoughts. Linette's words had brought back his fear of living through the nightmare of seeing another Restorer die. I hurried to sit beside him on the couch, wanting to reassure him.

My husband shook off his mood and stood. "Wade,

guardian of Braide Wood, will you protect my house?" His tone was formal.

Wade sprang up and stood stiffly in front of him. "Markkel, councilmember of Rendor, it will be my honor to protect your house with my life."

"What house?" I whispered to Linette, looking around the borrowed rooms we were using. It sounded as if they were saying something important, but I didn't quite understand.

"He means you," she whispered back to me. "His house is his family."

Mark turned to me, and I couldn't find my easy-going husband in his stern face for a moment. "Susan, when word gets out that I'm back, my life will be in danger again. If the Council believes you to be the Restorer, your life will be in danger — from Kahlarean assassins or from the role you'll fill. Either way, you need a protector. I never finished my guardian training. Besides, it's been years since I used a sword."

I nodded my understanding. This reminder of the threats we would both be facing frightened me. I was touched by Mark's concern and Wade's eagerness to pledge his aid. Also, I was impressed by Mark's humility in asking for help to protect me. I had a feeling he wasn't half bad with his sword and would have enjoyed the role of my sole protector. Along with that mix of feelings, a wave of fatigue washed through me, pulling all the energy down from my head, through my chest — which was aching again — and out through my toes. I tilted my head back against the couch and closed my eyes. Mark and Wade talked for a while in quiet tones, and then Wade left to stand guard outside the door of our borrowed rooms. I heard Mark and Linette speaking, but tried to ignore them.

"She's so tired. I think using her gifts is hard on her," Linette was saying. "Maybe this isn't the best time."

"We don't have any more time," Mark said, his own voice sounding weary. "Tomorrow she'll begin to meet the council-members." I wanted to scold them for talking about me when I was sitting right there, but it seemed like too much effort.

"Susan," Mark's voice was close to my ear.

"Hm?"

"Susan, wake up." Mark's words grew more insistent. "We'll go to bed soon."

I started to smile in answer to that, but remembered that Linette was still in the room. I sighed and forced my head up and my eyes open. "What?" I asked, a bit cranky.

Mark smiled at my bleary eyes and placed a light kiss on my forehead. Then he rested his forehead against mine for a moment before sitting back. "Susan, Linette is going to search for any poison in you. I'll try to help her. I know I don't have Restorer powers, but I can sing with her."

I was wide-awake now. "Wait a minute. You were with me at the tower. The One spoke to me. I'm fine now." I curled up more firmly into the corner of the couch, tucking my feet under me. I didn't know why his suggestion bothered me so much, but it did.

"Susan, Markkel is right. It's a wise precaution." Linette's voice was timid, and I knew she wouldn't push the issue.

I turned toward Mark. "You're just doing this to get back at me because I didn't trust you at first," I accused. I ignored the hurt on his face and pulled my knees up in front of me, hugging my shins. After what Cameron had done to me, I didn't want anyone poking around in my soul, finding things, uncovering things.

He moved closer to me on the couch but didn't touch me. "Susan, I'm not Cameron," he said, his voice low. "We aren't

Rhusicans. We won't do anything to hurt you."

I met his eyes. Tears welled up in mine, causing his face to blur. "Don't make me do this," I whispered.

"I can't let you face councilmembers who may be controlled by Rhusicans if I don't know you are as strong and healed as you can possibly be." Mark's jaw was set. "Do you want to go ahead with our plans tomorrow or not? We can go through the portal and leave instead."

I glared at him. "You know I can't do that."

"Then let us help you." His tone softened.

I felt betrayed all over again. He saw how frightened I was, but he was going to make me do this anyway. I squeezed my hands together to stop their trembling, locking them tighter around my shins. How could he not trust me after the day we had shared? Why would he demand this senseless test from me now, when I was so tired? I dropped my forehead to rest against my knees. "Go away."

"No," he answered simply.

I groaned in frustration, asking God why He had cursed me with such a stubborn man for a husband. "Fine." I lifted my chin. I couldn't look at Mark, but I faced Linette squarely.

Her skin flushed with worry and apology, but she pulled her chair closer and reached for my hands. "I'm sorry."

I clenched my jaw and didn't answer. I'd submit to this silly exercise, but I wasn't going to like it.

She sighed. "Repeat the Verses. I know you haven't learned them all. Say them after me." She began with the creed she had used with Mark.

I repeated each line, feeling Mark's eyes on me from where he sat nearby on the couch. I wanted to tell him to leave, but I knew he wouldn't.

Linette reached the part of the creed with the promise of the Restorer. I swallowed and recited the familiar words along with her. After that, Mark relaxed, settling back into the couch. Linette smiled gently and continued on to the promise of the Deliverer. "We wait in the darkness for the One who brings light. The Deliverer will come, and with His coming, all darkness will be defeated."

I opened my mouth to repeat the words.

A wall of pain slammed into me. My right arm began to burn, and my heart pounded. Linette's face and the room around me disappeared. A gray mist covered me.

I tried to scream, but couldn't breathe. "No!" The moan was all my clogged throat could manage.

In the fog, auburn curls framed the smiling face of the Rhusican woman. *Do you think if your god could hear you, he would have let us take you? Wouldn't he have stopped the pain? He didn't rescue you. He gave you to us.* There was no Deliverer. I was alone on the edge of a chasm. Nothing but darkness and emptiness stretched before me.

"Not again," I gasped. "Please God, not again." I heard Cameron's laughter, but then the sound changed. It wasn't his voice. It was the Rhusican I had killed, mocking me with an eerie overlay of low, growling laughter and high shrieks. I cringed as far back as I could. "Help me. Someone stop them." Suddenly I was kneeling by Bekkah's body, acrid yellow smoke stinging my eyes as I rolled her over. But this time, as the lifeless face became visible, it was my face. And then I was back in Cameron's office, trapped and abandoned. He was standing over me, holding my sword. "No!"

For a moment I was aware of Linette. Her voice was edged with panic. "Nothing is helping, Markkel. I'm sorry. I don't know what to do."

I felt myself sinking away from her voice and remembered the long battle on the path to Braide Wood. I couldn't face that tug-of-war again. I tried to squeeze her hand in mine, but couldn't feel anything. I was limbless, formless, slipping away. Her voice faded completely, and a crushing weight of emptiness pressed against my heart, holding it back from beating with life. The gray mist became spotted with black.

"Even though I walk through the valley of the shadow of death, I will fear no evil, for you are with me." The words were spoken in a strong baritone, but as if from a great distance.

I recognized them and some part of me reached out.

"Your rod and your staff, they comfort me. You prepare a table before me in the presence of my enemies. You anoint my head with oil; my cup overflows. Surely goodness and love will follow me all the days of my life." The words floated under and around me and held me—a warm cocoon forming within the cold mist.

My mouth was able to move again. I managed a small breath. "I will dwell in the house of the Lord forever," I whispered.

"That's right, Susan." Mark's voice was firm. "He will never forget you. He will never lose you or abandon you." Strong arms surrounded me. Someone was holding me, rocking me. "The Lord is my shepherd, I shall not be in want."

"The Lord is my shepherd," I repeated. The crushing pain was easing. Had it happened again, or was it just a memory of earlier torture? I could feel my hands again. Linette pulled hers away for a moment, and I heard her moving across the room. Mark's voice continued, and I rested, letting the strength of the verses from my own world cut through the ties of the Rhusican lies. One by one, the cords were breaking away, and the pull toward the chasm was lessening.

Something cold pressed against my palm. Linette had brought me my sword. I was able to open my eyes to stare at the shimmering blade. Linette's face reflected in its luster. Her eyes were full of tears, and she looked shaken.

"The Lord is my shepherd," Mark said again. I repeated it after him, slowly feeling strength returning. "I shall not be in want. He makes me lie down in green pastures." I recited the words with him, letting myself relax into his arms. "He leads me beside quiet waters." He stopped suddenly, and I tilted my face up to look into his. His eyes were wide as we spoke the next words together, a new understanding hitting us both.

"He restores my soul."

The One was my Restorer. I had wanted to bury the pain and doubt, never to go back to face it. But the One had let me see the hurt that still cut a fissure through my faith. He showed me that He had been with me, even in the valley of the shadow of death. He drew out the poison and washed it away with anointing oil. And I understood: I could only be a Restorer when I let the One continue to restore my soul.

The mist could have stayed hidden in the background for years. Or it might have welled up when I tried to discern poison in others tomorrow. If Mark hadn't insisted . . .

I dropped my sword and pulled myself up to turn and hug Mark. When I leaned back, I saw how pale he looked.

"I didn't realize," he said, voice thick with regret. "I didn't know until I heard you—how bad it had been."

"I'm all right."

"And then we didn't know how to bring you back. What if . . ."

"Shh. Mark, stop it. He won't abandon me. He gave you the words to say. He knew what I needed to be healed."

Mark gathered me close with a shuddering sigh, and we hugged each other tightly. He whispered the words again, his face pressed against my hair.

"He restores my soul."

Chapter Twenty-five

LINETTE SPENT THE NIGHT ON THE couch. With her cultural unease at venturing out after dark, she was more comfortable remaining with us, even when Wade offered to escort her to the songkeepers' lodge where she had been staying. I think she really wanted to stay close to the Records.

My sleep was deep and dreamless, and I woke surprised by my level of energy. We had a clear plan, I knew my role, and I was eager to get on with it. Time might not have been rushing on at the same pace in our home world, but I worried about our children. I wanted to solve whatever problems I could and get home to them.

"Mark, couldn't we just pop through the portal for a few minutes to be sure everything is okay back at our house?" I asked him over breakfast.

He choked on his juice.

"It's not that easy," he said when he caught his breath. "It's not like people here go popping through portal stones every day. And please don't talk about it anymore," he added in a quiet voice, though Linette had left already to change clothes at her lodging. "Very few people know about them. It's dangerous to talk about them too freely."

"But at Braide Wood, no one thought it was strange I was from another world."

"Sure, but that doesn't mean they knew about how you got here. Can you imagine what would happen if someone like Cameron discovered a portal? It was only desperation that led the eldest songkeeper to teach me how to use it. We'll only use it once more. When we leave here, it will be for good. Promise me you won't talk about it with anyone?"

"Okay, don't worry so much. I won't say anything." In contrast to my confidence this morning, Mark seemed anxious.

"Susan, we have to talk." He rubbed his jaw. "You've done a great job adjusting to life here, but . . ." He seemed to be struggling to find the right words.

"Out with it. If you've got something to say, say it."

"Well, there's a lot of protocol involved in conversations with chief councilmembers. I wish I had more time to go over things with you. You can't just treat these people like . . . well, like your friends back home."

"Okay. Fill me in." I tore off a piece of bread and popped it in my mouth.

He smiled, grateful I wasn't taking offense at his coaching. "Please be respectful no matter how upset you feel about something. The proper title of address is 'Chief Councilmember,' with or without the clan name added." Mark continued to give me a crash course in the rules of Council interaction. I tried to pay attention, but a lot of the policies seemed silly and arbitrary.

"I sent a message this morning to my Rendor friends," Mark continued. "I asked them to send an official tunic for you. I might be able to get you in based on my status, but it will help if you're dressed right." He pushed a piece of fruit around on his plate.

"Mark, settle down. It's going to be fine. I'll let you do all the talking until I'm needed."

"I haven't figured out how I should introduce you. I don't want it known that you are the Restorer. But I may have to tell them to convince them to listen to us."

"Then tell them."

"No. If they keep thinking that I'm the Restorer, you'll be safer."

"But *you* won't be. That idea's no better. At least I have Restorer gifts. If any Kahlareans come after me, I won't be easy to kill." I was hoping my bravado would comfort Mark. Truthfully, I wasn't sure of the extent of my ability to heal, and didn't plan to test those limits if I could help it.

Mark shook his head. He wanted to protect me from the role as long as possible. As if to confirm his fears, a sudden scuffle outside interrupted us.

Wade burst through the door, dragging a young boy by the back of his collar. "Councilmember Markkel, are you expecting a delivery from Rendor Council? Should I let him in? He has no weapons." It was clear that Wade was having fun being our house protector.

I hoped he wouldn't have to ward off anyone more dangerous than the irritated young messenger in his grip.

Mark quickly stepped forward to thank the boy and accept the package, and Wade whisked him back out the door. Mark untied the cloth bundle and shook out a long, rust-colored tunic. It was similar to the one he wore, but his had two short stripes running vertically down from one shoulder, and mine had one. Mark's mentor had granted him full first-level status on his return. I was being allowed to pose as an apprentice. I'd already tried guardian training. Now I was stepping into a place, albeit a lowly one, on the Council. Perhaps if I stayed here long enough, I'd get to try becoming a songkeeper. That was a calling I'd really enjoy.

I changed into the unfamiliar uniform as if getting costumed for a play. Would I know my lines when the curtain rose?

When I walked back out to the common room, Mark gave me a nod of approval, but he seemed distracted. He was carefully bundling the Records and hiding them in a pack to carry with us. Linette arrived a few minutes later, and we set out for the Council offices.

We began with Mark's mentor, the Rendor Council chief. There were several people in his office when we arrived, but Mark led me directly to a tall man in a rust tunic with five stripes at the shoulder. He broke off his conversation and turned to us. Wavy silver hair hung down just past his broad shoulders.

"Chief Councilmember Jorgen, this is my wife, Susan, most recently of Braide Wood clan," Mark said.

"Greetings," Jorgen boomed, clasping my right forearm and holding on while he scrutinized me. His weathered face revealed long experience, but his enthusiasm was youthful and contagious.

No wonder Mark had such respect for his mentor. I found myself wanting approval from this man who had been a father figure in Mark's life. "Thank you for seeing us, Chief Councilmember," I said, meeting his eyes.

Jorgen seemed satisfied. He released my arm and smiled at Mark. "The One has provided a suitable wife for Markkel, son of the prophecy."

Mark bowed his head in acknowledgment, but a muscle in his jaw clenched. He beckoned Linette forward and introduced her. Then Mark and Linette explained the Rhusican threat, and the experience we had gathered that proved their danger. After hearing our story, Jorgen was happy to recite Verses with Linette. No Rhusicans had traveled as far as Rendor, and we found no sign that he was affected. Jorgen was grateful and relieved when Mark handed him the carefully wrapped Rendor copy of the Records.

"My eldest songkeeper was already in Lyric preparing for the Feast when Cameron's guards showed up in Rendor and took these. But other songkeepers sent me word immediately. I confronted Cameron, and he said the Records would all be safer in a central location, since war is coming."

"So that's his lame excuse," I muttered.

"Cameron holds the loyalty of all the Council guards, so I didn't want to oppose him directly. I planned to bring this before the whole Council at the session. Thank you for returning these." The Rendor leader patted Mark's back, then steered us toward the door. We thanked him again for his time. "It's good to have you back, Markkel," he said with genuine affection. Jorgen's support encouraged us as we set out on our campaign to see the other chief councilmembers.

The day passed in a blur of waiting in outer offices, introductions that made my head spin, and meeting after meeting. Almost all the clans' Council chiefs agreed to meet us, especially when they heard Markkel was back in Lyric. The official word when he disappeared two years before was that he had been sent as an ambassador to the lost clans beyond Morsal Plains. Only Jorgen and the eldest songkeeper of Lyric knew where he had really gone. Curiosity about Markkel got us in the door.

Time after time, Mark and Linette explained our concerns about Rhusican poison and asked cooperation to test for its presence. Each time we persuaded a chief councilmember to recite Verses with Linette, I saw swirling visions indicating fear, doubt in the Verses, and a desire for alliances and weapons for protection. We were able to bring the poison thoughts to the surface and see an instant change. The Braide Wood Council chief shook himself as if waking from a nap and straightened up with clearing eyes, but not everyone appreciated our visit.

Though the majority of Shamgar's clan had been destroyed when the city was taken by Hazor years before, the clan still had a chief councilmember who represented scattered pockets of people living in the Gray Hills. I was surprised at the hostility we encountered from him. He was clearly gripped by anger toward the other clans because they had not done more for Shamgar. Given Shamgar's sorry past, I could understand his desperation to create weapons against future Hazorite threats, but I couldn't help him, because he scoffed at our request to recite Verses and threw us out of his office.

At the end of the afternoon, we could count on five clans that were free of poison. No guarantee they would vote to banish the Rhusicans or to protect Braide Wood, but at least they weren't being influenced directly by Cameron. We had already known that Lyric was firmly in Cameron's grasp. From our visits we learned that Shamgar and Corros Fields were in his pocket as well. That left two chief councilmembers that refused to see us. We had no clear idea where they stood, but we'd done all we could.

Mark followed through on his plan to return each clan's copy of the Records. Five had been placed in the hands of their Council chiefs. That act alone won us a great deal of allegiance on the Council. All the councilmembers had been livid at having their clan copy of the Records brought to Lyric, but none had been ready to openly confront Cameron. When we couldn't see the remaining councilmembers, Linette informed each clan's eldest songkeeper, and the other five Records were turned over to them.

Linette and I were mentally drained, and I was chafing from a long day of following strange and annoying protocols. As we walked out of the building housing the Council offices, I tugged at the neck of my tunic. Mark was pensive, and I was preoccupied with my worries about the big Council session to come. Sitting in our borrowed rooms stewing about our problems wasn't an inviting prospect.

Wade provided an unexpected outlet for my restlessness. "Susan, when did you last train?"

I shrugged. "I'm not sure. It was before the attack on Braide Wood. Before Kendra was healed. Oh yeah, I guess the last time was . . ." I caught myself before mentioning Kieran to Wade. Though secrecy probably didn't matter anymore. I'd already told Kendra, Cameron, and Mark about Kieran's short visit to Braide Wood before his journey to Hazor. "It was the day after the Rhusican attacked me in front of your house, when Tristan worked with me."

Wade frowned. "You mean you've only trained once since I was working with you?" Wade turned to Mark. "One way or another, war is coming. She needs to be training every day."

Mark looked at me, and I grinned. After a day of arguing with politicians, my hand itched to work with my sword.

"Sounds like a good idea," Mark told Wade.

Wade was able to get us into the guardian training tower because it was late in the afternoon and most of the first-years were finished for the day. Mark was as eager as I was to refresh his sword skills, so he came, too. He still wore his Council tunic, but I had insisted that we stop by his rooms so I could change into my old, comfortable clothes. Wade and I quickly fell into our old routine of sparring, and reviewed set patterns with wooden swords borrowed from the racks lining the sides of the practice hall. After some energetic passes, the lingering pain returned to my chest, and I grew short of breath. Mark looked concerned.

I waved him away as I plopped on a bench to rest. "Just out of shape," I said between gasps.

While I took a break, Wade put Mark through his paces. The skill must have been something like riding a bike, because Mark looked very natural, the blunt blade almost an extension of his arm as he worked through the forms.

I pulled out my true sword and examined it for nicks, admiring the play of light on the blade. After Wade gave Mark some tips and they circled the room a few times in a volley of parries and blocks, I was ready to play again.

Wade lifted his sword in salute to Mark. "Not bad for a councilmember," he said, grinning. Mark tried to hold a fierce frown, but the corner of his mouth twitched.

I stepped forward, holding my sword at the ready.

"Whoa. Are you sure you want to try that?" Wade asked.

"You said it yourself, Wade. War is coming, and I need to learn to use my real sword."

"All right, but let's take it slow." He grabbed a blunt-edged blade from the wall rack. We reviewed standard patterns again, in slow motion. Gradually picking up the tempo, Wade called out changes as we circled.

My own sword was more comfortable in my hand than any practice weapon. Strength seemed to flow from the steel through my arm. Even my frantic, clumsy sparring with Kieran was stored in my muscle memory, and I found myself blocking with different edges and countering with aggressive strikes.

Wade was impressed. "Tristan'll be surprised when he sees you next."

Mark stepped forward. "Want to take me on?" He winked.

"You can always try." I brushed wisps of hair out of my eyes and grinned.

Wade placed his sword back in the rack. "I'm going to find something to drink." Then he paused, as if remembering his new role as our house protector.

"Go ahead," Mark told him.

"I won't be far," Wade said. "Call if you need me."

Hints of anxiety trickled through my confidence. Every time I noticed how hard Wade was working to protect us, it reminded me of all the dangers we needed protection from. I didn't like that reminder.

"Come on, show me what you've learned," Mark invited, pulling me away from my worries. We started slowly, tracing careful patterns, and pulling our strikes. My sword felt balanced in my hand, and the movements became more effortless. I loved the admiration on Mark's face. I also realized that proving some level of skill in fighting would ease a little of his worry for my safety.

We were building our tempo and beginning to move around the room when I thought I heard a sound from the hall. I paused to listen but must have imagined it. We resumed, but I was starting to get distracted. I wondered why Wade hadn't come back yet.

Mark spun and came under my guard at an angle, anticipating my block. My response was sluggish, and he accidentally nicked my shoulder.

I gave an inadvertent yelp.

A dark shape flew past from the hallway behind me. At first I thought it was Wade, mistakenly thinking I needed rescuing. But Wade didn't move that fast. This man was leaner, and his sword work was lethal. He attacked Mark before I could move and disarmed him in three blows. Mark's sword flew from his hand, and the stranger grabbed the front of Mark's tunic and shoved him against the wall, his blade against Mark's throat.

"Wait!" I shouted, running toward them.

"Who are you?" the man snarled at Mark.

I knew that voice. I swung my weapon down, crashing the flat of the blade with all my power against the man's sword arm.

He released Mark as his arm dropped, but he didn't lose his grip on the sword.

"Kieran, stop. This is my husband."

Kieran pulled back a few steps so he could cover us both with his sword. His travel cloak was splotched with mud; his face was unshaven and flushed. The same feverish look burned in his eyes, but his voice was icy. "You never told me your husband was on the Council. In fact, I seem to recall you went to great lengths to convince me that you didn't know anyone in this world."

Great. How could I explain this fast enough to keep his sword at a distance? "This is Mark. He came through a port—"

"I came to rescue her," Mark cut in. He rubbed his wrist, which he had wrenched when Kieran knocked his sword from his hand. "We were sparring."

Kieran eyed the two stripes on Mark's tunic. "You came to protect her?" He didn't bother to hide his sneer. He shifted the grip of his sword and turned to me. "Susan, he's on the Council."

"I know, but he's here to help. Really."

Kieran's face was unreadable, but he sheathed his sword.

I sighed with relief and slid my weapon into the loop on the baldric he had given me.

"Can you get me into the Council session?" Kieran asked Mark.

Mark studied Kieran's intense expression and frowned. "Go see your clan's Council chief. You know the protocol."

"Tried that. Takes too long to go through channels." Kieran turned to glare at me. "So all this time, you really were working for the Council."

Mark didn't want me talking about the portal or our other world, so how could I explain this? "I didn't lie to you. It's hard to explain. I didn't know Mark was on the Council. . . ."

He turned away from me. "Which clan?" he asked Mark.

"Rendor." Mark tugged his sleeves into place.

Kieran nodded. "And you really have a standing on the Council?" He was stuck on that topic.

I interrupted. "Let's go somewhere to talk, and I'll explain everything."

He continued to ignore me and stare at Mark.

"I have some standing," Mark answered. "Why do you want to approach the Council?"

Kieran's eyes narrowed with suspicion. "You don't need to know that."

"Then I can't help you." Mark crossed his arms. He was being calmly stubborn in the way that always drove me crazy.

Kieran didn't look very cheerful either. "You won't help me?"

"Not without knowing what you're planning."

"You really are Susan's husband?" Kieran clarified once more, confusing me with the change of subject.

Mark glanced at me, and his face softened before he answered. "Yes."

"That works." Kieran stepped within arm's reach of me. Too late, Mark realized his intention and moved in to shield me. In the space of a second, Kieran grabbed me and pressed the blade of his dagger against my throat.

Mark pulled up short.

"Move and she dies," Kieran promised evenly.

Rage and horror dueled on Mark's face, but he gritted his teeth and held his ground. "What do you think you're doing?"

Kieran shifted the dagger slightly in warning. "You are going to get me into the Council session tomorrow," he told Mark.

I couldn't swallow and could barely breathe with the sharp edge of the knife against my skin. I remained frozen, hoping Kieran's hand stayed steady. Could a Restorer recover from a slit throat? I didn't want to find out.

Mark's eyes widened for a second, but then focused back on the dagger at my throat. "Let her go, and we'll talk about this," he promised, trying to keep Kieran calm.

That's right. Keep him talking. Wade had to be around somewhere. I stretched my hearing, but there was no sound from the outer hall. I heard someone's heart beating way too fast. Probably mine.

Kieran ignored Mark's comment and spoke to me, his voice coming from somewhere behind my right ear. "I see you forgot lesson one," he taunted. "Stay on guard."

That did it.

I twisted in his grip, letting the dagger pierce my skin and surprising him enough to give me an advantage. While turning, I slammed my elbow into his chest, knocking him back. With my focus on his dagger, I grabbed at his arm. I couldn't break his grip, but I held the blade away from me.

Mark ran to snatch up his own sword from where it had fallen. As he ran up behind Kieran, I thought he planned to cut him in two as he swung in an arc. But he used the flat of the blade to knock Kieran's legs out from under him.

Kieran fell backward.

With the force of the fall, I was able to knock the dagger from his hand.

Mark planted a foot on Kieran's chest and positioned the tip of his sword right under his chin. "Are you hurt?" My husband spared a quick glance my direction.

I touched my throat, and my hand came away covered with blood. But the gash was healing. "I'm fine."

Kieran's eyes burned with hatred as he glared up at Mark. We didn't need this. Our list of enemies was too long already.

"Should I kill him now or turn him over to the Council Guard?" Mark asked.

I knew he wouldn't actually kill Kieran. At least I was pretty sure he wouldn't. He looked capable of it at the moment. "Mark, we can't trust the Council Guard."

"He was ready to murder you," Mark argued. "Let them deal with him."

Kieran braced himself on his elbows, trying to ease his torso up. Mark shoved him back down with his foot.

"I have to talk to the Council tomorrow," Kieran grated out. His focus shifted over to me. Desperation lurked behind the fevered rage that gripped him.

I stepped closer. "Why?"

He looked straight up at the ceiling, then closed his eyes, saying nothing.

"Kieran, I'm not your enemy."

He laughed, an ugly sound. His eyes popped open again, and he turned his head toward me. "Try saying that when you don't have a sword to my throat."

"You started it," I protested, then winced at how childish that sounded. "Why did you attack me?"

"He's on the Council. He can get me in. You're leverage."

The way his mind worked amazed me. Absorb facts. Change plans. Practical. Ruthless.

"Well, you don't have any leverage now. So tell us why you need to talk to the Council."

He ignored me.

I looked at Mark and shrugged. Kieran could be a dangerous enemy or a valuable ally. I honestly didn't know what he was up to, but we wouldn't get anywhere with him pinned to the floor. I walked over to a cubby near the hallway door and rummaged through it until I found some rope. I tossed it to Mark. "We'll have to tie him up and take him with us to look for Wade."

It took both of us to disarm him and tie his wrists behind him. Even bound, Kieran looked about as harmless as a wolverine.

"Where's Wade?" I asked as Mark hauled him to his feet.

He gave a snort of amusement but wouldn't answer.

Since we couldn't find anything to secure him to, we dragged him along with us down the hallway, checking all the side doors in our search. I felt the coiled tension in Kieran and expected him to try to break free at any moment.

After a good deal of searching, we found Wade tied and gagged in a closet near the main entrance. I quickly cut him free. I wasn't sure if he was angrier with himself or with Kieran, but I'd never seen such a vicious look on Wade's face before.

He bounded to his feet and threw a right hook to Kieran's face that knocked him out of Mark's grip.

"Wade!" I protested.

Kieran stumbled and crashed against the wall, looking dazed.

Wade grabbed the front of Kieran's shirt and hauled him closer, until their noses were only inches apart. "The only reason I don't kill you now is that you're Tristan's family," Wade warned. "But if you do anything to harm Councilmember Markkel or Susan, I won't let that stop me again."

Kieran jerked in surprise when he heard Mark's name. He darted a sideways look at Mark.

Of course. He would know the story of the Restorer's son and the prophecy. I saw him putting together the pieces, studying both of us.

Wade turned to Mark and began an elaborate apology for failing to protect us, but Mark interrupted. "Wade, just take him to the Council Guard. We need to get home."

"Wait." I pulled Mark a short way down the hall. "I don't think he really meant to hurt me. He's just desperate to get into tomorrow's session."

Mark looked at the blood splattered on my shirt. "Susan, I'd like to trust your instincts, but if he won't tell us why he wants to get into the Council session, we can't let him in. Maybe he just wants to address the Council, but if so, why doesn't he tell us?"

"He doesn't trust us. He despises the Council."

"All the more reason to be careful. He could be an assassin. He could be spying for Hazor. You told me yourself his mother was Hazorite. Who knows where his loyalties lie?"

I shook my head and walked back to our prisoner. Trussed

up and bleeding from Wade's blow, Kieran nonetheless emanated danger like radiation. "Just tell us why you need to get in tomorrow." It was a reasonable request, and I tried to infuse my voice with Restorer power — or, if that failed, at least to coax him into trusting us.

The corner of his mouth quirked in a bitter half-smile. "I know better than to trust anyone working for the Council, Susan of Ridgeview Drive."

I turned back to Mark in frustration. "Maybe Wade could keep him under guard at your place until after the session tomorrow."

Mark shook his head. "We need Wade to testify on your behalf. Cameron could ask the Council to try you for the murder of the Rhusican. We really don't have any options. We have to turn him over to the guardians."

I started to object, but Wade spoke up. "Susan, I'll take him personally to the captain of the Lyric guardians. I'll be sure Cameron's Council guards don't find out anything about him."

I appreciated his effort to find a solution I could live with, especially when I knew how angry he was at Kieran. I nodded in relief.

Wade grabbed his prisoner's arm and headed down the hall.

Kieran jerked away and turned to look at me. "I have to be at the session tomorrow." His feverish eyes were angry, but there was desperation along with the snarl of warning in his tone. "You're making a mistake."

Wade shoved him toward the door.

Kieran kept his footing and tried once more. This time he looked at Mark. "You don't want me for an enemy, Markkel of Rendor," he said. "Don't do this."

A chill of dread ran through me.

Mark faced him calmly, his own eyes glacial. "You lost any chance of my help when you touched my wife." He nodded to Wade, who hauled Kieran from the building.

Mark had hidden his anxiety well when a tornado approached our neighborhood one summer, and when the city was planning to assess our street for a new sidewalk we couldn't afford, and when Anne's birth had run into complications. But his courage today impressed me on a new level. It was only when Wade and Kieran were out of sight that he rubbed his face, as if trying to erase the worry that was settling into the lines there.

Hazorites, Rhusicans, Cameron, and now Kieran. We were heading into the Council session with one more threat added to the list confronting us. Heading back through the portal was beginning to sound like a very good idea.

Chapter Twenty-Six

MARK LED ME UNDER THE VAULTING arches of the Council hall entry. The grandeur of the black onyx floors and crystal-lined walls brought home to me the gravity of what we were facing today. Why were government buildings always so obviously designed to make an individual feel insignificant? The scale of the foyer dwarfed us. Our footsteps echoed as we crossed to the entrance for the Council chambers.

Mark looked at ease in his rust tunic and black trousers. He carried himself with confidence. I tugged at the hem of my own apprentice garb, feeling conspicuous. My hair was neatly braided back from my face, and I kept touching it, checking that it was still in place.

The reassuring bulk of Wade's presence hovered behind us. Linette walked to my right with youthful grace, unawed by the setting. She served a more powerful master than the Council.

I reminded myself that I did, too.

My first hurdle came at the door into the inner tower. Several Council guards stood beside the entrance, complete with black vests and abundant weaponry. I recognized one of them from the group that had taken me from Braide Wood, and my feet slowed, as if of their own accord.

Mark noticed and put a hand on the small of my back, guiding me forward. He announced our titles as Rendor councilmembers. There was some question about whether Linette and Wade would be allowed inside, but Mark insisted that they were under the sponsorship of Rendor for this session because they would be testifying. The guards let us pass, and I began to breathe normally again.

We entered a hall that curved around the outside of the chamber. Mark had explained to me that there were twelve doors leading from this hall. The doors opened to the outer office delegated to each clan. Two doors had remained unused for many years, since the clans beyond Morsal Plains had withdrawn from the Council.

The other ten offices were used as places to meet and discuss votes. They also served as waiting areas for guests that were going to be called to testify. These outer offices also held the doors into the central Council chamber.

When Mark slid the door open for the Rendor outer office, we counted about a half a dozen people in the room, including Jorgen.

Though I had met him yesterday, there was protocol to observe today for my first public appearance as a Rendor apprentice. "It is an honor to address you, Chief Councilmember of Rendor. I am grateful for your sponsorship and am happy to serve you as an apprentice councilmember."

It was the formal greeting Mark had taught me. I wished I could say what I was really thinking. "Thank you for seeing us yesterday, for taking this risk, for bending the rules, for getting Mark back on the Council, and for providing a way for me to get in. We won't let you down." But I kept those words to myself.

When Jorgen spoke to the room at large, I thought how well he would fit in a Wagner opera—complete with Viking helmet. His whole bearing was larger than life. "Welcome her into Rendor clan," he proclaimed. This announcement formally ensured my status and brought a flurry of introductions and greetings from other Rendor councilmembers in the room.

I struggled to remember names and give innocuous answers to questions about where I had met Mark and why Jorgen had chosen to sponsor an apprentice who had never even visited Rendor. It was almost a relief to hear the clarion sound of a signaler from within the central chambers. The tone played for a few seconds, stopped, resumed, and continued the pattern. Like a tolling bell, its twelve chimes represented a call to the twelve clans. Though only ten clans remained, the tradition was never changed.

All conversation stopped, and Jorgen walked to the door that led into the Council chamber. The other people wearing the uniform of the Council lined up behind him.

Other than a handful of guards, only actual councilmembers were allowed to continue from these outer offices into the Council chamber. Wade and Linette would wait in the Rendor office until they were called as witnesses. When the last tone finished its high, clear call, Jorgen shoved the heavy sliding door open and stepped forward.

He led the Rendor contingent into the chamber. Mark and I stayed at the end of the column, and Mark slid the door closed behind us once all the councilmembers had passed through.

I was grateful that our low status meant we were in a back row of chairs. I took the opportunity provided by our anonymity to look around the room without feeling conspicuous.

Delegations from each of the other clans were entering their own area of the tower. Twelve segments were partitioned off with wooden railings to form low balconies, with a raked floor leading down toward the middle of the room, where arguments were made and testimonies given. The number of delegates in each section varied. Some had groups of close to twenty members; others had three or four people representing the clan. Mark had explained to me that each clan controlled one vote, cast by the chief councilmember of the clan. It was up to each clan to decide how many other representatives they sent to the session.

The Corros Fields Council chief, Landon, stood in the center of the room and called the roll. The short, round man's black trousers disappeared against the polished stone floor, giving the appearance of his rust tunic hovering like a fat, disembodied ghost. He was the head of today's session. Every clan took turns in rotation at conducting a day's session.

I wished it were Jorgen's turn. I stayed low in my chair, peeking between the shoulders of the delegates in front of me. I spotted Cameron in the Lyric segment of the tower and had to clench my hands together in my lap to stop their sudden trembling.

Each clan's chief councilmember stood and announced the presence of his clan, along with the name and sponsorship of each member present. As Cameron spoke for Lyric in his resonant voice, my breathing became short and shallow, despite my best efforts to remain calm. Mark reached over for my hand. Grateful, I nestled my cold fingers into his warm palm. His eyes were fixed and hard; his jaw muscles worked as he stared across the room.

Focused on getting my feelings of panic under control, I almost missed the first issue addressed.

"Blue Knoll brings a case against Vaughn of Shamgar.

Bardon of Blue Knoll was traveling in the Gray Hills and was attacked and robbed." The Blue Knoll Council chief introduced Bardon, as well as a witness who had traveled with him. They gave a quick explanation of what happened. A few delegates asked clarifying questions, the Blue Knoll Council chief asked for banishment, a quick vote was passed, and the two witnesses left the room.

"Mark," I whispered, "what about the guy they accused? He didn't get to say anything. He didn't get to confront his accuser."

"This isn't our world," he said quietly.

"What will happen now?"

"They've already made the decision. Now they'll send two Council guards to find him and escort him to the closest border."

"But that would be Hazor!" I had a million more questions, but one of the women on the Rendor Council turned and glared at us over her shoulder.

"Lyric brings a case against Tristan of Braide Wood." Cameron had taken center stage, and I bit my lower lip. There was a low murmur through the room. "I have the testimony of Susan of Braide Wood, given before my witness, who is an honored guest to Lyric, Medea of the Rhusican people." There were more undercurrents of conversation as the woman I had seen in Cameron's office was ushered into the room.

She wore a long, loose tunic in variegated shades of green. Her gaze traveled around the room, making effective eye contact with each chief councilmember as she shared how her husband had disappeared and how she had worked tirelessly to find him. All around, councilmembers leaned forward, nodding with sympathy.

Furious and worried, I grabbed Mark's arm. He rested his hand over mine, the warm pressure giving me fleeting comfort. Then the tension in his muscles and growing worry lines on his face as he watched the proceedings stole the moment of reassurance away.

Cameron thanked her and addressed the Council once again. "I was able to find out the truth about what happened to Medea's husband. He was murdered by a Braide Wood guardian . . . a man sworn to uphold the word of the Council and protect guests within our borders. Susan of Braide Wood witnessed the murder and revealed the truth under questioning. Tristan tracked him down for the sole purpose of revenge and killed him. The law leaves no question; Tristan must be banished."

Landon called for a vote, and I realized that legal events in Lyric moved at lightning speed compared to my world. In mere seconds Tristan's entire life would be over. He'd be banished, and Braide Wood would lose the captain of their guardians when they needed him most.

I jumped to my feet, pushed between two of the chairs in the front row, and grabbed the railing in front of the Rendor section of the tower. "Wait!" I shouted. "You don't have all the information."

Dozens of eyes turned toward me, and several voices responded in outrage to the interruption. Mark had tried to teach me protocol, but there were too many rules to remember.

"Identify yourself." Landon's voice screeched over the grumbling conversations. Medea smiled at me, tilting her head.

"I'm Susan of Braide Wood."

"Then you have no standing with Rendor," Landon said.

"Remove her." He turned his head to signal some of the leather-vested Council guards that were scattered throughout the tower.

"She has standing as a full member of Rendor clan." Mark's rich baritone voice rang out in the hall. He stepped up beside me. "I am Markkel of Rendor. She is my wife and an apprentice with sponsorship of Chief Councilmember Jorgen."

Cameron sneered. "Then let her step forward to testify. You can hear for yourself how she witnessed Tristan commit murder."

By now the room was in an uproar. Could I walk down the inclined floor to the center of the tower? Could I stand near Cameron and his Rhusican ally? Could I keep them from twisting my words?

"I'm not allowed to go with you," Mark whispered. "But the One will be by your side. Just don't break any more rules. I'm surprised they didn't throw you out. Stay within protocol."

I smoothed down my tunic and left the haven of the Rendor balcony. Making my way quickly down the ramp to the center of the chamber, I looked up at the faces all around. Not wanting to give Cameron a chance to take control, I spoke out immediately. "Yes, I was in Shamgar. Yes, I saw Tristan. A Rhusican with a sword was attacking him. He was defending himself."

Cameron interrupted. "You saw him kill the man?"

"Yes, but—"

"Then there is nothing more to say."

"I heard the Rhusican man. He bragged about what he had done to Tristan's wife, Kendra." Cameron tried to cut me off, but I shouted over the agitated discussion in the room. "The man said, 'It won't do any good, Tristan. Kendra won't be coming back.' He was the man who poisoned Kendra."

The chatter stopped, and shocked silence seized the room.

The Braide Wood Council chief stood, fists pressing down against the railing in front of him. "I can testify that Kendra was taken ill with a strange poison of the mind. She has suffered for two seasons, and the healers haven't been able to help her."

The Rhusican woman took a step toward the Braide Wood section of the tower. "We are new to your lands and have been grieved to learn about the illnesses your people endure. When we offered our alliance to you, we hoped to help you with this problem, as well as with others you face." Her voice was soothing and mesmerizing. The mood in the chamber began to shift. She looked around the room and continued. "You can imagine how distressed I am that my husband, who was brutally murdered within your borders, is now being accused of something so reprehensible." She played the sweet, frail victim with amazing skill. Next she'd be saying, "I've always depended on the kindness of strangers" in a southern, Blanche DuBois accent.

She turned to me, hypnotic color twirling in her irises.

I quickly looked away.

Cameron took a step to stand beside Medea. "We don't need to go back over old ground. The last session agreed to an alliance with the Rhusican people. They are our allies. We owe them justice. In fact, since Tristan murdered one of their people, I recommend that, instead of banishment, we turn him over to the Rhusican people. They can try him in their own land." A rumble of agreement moved throughout the cavernous room.

Cameron was succeeding. Medea was using her Rhusican ability to twist the truth, and I could feel sympathy for her growing in the hall. And because of the rules of their Council, Tristan couldn't even be here to defend himself. Not that he would. He'd probably loyally surrender his sword and his life to his precious Council, no matter how confused and manipulated they had become.

And Cameron wasn't finished.

"I realize that this isn't normal protocol, but there is another case I need to present, and since they are linked, with the permission of the Corros Fields Council chief, I will share it now."

Landon nodded his approval, and Cameron turned to me, showing his teeth. "There has been another murder."

Gasps and frenzied whispers circulated through the room. "Lyric, on behalf of our allies, the Rhusicans, brings a case again Susan of Braide Wood . . . or Rendor, or whatever loyalties she claims at the moment." Disdain dripped from his words. "A Rhusican man with the welcome and protection of the Council visited Braide Wood. He was in quiet conversation with two young people when this foreigner"—he pointed at me—"attacked him and stabbed him with her sword. He was unarmed. I call for a vote. Lyric demands she be turned over to the Rhusican people for their justice."

Two of the Council guards moved a few steps closer, preparing for the foregone conclusion. My heart raced. The faces around the room were a wall of hostility.

Jorgen lumbered to his feet. "Rendor has a witness to present." His strong, calm voice slowed the current of animosity. Wade and Linette were each brought in, in turn. Cameron forced them to admit that their memories of the event were foggy and uncertain. I knew it was because of the strange mental sleep the Rhusican had cast on them, but the Council wasn't going to believe that. Mark had sent a messenger to find Kyle, but he hadn't returned yet. My only reliable witness wasn't here, and my fear grew. Before Cameron could again call for a vote, the Braide Wood Council chief rose.

"I speak for Bekkah of Braide Wood. She is not able to be here, but she investigated this incident as a trusted member of the guardians. She questioned Kyle of Braide Wood, who confirmed that the man attacked Susan. She lifted her sword in defense, and the Rhusican's own momentum impaled him."

Medea's laughter tinkled through the room. "Well, this will not be a difficult decision for all you wise councilmembers." She turned slowly, again looking at each chief councilmember with a conspiratorial smile. "She talks with an unarmed man, and moments later he is dead with her sword in his chest. None of the witnesses denies that fact."

A wave of despair crashed against my resolve. She was even convincing me that my defense was implausible. I was a murderer, and so was Tristan. I was going to be dragged away and given over to the Rhusicans. I looked up toward the Rendor balcony.

Mark stood and gripped the balcony railing with such force that the muscles of his arms bulged against his tunic sleeves. He was leaning forward.

I let him see the hopelessness in my face.

His mouth moved. What was he saying? I let my hearing stretch and focused on his words that were too soft for anyone else to hear. "The Verses."

I blinked and shook myself. "Honored councilmembers," I said before Landon could call for a vote. "Like Medea, I come from another land. But my people serve the One, just as you do. We also have Verses."

Cameron moved toward me to interrupt.

I held up my hand and continued. "They tell the story of a great Council leader, who was also a guardian who fought for his people. Enemies with greater might surrounded them on all sides. But this leader reminded the people that their strength came from fearing the One and serving only Him. He spoke to the whole nation and said, 'Choose for yourselves this day whom you will serve, whether the gods your forefathers served beyond the River, or the gods of the Amorites, in whose land you are living. But as for me and my household, we will serve the Lord.'"

I looked around at the faces of the various councilmembers. I felt their decision balancing on the edge of a blade. "You are the People of the Verses. You follow the One. You must stand against the voices that lie and control your minds. Cameron said earlier that you don't need to go back over old ground. He's wrong. Last session you established an alliance with the Rhusicans, though such ties are forbidden in the Verses. Choose this day whom you will serve. You can't have both."

Medea laughed sweetly. "Such a childish way to look at things. Of course you can have both. We are only here to help you where your One hasn't been able to."

I scanned the room. Too many eyes were still clouded with confusion. I didn't know how to fight the control Medea had over so many in the Council. But I had to try. "Honored Council, because I'm a newcomer, I haven't yet learned all your Verses. Would you please indulge me? What do the Verses say? 'Awesome in majesty . . .'"

"Is the One eternal," the councilmembers responded automatically.

"Perfect in His might and power," Mark projected clearly into the room, still on his feet.

Jorgen rose to stand beside him in the Rendor balcony and bellowed, "The only truth and only source."

"He made all that is and loves all He made," the answering voices proclaimed in unison.

"His works are beyond our understanding." The

councilmembers continued reciting these core truths; one by one people rose to their feet as the words continued, and the strength in their voices grew.

The current had turned. The hostility and fear faded from the faces around the room. They were no longer focusing on Cameron, Medea, or me. They looked across the chamber at their fellow clans, reveling in the unity they shared, drawing strength from the Verses.

I soaked in the power of their words.

They continued on to the promise of the Deliverer to come. Then Jorgen began singing the hymn I had heard two days earlier at the gathering. The entire Council joined him. I even saw a few of the Council guards moving their mouths.

> *Awesome in majesty, perfect in power,*
> *One to deliver us, He is our tower.*
> *Enemies circle us, darkness descending;*
> *He is the Morning Light, love without ending.*

I was lost in the beauty of the hymn resonating through the room and almost missed the sudden blur of movement at my side. I turned.

Medea ran at me with something in her raised hand. Her face contorted with rage.

I stumbled back, but everything happened too fast. Her fist came down, and I realized as a razor-sharp blade cut into my chest that the object in her hand was a knife.

I collapsed to my knees from the force of her attack. Time stopped, and I turned my head to watch Mark catapult over the railing to race toward me. In the second of shock before I felt pain, two Council guards ran forward to pull Medea away. Her face twisted in a snarling scream, but I didn't hear the sound. It was like watching a muted television from far away. It didn't seem real.

I fell back and knew Mark was there. His arms supported me. I wanted to thank him. The pain exploded, and I couldn't speak.

He pulled the knife from my chest. I noticed from a strange mental distance that the curved blade was beautifully designed. My lungs gurgled when I tried to breathe.

Mark's eyes were wide with panic and anguish. His lips moved, calling my name, but I couldn't hear anything but a roaring hum. I wanted to tell him I'd be all right, but I was swallowed up in darkness. As his face faded from my sight, I wondered how many rules of protocol had just been broken.

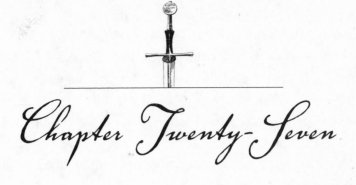

Chapter Twenty-Seven

"SUSAN, CAN YOU HEAR ME?" THERE was a tickle by my ear. I reached up to brush it away, and my hand whacked something warm and scratchy.

"Ow! Look out!" Mark protested.

My eyes popped open.

I had flailed my knuckles into his whisker-stubbled face. His blue-gray eyes were inches from mine. They shimmered, and I almost thought they filled with tears.

I couldn't study them long enough to figure it out, because Mark pulled me close, burying my face against him with a groan of relief. "I wasn't sure you would heal," he whispered.

"Where are we?" I squeaked, thinking that if he squeezed me much harder, I'd pass out again.

He loosened his grip so I could look around. "The outer Rendor office. They sent for a Lyric healer. How do you feel?"

I tried to assess that. "A little sore, but I can breathe again. That's an improvement." I touched the furrows on Mark's forehead, trying to smooth away his worry. "Did that Rhusican really go crazy and stab me?"

"Mm hmm," Mark answered, checking the cloth he had pressed against my sternum. "Looks like the bleeding has stopped."

"So what did the Council do? Are they finally figuring out what the Rhusicans have been doing to them?"

Mark nodded. "After the guards dragged Medea off, I carried you out here, and they sent for help. There was so much chaos in the chamber, they almost decided to stop for the day, but Jorgen convinced them without too much trouble that it was important to move ahead on some decisions."

"Good. When they were singing, I could see them waking up. I wouldn't want them to lose that."

Mark stroked the hair back from my forehead. "Don't worry. They felt terrible about the attack, but they were way too stirred up to walk away for the day. They had quite the discussion. One of the apprentices slipped out to tell me about it. The Songs really broke the hold the Rhusicans had on so many in the Council. And seeing Medea lose control and attack you helped, too. Chief councilmembers started reporting all sorts of strange problems that happened in any clan visited by the Rhusicans. They've come to their senses and voted to revoke their welcome to any Rhusicans in our borders."

I nodded and felt a rush of satisfaction. I was so tired of battling their lies. Strength surged back into me as I thought of them being sent back to where they came from. The People of the Verses still faced some powerful enemies, but with their hearts twisted and controlled, there hadn't been any hope at all. Now we could move forward. "And did they kick out Cameron, too?" I asked.

"No, Cameron acted shocked at Medea's actions and convinced the Council that he really believed they meant to help us." Mark shrugged. "Who knows? Maybe he was deceived by them, too."

I pushed myself up on my elbows and looked down at my

tunic. The rust color didn't do much to hide the blood all over it or the gash over my heart. "Um, Mark? I think I'll need a new tunic."

He started chuckling, and I joined him. Our giddy relief made everything seem funny. We were still laughing helplessly when the door to the outer hall burst open. Wade rushed in, dragging a woman by the arm. When he released her, she glared at him and took a split-second to smooth her crisp green tunic and touch her hair, which was pulled back into a neat braid. Then she lifted her cloth bag and hurried toward us.

"Step aside," she ordered in a calm, businesslike voice. She knelt on the floor beside me and began efficiently pulling items from her bag, though she spared a moment to glare at Mark. "You pulled the knife out?" When he nodded, she shook her head. "Next time leave it until help arrives. You can cause more bleeding and damage by removing it."

"Next time?" I gasped. That struck me as so funny that I started giggling again.

The healer looked at me in alarm. Wade slipped outside to stand guard, and Mark hovered while the healer examined a wound that had already closed. "I don't understand. I thought you were attacked." Her eyes took in the sticky blood on my skin and tunic, and turned back to the gash that was fading to a thin scar.

I looked at Mark, not sure what to say.

She didn't wait for an explanation, but pulled something that looked like a light cube from her bag. Attaching small patches to several places over my heart, she studied the cube in her hand. With a professional smile that didn't match the worry in her eyes, she patted my shoulder. "Just rest here. This will keep you warm to prevent shock." She pulled a paper-thin sheet of fabric from her bag and unfurled it over me.

I instantly felt as if I were bundled in a huge heating pad and sighed with pleasure.

The Lyric healer pulled Mark to the far side of the room and held the cube in her hands up to him. She spoke in low tones, but I had no trouble eavesdropping.

"You can see where the knife blade entered the heart. It's healed well." She paused, waiting for an explanation from Mark, but he didn't say anything, so she continued. "But look at this." She pointed to something else.

"What does it mean?" Mark asked her, all levity gone from his voice.

"I'm not sure. There is some kind of scarring from a past injury. Has she had any other symptoms?"

"She's been short of breath sometimes . . . seemed to have some chest pain."

"I'm surprised she's been walking around at all. Her heart is severely damaged."

She had the sympathetic but aloof expression that I remembered from the doctor who told our family that my dad's cancer was terminal.

Mark recognized the look as well, and the color washed from his face. "How is that possible?"

The healer started to explain again, but Mark shook his head. "You don't understand. She's the Restorer."

The healer fumbled the cube in her hands and nearly dropped it. "What did you say?" Her medical poise crumbled. She pulled Mark farther away and sank into a chair. "Are you sure?"

"Yes, I'm sure." He looked at her without blinking. "I know a little bit about the signs of a Restorer. Can you help her?"

The healer rubbed her forehead. "I don't know. Was she

injured before her Restorer powers began to work? Do you know what caused this damage?"

"I think it was Cameron. He interrogated her with drugs."

The healer bristled. "I've told the Council time and again that they shouldn't be using those chemicals without a healer present. Who knows how they might affect the people he interviews from foreign nations? I don't care how much he insists that he's only protecting our security, it's wrong to be using drugs for those purposes."

Mark interrupted before she could step farther up onto her soapbox. "She was already manifesting Restorer healing before he questioned her. I don't understand why the damage hasn't healed."

"I don't know what to tell you." The healer glanced over at me and seemed to realize that I was following their conversation. "The only other Restorer in my lifetime was Mikkel, but I never saw him. Maybe a Rendor healer would have more information. In the meantime, make sure she gets lots of rest and avoids putting strain on her heart. I have some herbs that are helpful in promoting healing."

It was tempting to keep resting under the warm sheet, but I knew I had to get moving. From the time he found out I was the Restorer, Mark had lived with worry and fear. In the past few days he had become resigned to my role and determined to help. In the process his anxiety had gradually eased somewhat. I didn't want to lose that ground to vague worries about my health.

"Mark, could you send Wade to get a new tunic for me?" I pushed the sheet aside and levered myself to my feet. "What is the Council discussing right now?"

He hurried over to me, opening his mouth to argue.

I held up a hand to interrupt him. "Mark, we'll go crazy if we try to figure this out. I feel fine, and we have work to do."

He pressed his lips together, holding back his obvious objections. Finally, his shoulders hunched with resignation. "I think they were planning to move on to a protest against Cameron for removing the Records to Lyric."

I wrapped the warm sheet around me like a cloak and smiled at the healer. "Thanks for your help. Can I keep this?"

She nodded, a bit dazed at having a patient walk around minutes after having a knife removed from her heart. Mark walked her to the door and paused to talk to Wade.

I stared at the closed door into the inner Council chamber and focused my hearing.

"We have no idea what Kahlarea is planning, and we know that Hazor's power is beyond anything we can fight." It was Cameron's voice raised in protest. "Lyric is the best place to keep our historic treasures. The Council Guard could protect them if they were all in one place." Several other voices shouted in disagreement, and I heard Landon trying to maintain order.

Then I made out Jorgen's rich bass voice. "If your Council Guard is so good at protecting them, how is it they were returned to us so quickly?"

"Who returned them to you?" Cameron demanded.

"You need to be answering our questions, not asking them, Councilmember. You are the one who took unauthorized action. There is not one chief councilmember here that will support your wishes to keep all the Records in Lyric."

"I admit I acted in haste, but only out of a desire to protect the Records. Of course I was planning to return them to each of you if you disagreed with my decision," Cameron said.

Mark came to stand behind me.

"Cameron is back-pedaling fast," I said, grinning. Then my smile faded. "He's lost his Rhusican allies, and his plan to change the Records didn't work. He's going to hate us."

Mark reached up to massage the muscles in my shoulders. "But he's losing his power in the Council. He won't be able to hurt you."

I could tell Mark was trying to convince himself more than me, but I leaned back against him and tried to believe him.

"Susan?" He turned me to face him. "Everyone in there saw you take a dagger to the heart. If you go back in, they will all know that you are the Restorer. I don't know why Cameron didn't tell them. Maybe he thought it would give you too much credibility. At any rate, there's no hiding it now."

Determination bolstered my courage. I met Mark's eyes. "Then it's time for them to know the truth. We need to get back in there before they start discussing Braide Wood and Hazor."

"They'll be taking a break soon. We'll get cleaned up and go in then. Jorgen can address the Council when the time is right."

I was happy to follow his advice on how to approach the Council. Most of their operating procedures were inexplicable to me.

Mark's brows lowered. "Are you sure you're up for this?"

"I don't have a choice."

He nodded and gathered me into a gentle hug. I stayed in his arms until Wade returned with a new tunic for me.

"Braide Wood requests the help of the Council." The Braide Wood Council chief had a voice as thin as his fragile frame. Then he recounted the message that Nolan had delivered. I was amazed once again at the skill these people had for memorizing. Nolan had recited the threat and terms to Tristan. Tristan gave the information to a messenger who traveled to Lyric and reported to the Braide Wood Council chief. As far as I could remember them, he had the terms down word for word. I hated hearing them again and shifted in my chair, careful to stay hidden.

When Jorgen and the other Rendor councilmembers had come out for a break, Mark had quickly explained to them why I was on my feet and relatively whole. Watching the play of emotions on Jorgen's face gave me a good indication of what I'd face in the Council. He was awed and glad that I had survived. But his eyes darted to Mark, his mind clearly on the prophecy that had seemed to say Mikkel's son would be the next Restorer. As Mark explained further, Jorgen measured me with his eyes, and he couldn't hide his disappointment. The People needed a Restorer/guardian to protect their borders. Instead, Jorgen saw a thin slip of a woman with little training or skill. His doubts were evident. Perhaps this time the One had made a mistake.

Still, he agreed to present my claim to the Council at the appropriate time, which would enable me to speak to the Council. To avoid further disturbing the order of the session, when the Rendor group entered the inner chamber, I was tucked in the back row again, sandwiched between Mark and another tall man. Keeping my head down, I was able to listen to everything going on, but others in the low balconies around the tower would only see one more rust-clad shape in the background.

". . . unless, within the time of twenty days, Braide Wood delivers tribute to Zarek, King of Hazor, in Sidian." He was wrapping up. "The tribute demanded is for you to give each Braide Wood child of fewer than twelve years to Sidian as a surety. Deliver them before nightfall of the twentieth day, and they will live and Braide Wood will be unharmed. If the tribute is not met, they will die along with every other soul in Braide Wood."

"How strong is Hazor? Do we have enough guardians to defend Braide Wood?" Jorgen asked.

"What good will a few hundred guardians do against their weapons? Even if we matched their numbers, it would be hopeless," another chief councilmember spoke out.

"How many children would it be? It seems like a small price to pay to maintain peace with Hazor," someone else interrupted.

I stiffened, but Mark patted my knee, and I squeezed my lips together to keep from blurting out an argument.

The Shamgar Council chief rose to his feet. "Raise an army and attack Hazor now."

I was surprised to find myself on the same side of an issue with him. The People of the Verses couldn't surrender their children. The One promised them protection if they turned to Him. There had to be a way to hold back the Hazorite armies.

"The Shamgar Council chief certainly knows what can happen to a clan that Hazor decides to attack." Cameron crossed his arms and projected his charisma. He was almost as dangerous as the Rhusicans.

"That happened because Shamgar forgot the Verses," I hissed.

"Shh," Mark warned.

Cameron leaned forward with an oily smile. "With the aid of the chief councilmembers of Shamgar and of Corros Fields, I have anticipated this danger and have been able to buy syncbeams for our use. I have a team of transtechs studying them and reproducing more as well. We will soon be on equal footing with the nations around us, able to defend or even expand our borders." Lyric's chief councilmember had bounced back from the earlier rebuke of the Council. His voice was thick with pride as he presented himself as the forward-thinking hero who could provide the solution to this problem. But the Verses forbade everything Cameron had been doing. "Of course, it will take several seasons to be fully armed, so I agree that for the time being, it makes sense to surrender the children. Choose two guardians to escort them to Sidian and be sure that they arrive safely."

The room buzzed with discussion, every cluster of councilmembers taking time to deliberate within their delegation. After a time, Landon asked each chief councilmember to present the opinion of their clan.

I was dismayed to hear how much consensus was growing to appease Hazor until the People could build up more strength. They would address the issue of developing long-range weapons later—there was still lively disagreement about that—but Landon seemed ready to call a vote on the issue of Hazor's demands.

When Cameron rose to speak, he thanked everyone for supporting his suggestion—again revealing his power to sway the Council, even without a Rhusican to help him cloud minds. "In my trade negotiations with the people of Hazor, I have found them to be an enlightened nation, and it will be a benefit to both our peoples to send children to live within their borders. I'm sure that it will open the door for an ongoing relationship with Hazor. We need their alliance to hold Kahlarea back beyond the River Borders. Think of it as a kind of apprenticeship, as the Braide Wood children have the opportunity to learn new things to benefit all of the clans one day."

I didn't want to embarrass Jorgen by breaking more rules,

but I couldn't listen to this anymore. I leaned forward, about to push myself to my feet, when I heard someone across the room gasp, "Look!"

"Except that isn't what Hazor plans for your children," said a cold, clear voice. I knew that voice.

I peeked around the shoulders of the councilmember in front of me, trying to see.

Most of the heads were turning toward one of the empty balconies held open for the two clans that had withdrawn from the Council years ago. The light-walls for those two segments of the tower were off, and darkness shielded the cloaked and hooded man until he stepped forward toward the railing.

"Identify yourself," Landon shouted, as murmurs of surprise, anger, and speculation grew throughout the chamber.

"Kieran of Braide Wood," he said, calmly ignoring the uproar he was causing.

Mark and I gasped in unison. How did he get here? How had he escaped the Lyric guardians? He must have slipped through the unused clan office, but how had he made it into the chamber unseen? Landon looked over to the skinny Braide Wood Council chief, who shook his head.

"He is not under our sponsorship," he stammered, not wanting blame for this unexpected interruption. "He did not petition us."

"Then he has no right to speak. Remove him." Two Council guards marched toward the dark balcony.

Kieran ran down the ramp to the center of the tower, drawing his sword and tossing aside his cloak. "If you won't hear me as a son of Braide Wood, then I claim audience as a representative of Hazor." He was wearing a short gray tunic with a jagged black emblem across the chest, and he kept his sword raised.

His eyes still looked glassy with fever, and his angular face projected a dangerous force of will. The Council guards looked to Landon, not eager to advance on Kieran. The tableau froze for a moment while a flustered Landon took a few steps back.

"All right," he decided at last, gesturing the guards back. "If you can support your claim, we will hear you."

The whole Council burst into conversation now, so it was easy for me to talk to Mark without risk of discovery. "What on earth is he doing?"

"Clever." Mark leaned forward and watched the action in the middle of the room. "It forces the Council to allow him to speak. But if he claims to represent Hazor now, he's renouncing his place in Braide Wood clan, and the People."

I knew Kieran had isolated himself from his people and was estranged from his father. But I had seen him looking down on the rooftops of his village with his soul in his eyes. He loved his clan. What could drive him to do this?

"I am Hazorite by birth, on my mother's side. I have spent the recent days in Sidian. I am here to tell you exactly what Zarek plans for your children." Kieran's eyes burned as he glared at the Braide Wood delegation.

"We will hear you." Landon backed away slowly as if he were in the presence of a rabid dog. "But you are no messenger under flag of truce. We will hear you, but we will not guarantee amnesty."

"Fine." Kieran sheathed his sword in a fluid motion. He was clearly long past caring what would happen to him after this. All he focused on was this opportunity to address the Council.

"Honored councilmembers." He used the correct terms and almost managed to hide his sarcasm. "You are debating something you know nothing about."

More murmurs rumbled though the room. Wearing the emblem of Hazor, interrupting the Council, and now insulting them—he wasn't winning friends here.

"Hazor worships the hill gods." The room quieted in confusion at this detour in his speech. What did that have to do with anything? "Until Shamgar fell, Hazor feared the rumors of the One who was all-powerful and protected the People of the Verses. They stayed behind their borders. They heard about the Restorers that had been sent to drive back Kahlarea. And they waited. But once they were able to defeat Shamgar, their thinking changed. During his reign, Zarek has called all of Hazor to serve the hill gods with new fervor, in preparation for conquering both the People and Kahlarea."

Most of the faces around the room looked as confused as I felt.

"But Zarek had a problem." Kieran turned slowly, addressing each part of the tower. "The hill gods require frequent sacrifices, and that didn't fit well with Zarek's plan to build an army." He paused and waited for a response, but the councilmembers shifted and looked at each other, bewildered.

"Idiots," Kieran snapped under his breath. Then he spoke loudly again. "The Hazorites sacrifice their children to the hill gods." He paused to watch the councilmembers recoil. "To build his next generation of armies, Zarek needs to find a new source for the sacrifices. That's why he has demanded a tribute of children from Braide Wood."

"No." A man from Blue Knoll stood, seeming more offended by Kieran's revealing the facts than by the facts themselves. "That can't be true."

"I was there. I heard Zarek's plans," Kieran answered, expressionless.

"We would have heard something if this were really going on," a woman in one of the balconies protested.

"No one here has had dealings with Hazor." Kieran rubbed his right temple. "Except Cameron, and it didn't suit his purposes to tell you . . . if he even bothered to find out."

Cameron stayed silent, and discussion began to swirl around the room again.

"I've seen it," Kieran said, his jaw clenching. "I've seen them bind their own children and drag them into their dark temple. And they let the children know what's going to come. They want them to scream. They believe it gets the attention of the hill gods."

I sank back into my seat, stomach roiling. Nolan had told me about Hazor's plans and the growing boldness of his nation. It made sense. But as I glanced around the tower, I saw that most people were too shocked to believe Kieran.

He saw it too. He pulled himself up taller. "There's more."

The conversation stopped and all eyes turned to him again.

"Shamgar was destroyed when I was young. We were taught the story about the destruction and how every adult was killed and the children were carried away. Both Tristan and I had cousins among the children who were taken. After I grew up, I decided to search for them. Against the wishes of my clan and my family, I began to travel into Hazor, trying to find out what happened to the Shamgar children. That's when I found out they all had been used in sacrifices years earlier."

"You've already declared yourself to be a Hazorite and an enemy of our people." Landon stepped forward, showing irritation that once again the Council meeting had spiraled out of his control. "We have no one's word but your own."

Kieran was in an impossible position. He'd been working in

secret for so long that he had no one to vouch for him.

"You have *my* word." Tristan stepped forward from the back rows of the Braide Wood Council balcony, his commanding voice edged with exhaustion.

How many other people were hiding in the wings today? I grinned.

Landon's expression turned livid at yet another disruption. "Identify your —"

"I am Tristan, captain of the guardians of Braide Wood." More buzzing hit the room, but before Landon could object, Tristan continued. "I am here at the request of the Council. I was asked to search the River Borders by Cauldron Falls and bring a report to the Council."

"But you aren't scheduled to report for several days."

"I'm early," Tristan said dryly. He left the balcony, limping heavily as he walked down the ramp. He looked as if he hadn't slept since I saw him last. Though he was battered, grubby, and very cranky, it was wonderful to see him.

He stood beside his friend. I could hear Kieran's angry whisper, though his lips didn't move. "What do you think you're doing?"

Tristan returned his glare and spoke almost inaudibly through gritted teeth. "I'm helping." Then Tristan addressed Landon. "Although I am here to give my report, the Council will surely allow me also to give testimony where it is needed. I've known about Kieran's trips into Hazor for several years —"

"More evidence that Tristan is unfit to be a guardian!" Cameron shouted. "He was aware of these illegal acts and didn't report them." But everyone was too anxious to find out the truth, and they ignored Cameron.

"Everything Kieran told you is true." Tristan paused to

let that sink in. Dismay hit the surrounding faces as they lost their last hope of denial. "You cannot surrender the children to Hazor." Tristan planted his feet, rested his hand on his sword hilt, and took a deep breath. "Who will stand with Braide Wood?"

Heavy silence fell over the room. This was the moment when the clans should leap to their feet and offer unified support. Instead, someone coughed; someone else shuffled his feet.

It looked like Kieran's assessment was correct. They were a bunch of idiots. I pushed to my feet and elbowed my way to the railing. "I will!" I drew my sword and lifted it.

All eyes turned toward me, and gasps sounded from every direction. Landon looked apoplectic at yet another interruption.

"In every time of great need, a Restorer is sent to fight for the people and help the guardians," I recited. "'The Restorer is empowered with gifts to defeat our enemies and turn the people's hearts back to the Verses.' I stand with Braide Wood and the People of the Verses."

As far as dramatic entrances go, I thought it was very effective.

Chapter Twenty-Eight

FOR A FROZEN MOMENT, I ABSORBED the silence in the tower chamber.

Tristan didn't show his surprise, but the corner of his mouth twitched and he nodded. Kieran's eyes narrowed as he looked at me speculatively. Shock radiated off every other face. No matter how much they may have wanted to dismiss my statement as ridiculous, they had all seen me take a knife to the heart. And now I stood before them again. On their faces disbelief gave way to confusion.

The Shamgar chief councilmember spoke first. "But the prophecy said Mikkel's son would bring restoration."

Jorgen stepped forward and frowned at me until I lowered my sword and moved aside.

"This will be interesting," Kieran said to Tristan out of the side of his mouth.

"I apologize for this unconventional presentation," Jorgen said to the room at large. "It was my plan to introduce her to the Council at the proper time. Susan of Rendor, wife of Markkel, is a Restorer. I ask that she be given the right to leadership as part of the Council, and be allowed to address the Council." He scowled in my direction. "Within our guidelines."

"She's not one of our people," someone objected loudly. Cameron. What a surprise.

Mark stepped forward and touched Jorgen's arm. Jorgen nodded slightly to acknowledge him before he spoke to the Council again. "I ask that you hear the testimony of Markkel, son of Mikkel, councilmember of Rendor."

Landon threw up his hands and backed away as Mark walked slowly to the center of the room. Tristan also stepped back, his gaze ping-ponging between Mark and me in confusion. He'd only heard me speak of my husband Mark as someone from my own world.

Mark stopped dead center, a wary distance from Kieran, and looked up at the ring of faces. "I am Markkel. You know who my father was, and you know the prophecy."

How did he keep his voice so calm and even? He sounded like he was giving a corporate project report to his team at the office.

"Everyone assumed I would be the next Restorer, including the Kahlareans. Many of you have heard about the assassins they sent to kill me. Because of the danger, I was sent away until the time when I would be needed and when my gifts would become evident. That's where I met Susan. By marriage she *is* one of our people. The prophecy has been fulfilled. I am Mikkel's son, and I have brought you a Restorer. She has the signs and the gifts and is ready to guide you as you prepare to answer the threat of Hazor."

"Rendor welcomes the Restorer to our Council," Jorgen said in his Viking voice. One by one the other clan chief councilmembers declared their acceptance with varying degrees of enthusiasm. Some that I had met the day before looked genuinely hopeful. Others clearly weren't impressed. But since the

Verses didn't give them an option of upgrading to a Restorer more to their liking, they muttered a declaration of welcome.

Cameron was the last to speak. He leaned heavily on the railing that banded the Lyric section, his eyes scorching me like syncbeams. "Lyric is happy to accept a Restorer ready to give up her life to defend our people. May you, like Mikkel, defeat hundreds of our enemies before you die." There was venom in his tone, and he smiled as he said the last word.

Mark stiffened and turned toward Cameron.

Tristan stepped toward my husband. He placed a friendly hand on Mark's shoulder, but effectively held him back at the same time. "Every Restorer of our people has been unique." Tristan turned as he addressed each clan. "A gift from the One, used for His purpose. We don't know what role this Restorer will have." He paused in his slow circle and glared at Cameron. "But the guardians of Braide Wood are honored to accept her aid. May He guide our steps and preserve us all from darkness."

"So shall it be," the Council answered in one voice.

Mark nodded at Tristan and walked back to the Rendor balcony. Landon moved forward to take back control of the session. Two Council guards flanked him, aiming for Kieran.

But Tristan hadn't finished. "Chief Councilmember, please allow me to present my report." Tristan addressed Landon, bowing his head. "I have information that needs to be heard by the Council before more decisions are made."

Landon hesitated. He glared over at the Rendor balcony. "You have permission to present your report. But if any further interruptions or unsanctioned appearances occur, this Council session will be ended."

I bit my lip, feeling like I was back in seventh grade when

Mrs. Lynn caught me passing notes in class. Mark and I quickly took our seats in the back row.

Tristan drew a deep breath. "As ordered by the Council, I traveled to the River Borders and joined the patrols to search for a young guardian missing near Cauldron Falls. I found him."

I gripped Mark's arm and beamed. "Linette will be so relieved," I whispered.

Tristan's eyes looked weary as he continued. "He had been murdered while defending Cauldron Pass."

I gasped, then pressed my fist over my mouth. I thought of all the dreams Linette had shared with me about her fiancé. I pictured her radiant face as she led worshipers at the Feast day gathering in the tower. She was so young and full of trust and hope. Dylan would never get to hear the song she had composed for him during their long separation. She would never have the heart to sing it again. I didn't try to stop the tears that sprang up, but knuckled them aside in anger as they hit my cheeks.

"He was killed with a long-range syncbeam, by Kahlareans slipping across our border." Tristan stopped to let the Council absorb those facts. The death of one guardian saddened them but was an expected part of life for those on patrol along the River Borders. However, the knowledge that the Kahlareans also had syncbeams was devastating. Tristan used this opportunity to tell the Council all that I had found out from Nolan about the reason Hazor was happy to provide Lyric with syncbeams. Hazor had given their technology to Kahlarea as well, which made it clear Hazor planned to let the People and Kahlarea decimate each other, leaving the Hazorites a clear field for expansion.

"So we build better ones. We build more. We have transtechs who can do it, if the Council stops holding on to outdated rules," said the Corros Fields Council chief.

A buzz traveled around the room, growing in volume.

I looked out at the curving balconies full of leaders from each clan. They may be free of Rhusican mind control, but they certainly weren't immune to fear. For a moment, I saw a vision of desperation like translucent masks in front of the faces around the room. What comfort was there in holding on to the Verses if it held them back from progress? How important was the commandment against long-range weapons, really? I could feel the tide of panic growing. If it continued to swell, it would sweep away the fragile remnants of faith that the People were hanging on to.

I jumped to my feet. The balcony railing felt slick under my sweating palms.

Jorgen glared at me in warning. This time I waited respect-fully until Landon acknowledged me. The tower chamber slowly quieted, and I felt the stares of curiosity and hostility burn into me.

I focused on a spot on the obsidian floor in the center of the room. I couldn't scan the room anymore. I knew. I *knew* how close they were to breaking their covenant with the One. My world was different. My history was different. But the decision they were facing wasn't unique to them. I cleared my throat.

"In the Verses of my home, there were many times when greater forces threatened the One's own people." My voice sounded high and wispy in my own ears. *Father, please speak to these people.*

"They were tempted to make alliances, to build weapons, to rely on their own power. But those things could never save them." As had happened when I was talking with Kieran in the clearing overlooking Braide Wood, I felt the sense of words coming from outside of myself. A power that had nothing to do with me was speaking to the room. My voice grew stronger and more confident. "When they turned their hearts back to the One, He fought on their behalf."

At last I was able to lift my gaze. I paused and looked into the eyes of one after another of the councilmembers around the room. "You don't need to be afraid. You don't need to scramble to create weapons the One has forbidden. Trust Him. If you ever meant a single word of the Songs you've sung in the Lyric tower, then trust Him. If you've ever truly believed the Verses you recite every night, trust Him now. He is our strong tower."

The tide of fear had stopped advancing, but had it turned? There was an expectant stillness in the room. I was tempted to say more, to plead and cajole. But I held my ground and waited.

Tristan's eyes widened as he watched me from his place in the center of the chamber. He took a slow breath in. His torso lifted and he grew taller. "We've been given the promised Restorer. We will fight with our swords and with the power of the Verses, as the Songs tell us. Who will stand with Braide Wood?"

This time each chief councilmember rose to his feet.

"We will!"

"Blue Knoll answers!"

"We are united."

Jorgen stood next to me and added his voice to the room. "We will stay true to the Verses. The One is our Defender."

Discussion started up again. Most clans offered to send all their guardians to defend Braide Wood against Hazor. Corros Fields said they would need time to discuss it within the clan. Shamgar's chief scowled. "No one came to our defense. We have no resources now. Destroy Hazor if you're able, but we can't help you."

Cameron spoke for Lyric. "Our role is too vital. We cannot

risk Lyric remaining defenseless. The Council Guard cannot be spared, nor can the Lyric guardians."

It wasn't a unilateral show of support, but it was a start.

Tristan faced the Braide Wood wedge of the circle. "I also ask that Kieran be accepted back into Braide Wood clan. His dealings with Hazor weren't sanctioned, but we need the help and information he can provide."

The scrawny Braide Wood Council chief agreed, eager to accept any ally, even one who broke so many rules.

Kieran gave Tristan a hard look. "I didn't ask you to do this," he said in a low voice.

Tristan ignored him and thanked Landon for allowing him to speak. With evident relief that his turn to moderate was over, Landon nodded to Tristan and officially closed the day's meeting.

As everyone rose to file out to the clan offices, I risked one more break in protocol. I ran down the ramp to the tower's center, dragging Mark behind me. "Tristan, I'm so glad you're back." I threw my arms around the startled guardian in a quick hug.

Tristan stood as if frozen, and Kieran gave a strangled cough.

I stepped back and kept talking. "We have so much to tell you. Were you injured? I saw you limping. Oh, this is my husband, Mark."

Tristan shook his head slowly. Mark stepped forward with a grin and offered his hand. "Would you join us for our evening meal?" he asked formally.

The guardian gripped my husband's forearm and nodded. "Thank you. I obviously missed a few things while I was gone."

My giddy relief at seeing Tristan gave way to heaviness at the news he'd shared, and I sobered. "We have to go to Linette.

She's been waiting for news for so long, and she should hear it from you."

Mark nodded. "She's waiting at my apartments."

Tristan noticed Kieran sidling away and grabbed his arm. "You're under my care, so you're coming, too."

Mark frowned, but didn't say anything.

I stepped closer to Kieran.

He stiffened and leaned away.

I was so relieved at the way the Council session had gone that I wanted to throw my arms around everyone; since that would probably give Kieran a coronary, I offered him my hand instead. "Thank you for finding out the truth."

He frowned, but clasped my forearm, releasing me quickly. Even through the sleeve of his tunic, I could feel the dry heat of his skin. His eyes still looked glassy.

Tristan and Kieran walked ahead of us out of the chamber. Tristan continued to favor one leg and move slowly. Kieran slouched as his adrenaline leached away.

"Mark," I said quietly, "could you send someone for the healer?"

"Good idea," he said, watching them. He rested his arm across my shoulders and pulled me closer. "And how are *you* feeling?"

I thought about it. "Remember when I went into labor with Jake?"

Mark raised his eyebrows, but nodded.

"He was early. I was excited. I thought I was ready for it. But I also felt . . . pure terror. All of a sudden, I couldn't remember anything we had learned in birthing classes, and I wanted to stop, to call it off. But it was too late. There was no way to go but forward."

Mark stopped and turned me toward him. "And we did. We

went forward." He rested his forehead against mine, and I felt his strength.

When we stepped out into the hallway, Mark spotted Wade and went to send him for the healer.

"What do you think you've accomplished?" a voice hissed behind my left ear.

I whirled around.

Cameron glared at me from only a few feet away. "I told you the truth," he said. "My job is to protect these people. All you've done is to ensure they will all be destroyed."

My pulse was racing, but I wasn't about to let him intimidate me. "No, you were the one harming the People." My hand clenched on my sword grip. "Destroying the Verses or the People's faith in them isn't a solution."

He gave a mirthless laugh. Mark turned to look in our direction from down the hallway. His eyes widened, and he headed our way fast.

"We'll see what kind of solution you come up with," Cameron said, "when you're watching the guardians being incinerated by syncbeams and Braide Wood being overrun by Hazor."

Mark stepped in front of me.

Cameron didn't even blink. "Councilmember Markkel, why didn't you tell me earlier that the person I had invited to Lyric was your wife? No, never mind. Don't explain it to me." A slow smile stretched across his face. "Try explaining to her that if you had told me the truth sooner, I never would have questioned her."

"I know what you did." A tendon jumped along Mark's jaw line. "This isn't over."

"Are you threatening a fellow councilmember?" Cameron

asked. "I'd expect something like that from Tristan. I thought folks in Rendor were more civilized."

"Mark, let's go." I rested my hand on his arm, feeling his muscles knotted with tension beneath his tunic. From the doorway of the lobby area, Tristan and Kieran walked back toward us.

Cameron saw them, too. "Tristan, we were just discussing you. And how is that lovely wife of yours?"

In two strides Tristan came nose to nose with Cameron. Kieran reached for his dagger.

I held Mark's arm with both hands now, still worried about the rage bundled in him. I was the one who wanted vengeance on Cameron, so why was I the only person staying calm now? The pressure in the hallway mounted with rising waves of male hostility, and I was afraid an explosion would destroy the progress we'd made today.

Then, with an obvious effort of self-control, Tristan took a step back. "Thank you for asking. She's recovered."

Cameron frowned. "I hadn't heard." He gave us all one last sour look and walked away.

Kieran grabbed Tristan's arm and spun his friend to face him. "Is it true? She's better?" Desperate hope played across his face, and he held his breath as he waited for his friend's answer.

Tristan nodded, and his face softened with the first genuine smile I'd seen from him today.

Kieran's grip tightened. "And just when did you plan to tell me about this?" He looked ready to throttle his friend. "You didn't think that was important news?"

Tristan tugged his arm away. "I wanted to let Susan tell you. She's the one who brought her back." Kieran's eyebrows all but disappeared under his cropped bangs.

I sagged against Mark. "Can we please have this discussion somewhere else?"

Mark put a protective arm around me as we walked out to the lobby. "He was right," he said quietly.

"What?" I asked.

"If I had told Cameron you were my wife when I first came to Lyric, he wouldn't have taken you. You technically weren't a foreigner. He had no right." Mark's feet were dragging as we left the Council building.

I stopped and faced him. "Cameron has been doing a lot of things he has no right to do. Who knows what he would have done if you'd told him sooner? He wants me to blame you, but we aren't going to play his game. It wasn't your fault." I touched Mark's face, stroking his whiskered cheeks. "I'm all right." It was almost true. True enough.

Tristan and Kieran had walked ahead of us down the street, but we could still hear them arguing. Kieran was scolding and complaining, and Tristan was growling and waving his arms. There were no other people on the street, which cut a wide, curving path past the large towers of Lyric's heart.

"Look at them." I shook my head. "Kieran can't just show how happy he is to hear about Kendra, and Tristan won't let Kieran see how glad he is to have him back here. Men."

"Hey, wait a minute." Mark poked my ribs and found the one spot I'm ticklish.

I pulled away, laughing, just as a gust of wind swept by. Odd—in all the time I'd been in this world, there had never been any wind. I blinked and realized that what I had felt was a person rushing past. Dressed in gray, head covered in a hooded mask, the shape flew across the distance separating Tristan and Kieran from Mark and me. He leaped at Tristan, knocking him down. Metal flashed, and I ran forward to help, but more gray-clad shapes had appeared in total silence. Kieran drew his sword and engaged one of the attackers.

I turned to Mark, but he wasn't there. Two dark figures were pulling him away toward an alley.

The silence and suddenness of the attack left me stunned. It was several seconds before the sounds registered in my mind. Clanging metal. The thud of bodies taking blows and hitting the ground.

When I finally took in what was happening, I screamed. I tugged my sword free, but felt the nightmarish sense of moving through molasses. I ran toward Mark.

"Susan, look out!" he shouted, even as he struggled in the grip of his two attackers.

Something rammed into me from the side.

As I fell, I remembered to tuck my shoulder and roll. I kept a hold on my sword and scrambled to my feet. One of the masked attackers moved toward me. With a two-fisted grip, I swung my blade back and forth in front of me, hearing it whistle through the air. The man jumped back.

"Mark!" I had the space of a second to check on him.

The two men dragged him farther toward the alley along-side the Council building. I was vaguely aware that Tristan and Kieran were also fighting, but I couldn't keep track of how many people were attacking us.

When I started toward Mark again, my attacker moved in from the side. This time I closed my eyes and swung my sword like a baseball bat.

It made contact with something. Someone grunted and moaned.

I didn't stop to see what I had done. I ran toward Mark

and gained some ground, although he was close to disappearing around the corner of the building. As I drew near, one of the men dragging Mark lifted his free hand. Metal glinted.

My heart lurched like a startled lehkan. "God, no!" I shouted the prayer. I sprinted forward, sword raised.

The attacker gripped the hilt of a long, twisted blade. He plunged the knife straight down at Mark.

Chapter Twenty-Nine

IT TOOK A HALF-SECOND FOR the horrible truth to grab me. I couldn't reach Mark in time. My legs kept moving me forward, but I felt my life shattering. My husband was about to be murdered in front of my eyes, and there was nothing I could do to stop it.

In that same compressed second of time, Mark's head angled upward and he pulled against one of the men who held him. He saw the blade in his second captor's hand.

My gaze clung to every detail of his face. I knew in that moment that I had never known any man more noble or unselfish. I was desperate to tell him one more time how much I loved him.

The blade flashed downward.

Wade barreled out of the alley and launched himself at the man with the knife, propelling him away from Mark. The weapon flew from the assassin's hand before it could reach its target. I ran at the hooded man who still held Mark on the other side, and slammed the flat of my blade into his shoulder. The force of the swing jarred my wrists, but the impact was successful in making the man release his grip on Mark.

Mark was finally able to draw his own sword. He finished

off the man I had attacked with a single efficient thrust.

I froze, stunned at the sight of my easy-going suburban husband transformed into a warrior. Once I stopped moving, instinct deserted me, and I wobbled on my feet, unsure what to do next.

Mark pulled his sword free and turned to check on Wade. The burly guardian pummeled his opponent into the ground and delivered a meaty right cross. The attacker's head bounced against the pavement, and he stopped moving. Wade sprinted down the street toward Tristan and Kieran, hurdling over the crumpled form of the first man I had fought out in the street.

I stared at the lifeless body at my feet, dazed.

Mark never stopped moving. He pulled the hooded mask off the man's head. The enemy's skin was ashen white, with a sunken chin and large black eyes that seemed frozen open in surprise. "He's Kahlarean," Mark said in disgust.

I closed my eyes but couldn't escape the image of the lifeless face looking up at me. I wrapped my arms around my ribs, curling in around the shock that gripped me.

"Susan, stay with me." Mark's voice was terse. He was checking Wade's opponent for weapons. At least that man was still breathing. "Come on. We're not done yet."

I followed Mark back out to the street in time to see the other attackers disappear into the twilight. Tristan took a few lurching steps after them, but their speed would have made them impossible to catch, even if Tristan weren't already hobbling from a recent injury. Wade gave chase a little longer, but soon gave up and headed back toward us. Kieran was on the ground, and Tristan offered him a hand and helped him up.

"Are you all right?" I asked them as Mark and I drew close.

"Just great," Kieran snapped.

"Thanks to me." Wade grinned at us. "The man had a ven-blade two inches from Kieran's neck when I got here."

"I was taking care of it." Kieran scowled at Wade.

Wade's smile broadened. He was enjoying the thought of Kieran owing him his life.

"Who were they?" I still had my sword in my hand, but the blade seemed to be shaking. Tristan and Mark exchanged a look.

"Kahlarean assassins," Mark said.

"They've heard Markkel has returned," Tristan said. "That's going to be a problem."

I loved his gift for understatement. "But Mark isn't the Restorer," I said.

Mark moved closer to me and gently pried my fingers away from my sword hilt. I realized it wasn't the sword that was trembling. It was my hand. "They don't know that," he said.

"Yet," Kieran said. "But they will soon." He looked at me. For a moment I thought I saw sympathy or even admiration in his dark eyes. "You made yourself a target today."

"Don't even pretend that it matters to you." Mark turned his back on Kieran and helped me get my sword back into its loop.

Mark's anger worried me. I knew he hadn't forgiven Kieran for trying to use me as a hostage, but he had to give the dark-haired man some credit for what he'd done today in the Council session. "We're all on the same side," I said quietly.

Mark ignored me. "Tristan, will you and Wade take Susan back to my rooms? Kieran, you can help me take care of them." Mark jerked his head toward the street. Kieran's eyes narrowed. Then he shrugged and walked over to the nearest corpse.

Two dead bodies and an unconscious assassin. The Lyric guardians were going to love this. Wade and Tristan led me down the street and through an alley to the building where Mark and I were staying. It was getting too dark to see, and of course there were no lights. No one ventured out after dark. No one but assassins.

"I'm really not cut out for this," I said suddenly. "When Anne's hamster died, I couldn't even look at it. Mark had to put it in the shoebox and arrange the funeral. Sure, I told the One that I want to fight evil. But I was thinking maybe I'd volunteer at the drug rehab center downtown as a counselor or something. I really, really didn't plan on Rhusicans or assassins or war." My words came faster and faster. Wade and Tristan exchanged a worried look, but I didn't care. Babbling helped me process the flood of horrified feelings that threatened to drown me.

"You know, I've done what I was supposed to. The Council is going to honor the Verses, and the guardians are going to protect Braide Wood. Maybe that's all I need to do. We really have to get Mark away from here before they try again. And I don't want anyone else getting hurt because of us. We should leave. And who knows if Jake has gotten home from work yet. What if he finds the house empty? I didn't even leave a note. I don't want to fight anymore. My children need me. And I can't do this anymore." Anxiety spiraled into tighter and tighter coils and the shaking in my hands was moving up my arms.

Tristan limped to a halt in the doorway of the building. He waited until I met his eyes to speak. "You fought as bravely as any of my guardians tonight. Now put it aside. Linette is in there. She's going to need your help."

The words stung me like a slap across the face. I'd forgotten. My face heated. I sounded completely self-absorbed. This was hard for me, but Linette had lost her fiancé and didn't know it yet. I took a slow breath and nodded.

She was curled on the couch, holding a small wooden flute, silently running her fingers through some drills. As I came in the door, she smiled at me and unwound to stand. Then she saw the man behind me.

"Tristan! Are you all right? Did you find him?" She ran toward him on light feet, but read his expression and stopped short in the middle of the room. The hope poured out of her face like water swirling down a drain. Her long, graceful body began to crumble.

I ran forward to gather her in a hug as her knees collapsed. We both sank to the floor, and I held her while she cried. My own tears dripped down onto her hair. The cold floor sent a remorseless chill into my muscles, but I feared if I loosened my grip, she'd curl so deeply into herself that she'd disappear from sight. I held on, trying to siphon some of her pain into my own heart and ease her grief by a tiny fraction.

Wade fidgeted in the doorway, but Tristan walked over to us. He knelt down and touched the side of Linette's face. She looked at him, holding her breath to still her sobs.

"I'm sorry. He gave his life defending all of us." Tristan offered the only comfort he could. Dylan was gone, but in Braide Wood he would be remembered as a hero. I thought of how little comfort that had been to Mark when his father was killed.

Linette's face contorted in pain. "Thank you," she whispered. Then she lowered her head and sobbed, and I drew her close again.

It was much later that Linette's fragile body stopped shaking with tears. I helped her up and led her to the couch.

She wavered on her feet, but didn't sit down. "I need to go back to the songkeepers' lodge."

"Are you sure? It's late. You're welcome to stay with us." I knew that normally she cherished the traditional boundaries, including restrictions against going out at night.

She shook her head. "No. I . . . I want to go back."

I walked with her to the door. She moved as slowly as Lukyan, as though her grief were arthritis gripping her every joint. Wade had taken up a guard position outside the room. I asked him to escort Linette home.

He looked at her uncertainly and rested a clumsy hand on her thin shoulder. "I'm really sorry. Dylan was a good friend. Did he ever tell you about the time he pulled me out of the river when we were first-years?"

Linette gave him a watery smile, and as they walked away, Wade quietly offered a tribute to Dylan with his stories.

I hoped it would help her. I stepped back into the room with a sigh but stopped short at the sight of Tristan, who had collapsed into a chair, his injured leg stretched out in front of him. He was watching me with something close to anger in his eyes.

"Tristan?" I pulled a chair up and sat down slowly. "What's wrong?"

"You aren't from here—"

"I think we've established that."

He scowled, his long, uncombed hair adding to his fierce aura. "And I wanted to be sure you understand what you did today."

I rolled my shoulders and frowned. It had been a full day. I'd interrupted a Council session, been stabbed in the heart, and fought off Kahlarean assassins. I used to think running errands and driving to soccer practice was a lot of work. "What do you mean?"

"Susan, what does a person's word mean in your world?"

My eyebrows pulled together as I tried to understand where this was going. "Are you asking me if you can trust me? Don't you know that by now?" He didn't answer, and I felt a cold congestion in my throat, as if I had swallowed a piece of ice.

"I know you were upset earlier," he said slowly. "But you talked about going back to your world. You said you didn't want to fight. Do you understand what you did in the Council today?"

"When? I mean, which thing? Tristan, what are you talking about?"

"Did you promise to stand with Braide Wood as a Restorer?" There was an impatient edge to his voice.

"Yes, of course."

"By those words, you promised to ride with the guardians and defend our clan. Did you know what you were pledging? Do you plan to honor your word?"

I opened my mouth, insulted. I closed my mouth, ashamed. He was right. I hadn't fully realized what I was promising. I had intended to give my moral support—proclaim my loyalty. I hadn't thought about what would be expected of me now. I was great with motivational speeches, but not so great with the thought of riding into battle.

Stricken, I met Tristan's hard stare. "I'm sorry. I wasn't thinking. But you do have my word." I straightened in the chair. "If that's what the Restorer is supposed to do, I'll ride with the guardians against Hazor."

"No, she won't." Mark spoke loudly from the open doorway, glaring at Tristan. Kieran hovered behind him, watching with keen interest.

Tristan pushed himself to his feet, and I expected him to

argue with Mark. But he inclined his head. "We'll leave you to talk." He limped toward the door and paused. "I know you understand this, Markkel. The guardians won't unite without the Restorer." He waited, but Mark stared straight ahead, lips pressed in a thin, silent line. Tristan shook his head and walked out to the hall with Kieran.

Mark had turned into an angry statue.

"Okay. I'm not thrilled about going into battle." I tried to make my words soothing. "But you'll be with me. We make a great team. And it's what the Restorer is supposed to do. Mark, what's wrong?"

He turned his head stiffly, as if it hurt to move. "Susan, I just talked to Jorgen. He's ordered me to remain in Lyric to coordinate the Council's part in gathering the army."

"Tell him you can't." I sprang from my chair.

"When he reinstated me to the Council, I pledged to serve where he asks as long as we're here. I don't have a choice."

"Neither do I."

"Susan, I don't want you to go."

"And I don't want you to stay here. Would it help if I went and begged Jorgen to let you come with me?"

"I gave him my word. He needs me to keep the Council on track with collecting supplies and organizing the clan guardians that are going to help. And he's asked for my help to keep Cameron from regaining control of the Council." Mark was holding himself so still that I was afraid he'd shatter if I touched him.

I stepped closer anyway and rested my head against his chest. "I'm the Restorer. This is what I'm here to do."

His chin rested on the top of my head, and he blew out an uneven breath. "You have something wrong with your heart, and you've hardly had any training. The Hazorites have syncbeams. I don't care how fast you heal; it's too dangerous." His words became muffled against my hair.

I wrapped my arms around his waist. "I'm sorry." I looked up at his strained face and tried to understand what had triggered this renewed fear in him. Together we moved to the couch and sank down beside each other. Mark leaned forward and buried his face in his hands. I waited.

"They're just like the ones who came before," he said in a tight voice.

"Who?" I rested my hand lightly on his back.

"The Kahlareans. The assassins. I didn't see the ones who killed my mother, but I saw them the last time they tried to kill me. Before I was sent through the portal. They slip in. Silent, gray death. My father, my mother, me, you."

I rubbed his back and let him talk. The attack tonight had been a slingshot into the most terrible moments of his past. I floundered for words that could comfort him. When Wade walked Linette home, he made an effort to share treasured memories. "Tell me about your father. What do you remember about him? What was he like?"

He lifted his head. He had never been able to tell me about his father, except in a very vague way. Now that I knew his history, he finally had someone he could talk to. It was the best gift I could give him.

"When I was four, he took me hunting along the river. We hiked all day to reach an outpost. When I got tired, I rode on his shoulders. . . ."

As he spoke, his tension melted, and he relaxed back into the couch. I think he would have talked all night if the door hadn't opened.

Wade stuck his head in from the outer hall. "The healer is here." The door opened farther as the woman I had met earlier pushed past Wade and into the room. Her green tunic wasn't as freshly creased as it had been earlier in the day. She still carried a large bag. Wade tried to grab her arm and stop her, but he was swept aside by Tristan and Kieran, who also strode into the room. Wade crossed his arms and glared at them. He took his bouncer duties seriously and didn't like seeing so many visitors. He scowled with extra venom at Kieran, though Kieran deliberately turned his back.

"This couldn't wait until morning?" The healer set her bag on the table.

Mark smiled bleakly. "We appreciate your coming. Tristan just returned from a patrol on the River Borders. Would you take care of his injuries first? And I want you to check Susan again."

The healer was already eyeing Tristan with a frown. Kieran slumped into one of the chairs at the table and dropped his head down to rest on his arms. He looked oddly like a first grader resting at his desk during story time.

"Oh, and something's wrong with him, too." Mark gestured toward Kieran. "He'd better not be contagious," he added to me in a low voice.

I swatted his arm. "Mark, be nice." I got up and showed Tristan and the healer to the back room, and brought her a bowl of water from the kitchen. Wade went back out to the hall to stand watch at the door. I had just settled back on the couch with Mark when we heard a loud bellow from the back room. Kieran's head lifted heavily, and he looked around with bleary eyes before letting his forehead drop back down onto his arms with a thud.

Wade stuck his head in the door. "Everything all right?"

There was another yelp from Tristan.

"The healer is patching up Tristan," I explained.

Wade chuckled as he ducked back out.

Later, the healer examined me and seemed as worried as she had been earlier. She gave me a bag of herbs and explained how to brew them and how much to drink each day. Kieran got a scolding for picking up a nasty clay-field fever and not taking care of it sooner. She slapped a drug patch on his arm and told him to rest and to drink plenty of water. Mark rolled some pallets out on the common room floor for Tristan and Kieran. With assassins still on the loose, we were safer sticking together. Tristan planned to relieve Wade on watch halfway through the night, but Kieran wouldn't be any help. As soon as the healer helped him to the pallet, he stretched out and fell asleep.

Linette had started an evening meal earlier. There was a pot of vegetable stew simmering on a heat trivet. Mark and I brought that out, along with anything else edible we could find in the kitchen cubby. I didn't have much appetite, but Wade and Tristan ate everything on the table. Even Mark dug in. He must have found comfort in the flavors from his childhood. It had been twenty years since he'd had some of these vegetables and spices.

Tristan nudged Kieran with his foot. "You want something to eat?"

Kieran didn't move. He was out cold. In sleep, all the hard lines of his face had relaxed. With his cheeks flushed from the fever and his mouth partway open, he looked much younger. He reminded me of Nolan. I wondered briefly how the young messenger was adjusting to life in Tara's home, before I tuned back in to the conversation around the table.

"You'll need his protection," Tristan was saying.

"No, I'd rather send him with Susan," Mark said. Wade's chest was puffed out with pride.

I realized they were debating where to send our house protector. "Mark, keep Wade here with you." I reached for my husband's hand. "The assassins are still out there, and I don't trust the Council Guard to be much help."

Tristan leaned forward and looked straight into Mark's eyes. "I owe her my life. She brought Kendra back. You know what that means to me. I promise you, I'll protect her."

"Your vow?" Mark asked. The intensity in the faces of both men reminded me again of how important words were in this land.

"With my life."

Mark studied Tristan's face. I could follow his thoughts. Tristan loved his wife so much that watching Kendra suffer had caused a visceral response. It overpowered his training, his duty, and his other loyalties. He knew exactly what Mark was facing in letting me go to this war. He also knew what it would cost his people if I didn't. So did Mark.

"All right." Mark slumped back into his chair. I knew he was agreeing to more than keeping Wade with him in Lyric.

I began gathering up the dishes. "When will we head back to Braide Wood?" I wanted to meet the eldest songkeeper of Lyric, who had sent Mark through the portal. I wanted to spend some time with Mark in his favorite grove outside the city. When Tristan didn't answer right away, I looked up from the bowls I was stacking.

Tristan looked at Mark as he spoke. "Tomorrow," he said quietly. "First light."

Mark squeezed his eyes shut.

Chapter Thirty

"I CAN'T DO THIS. I WANT to go home." I moaned the words into Mark's shoulder.

It was just past first light, and the morning air was cold. A low fog muted the edges of the trees and gave the impression that all existence ended fifty yards out in any direction. The Lyric station was empty except for Tristan, Kieran, Linette, and Wade. A sleek transport was parked along the road, engine off. Mark and I had walked a distance away from the others to say our goodbyes.

We had spent the night in each other's arms, talking, praying, and sometimes dozing for short stretches of time.

He squeezed me now, and his chest moved as he chuckled. "You're right. You did sound like this each time you went into labor." He cupped my chin in one hand and tilted my head up. "Remember? When you can't go back, you go forward. The One . . ." He swallowed. "The One will protect you. You can do this."

"I'll try." I wanted to be brave for him, but it was taking all my strength not to grab him and beg him to come with me. Part of me wanted to suggest that we forget about honor and duty and go back through the portal and leave this strange world to its own problems.

Mark kept staring into my eyes. "Susan . . . thank you for what you're doing for my people."

"Our people."

He kissed me, and I breathed in the smell of his skin. I soaked in strength from the feeling of his arms around me. Then we heard the hum of an engine powering up. The transport doors slid upward into the curved roof with a whoosh.

He pulled his head back. "Have you got the herbs from the healer?" He smoothed a strand of my hair back and tucked it behind my ear.

"Yes, and I promise I'll stop in and see the Braide Wood healer, too."

"Here." He pressed a folded fabric square into my hands.

"What's this?" I shook it open and discovered an appliqué of a blue-gray waterfall tumbling over rocks.

"It's the Rendor clan emblem. To wear into battle. Be careful."

I squeezed the fabric against my chest. "I will. You, too. Keep Wade close."

"Don't worry. The Council Guard will find out what the Kahlareans have planned. It's good we caught one of them alive. I don't think they'll try again soon." Mark was deliberately infusing confidence into his voice, but I was grateful.

Over at the transport, Wade had already helped Linette to board, and Kieran was following.

"Susan, stay away from Kieran," Mark said in a low voice. "I don't trust him."

I sighed. "You worry too much."

Tristan and Wade stood by the transport door and waited for us. We walked toward them, my dread growing with each step. It was easy to assert that I needed to follow my calling. It was much harder to step out of Mark's arms and onto the transport that would carry me to war.

Wade rubbed his hands up and down his arms to warm them in the chill air and shifted his weight from side to side. I was glad he would be staying with Mark. He may be just an overgrown boy, but he was completely trustworthy and fiercely determined to help.

"Wade, please take care of him."

His jovial face sobered. "You have my word."

Mark and I stood in front of the transport door. "I love you," I whispered.

He hugged me one last time, hard. "I love you, too. Go with the One."

I boarded and sat beside Linette. Mark and Tristan exchanged a few words, and then Tristan stepped into the car, allowing the curved door to slide downward. The transport surged forward, pulling me away from Mark. I looked out the window. He stood, chin raised, with Wade behind him. I watched them until we crested a hill and the Lyric station disappeared into the fog.

It took a moment to swallow the fear and loneliness that I tasted. Then I turned to Linette. "How are you?"

She was staring out the window, but pulled her gaze away and looked at me. Her eyes were red and swollen in her pale face, and even when she answered me, part of her wasn't really there. "I'm all right. I want to be home."

I nodded. Her family in Braide Wood would be able to bring her some comfort. Her gaze shifted back out the window. She had gone inside herself somewhere, her withdrawal reminding me of the effects of Rhusican poison. But reciting Verses wouldn't make this go away. This was pure grief.

Tristan rose from his seat to scan the road ahead of us. He sat down again, but a few minutes later he was back on his feet.

Kieran watched him and smirked. "The transport won't go any faster if you're standing." The full night's sleep and the healer's drug patch had helped him. His eyes were no longer glazed, and even though he sprawled across the bench, there was tightly wound energy in his muscles again.

Tristan looked over his shoulder at Kieran, and his focus latched onto the Hazor emblem still attached to the front of Kieran's tunic. "Get rid of that thing."

Kieran shrugged and pulled out his dagger to slice the threads holding it in place. "I'm only coming with you because I want to see Kendra for myself." He cut the bottom stitches free.

"You're coming with me because I need help planning our defense against Hazor," Tristan said, turning to look out the window again.

Kieran ignored him and tried to line his blade up to cut the top threads of the emblem. He was looking down, cross-eyed, but couldn't see what he was doing.

"Here, let me help." I leaned across the aisle and reached for his dagger.

He looked at me and then at the blade he was holding just under his own throat. "Oh, I don't think so." He put away his knife and ripped the emblem off the rest of the way.

I sat back and glared at him. "You give new definition to the word paranoid."

He bunched up the fabric emblem and stuffed it into his pack. "It's worked for me so far."

My irritation at him took the edge off the ache I'd been

feeling. Good. I'd concentrate on being annoyed instead of lonely and afraid.

We reached Tristan's house around lunchtime. It felt like *déjà vu* as the door flew open and Tara ran out. Today, instead of rushing toward Tristan, she stepped aside. Kendra catapulted from the house and into Tristan's arms. It took her several seconds to notice Kieran and me standing nearby.

"Kieran? Oh thank the One." She threw her arms around him.

He returned her hug and then grabbed her shoulders and held her at arm's length, searching her face. "Are you really back?"

I looked back and forth between them and smiled. I could see the family resemblance in the black hair, dark eyes, and angular cheekbones. Turned toward his sister, Kieran's face lost some of its perpetual cynicism. His grin was a mirror of hers.

Tara circled around them to come and greet me. "Are you all right? I was so worried when Tristan told me the Council Guard had taken you."

I blinked several times, my eyes stinging with the threat of tears. When I left, I hadn't known if I'd ever see her again. It felt so good to be back.

She must have realized that her compassionate welcome was about to do me in. She changed her tone. "Come on, everyone. Don't let moths in the house. I was just starting lunch."

I followed her through the doorway with a sense of coming home.

Nolan sat at the table with Dustin and Aubrey, playing a

game involving black and white stones. The bruises on his face had faded. He looked up and blanched as Tristan and Kieran followed me into the room. Tara quickly went to stand by him and laid a quieting hand on Nolan's shoulder. "You three go get washed up. It's almost lunch time."

Dustin and Aubrey gave Tristan a quick hug and disappeared down the hallway. Nolan followed them, glancing over his shoulder with a worried frown.

"That's the messenger from Hazor?" Kieran asked Tristan. "And you kept him alive. You're getting smarter. We can use him."

Kendra slugged her brother in the arm hard enough to make him stagger. "Don't you touch him."

Her prickly defense of Nolan and her ability to keep Kieran in his place made me smile.

"Kendra, don't be an idiot." Kieran tossed his pack to her. "They've declared war. We'll do whatever we have to."

Tristan put an arm around his wife. "She knows that. Let's not talk about this right now."

Kendra glanced at me and I nodded. Between the two of us, we'd look out for Nolan.

Tristan pulled Kendra closer and looked around the crowded room. Large family groups made a private reunion difficult, and they'd had almost no time together since her healing. "We'll be back soon," Tristan told his mother abruptly. "Don't wait on us for lunch." He grabbed Kendra's hand and hurried her out the front door.

"Strange time to go for a walk," Kieran said dryly. "I thought he was hungry."

Insensitive clod. I ignored him and sighed, half in appreciation of Tristan and Kendra's regained romance, half in response to the ache I felt to be in Mark's arms right now. Was he already meeting with councilmembers to procure supplies? Was Wade sticking close to protect him?

"Pining for your Rendor bureaucrat?" Kieran murmured by my ear. He'd slipped up behind me while I stood lost in thought.

"That," I said, rounding on him, "is none of your business." I stalked away to help Tara get lunch finished, but his low chuckle followed me. Tara took her time adding more ingredients to the large bowl of stew simmering on a heat trivet, and I told her about the drama in the Council meeting. We managed to stall lunch for nearly an hour until Kendra and Tristan returned. Kendra's skin was flushed from whisker burn, and Tristan sauntered across the great room with almost no limp, clearly in a much better mood.

I made a point of sitting beside Nolan. In spite of that, the boy didn't eat anything. I tried to talk to him, but he answered me with shrugs and monosyllables. If he'd started to relax under Tara's care, Tristan's return had ruined that progress.

"Where's Gareth?" Tristan asked his mother.

"He and Talia joined a party from Blue Knoll to head out and do some hunting. We need something to get us through next season." Tara stood up to refill the water pitcher, and Tristan followed her to the kitchen alcove.

"He's supposed to be guarding Nolan," Tristan said, rubbing his forehead, as if a headache were blooming.

I watched them huddle in conversation and hoped that it was only my keen hearing that allowed me to follow. Nolan already looked miserable slouched beside me.

Tara's smile made her look like an imp in a grandmother's body. "Finding food is more important. And do you really think

Kendra and I can't handle one skinny teenage boy?" She patted her belt. She was wearing a dagger—small and ornate, but definitely a weapon. Tristan sighed and let the subject drop as they returned to the table.

After lunch, Dustin, Aubrey, and Nolan settled in the corner of the room with their game.

Tristan and Kendra sat together at the table, oblivious as Tara and I moved around them to clear away the dishes. They carried on a quiet conversation with small movements that looked like a dance. She smoothed the shoulder seam of his tunic. He traced circles on the back of her hand. She rubbed away a streak of dirt from his cheek. He touched her hair. Tara grinned at me and shook her head. Kieran sat across the table from them. I waited for a sarcastic comment from him, but he just watched Kendra, relaxed and content.

"I was planning to visit Father this afternoon," Kendra said, picking lint from the sleeve of Tristan's tunic. "But I could do it another day."

"Go ahead." Tristan's voice lowered in volume, and he glanced at Nolan to be sure the boy was still immersed in his game with the children. "I need to check in with the replacement captain and start making plans for the other clan guardians. They'll start arriving soon. But I'll be home before nightfall." They smiled at each other.

Kendra glanced across the table at Kieran. "You can come with me. Father would—"

"No." Kieran pushed his chair back and stood. His face hardened.

"It would do him good. He misses you. I know you want to see him."

Kieran shoved his empty chair under the table with

unnecessary force, making his sister jump. "I said no."

Tristan rested his elbows on the table to lean forward and glare at his friend. But when he spoke, his voice was gentle. "We need Skyler's help. I know how you feel. But we're going to need him. Please talk to him."

Kieran paced away, then turned and looked at Kendra and Tristan. "Later. Maybe. Not today."

Tristan nodded. The couple rose from their chairs, and Kendra left Tristan's side to circle the table and give her brother a hug. "I'll tell him you're back. Maybe we can visit him together tomorrow."

He shook his head and turned away.

Tara brought a basket covered with cloth out to Kendra. "The stew's still hot, and I made him some of the caradoc rolls he likes."

"Thank you." Kendra gave Tristan one more kiss and left. Tara grabbed her cloak and called to Nolan and her grandchildren.

"Where are you going?" Tristan asked her. His cheerful mood had traveled right out the door with Kendra.

"The little ones are helping me find berries," Tara said, as Dustin and Aubrey ran past her son and outside.

Nolan followed the children, but Tristan's hand shot out and grabbed him by the arm. "Not him. I need to talk to him," Tristan said. Then he noticed me hovering by the kitchen. "Susan can go with you."

"I don't think so." I crossed my arms. "I'm staying right here."

"You had better leave for a while." Tristan's face was unreadable.

My stomach tightened. Whatever he and Kieran were planning, I had no intention of leaving them alone with Nolan.

"I'm not going anywhere." I leaned against the entry into the kitchen alcove.

Tara smiled at me and followed her grandchildren out the door. As soon as the door shut, Tristan shoved Nolan into a chair.

"Hey." I stepped forward.

Tristan stopped me with a stony glare. "If you want to stay, then sit down and don't say anything." His harsh tone startled me.

"But he's willing to talk to you. He answered every question I asked him."

"We'll see." Kieran pulled up a chair across from Nolan.

Worried by the hard resolve in both men, I took another step closer.

"Don't interfere," Tristan warned. "If you don't have the stomach for this, get out."

I stumbled a few steps back and perched on the edge of the table, planning every scathing word I would say to him later. Since I didn't want to leave Nolan alone with these two, I kept my mouth shut.

"Nolan, which part of Hazor are you from?" Kieran slouched back in his chair, his voice almost casual.

Nolan stared hard at the floor. He swallowed.

"Come on. This is an easy one. Where were you born?"

"I'm from Trezald," Nolan said softly.

Kieran grabbed Nolan's chin and tilted his head up, his eyes hard. "Don't lie to me again." His tone was lethal in its blandness.

Nolan's eyes widened, and he pulled back. Tristan stood behind him and clamped his hands down on the boy's shoulders.

"I've been to Trezald," Kieran said. "Let's try again. Where are you from?"

Nolan looked down again, his chest moving in and out faster. I was breathing harder, too. "Sidian," he mumbled.

"Hmm. And how many troops does Zarek command in Sidian?"

"I don't know."

The words were barely out of Nolan's mouth before Kieran backhanded him across the face. Tristan kept his grip on Nolan's shoulders to keep him from falling out of the chair. I jumped up.

Tristan pointed at me. "I'm serious, Susan. Don't interfere."

My mouth hung open. They couldn't be doing this. They were supposed to be the good guys.

Kieran didn't even acknowledge that I was in the room. He sat back casually and kept his eyes on Nolan. "How many troops in Sidian?"

"Maybe two thousand. A little more." Nolan closed his eyes.

"Is he bringing in his army from the Gray Hills, or just using his Sidian troops for the attack on Braide Wood?"

Nolan's face was pinched with fear. "I don't . . . I mean, yes. Yes, he's called in the Gray Hills army."

"What are the numbers?" Kieran's voice was smooth, insistent.

Nolan opened his eyes wide. "I don't know. Really. I don't."

Kieran shook his head. "We'll come back to that. Why does Zarek want the Braide Wood children?"

Sweat beaded on Nolan's forehead. He looked at Kieran's eyes and started shaking.

"It's a surety. To prevent war." Nolan squeezed his eyes shut again, shrinking as far down as Tristan's grip would let him.

"So what do you think?" Tristan said in a loud voice that made Nolan and me jump.

Kieran shrugged. "He could be telling the truth. It's a good thing the Council voted to surrender the children. There's no way we could stand up against those numbers."

I blinked, confused. Tristan shot me a warning look.

"We can barely muster a hundred guardians. We'd never be able to defend the Wood," Tristan said to Kieran. "But are you sure he's telling the truth?"

"I will be." Kieran slid the dagger from his boot sheath and eyed its edge. "And I'm sure there's more he can tell us." He turned his gaze to Nolan. Kieran's expression was set, remorseless. Nolan cringed and looked over at me, his eyes pleading.

I shivered. My heart ached for the terror the boy must feel.

"Not here," Tristan said.

Kieran shrugged. "Fine. I'll take him up to the caves. I'll be back before nightfall. Come on." Kieran jerked Nolan to his feet and propelled him toward the door.

"Tristan, no," I said. "Don't let him do this." I tried to follow Kieran.

Tristan grabbed me and pulled me back. "He'll do what has to be done."

"He's going to kill him," I shouted, turning on Tristan. "How can you let him do this?" I was so furious when he didn't release my arm that I threw an uppercut with my free hand and hit Tristan squarely on the jaw.

"Ow!" He let go of me in surprise.

Shaking my throbbing hand, I turned to storm out of the house, but Tristan grabbed me again. "Susan, listen." His voice dropped to a whisper. "He's not going to kill the boy. He's going to let him escape."

I froze. "What?"

Tristan let go of me and rubbed his jaw. "I told you not to stay and watch." He turned away and muttered under his breath. "Messengers of the One, deliver me from women Restorers."

"Would you just explain this to me?" I yelled.

Tristan winced and rubbed his ear. "Kieran will get all the information he can from him, then get careless and let him escape. We needed him scared enough so he would risk running. He'll head straight back to Hazor and tell them our Council voted to surrender the children, and we have less than a hundred troops. It'll buy us some time, and it might even mean that Zarek won't call up his Gray Hills troops."

I collapsed onto a chair by the table and lowered my head into my hands. "And you couldn't have explained this to me?"

"I told you to leave. When you insisted on staying, I figured you'd catch on. All we did was shake him up a little." Tristan sat down at the table, concern on his face. "You're as white as a Kahlarean. Are you all right?"

"No thanks to you and the Braide Wood repertory company," I snarled. "Why didn't you just send him back to Hazor with a message that we agreed to their terms?"

"They'd know it was a lie. If he escapes and brings them information he overheard, they might believe it . . . if they don't have spies in the Council to give them the truth."

"But what's going to happen to him back there?"

Tristan shrugged and didn't try to answer.

I didn't know what I had expected. Maybe I thought Tara could adopt Nolan and he could learn the Verses and live a happy life in Braide Wood. Of course, that fantasy was built on the hope that the village would still be standing a few weeks from now. Tristan was doing everything he could to see that it would be.

Tristan rubbed his chin again and waggled his jaw side to side. "Well, your arm is getting stronger. That's good. You'll start training with the other guardians tomorrow. Now that we don't have to keep you a secret, you can work with everyone else." He grabbed his pack and started gathering supplies and cleaning his weapons.

I sat and seethed. The scene I had watched was a ploy. But when Kieran told Kendra, "We'll do whatever we have to," he had been dead serious. They didn't question the equation. Cruelty to one enemy boy didn't budge the scale when weighed against the defense of their home.

Tristan ignored my sulking. He whistled as he moved around the room preparing to head out to his troops. Halfway to the door, he stopped and turned to me. "If I had told you what we were planning, Nolan would have taken one look at your face and known. You aren't much good at hiding your thoughts." He wasn't apologetic, but his eyes were compassionate.

I remembered the moment he had handed me my sword in the doorway of the house in Shamgar. That felt like years ago. Even that first day, he had guessed at my purpose. Then, as now, his face had reflected a weary resignation for the things I would probably have to face.

The afternoon rain began to fall. Scattered drops slapped the ground with a sound like bugs bumping into a screen. The rhythm quickened steadily, until the sounds of the rain melded into a continuous rippling noise. Tristan shouldered his pack and left, closing the door behind him.

I lowered my head to rest on my arms. *You'll have to make*

me strong, I prayed. *I don't know how to be tough enough for what's coming. I'm not even sure I want to be. I need your help.*

The rain continued to permeate the earth and drum against the roof. I dozed, my sleep plagued by fitful dreams.

Some time later, Kendra came back in, carrying the empty basket. She shook the rain from her cloak and hung it near the door. My lids felt dry and tired, and I watched her but didn't lift my head.

"Where is everyone?" she asked.

I sat up, rubbing my eyes. "Kieran took Nolan out to the cave clearing. He and Tristan have some plan to interrogate him, give him false information, and let him escape."

To my surprise Kendra nodded. "I'm glad they found a way to let him live." She sat down at the table with a sigh, stretching her legs out on a second chair.

"How was your visit?" I asked.

She ran a hand through her hair, which was damp from the rain. "Not great. Father was never easy to live with. And lately . . . I don't know. The tension with Hazor makes it worse. But he's getting used to me being well again." She smiled. "It's one less grudge he can hold against Tristan."

"They don't get along?"

"Father doesn't get along with anyone. The only things he has a real affection for are his magchips and machines. He doesn't understand Tristan."

"You and Tristan are perfect for each other. Anyone could see that."

She jumped up and patted my shoulder. "I know. Want some clavo? I'm cold."

"Sure. No, wait. I'm supposed to make an herb medicine to drink every day. I promised Mark. Will you help me make it?"

"Of course."

I got up and dug through my pack, pulling out the cloth bag of herbs.

Kendra sniffed it and groaned. "I think the healers search the woods for the most foul-tasting plants they can find." We both laughed, and she adjusted a heat trivet and started some water warming. "Susan, are you all right? I mean, is it something serious?"

I would have loved to toss off a blithe reassurance, but I didn't want to lie to her. "I don't know. The Lyric healer seemed to think so, but it doesn't make sense. Every injury I've had since I've been here has healed so fast. I really don't know what's going on." The hike up from the Braide Wood station had been a sharp reminder that something was wrong. I had been short of breath, though I tried to hide how quickly I grew tired. Yet most of the time, I felt fine. I wondered how I would do with training tomorrow.

Kendra put an arm around my shoulders and squeezed. "Let me know if I can help. With anything. All right?" She ladled the brew into a mug and handed it to me.

"How about if you drink this mud for me?"

"Oh, no. I'm not *that* good of a friend." We walked back out to the table, and Kendra grinned when I sipped my herb concoction and shuddered. "Susan, would you help me with something?" she asked, becoming serious.

"Of course. What do you need?"

"Will you convince Kieran to ask our father for help?"

I choked on a swallow of tea, and it took a minute of coughing to catch my breath. "What good would that do?"

"We think my father could develop a defense against the syncbeams." She saw my eyebrows go up and spoke faster.

"Nothing forbidden in the Verses. Not a long-range weapon. Just some kind of field to keep their weapons from working."

"Okay, but what I meant was what good would it do for me to talk to Kieran? He won't listen to anything I say." I sipped more of the herb drink. The marshy flavor must be an acquired taste—and I doubted I'd ever acquire it.

"I think you're wrong. He respects you. He doesn't have many friends—"

I snorted. "I'm not his friend."

Kendra frowned.

"His words, not mine," I said quickly. "He doesn't trust me, he doesn't like me, and he wouldn't listen to anything I had to say." The damp cold of the day was soaking into my bones. I went to dig through my pack for a sweater.

"The thing about Kieran is you have to ignore half of what he says and pay attention to the things he doesn't say," she said. "I do think he'd listen to you. Please try?"

"How about if I visit your father with you tomorrow? I could try to convince him to help."

"He doesn't like strangers. Even more than he doesn't like people he knows. But Kieran's been gone so long. I think seeing him would really make a difference."

I pulled the sweater over my head. "If I get a chance, I'll see what I can do." I had a few other things I planned to say to Kieran when he got back, especially if he had done anything else to hurt Nolan.

Kendra pulled out a basket of fibers from a cubby in the common room. The earth-toned strips reminded me of strands of yarn. She had started making a new sweater for Tristan, and she showed me the technique for weaving together the strands. It looked like way too much work to me, but she smiled as her fingers moved over the fabric. I dug into my own pack and pulled out the Rendor emblem Mark had given me. Kendra helped me sew it onto my best tunic. We were just finishing when the door swung open and Kieran walked in, looking grim.

"Did it work?" Kendra asked.

He let his breath out in a huff. "He's gone. I don't know if it will work."

"Well, I'm getting tired. I think I'll go lie down for a little bit before supper." Kendra smiled at me and slipped out of the room.

"What's wrong? Is she all right?" Kieran's face darkened with worry.

It took me a moment to realize that to him, Kendra's return to sanity and health was still a new and fragile miracle. "She's fine. It'll take a while for her to get her strength back, but she's doing great." I set Kendra's basket back in the cubby she had drawn it from. "And she knew I wanted to talk to you."

He sank into a chair in the corner of the room and let his head tilt back so that he was staring at the ceiling. "About?"

I walked over to him and crossed my arms, waiting for him to lift his head and look at me. "What did you do to Nolan?"

"You don't want to know." He gave me a level look and then dropped his head against the high back of the chair again and closed his eyes.

"If I didn't want to know, I wouldn't be asking. Did you hurt him?" I dropped my arms to my sides and clenched my fists. Kieran wasn't the only one I was angry with. I was frustrated at the impossible situation we all faced. But I couldn't confront Zarek. I couldn't yell at Cameron. On the other hand, Kieran was right in front of me.

He opened one eye. When I didn't go away, he sighed

and pushed himself out of the chair. He went to stand by the window and looked out at the trees. "Yes." His voice was almost inaudible.

My stomach lurched.

"Happy now?" He continued looking out the window. "I hurt him. I scared him. He stopped lying. I got plenty of information. Some of it I already knew, but some could help us. Then I let him escape." His shoulders tensed. He turned around slowly; fury lay in a thin mask over the pain in his face.

I couldn't speak.

"Satisfied?" His voice was hoarse. "I hurt a scared, unarmed kid. I didn't enjoy it." His eyes were glassy again.

I stepped closer and pressed the back of my hand against his forehead.

He swatted my hand away. "What are you doing?"

"Your fever's back. Where's your medicine?"

He blinked at the change in subject and walked heavily over to his pack near the chair. He crouched to rummage in it, but swayed and finally sank to the floor, leaning on a wall for support.

I went to get him a mug of water, and when I came back, he was still fumbling with the drug patch he had unearthed. I shook my head, took it from his hand, and slapped it onto his arm in the same place the healer had yesterday.

He drank most of the water I handed him, watching me over the rim of the mug. "You are the oddest person I've ever met." He handed the cup back to me.

"Why?"

"Never mind." He closed his eyes.

"Don't worry, I'm still furious. But I'll argue with you later.

It wouldn't be a fair fight right now."

The corner of his mouth turned up as he leaned his head back against the wall, eyes still closed. "Just like Tristan. Have to keep things fair. Wouldn't be honorable otherwise." His voice dropped to a mumble. "Bunch of dimwits."

Kieran's fever had peeled away a few layers of the aloof distrust that usually surrounded him. It occurred to me that he might be easier to talk to right now.

I sat down next to him against the wall and planned my attack. So much for fighting fairly. "Why won't you go talk to your father?" I asked in what I hoped was a casual voice.

His head came up, and he turned to glare at me. Every plane and angle on his face became sharp-edged again. "Don't."

I swallowed. This was like poking a stick at a wounded, snarling tiger. Kendra was going to owe me. I took a moment to breathe before I met his glare. "Look, I don't know the whole story. I don't need to know. But if you and Skyler can come up with some way to disable their syncbeams, it could save a lot of lives."

"Why bother? Maybe the One will just—zing!—make them disappear right out of their hands." Kieran waved one hand around.

"Maybe He will. But maybe He wants to use you."

He sneered and turned away without answering.

Time for a new tactic. "Kieran, you may be paranoid, selfish, and pretty much heartless, but I didn't think you were a coward." I steeled myself to face his rage.

Instead, his shoulders moved, and he coughed. The cough changed into a low chuckle. Finally, he was laughing so hard that he had to wipe his eyes.

I gave him my fiercest frown.

He looked over and started laughing again. "That was —" he coughed and shook his head. "That was a good try. Really. You're learning. The glare needs a little work, though."

So much for my feeble attempt to manipulate someone who could have coached Machiavelli. Still, I wasn't going to back down. "This is serious. You're going to have to convince him to help us. Kendra's already tried."

Kieran gave a long sigh and shifted his body to face me. "I know. I planned to talk to him tomorrow."

"Well, why didn't you just say so?"

He ducked his head down to dig in his pack, but didn't answer until he produced a shiny black half-sphere. "Here. This will help." The device was a little too large to fit comfortably in the palm of a hand. As Kieran turned it, I could see the inside was hollowed out and lined with crystals, like a geode.

I tore my eyes away and looked up at him.

"It's a syncbeam. Not the garbage they sold Cameron either. This is the kind they'll be using when they attack."

"How did you get it?" I admired the jagged facets in the center of the weapon.

"Picked it up a couple days ago, when I was in Sidian."

There was probably an interesting story behind that comment. I was sure the Hazorite army didn't leave these lying around. "So you'll show it to Skyler tomorrow?"

He nodded and put the syncbeam away.

"Thank you," I said. "You're helping a lot of people, Kieran. I know things have been hard for you."

"For pity's sake," he said, wincing. "I said I'd do it. Now would you please go away?" He slouched against the wall and closed his eyes again.

I looked at the mug in my hand and considered pouring the rest of the water over his head, but decided to quit while I was ahead.

Chapter Thirty-One

MARK WAS RIGHT. TIME WAS RELATIVE. Now that every day was so vital, the hours hurtled ahead like a lehkan with no rider. Tristan guessed that we had about fifteen days to prepare for Hazor's attack, provided they stuck to the timeline in their ultimatum. There was always the chance that they would discover that Braide Wood wasn't going to meet their terms and decide to attack early.

New guardians arrived daily, and the numbers swelled to nearly four hundred. Thanks to Mark's work in Lyric, they came well supplied and organized. Still, from the information Kieran had gathered during his recent travels in Hazor and his interrogation of Nolan, he estimated that we could be outnumbered ten to one. Hazor would send at least two thousand troops from Sidian, and most likely other regiments as well. Kieran warned Tristan to prepare for an army of four thousand to advance over the mountains.

Tristan had set up camps for the various clans in the woods near the lehkan plateau. Trying to keep the reinforcements hidden as much as possible complicated the task. As training began in earnest, secrecy became a lost cause. If Hazorite spies made it across the mountains, they would see obvious signs that we were preparing for war.

Tristan sent out his own spies. Kieran wanted to go, but was too busy working with Skyler each day. Ever the pragmatist, he had found some way to get along with his father so they could dissect the syncbeam and develop a defense. I guessed that it had been the allure of analyzing the syncbeam, rather than Kieran's winning personality, that convinced Skyler to help. Kendra had joined them. Apparently she also had a keen mind for technology. Every night I'd ask how the work was progressing. Though Kieran was too irritable and preoccupied to say much, Kendra told me she was sure they could come up with something if they had more time.

Guardian training was a happy surprise to me. I grew stronger and faster almost by the hour. More than that, I developed an instinct for sword work. On the first morning I joined the other guardians to train, I read mockery on the faces of some of the experienced troops. The skepticism disappeared within hours, and I never saw it again. Tristan started me on drills with first-years, but by afternoon had me sparring with some of his best men and women. The hint of Restorer skill that had flickered to life when I'd fought in the past now blossomed into blazing power. I was clear, sharp, and agile, and my sword no longer felt heavy in my hand. The feeling of strength was exhilarating.

The training also gave me a place to focus my emotions. I missed my children and worried about them constantly. I also felt deep anger at Bekkah's death and Dylan's, at the ruined fields, and at the feeling of dread that had soaked into the life of the village along with the chemicals. I ached when I thought of Nolan and all the children in Hazor. Most of all, I missed Mark and worried about the Kahlarean assassins. Clanging my sword against an opponent's again and again was the best remedy for my fears. My arm never seemed to grow tired. Even during the afternoon rain, when we skidded in mud under the low gray skies and maneuvered over the uneven terrain of the plateau, I never felt the cold or the recurring ache within my ribcage.

Walking back to Tara's home in the evening, though, the odd weakness often returned. My chest hurt when I took a deep breath. Sometimes dizziness would hit me, and I'd stop and lean forward, hands grabbing my knees, trying to push the black spots away from my vision by sheer force of will. I faithfully downed mugs of the healer's concoction each day, but it had been seven days now, and it didn't seem to be helping.

One night I washed the mud out of my hair and prepared for bed, but realized I'd forgotten to drink my vile herbs. I padded out to the common room. Tristan and Kieran were at the table, speaking in low tones. Each night, when everyone else headed to bed, they would sit and strategize, sometimes pushing Dustin's black and white pebbles around in patterns on the table.

"I'm guessing they'll come at twilight. That's their pattern," Kieran was saying.

"How many, do you think?" Tristan asked. I assumed they were deep into their usual analysis of Hazor's army. Kieran saw me walk into the room and nudged Tristan. They both stopped talking.

I walked past them toward the kitchen, then pulled to a halt and turned back. "What's wrong?"

Kieran shook his head.

Tristan sighed. "Come and sit down."

I pulled out a chair and saw that the little stones from Dustin's game weren't on the table. I sat down slowly.

"The messenger from Lyric today—"

My heart stopped beating, and I grabbed Tristan's arm. "Is

Mark all right? What happened?"

"He's fine," Tristan said quickly. "There haven't been any more attacks. I didn't mean to scare you."

"But that's the problem," Kieran said. "No more attacks. Wade and Markkel even set up a trap . . . tried to draw them out. Nothing."

"That's good," I said, glaring at him. Did he really think we needed more excitement?

He drummed his fingers on the table. "It means they know Markkel isn't the Restorer." He paused, and I looked at both men questioningly. Kieran leaned forward, and his voice was matter-of-fact. "It means they'll be coming for you."

I was still feeling the bravado of another great day of riding and sword fighting. "Let them come."

"Don't be stupid," Kieran snapped.

I'd had it with his insults. All he did was mock and belittle me. I shoved my chair back and stalked away.

Kieran sprang up like a panther and blocked my path before I'd taken three steps. "Think. What will happen if they come for you here?"

I looked down the hallway to the back rooms. Tristan's family. They were all in danger. My spine lost its stiffening, and I melted back into the chair. "Where should I go?"

"Don't look like that," Tristan said. "We're not throwing you out the door. We just need to make a plan." Kieran walked away to the kitchen, leaving Tristan to comfort me. "You're safest during the day. They won't attack when you're surrounded by guardians. We think they'll come at night. I can assign some of my best guardians to stay with you constantly. I want to move you out to the caves on the ridge."

The common room had been my haven. Comfortable

chairs, warm light panels hanging on each wall like artwork. Even some drooping wildflowers in a mug on the table. I loved this home. I sighed. "When?"

"Now."

Kieran walked back into the room and handed me a steaming cup. I sniffed it. It was my medicine. Had he noticed I'd forgotten to take any today? He didn't miss much.

"No," Kieran said. "Better make it tomorrow, in daylight . . . and make sure everyone knows about it. You want to make it clear she's not here anymore."

Tristan nodded.

I drank a swallow of the bitter sludge and set the cup on the table. My hand shook, and I quickly pulled it into my lap. I had become two people. I was the Restorer. With a sword in my hand, I felt no fear. Strong and relentless, my presence inspired confidence in the other guardians. I could wheel my lehkan around with a nudge of my knee, raise my sword over my head, and shout out one of the Verses. Hundreds of warriors would roar in answer and charge across the plateau. Watching them, it was easy to believe that somehow we would defend Braide Wood.

But I was also Susan. My eyes welled up when Tara told her grandchildren bedtime stories. Spiders scared me. I missed Mark and my children. And I was terrified at the thought of watching my friends die. The odds we faced were hopeless. And even when my faith was strong enough to believe the One *could* save us, I wasn't totally sure that He *would*. He promised to be with us, but He gave no guarantees that everything would go the way I wanted. Lukyan would say that the "not knowing" was where my obedience was tested. I suddenly didn't feel up to the test.

I lifted my eyes to look at Kieran, who was slumped in his

chair again, across the table from me. "You said I'd die and cause the deaths of others," I said softly. "Back in Shamgar. The day after I arrived. I heard you tell Tristan."

"Do I look like a songkeeper or a prophet? What do I know?" he scoffed.

When I didn't react to his attempt at humor, he shifted forward and leaned on his elbows. "Susan, tell me one of the Verses from your world."

I rubbed my eyes and squinted at him. "But you don't believe in the Verses."

"What's wrong? Can't think of any?" he taunted.

"I'm not in the mood for your games." I took another drink and thumped the mug back onto the table.

Kieran's eyebrows lifted and he waited. Even Tristan watched me expectantly.

"Fine." I closed my eyes and let my mind page through a mental Bible. Hebrews. Something in there about faith. "Now faith is being sure of what we hope for and certain of what we do not see. This is what the ancients were commended for." I started the words flippantly, but they coursed into my blood and I felt their power. I began to remember the ancients that this chapter commended: Abraham, Joseph, Moses, Gideon, Samson, Daniel. A roll call of faith.

"Therefore, since we are surrounded by such a great cloud of witnesses, let us throw off everything that hinders and the sin that so easily entangles, and let us run with perseverance the race marked out for us. Let us fix our eyes on Jesus, the author and perfecter of our faith. . . ." I opened my eyes. Warmth had filled me. These people still waited for their Deliverer. They didn't know Him yet. But I did. And the One was big enough to work out His purposes, even in the frightening days ahead. I smiled.

"Thank you," Tristan said quietly to his friend. Kieran nodded, but pushed his chair back and avoided my eyes. He had accomplished his goal. I wasn't sinking into defeat anymore. But Kieran looked uneasy. The verses had unleashed the sense of the One's presence. Even Kieran must have felt it. I smiled more widely.

Kieran refused to acknowledge me. "Give her some drills on Kahlarean weapons tomorrow." He rose and practically ran from the room.

I swallowed the rest of my drink and looked at Tristan. "It's going to be all right."

He gave me a tired nod.

Staying up at the caves wasn't as bad as I had expected. The walls were damp and there were bugs, but I was too tired by nightfall to pay much attention. The cave where I slept had a familiar reek; it smelled the way the lining of my kids' boots do by the end of winter. I grew accustomed to the murky air—the hard part was the paradox of being lonely but never alone.

I wanted to spend time with Linette and visit Lukyan. I wanted to bake bread with Tara and chat with Kendra. But anyone I spent time with would be in danger. We didn't know if the assassins were on their way or already here, watching my movements and waiting for the right moment to attack. I didn't dare go near anyone in the village.

At the same time, three or four guardians, hand-picked by Tristan, constantly surrounded me. They stood guard at the caves, and walked with me to training each morning. Even while we drilled, they followed me everywhere like a kite tail.

For the first day or so, I was comforted by their presence. After a while I felt claustrophobic.

The threat from the Kahlareans didn't seem real. For all we knew, the few assassins who had escaped from the attack on Mark had already retreated across the River Borders. I was much more focused on preparing for the war with Hazor.

Each morning I rode with Tristan as he spoke with the captains of each group of guardians. The Council had appointed Tristan to lead this defense.

As the head guardian of the clan most directly threatened by the enemy, it was his place to defend Braide Wood. But he took no satisfaction from the honor. In reality, until the moment arrived when he would ride into battle with his troops, leadership consisted mostly of arbitrating conflicts between clans, checking on weapons and supplies, planning our desperate strategy, and, above all, praying to the One for mercy and guidance. By his side every day, I saw the burden of leadership etched on his face and wondered if the lines of my own face were hardening as well.

Late one afternoon Tristan asked me to sit in on his war council. Time was running out. "I got word from the patrol this morning. Hazor's army is approaching. We ride out to meet them tomorrow," he told me. Under a hastily constructed tent, soggy with afternoon rain, he and his captains pushed stones around in the dirt. They drew terrain lines and argued, heads together over diagrams of mountains, forests, and plains. Some of the captains were young. They were eager and restless, and suggested bold direct attacks. Others were grizzled and time hardened. They understood the hopeless odds but chose to ignore them. They spoke of the need for a line of protection closer to the village, in case Hazor moved forward on two fronts.

While the captains argued about whether they could spread their troops so thinly, I noticed how much they looked like Jon's grade-school football team, huddled together and mapping out their plans. But some of the men in this group wouldn't survive the face-off ahead. Maybe none of them would.

"What do you think?" Tristan's voice snapped me back to attention. He was looking at me, hopeful for a little Restorer guidance.

I shook my head. "I'm sorry. I really don't know. Do what you think is best." I saw discouragement in the heavy shoulders and downcast eyes around the tent. "Just put a sword in my hand and point me in the right direction," I added with a grin. A few faces looked up, startled. A couple of the captains chuckled.

Tristan clapped a hand on my shoulder, almost as if I were one of them. "Not a bad motto." He led me out of the tent and turned me over to my bodyguards. "Thank you for that. If you see or hear anything . . . I mean, if you sense any direction from the One . . ."

"I'll tell you right away. But I haven't." I rubbed my neck, more out of habit than for any actual stiffness. "No visions. No voices. All I know is that we have to defend Braide Wood, and I know He'll be with us. You're doing what you can. We all are. That's all we can do right now."

He nodded and turned to go back into the tent.

I followed my contingent of guardians along the ridgeline toward the caves, lost in thought. As we drew closer to the clearing, the man in the lead shouted something, drew his sword, and raced forward. Blades clashed.

I raced toward the sound, bounding up the trail and into the clearing close on the heels of another of my guardian protectors. One of my men was sprawled on the ground, struggling to roll back onto his feet. His sword lay several yards away. A second guardian faced off against an attacker . . . who wasn't a Kahlarean. He wasn't even an attacker. It was Kieran, and he was grinning.

"Hold!" I shouted.

The guardian facing Kieran took a step back but kept his sword up.

"Your protectors are a little jumpy, aren't they?" Kieran asked as he sheathed his sword.

"You could have told them who you were." I strode forward. My protectors today were from Rendor clan and didn't know him. "Put up your swords, he's a friend," I told them. "Heaven help us," I added under my breath.

Kieran pulled the first man to his feet. "Sorry," he said with a laugh. "Just keeping in practice." The young Rendor guardian picked up his sword and glared at Kieran. My bodyguards moved off, checking the surroundings and keeping an uneasy watch on us. Kieran and I sat down on the boulder and looked down at the village roofs.

"You're in a good mood today," I said.

"We think we have it figured out. A way to project a field that will suppress the magchips in their syncbeams." He continued explaining, and I suppose the words must have made sense to him, but I tuned him out. Skyler, Kendra, and Kieran had done nothing but work on the problem for days now. There was a fanatical gleam in his eyes. It reminded me of the excitement Mark had displayed when he figured out a way to rewire something in our house circuits so we wouldn't blow a fuse every time I turned on the toaster at the same time that the refrigerator was running.

"I lost you. Should I explain it again?"

"No. Please don't," I said quickly.

He grinned. "Kendra asked me to come. She wanted you to know we'll be there tomorrow morning with our invention, out of sight on the edge of the forest." His mood sobered. "She also said I should tell you to be careful . . . and to take care of Tristan for her."

"Tell her I will."

"Oh, and she sent you this." Kieran handed me a palm-sized device with a loop for attaching it to a belt and a few hidden panels. It looked like a smooth, white skipping stone. "It's a signaler. You press here to get it to sound."

I turned it around in my hand. Tristan had carried a signaler that looked similar to this. With a nod I linked it onto my belt and then looked back out over Braide Wood, swinging one leg against the boulder.

"Use it," Kieran said.

I turned to look at him, forgetting what he had been talking about.

He frowned. "The signaler. Use it if you need help tomorrow."

I nodded. Time had been rushing, then stalling, then hurtling forward again like a bizarre carnival ride. Now we were poised on a tall pinnacle about to plummet. There was no way back. "So we go forward," I said softly, thinking of Mark.

I had wondered how I would feel when this day before the battle came. I didn't have the fear and wavering I had expected. But I didn't feel excitement or confidence either. I was relieved that the waiting was almost over. I felt resolve. This was the path I had to follow, and with the help of the One, I would walk it tomorrow. And I felt tired.

"Did you hear what Linette is planning?" Kieran asked.

I straightened and looked at him, pulling myself out of my

thoughts with an effort. "How is she?"

"She's . . . focused. She's working with Lukyan. They've called for everyone in the village to gather at first light to sing the Verses."

"That's terrific!"

Kieran shrugged. "I suppose it will keep folks from panicking . . . keep them out of trouble."

I knew he was needling me on purpose, waiting for my reaction, but I couldn't stop myself. I stood up and glared down at him. "One of these days you're going to admit how powerful the One is, and how important His Verses are, Kieran of Braide Wood."

The smile he gave me had genuine affection in it. "Please tell me that's just your opinion and not some Restorer prophecy."

I couldn't hold on to my frown. I laughed and shook my head.

He pushed himself off the boulder and stood in front of me, offering his hand. We clasped forearms. "Fight well tomorrow. Watch your back," he said, then released me and disappeared among the trees.

I realized that I should have sent a message back with him. There were things I wanted to tell Tara, and Kendra, and Linette. But he was gone.

Tomorrow I'd have my chance to let them know how much the One loved them. How much I loved them. I looked down on Braide Wood one last time.

The Restorer would *be* the message.

Chapter Thirty-Two

THE MURMUR OF VOICES WOKE ME well before first light. I had dozed restlessly throughout the night and kept dreaming about the attic.

Mark was hammering the flooring into place, with a supply of nails pressed between his lips and a frown of concentration on his face. He drove the last nail home and turned to me and smiled. I ran to hug him and smelled the sawdust on his clothes.

Then I'd roll over and a rock would jab my ribs, and I'd wake up to the reality of the dank cave.

My fingers fumbled in the darkness for a heat trivet. I thumbed the lever and a soft glow lit up a bubble of space around me. My clothes and weapons were lined up along the wall of the cave. I moved slowly, as if enacting a ceremony as I dressed and armed myself. The tunic went on first, and I smoothed down the emblem of Rendor that was sewn in place over my chest. Mark would be riding with me today, if only in his symbol near my heart. I slipped on the trousers that Tara had loaned me, and pulled on the boots that were a constant reminder of Bekkah. Kieran's baldric slipped over my shoulder, and I cinched the belt. I slipped the sword I had carried with me from home into the loop and clipped Kendra's signaler to my belt. I drew on the cloak Tristan gave me the day we left Shamgar. There were still holes in it from the attack on Morsal Plains, and I fingered them, remembering that day. I picked up the gauntlets from Wade and pulled them on, tugging the ties into a knot with my teeth. Before leaving the cave, I dropped to my knees.

"Any road, Lord," I said aloud. "Any road You choose. But I won't go without You." His presence filled the cave like a wave of heat from an open oven door. Warmth and strength enfolded me, and I rested in that awareness for a precious minute. Then I pushed myself to my feet and walked out of the cave.

Tristan stood in the clearing, talking with one of the guardians. I could barely make out his features in the dark gray of pre-morning, but felt his energy and strength. He watched me stride forward and the corners of his mouth pulled upward.

"What?"

"I was just thinking about the first time I saw you in that alley in Shamgar." He shook his head. "I didn't know what to make of you."

"But you helped me. You didn't know if you could trust me, but you gave me protection."

"I never told you, but I had begun to wonder if the One even heard us anymore. So much was going wrong . . . the Council, Hazor, Kendra . . ." Tristan cleared his throat. "I'm glad He sent you to us."

I nodded. "What are you doing up here?"

"I came to walk you to the field." He looked at the emblem on my tunic. "I know you're officially of Rendor clan now, but you'll be riding with me. Whatever happens today, stay close."

"Mm hmm." I was watching the bodyguards break camp and gear up, ready to walk to the plateau with us.

"Susan." Tristan's voice changed from big brother to commander. "I mean it. Promise me you'll stay right behind me."

I acknowledged the focused intensity in his eyes. "I will. Besides, I promised Kendra I'd watch out for you." I grinned.

"Oh, great. Well, at least you listen to her."

I walked over to the boulder and looked down over the village. It was still dark, and fog floated over the space where the homes should have been visible. In a little while, young and old from the Braide Wood clan would gather with the songkeepers and begin to recite the Verses. I drew strength from that knowledge and followed Tristan out of the clearing and along the path.

The plateau was high enough to be barely touched by morning mist. The dawning sky was gray and overcast. No surprise there. Other than slight fluctuations in temperature, weather was a non-issue on this world. I had missed the surprise of waking up to a wet March wind rattling the windows, or a sullen August heat wave, or a crackling, booming thunderstorm. Today I was glad of one area where we knew what to expect: cool morning, moderate day, heavy gray skies, placid afternoon rain.

The guardians were preparing in muffled silence. Hundreds of men and women spread out across the field, but there was no chatting, laughter, or arguing, as there would be on a morning of training exercises. Tack rattled as it was adjusted. Saddle girths tightened with a creak of leather. Lehkan pawed and stamped and took nervous side steps. Stone scraped metal as a few of the younger guardians sharpened their blades nervously one last time. Occasional quiet orders directed the troops into their formations.

Tristan had agreed to let me ride Mara, my lehkan doe, into

battle. She didn't have fierce antlers to use as a weapon, but I knew how she moved. I was comfortable with her. After checking her saddle, I paused to rest my face against her soft-haired neck. Then I hoisted myself onto her back and adjusted my sword against my hip. I looked out at the army. Braide Wood's lehkan cavalry had grown from two dozen to nearly a hundred. About three hundred other guardians would fight on foot. We knew Hazor would rely primarily on foot soldiers and their syncbeams, although if they managed to maneuver some of their own lehkan over the mountains, we would also face a formidable cavalry.

I waited while Tristan made his rounds talking with each captain. He was grim, but took time to stop and exchange a few words with individual guardians as they finished their preparations. He thumped one young guardian on the back and paused to watch another hone the edge of a sword. He nodded his approval and moved on. Every place he walked, faces lightened with something more than the dawning morning glow. He fed them strength and courage.

In a few minutes he returned and mounted, nudging his lehkan into position beside mine. We faced the guardians and Tristan nodded to me.

My heart filled with resolve and gratitude as I studied the army before me. Slowly hands stopped tugging at saddles, weapons were stowed, all movement stilled, and four hundred faces turned toward us, ready.

"Guardians of all our clans," I shouted, "you have heard the voice of the One in your Records. You have felt His presence in the Lyric tower on Feast days. You have seen His promises fulfilled in your history. But He does not only live in the Records, or in the tower, or in the Songs of history. He is here as well. He is with every one of you." My voice broke, as I had a flash of seeing with other eyes. For just a moment I saw them the way the One saw them, and felt love that was so deep it made me tremble. I took a steadying breath. "We do not fight alone today."

Tristan edged his lehkan next to me. Confidence and nobility held his shoulders square. His face was devoid of any levity. His men, his clan, his own family faced the threat of death today. But even with the grim set of his face, he exuded hope and determination. "Awesome in majesty, perfect in power," he shouted.

"One to Deliver us, He is our tower!" roared four hundred strong voices. And we moved out.

One contingent on foot took the shortest route through the forest, down the steep trail toward Morsal Plains. It was the path we had scrambled down the day the farmland was attacked, but it wasn't a safe or efficient way to move large numbers of people. The bulk of the army, including cavalry, circled to the far side of the plateau and down a longer, more gradual slope toward Morsal Plains.

The light continued to grow as we traveled. By the time we arrived in the valley, I could see each broken stubble of grain and the sickly yellow tinge to the fields. Wisps of thin fog drifted in the lowest lying areas, stirred aside by the men who spread out into position. They faced the mountainous cliffs that stood between Hazor and us.

A runner approached Tristan from the forest. "Hazor is on the move," he said, gasping. "Two thousand strong."

"Good," Tristan nodded. "Not as many as we feared. Cavalry?"

"Yes. Not many. A few hundred. They already lost some on the steep trails," the runner said.

Tristan rested his hand on his sword hilt. "They'll lose more soon. And Skyler?"

The young man nodded. "He's in place with Kieran and Kendra. They're ready."

Tristan's jaw tightened and he looked over to the forest line, close to the mountain ridges. He would have liked to tell Kendra to stay somewhere safe. But if this defense didn't hold, there would be no safe place. He pulled his gaze away and straightened in the saddle. His eyes scanned the rough peaks of the mountains above us.

Hazor would have the high ground, but we didn't have a choice. We couldn't wait on the hills of the forest and let them advance that close to Braide Wood. The rough terrain would work against them as they moved down from the mountain toward us. But the approach also gave them cover if their sync-beams worked. They could position themselves behind the high boulders, and pick off our men without ever coming into range of the guardians' swords. Skyler's invention had to succeed.

I stretched my hearing and strained my eyes, watching the gaps in the boulders for movement. Still nothing. I focused my vision toward the woods. It took a few minutes, but I spotted Skyler and Kieran and Kendra. They were partially hidden by the trees, but right along the edge of the attack line. Kendra watched the mountains, and the two men fidgeted with levers and switches that jutted out of a waist-high cube. I squinted harder to see their machine. Every bit of technology I'd seen so far on this world was seamless, sleek, and designed to meld into its setting unobtrusively. Their creation was a monstrosity. Odd pieces poked out at random angles. Skyler's head was bent over the machine in concentration, and Kieran was scowling.

Lord, let it work.

Then I heard a sound. I edged Mara a few steps without realizing it and leaned forward in the saddle. There it was again. A heavy sound . . . feet on a hard-packed trail. Thousands of feet. I glanced back at the guardians. My heightened Restorer senses weren't necessary today. Everyone was hyperalert. They heard it too. Hands gripped sword hilts, at the ready. Eyes wavered between the line of the mountain ridge and the captains. We waited.

Muscles tensed throughout my body, and I had to consciously relax so Mara wouldn't mistake the tightening as a signal to move.

Then I saw them. Picking their way around the rocks, pouring over the top of the mountain ridge. Hazorite soldiers. They had cropped black hair and gray tunics with the jagged emblem of Hazor cutting like a lightning strike across their chests. It was hard to judge size from this distance, but these men bore little resemblance to Nolan's wiry frame. They were huge, well-muscled, and heavily armed. I hoped that the others couldn't see as much detail as I could, because the fierce determination on their faces was terrifying.

My heart pounded, and I forced myself to take a deep breath. Tristan remained completely still. He watched the men pouring down over the mountain like lava, and narrowed his eyes.

Another deep breath shivered through me.

Tristan glanced in my direction. His lehkan shifted. "Steady," he said softly. He wasn't only quieting his mount.

I nodded and pulled myself up tall.

The guardian at my side watched the approaching army. As their first wave came down toward the plains, he drew his sword out slowly and raised it high. I heard the whisper of hundreds of other swords. Still he sat, poised, staring forward. Like the moment of suspended time before a high diver leaps, he waited.

"Forward!" Tristan shouted, bringing his sword down.

Instinct wanted me to kick Mara and spring ahead, but the plan was for the cavalry to hold back to engage its Hazorite counterpart, so I held her in check. The first line of guardians on foot began to run. Tristan held his position, eyes scanning the flanks.

As expected, the Hazorites didn't engage directly. The soldiers stopped on the lower slopes of the mountain and pulled out their glistening black half-spheres. They were awkward to hold, and although they began to fire immediately, the glaring beams scorched dirt and grain stubble. The weapons were long-range, but seemed to be difficult to direct and control. They soon refined their aim, and the first row of our men ran forward into the blasts.

Someone fell, and I stiffened, causing Mara to lurch a few steps forward.

Then a shrill buzzing sounded over the valley, like crazed bees rattling around inside a tin silo or the manic tapping of an MRI machine. The strange humming shot across the air for miles. I winced against the sound, but watched in relief as the syncbeams stopped firing. The Hazorites glared at their weapons, shook them, adjusted them. Our first wave of guardians used the distraction to advance and engage. They took out several Hazorites before the enemy could set aside their syncbeams to draw their swords.

As more and more Hazorites flooded down the mountain, our first line pulled back to fight them sword to sword on the plain. The valley filled with the sounds of shouting and clashing, along with the humming noise of the suppression field.

Our guardians held their own at first, but they were hopelessly outnumbered. Tristan prepared to move the next regiment in from the flank, when the buzzing noise sputtered and stopped.

Even the soldiers engaged in one-on-one combat glanced into the air, confused. I stared hard into the tree line and stretched my vision. Skyler was shaking the machine, and Kieran was twisting one of the jutting antennae. Kendra watched them, her mouth open in horror. It wasn't working. The field wasn't holding. The horrible noise burst out briefly, but stopped again.

The latest wave of Hazorites coming over the hill quickly engaged their syncbeams. Because of the unpredictable aim, they charred some of their own men as they began firing into the valley. But as the second regiment of our army moved in from the side, Hazor's weapons had a clear target.

The air filled with the strange rattling blasts of the syncbeams, and the unearthly sound of men screaming as they were hit.

God help us.

Panic rose in my throat.

Tristan studied the valley before us, resolute. His eyes moved the way they did when shuffling white and black stones around on the table. But there were so few white stones. And ever more black ones pouring in.

Then I heard a new sound. Familiar but unexpected. I had been away from home for so many weeks that it took me a moment to recognize it. Thunder. I glanced up at the sky, puzzled. The low rumble stopped, but was followed by a huge crack and a flare of lightning. Tristan's face turned sheet white. Our lehkan shuddered.

"It's all right. It's just a thunderstorm," I shouted over another rumble. It was clear by the faces of the cavalry corps that no one had experienced this before. "It's the armies of the One." I raised a triumphant fist. They stared at me wide-eyed, then looked to Tristan.

Another fork of lightning struck the ground, and a strange metallic smell sifted through the air. I looked ahead to the Hazorite army. Those in the valley continued to fight, but the reinforcements moving down the side of the mountain froze and stared at the sky in terror. Hazorites positioned behind the rocks continued to fire their syncbeams. The next crash of thunder rolled through, and the sky broke open with wave after wave of flickering lightning, unrivaled by any I had seen in my world. All at once the syncbeams stopped working, some crucial mechanism fried by the electrical storm.

"Tristan, look!" I shouted.

Our flanking troops were moving now, and, in the confusion, beating back Hazor to the edge of the prairie.

But over the top of the ridge, new shapes were appearing. Lehkan. It was the Hazorite cavalry. Our foot soldiers couldn't move forward to attack them while they were still on the precarious slope. Too many Hazorites stood between them and the mountain.

We watched, helpless, as hundreds of huge lehkans and their riders picked their way down the steep trails, unopposed, and gathered into a line at the bottom of the mountain. Lightning continued to cut across the sky. Random crashes of thunder spooked the Hazor lehkan. Several animals bolted, throwing their riders and scrambling back up the mountain, but the overall wave continued to move forward. Our mounts shied nervously with each new crackle from the sky, and I feared I wouldn't be able to hold Mara back much longer.

Tristan raised his sword again. It was our turn.

A wall of Hazorite riders charged forward. Away from the foot of the mountain. Past the men from both sides battling on foot. Into Morsal Plains.

Toward us.

I drew my sword and watched them come, keeping the corner of my eye on Tristan. My heart pounded in readiness and terror.

They thundered up the slight incline where we waited.

Tristan's arm came down and our army flew forward with a roar. I didn't have time to think as Mara bolted forward. Hooves chewed up the ground. My heart rose into my throat. The distance closed with bewildering speed and our cavalries collided.

A sword arced toward me and I swung, unseating a Hazorite with a blow, though there was no time to absorb that fact before I saw another man heading for Tristan. The guardian was exchanging heavy blows with a mounted Hazorite, and I kicked Mara forward to intercept the second soldier. I sliced downward, then sideways—inelegant, but effective.

Keep your eyes open. Don't drop your sword, I coached myself as I cleared a path around us. Mara helped. She kept turning, anticipating attacks. Several times an enemy sword whistled toward my head, but Mara pivoted in time for me to see it and block. The instincts that had developed in me over the past weeks were fully grown now. The enemy's blades seemed to move toward me in slow motion, giving me time to react and counter and attack repeatedly.

I was no longer aware of sounds. The clanging, shouting, screaming, trampling noises all became muted. Even the booming claps of thunder barely registered. My eyes were open, but didn't fully absorb the sights around me. Faces twisted with hatred and pain. Lehkans reared. Weapons flickered along with the lightning. Bodies fell. The images were a moving painting brushed with blood. Blood on the swords, blood on the men collapsing forward in the saddle, blood on my hands. Everything blurred as if I were seeing it underwater. I lost track of time. I might have been fighting for minutes or hours. Or for an eternity. I was trapped in an eternal nightmare of slashing and turning and shouting.

I spun and searched for Tristan. He was still nearby. I pulled up closer as his lehkan lowered its head and gored a Hazorite from the side. The soldier fell, and the lehkan he had been riding sprang away.

Tristan spared me a glance, scanning the field around us. We were in a tight knot of Braide Wood cavalry, and had beaten off twice our number of Hazorites. We had a moment to breathe, and Tristan rode closer to me. "You're hurt."

I shook my head, but then followed his gaze. The sleeve of my tunic was sliced open, and blood had poured down my arm. I never felt it. "It healed. What's next?"

He wheeled his lehkan and headed partway up the hill and I followed. We still had a large percentage of our cavalry, but our soldiers in the valley were being driven back. More and more Hazorites poured down the side of the mountain. And they were angling their attack toward the forest. Our last line of defense before Braide Wood.

Tristan shouted over the noise and thunder and moans. He held his sword high and all the riders gathered to follow. We rode hard to the edge of Morsal Plains near the woods, cutting off the advance of some of Hazor's soldiers. The hacking, spinning, shouting confusion resumed as we held the line. But Hazor kept coming.

"There's too many." Tristan's face was hard and set, even as he kept swinging, but despair edged his voice.

I nudged Mara forward and tried to work faster. The battle was like fighting the acid-spewing minitrans. I ignored anything that hit me and just kept whacking.

My efforts didn't seem to help. I could drive back soldier after soldier, but more replaced them. Some had already slipped past our line and begun to climb up through the forest toward Braide Wood. Tristan would call a retreat if he could, but there was nowhere to retreat to.

Several Hazorites on foot targeted him at the same time, and through sheer force of numbers got close enough to impale his lehkan. The animal screamed and its legs buckled. Tristan sprang from its back before he could be crushed and continued fighting on foot.

I moved closer to get between him and the next rows of Hazorite soldiers that continued to stream forward. Each time I could spare a glimpse back at Tristan, he had collected another wound and was moving a bit slower than the time before. I looked around our cavalry for help, but we were too few and too scattered.

Another flare of light burned my retinas, and a deafening crash shook the air. Some of the Hazorites pulled back, only to be urged forward by their captains. Rain burst from the sky in a torrent. I lifted my head for a second, eager to let the water wash away the sweat and blood that streaked my face. I drove back a few foot soldiers and continued to keep my seat, using my added height to give Tristan some aid. I heard more rumbling, but this time the sound continued on and on. I looked up, confused. It wasn't thunder. I squinted through the sheets of rain to peer across the battlefield.

From the far side of the plains, behind the advancing

Hazorite army, something was moving. It took a moment for the Hazorite army to notice, but the infantrymen farthest from us began to turn. At the same time, one of the Braide Wood riders finally fought his way close to us and leaped from his lehkan. He shouted to Tristan and offered him his mount. Tristan didn't argue. I moved in to cover him while he pulled himself into the saddle. From the back of the lehkan, he was able to look out across Morsal Plains with me and see what was coming.

It was a cloud of screaming banshees. At least a hundred mounted warriors. They rushed toward the rear lines of the Hazorite army and sliced through without pause. Mud spattered up from the heels of their lehkan. Grim, hardened men faced us over the field of Hazorite soldiers.

"Who are they?" I shouted over the confusion of the storm and the fighting.

I saw a flash of white on Tristan's face when he grinned. "It's the two lost clans! Forward!" His shout rang out and was echoed by the other cavalry still fighting. The guardians attacked with new energy.

The Hazorites became compressed between the two forces. They couldn't pull back, so they retreated to the side, back up the steep slopes of the mountain.

I stayed close to Tristan as he moved forward, aiming to meet the army that had come to our aid. My sword whirled, faster and faster. Something stabbed my leg, but I ignored it. Hands tried to pull me from the saddle, but I thrust my sword downward and broke free.

As Hazor began a full-fledged retreat, I scanned the faces of the clans heading our way, curious about these people who had left the Council years before. They looked very much like the men from Rendor or Braide Wood. In fact, one of them looked a little like Mark. I jerked and Mara pulled up short for a second.

It *was* Mark. The Rendor emblem covered the front of his tunic. His wavy hair was plastered to his head with rain, and he bounced crazily as his lehkan galloped forward. But if his riding was clumsy, his sword work was virtuosic. His blade flew side to side as he mowed his way through the Hazor army. Wade rode by his side, the Braide Wood emblem on his tunic.

I kicked Mara's sides and she jolted forward. I fought with new vigor, clearing a path toward my husband.

Mark saw me coming and grinned. "I could never get the hang of riding these things," he shouted. I quickly scanned the area around us. No Hazorites were left standing in the vicinity. They had all pulled back or fallen.

"We thought you could use a little help," Wade added with a wink. Tristan was nudging his mount toward us, through the mass of riders from various clans. I didn't know what to do with my arm now that I had nothing to swing at. I rode hard right toward Mark, causing his lehkan to startle and spring to the side, almost unseating my husband. While he struggled to calm his mount, I moved in again, slower this time.

Tears ran down my face. "How . . . who . . . what did you do?" I couldn't throw my arms around him from my saddle so I settled for reaching out my free hand.

He grabbed it. "After I helped Jorgen get the guardians supplied, I convinced him to let me go ask for help from the two lost tribes. The clans had to unite. Hazor would have targeted them next." We held on to each other's hand, struggling to stay together in the sea of moving riders. I kept snapping my head around, finding it hard to accept that we were out of danger. Nearby, Tristan was already greeting the captains of the other clans, giving them his thanks, and pledging his alliance.

The bulk of our army slowly moved toward the mountain. The Hazorites scrambled up and over the ridgeline like beetles skittering up a cave wall. Tristan ordered one patrol group to pursue, but only to the ridgeline, to assess whether they planned to try again. I strained my hearing and tried to pick up snatches of words from the retreating soldiers. It was hard to make sense of it, but the voices I overheard held terror and confusion. I reassured Tristan that they really were retreating.

"Susan, Markkel, head up the trails toward the village," Tristan said. "Some of their men got past us. Be careful." He didn't wait for our answer, but turned to snap orders to others among his men.

We rode slowly toward the forest. "Let's go on foot," Mark said. "I can't wait to get out of this saddle."

I quickly agreed. The steep and narrow trails up through the woods were difficult to navigate on lehkan. We left our mounts in the care of some of the Braide Wood cavalry and paused to hug each other fiercely before trudging toward the trees. Wade held off a discreet distance, but then followed like Mark's faithful shadow.

Mark was eager to get away from his lehkan. I was desperate to get away from the site of fallen guardians and bloody Hazorite bodies that littered the plains. I drew a deep, shuddering breath. Relief began to well up inside me. We had done it.

Mark paused again to turn me toward him. He rested his forehead against mine. "Thank the One you're still alive. When we came over the ridge, all I could see was the Hazor army pouring across Morsal Plains."

"You saved us all, Mark. How did you convince—"

I never got a chance to finish my question. A silent gray

shape dropped from a tree branch overhead and knocked Mark to the ground. Another slipped from between the trees and swung a sword at Wade.

I lifted my blade, but someone grabbed me from behind, and another shape moved in with inhuman speed. A dagger sliced into my sword arm, and I caught a glimpse of it. A ven-blade. My arm went numb as its poisons seeped into my system, and the sword fell from my hands. Something slammed into the side of my head, and I fell backward. Masked, hooded faces looked down at me. Kahlareans.

Chapter Thirty-Three

MARK AND WADE WRESTLED WITH THEIR attackers in a flurry of sounds out of my line of sight—crackling underbrush, grunts, and thuds.

I was desperate to help them, but numbness from the venblade was affecting more than my sword arm. One of the Kahlareans dragged me deeper into the trees by my armpits.

I couldn't feel the ground scraping past beneath me. My right arm dangled, useless, and traced a path through the pine needles. The paralysis terrified me. My left hand fumbled toward my belt. I found the signaler Kendra had given me and pressed the thumb-sized panel on it.

The clear tone shrieked and my captor dropped me. Another assassin found the device and yanked it from my belt. The two of them argued over the noise of the alarm, until one of them ground it under his foot. The sound stopped.

Had it been enough? The Braide Wood cavalry had been close to the edge of the woods. Help had to be coming.

"Are you sure it's her?" said a reedy voice.

"Just kill her. We have to leave."

Nearby, the sounds of fierce struggle continued.

God, please save Mark. The prayer screamed in my mind.

I looked up at the trees. The Kahlareans had been trying for a long time to kill the Restorer. Anger washed through me, that we should come through so much only to have it end like this. It wasn't fair. I pushed the thoughts away and with effort turned my head slightly. I wanted to see Mark one more time.

Instead, a gray-masked shape crouched beside me, venblade poised over my heart.

My right hand twitched. Some sensation was returning, but I couldn't force my body to move. I couldn't fight back. Despair tore at me. I didn't want to die this way.

A twig cracked and the ground vibrated under my head as pounding feet ran toward us. The Kahlarean near me stiffened and turned. Someone charged toward us, and a sword grazed the Kahlarean's arm, sending the dagger flying out of his hand. The assassin rolled away and came up with a sword, and immediately swung at the man who had interrupted him.

The man ducked and parried expertly. Kieran. His clothes were covered with mud and blood. He must have joined the battle after the syncbeam suppressor broke. If death weren't hovering so nearby, I would have enjoyed watching him fight. He never stopped moving. My eyes could barely follow the rapid strikes. He drew the Kahlarean back away from me, circled him, and blocked every attack with cold efficiency.

I struggled again to move. This time I could put some weight on my right arm. It felt dead, with the pins-and-needles feeling of a limb getting circulation back. I propped myself up on my right elbow.

The second Kahlarean ran from behind me to retrieve the venblade that had fallen onto the forest floor. His eyes tracked the duel for a second. Then he turned to advance on me, sword loose in his left hand, venblade raised in his right.

I pushed back with my hands and barely traveled a few inches.

The assassin took another silent step toward me. Protruding, relentless eyes targeted me through his gray mask. Beyond the man's shoulder, I caught a glimpse of Kieran as he struck a lethal blow to his opponent. Kieran didn't stop to breathe. He raced at the second Kahlarean. The man heard him coming and spun away from me. He threw his venblade at Kieran, who sidestepped. The dagger flew past him, just grazing his shoulder. The Kahlarean switched his sword to his right hand and ran forward to meet Kieran's attack. Swords clashed as the men circled each other.

Hope and adrenaline filled my veins. It would be over in a minute, and then we could go help Mark and Wade. I was already able to move the upper half of my body again. I managed to sit up, but couldn't get my legs to work yet.

Kieran again maneuvered his opponent away from me. He took a step back, drawing the Kahlarean forward, and swung a killing blow.

But the assassin was fast, and spun under the strike. He came in tight and cut Kieran across the torso. Kieran stumbled back.

I couldn't see how bad the wound was. Footsteps were approaching, and I prayed it wasn't more enemies.

Kieran swung again, and the Kahlarean blocked him.

Movement flickered in the dense forest. Mark and Wade dodged around the trees at a run, getting closer to us.

The Kahlarean saw them coming, too. He backed toward me.

Kieran tried to stop him. He launched himself forward.

The Kahlarean was ready for him, and dodged past, slicing

as he crossed Kieran's path. Kieran gasped, made a half turn toward the assassin, and fell to one knee. The Kahlarean thrust his sword straight into Kieran and pulled it out. Kieran collapsed onto the ground just as Mark and Wade reached us.

The hooded assassin ran. Wade immediately gave chase, while Mark paused beside me. "Are you all right?"

"Yes. Get him."

Mark followed Wade.

My legs still wouldn't support me, so I crawled the short distance over to Kieran. He had fallen forward, and I pulled on his shoulder, turning him. I was already mentally reviewing every Red Cross class I'd ever taken. Pressure on the wounds to stop the bleeding. Keep the victim warm to prevent shock. His body rolled back; blood covered him.

"Kieran. Stay with me. Help is coming."

His eyes were vacant, staring past me at nothing. He was already gone.

I couldn't move. I couldn't breathe. If I didn't move, this wouldn't be real. Time wouldn't move forward. This wouldn't have really happened.

Mark and Wade ran back through the trees toward me.

"We got him," Wade said. He and Mark skidded to a stop. "Is he . . . ?"

I closed my eyes and dropped my head. I couldn't speak. Mark was beside me in a second, his arm around me. My shoulders started shaking.

"He died because of me," I whispered.

"No," Mark murmured against my face. "No. A lot of people died today. It wasn't because of you." I heard more footfalls on the pine needles.

"What happened?" Tristan asked. "I heard the alarm."

"Kahlareans attacked us," Wade said. "They're all dead."

Tristan wasn't listening. He walked forward to look at the body next to where I was huddled. He hissed a sharp breath in, but when I looked up at him, his face was a hard mask of control.

Tears ran down my face. "He saved my life."

The guardian didn't look at me. Mark gently pulled me back to give Tristan room.

For the next hour I had no strength or desire to move. Mark sat with me, quietly reminding me that Braide Wood was safe, that many lives had been saved, that we had done what we were meant to do. I tried to feel something besides the shock and pain, but couldn't. We had won, but it didn't feel the way I thought it would.

Tristan had showed no emotion since the moment he knelt and closed Kieran's eyes. He sent Wade for two guardians to carry his friend's body. He continued directing troops in the final search of the woods for Hazorite stragglers. He organized help for the wounded. He made sure I had recovered from the paralysis of the venblade. But not once did he meet my eyes.

Later, when Wade and Tristan returned with two men and lifted Kieran's body onto a blanket to carry him up to the village, Mark rubbed my back. "We should go."

I nodded, but still couldn't muster the energy to rise. I picked up a twig and twisted it in my hands.

Ow. I hadn't seen the thorn. I shook my finger and a few drops of blood fell to the pine needles beneath us. I held the finger to my mouth, and then pulled it away to watch it heal.

I kept waiting. Another drop of blood welled up. I brushed it away. Another took its place.

"What's wrong?" Mark asked. I held my finger out to him, and it took him a moment to realize what he was supposed to notice. His eyes widened.

I looked through the trees toward Morsal Plains where some of the guardians were still helping the wounded. I squinted to focus my vision and see more detail. Nothing happened. I felt a quiet loss and moment of emptiness. "It's gone." Then incredible relief blossomed inside me. I looked at Mark.

The same relief bloomed on his face. He hadn't had to see another Restorer die.

Our time here was over. "I want to go home now," I said quietly.

He nodded. "We'll go back to Lyric and the portal in the morning." Mark's hand moved up and down my arm. "I just wish the People weren't still facing so many dangers. Cameron is still on the Council, the Kahlareans are still a threat . . ." Mark looked at me and stopped. "But we helped." He kissed my forehead and drew me closer.

Even with Mark's help, our pace was slow as we made our way back up the trail to the village. Without Mark's steadying arm around me, I would have curled up into the pine needles under the trees and never moved again. Tristan had sent word ahead, and when we approached his home, the door opened slowly.

Tristan carried Kieran's body into the house, while Tara held the door open, tears streaming down her face. Kendra rolled out a pallet at the side of the room. Tristan carefully lowered Kieran onto it, and Kendra knelt beside her brother's body. His earth-toned clothes were soaked with blood, and his skin was white and cold. Tristan turned away for a moment, unable to face his own pain coupled with the raw grief in Kendra's face.

Mark and I stepped closer. I couldn't believe Kieran was dead. He had sometimes frightened me, and often made me furious. But he'd been Tristan's loyal friend, Kendra's fiercely protective brother, and a true ally to me. Mark wrapped both his arms around me as my shoulders began to shake with silent sobs again.

Kendra smoothed back Kieran's hair and began talking to his lifeless body. Her voice murmured apologies for childhood wrongs: for the time she knocked him out of a tree when they were playing in the woods, for telling his father when he sneaked out after dark, and for ruining his best dagger by whittling with it. We waited in silence while she reminded him of times they had shared. "And I always believed in you," she whispered. "No matter what Father said. You know I understood. How can you do this? Please don't do this." Her hand stroked his face. "You can't leave like this."

Suddenly she gasped and skittered backward. "He moved. I saw him. He moved."

Tristan turned to look at her, his eyes full of compassion. He helped her to her feet and gathered her into his arms. "Shh. He didn't. Kendra, I'm so sorry. He's gone."

Tristan was right. The Kahlarean's sword had nearly cut Kieran in two. People didn't recover from wounds like that. My eyes filled again as I focused on a deep gash across his angular face—

I rubbed my eyes. I looked closer. "Mark . . . do you see that?" I stepped forward and knelt down. "Look at the cut on his face."

The wound was healing.

The edges met and sealed. I used the sleeve of my tunic to wipe the blood away from his cheek. There was a barely visible thin white scar. No wound.

Then he moaned. We all jumped.

I looked up at Mark and Tristan and Kendra, my mouth open. "What's happening?"

They all looked as frightened as I was.

I turned back to stare at Kieran. His chest moved as he took a deep breath in and gasped with pain. Instinctively I took his hand in mine. "Hang on," I whispered. "It will get better. I promise." Mark came and knelt beside me, an arm around my waist.

Kieran's eyes opened and struggled to focus. Confusion clouded his face. Kendra took a hesitant step closer, but held back, as if afraid she would do the wrong thing and this miracle would rewind. Tears were still running down her face.

Tristan found his voice first. "He's healing."

It was true. Color was easing back into Kieran's face, and he took another gasping breath. He squeezed his eyes shut against the pain, and rolled to his side, his free arm wrapping around his stomach. Tristan edged closer.

I looked up at him. "What does it mean?"

Tristan's eyes were wide. "I think," he swallowed, "that it is still a time of great need for our people."

I nodded. Hazor had been driven back, and Braide Wood was safe for the moment. But danger still crowded in around the People.

"You and Markkel need to return to your world," Tristan continued.

My head bobbed up and down. I wished we could do more to help, but I had no doubt that it was time for us to go home.

"So . . ." Tristan looked down at Kieran. "I think He's sent another Restorer."

I looked back at Kieran. He opened his eyes wide and stared at Tristan in alarm. He turned so pale that I thought we were losing him again.

"No. Impossible. Absolutely not," Kieran said through clenched teeth.

I sat back on the floor, letting go of his hand. I had glimpsed the One's deep love for this man on the day that we had sparred in the clearing. Kieran pretended he had no faith in the One and no allegiance to the Verses, but the One had plans for him. I had seen that much. But I would never have guessed this was part of the plan. I felt a wave of sympathy for him.

Mark and Kendra looked at each other, stunned. "Him?" they asked in unison.

I started to laugh. I couldn't help it. Kieran glared at me and pushed himself up to sit. I laughed harder and swiped at the tears running down my face. Mark straightened up and helped me to my feet.

I smiled at Tristan. "I'm glad we could meet the new Restorer before we leave."

Tristan looked down at his glowering friend and then grinned at me. "And I thought *you* were a strange Restorer."

The evening became something of a celebration. We all washed the grime of battle away and changed clothes. Tara served bowls of peppery soup and beamed at the faces around the table. She was delighted for a chance to get to know Mark and tried to unravel the mystery of his role in both worlds while they chatted. Kendra sat beside Tristan, taking every opportunity to lean against him, touch his arm, and tell him how proud she was of him. He had lost many good men today, but an impossible battle had been won. And Kieran had healed. As the evening continued, the hard set to Tristan's face began to soften.

I sympathized with Tristan. I had seen too many horrible things in the battle and after to allow myself to really celebrate. But as the reality of all the miracles sank in, I began to smile more too. I closed my eyes as the family recited the Verses for the evening, savoring every word. As everyone left the table, I helped Tara carry dishes to the kitchen. Mark and Tristan had their heads together, debating the strengths of various tribes, and how to build on the tentative new alliance with the lost clans. I noticed that Kieran had disappeared. He had been pensive during dinner. Tristan and Kendra had treated him with such awe at first he had threatened to leave. After that they slid back into their normal banter with him. When he didn't respond to their teasing, they eventually left him in peace.

"I'll be right back," I told Tara.

She nodded and patted my cheek. "Thank the One you survived the day."

I slipped out the door and found Kieran sitting on a bench against the front of the house. He was holding his dagger, and as I walked toward him, he idly sliced a small cut on his hand and watched it heal. He did it again. And again.

"Stop that," I said.

He looked up at me, his face passive. "It's a mistake, you know." He moved over, and I sat down beside him. I was worried by the unfocused look in his eyes. "I can't be a Restorer." He looked down and slid the knife across his hand again, drawing a thin line of blood.

I snatched the dagger out of his hand and tucked it in my belt.

He didn't even react. Rubbing away the blood, he stared at the place where the wound wasn't. He flexed his hand and sighed. "I can't be who they need." He sounded lost and overwhelmed. None of his cynicism or deliberate aloofness remained.

For a moment I worried that it wasn't really Kieran that had returned to us.

"I know," I said quietly. "But Kieran, this is something wonderful." He snorted, and I smiled at that small sign of his personality returning. "You're alive. Can't you at least be happy about that?"

He glared at me. "What am I supposed to do now?"

"Same as you've already done. Do what you can."

Kieran's shoulders sagged under the unwanted responsibility I knew he felt. "I can't do this."

"It's not about what you can do. It's about what the One is doing. Stop fighting Him." I thought of the quiet word that had burned into my heart on Feast day in the Lyric tower. *Surrender.* I wanted to tell him, to describe it to him in all its sweetness. But there was another One who would make him understand. Kieran frowned out at the dark trees. "Why don't you go talk to Him now?" I asked.

He looked at me, startled. Then his eyes narrowed. "I do have a few things to say to Him." His voice had the same resentful tone he had used in addressing the Council. I bit my lip to keep from smiling. This was going to be an interesting conversation. He held out his hand for his dagger. I returned it and he gave me a terse nod and strode off into the night, ignoring the fact that no one ventured out after dark.

God, you've called a very reluctant Restorer in that one. Please take care of him.

I went back into the house and pried Mark away from his discussion with Tristan, earning a grateful smile from Kendra.

"Mark, it's not our job anymore. Come on. Let's get some sleep." I took a deep breath, and a knob of pain tightened in my chest again.

Mark noticed me wince. "Still bad?"

I nodded. "I don't understand. Maybe it will heal when we go home. I hate feeling so weak."

"You weren't weak today."

"But that was special power from the One. It was Him working through me."

Mark smoothed the hair back from my temples and let his hands rest against the sides of my face. "It always is."

Warmth surged through me. He was right. The role of the Restorer wasn't all that different from the roles I had in my own world. In both worlds I felt discouraged by my weakness and very small against the needs and battles I faced. Yet, even weak or small, I wasn't on the road alone.

I pulled Mark's head down and rested my forehead against his. "Let's get some sleep. Tomorrow we have a transport to catch."

Chapter Thirty-four

WE SAID OUR GOODBYES IN TARA and Payton's home at first light. I soaked in the rustic warmth of the log walls behind the light panels, the long wooden table where I'd shared so many meals with the family, and the scent of freshly brewed clavo wafting from the kitchen. Talia and Gareth had a hard time hiding how glad they were to see me leave. But they nudged Dustin, who pulled a creation from behind his back with great flourish and offered it to me. A wooden frame carved with small ferns held a lumpy three-peg design.

"I made the weaving." Aubrey elbowed her brother aside.

My throat closed as I knelt to hug them both. "Thank you. It's beautiful."

When I stood, Tara held my face in her hands and touched her forehead to mine. "I'll have a bowl of clavo brewing for you if you ever want to visit." Even Payton gave me a gruff pat on the shoulder.

Kendra squeezed me in a tight embrace. "Thank you," she whispered.

I nodded, feeling my eyes sting. Then she turned and grabbed Mark in a quick hug as well. I could swear I saw him blush. Tristan walked out the door with us and offered Mark his hand. They clasped forearms.

"You'll always have an ally in Braide Wood, Markkel of Rendor," Tristan said.

Mark nodded. "May the One ride at your right hand." Respect and affection warmed the faces of both men.

My eyes stung again, and I swiped at a tear that escaped. "Tristan, thank you so much," I said as he turned to me. "You helped me, and trusted me, and trained me. You kept putting up with me when I made mistakes. You taught me so much—"

"Oh for pity's sake. Just say goodbye already," a voice drawled from behind Tristan. We both turned. Kieran slouched on the bench, one foot braced on the wooden seat. He levered himself to his feet.

"See what I have to put up with?" Tristan said, looking at me. "And he's going to be even worse now. Are you sure you can't stick around?"

I laughed and gave Tristan a quick hug. He patted my back awkwardly and stepped back. "Go with the One."

I walked over to Kieran. The skin under his eyes was smudged with dark shadows of fatigue.

"Rough night?" I asked.

His eyes narrowed. "I may not be able to forgive you for this."

"For what?" Tristan cut in. "Healing Kendra? Getting rid of the Rhusicans? Speaking to the Council? Uniting the clans?" His voice had a warning edge, which Kieran ignored as he continued to glare at me.

"It's not my fault." I fought to hide a smile, but my mouth twitched. "I didn't ask the One to make you the next Restorer."

"No, but you're enjoying this far too much," Kieran said.

I laughed and threw my arms around him before he could pull back. "You aren't alone," I said softly, before I let him go. He met my eyes and nodded.

Wade insisted on escorting us to Lyric—his last act as our house protector. Mark, Wade, and I stopped briefly at Linette's home on our way out of the village. She was so pale that she seemed translucent, but leading the singing yesterday had restored some of the ardor in her eyes. Faith glowed like a banked fire. One day her spirit would blaze again.

And then, as I had learned it was prone to do, time accelerated. The trail seemed like a brief hike. The transport flew. How could time move at such different rates?

We walked the short distance from the transport into Lyric, and then straight across the center of the city. My steps slowed as we passed the worship tower. The white walls glowed as they reached skyward. Would I ever again feel the presence of the One in such a tangible way as I had on the Feast day? Maybe the spiritual atmosphere of my world was so clouded that I'd have to be content with seeing through a glass darkly on this side of eternity, but I'd never forget how it felt to hear the One whisper to my heart in this place of clarity.

Mark led us to the hidden door that opened toward the grove on the far side of the city. "Wade, from here we need to go on alone."

Wade shifted his bulk from one foot to the other and back. "But I—"

"You've honored us with your service, but you've fulfilled your vow. Go back to Tristan and help him protect Braide Wood."

Still, Wade looked uncertain. Mark didn't want anyone else

knowing about the portal, so we had to convince our faithful protector to leave. "You'll need to hurry to get the transport back to Braide Wood before dark." I touched his arm where deep claw wounds had left scars. "You don't want to fight any more bears, do you?"

He grinned and rubbed his stubbly beard. "I wouldn't worry if I had you and your sword by my side."

I rested my hand on my sword hilt. "You were a good teacher. Go with the One."

Mark slid open the small door and we hurried through. Even then Wade lingered until Mark pulled the door closed, shutting out our view of his ruddy face along with the back streets of Lyric.

Hand in hand, Mark and I walked toward the grove. Somewhere along the way his arm moved to embrace my shoulders. I leaned into him. "You're sure you know where the portal is?"

"It's not something I'd forget." His gruff assurance calmed my nerves for about two seconds.

"But how do we know it'll work? What if the portal doesn't let us through? What if—"

"Susan, you've survived Kahlarean assassins and Hazorite cavalry. Now's not the time to get wimpy on me."

"Wimpy?" I pulled away in a huff. Then I saw his shoulders moving.

He laughed and gathered me close. His lips took mine with fierce possession, as if reclaiming me from this world that had taken me from him for so long. By the time I could breathe again, I'd forgotten about my worries.

"This way," he said, leading me between two trees with spiraling trunks.

Energy sparked along my skin and my hair drifted out with static, as if I'd rubbed it with a balloon. Then we were through. No trauma, no storms, no earthquakes.

The attic still smelled like fresh Sheetrock dust.

I ducked my head to avoid a rafter and turned to see Mark beside me. "Hey, look! It came through." I grinned as I held up the framed three-peg weaving Aubrey and Dustin had given to me that morning.

Mark didn't take time to respond. He picked up the three stones on our side of the portal and positioned them so no one could go back through. "I'll throw one of them in the pond. That should separate them enough."

I put a hand on his arm. "Wait. Don't do that. Put them someplace safe."

He hefted the smooth rock in his palm and looked up at me. "Are you sure?"

I shrugged. "It seems wrong to throw them away."

Mark gave me a slow smile. His Council tunic had been stained beyond repair in yesterday's battle, so he wore a hand woven sweater from Tristan. His sword rested at his hip. After a couple of weeks back in his world-of-origin, carrying a blade had become a habit.

All the bits of clothing and weaponry I had collected along my way had also returned with me. My hand moved to my sword hilt, and I laughed. I drew the sword and looked at it under the bare light bulb.

It was plastic again.

I held it out for Mark to see. "This wouldn't hold up long against the Hazorites."

"Thank the One you won't be needing a sword here." Mark pulled me into a hug.

I laid the sword in the toy bin and took off my cloak and folded it over the other costumes, giving it a gentle pat. I slid off my gauntlets and smiled at them.

I was glad for the reminders of my time in the other world. *Time.*

"Mark, what time is it? How much time went by?" I didn't wait for his answer, but scrambled down the pull-down stairs. I sprinted to the kitchen. The clock flashed the date and time. Same day, 8:00 p.m.

I leaned against the counter, breathing hard. I felt light-headed, and bent farther forward.

"Are you okay?" Mark asked, coming up beside me.

"It's still there. The pain. I guess that answers that question." I tried to smile. "Just another souvenir I brought back." Why would the same One who had provided Restorer powers allow this damage to remain and come through the portal with me? Although, if it saved Braide Wood, it was a small price to pay.

"You're going to the doctor first thing Monday morning, all right?" Mark stood beside me, and I turned and nuzzled my face against his chest.

He wrapped his arms around me, and we stayed there until our breaths were rising and falling in unison. "I guess I should drive over to your mom's and pick up Jon and Anne," he said at last.

My eyes suddenly flooded with tears. The yearning for my children these past weeks had been an aching emptiness like that of the haunting, deserted streets of Shamgar. Deep fear had slithered through every thought of them. Until this moment I hadn't known if I would really find my way back—if I would ever see them again.

I grabbed the car keys from the pegs by the door and tossed

them to Mark. "Let's go. Hurry up."

"Slow down, Mama Bear. I've missed them, too. But don't you think we should change first?" Mark leaned against the kitchen counter, rugged, unshaven, sword at his side. He seemed larger—or our kitchen seemed smaller. He'd definitely raise some eyebrows marching up to my mom's condo looking like that.

"Okay. We'll get changed, But come *on*." I grabbed Mark's hand and hurried down the hall. In a few minutes I'd have Jon and Anne in my arms again—every squabbling, loose-toothed, sticky-with-jam inch of them. Then Jake would get home from work and Karen from Amanda's, and we'd order pizza and let everyone stay up past bedtime. Joy spiraled its way up through my chest.

Then the hallway wavered.

I dropped Mark's hand and grabbed the wall. "Whoa."

"What's wrong?" Mark quickly held me up.

I waited for the vertigo to pass. "Just light-headed again. But that is *not* going to slow me down. I want to see the kids."

"Sure." Mark supported me subtly as we walked into our bedroom. "But you need to catch your breath. I'll go get them, and you can take your time changing. Rest. Take a bath."

Could I stand one more minute of waiting? Mark was already pulling on his jeans, leaving his Braide Wood clothes in a pile on the floor and his sword leaning against the wall. I sank onto the bed. Maybe a few minutes of rest would be a good idea.

"I suppose. But don't let my mom talk you into a piece of pie or anything." I curled up on the bed, amazed at how soft it felt.

Mark pulled a quilt up over me and gave me a quick kiss. "I promise. Sure you're okay?"

"Mm hmm. Just tired. Hurry."

I didn't need to prod him further. He was as anxious to see the kids again as I was. Probably wanted to reassure himself that the life he'd built in this world was still in place. I closed my eyes as the kitchen door closed and his car pulled out of the driveway.

Then, despite my fatigue, my brain came fully awake. I was really home. I shoved away the quilt, too excited to lie around. I prowled restlessly through the kitchen and living room. It would take at least ten minutes each way, plus a few minutes of chatting with my mom, before Mark and the kids would get back. I should have gone with him.

I got a drink of water in the kitchen and rubbed at a sticky spot of jam on the counter. Not so long ago, I'd been frustrated that I spent so much time cleaning up messes and muddling through tedious days. Now I felt incredible gratitude that I was back in my own home.

How had it all started? That's right, my Bible study. I'd been feeling depressed about the unimportance of my life while I read about everything Deborah did in the book of Judges.

A new burst of energy propelled me to the back hallway. That's what I could do while I waited for Mark and the kids. I could finally initiate the attic getaway spot that Mark had made for me.

I climbed the pull-down stairs and settled in my chair. Taking a deep breath, I sat quietly as I had done with Lukyan once and thanked the One for the gift of life and for being with me each step of my journey.

When I opened my eyes, something glinted near the base of the sewing mannequin.

I crouched and ducked under the eaves to reach for it.

Jake's iPod. That scamp *had* been up here snooping around.

He must have dropped it after our family meeting, before he left for work.

I settled back into my chair and opened my journal. My finger traced the notes I had scribbled about being a heroic woman of God.

I grabbed a pen. "I surrender," I wrote to God. "Help me follow You." When Mark had built this hideaway, I had hoped it would provide me a place to get closer to God. My lips quirked. It didn't work out quite the way I had expected—but that's how a lot of life is. Unexpected.

I turned the page and my breath caught.

My pencil drawing covered the page. The "Oak of Susan" looked a lot like the gnarly-branched trees of the Lyric grove. And underneath were a few words in Jake's unmistakable scrawl. *Hey, mom. Cool sketch. Love ya, Jake.*

He'd been up here. But it couldn't have been before he left for work. He'd left right after the family meeting.

The kitchen door slammed. "Susan?" Mark thumped through the living room.

"Up here," I called. He'd only been gone five minutes. Why was he back already?

He popped his head up through the floor opening. "Have you seen Jake? I was halfway to your mom's when I realized his car was out in front of the house, so he must be home from work. I thought I better come back and warn you so you could get changed before he sees you."

"He can't be here. There's no music coming from his room." The first thing Jake always did when he came home was to crank up his stereo.

"I'll check." Mark disappeared from view.

I picked up the iPod and turned it around in my hands.

Slowly, I eased my way down the steps to the hall. Mark met me, shaking his head. The silence of the house closed in on me.

"Maybe he came home and thought no one was here and went for a walk," Mark said.

Right. The day Jake went for a walk voluntarily would be the same day Karen decided to clean her room just for the fun of it. I checked the row of pegs by the kitchen door. "His keys are here. Even if a friend picked him up, he'd still have taken his house keys. He came home and didn't go back out again."

My heart was starting to pound. I ran to the stairs and scrambled into the attic. Mark was right behind me. The bare light bulb still cast a pool of light on my chair and end table. My journal still lay open on the table. I held the book up to Mark, my hands shaking. "He was up here in the attic. While we were gone. He got back from work and came up here."

"The portal was open." Mark took the journal, set it down, and fumbled for my hands. We looked at each other in panic.

Mark took a deep breath. "Okay, I'll go through and find him. He must be somewhere in Lyric." He was already pulling the stones out of hiding and positioning them.

My fear grew. There was no way I could watch my husband disappear through that portal. "We're both going." My voice shook, but I crossed my arms and stuck out my chin.

He glanced up at me and opened his mouth to argue, but then gave a staccato nod.

My mind raced. "Wait a second." I ran downstairs to the phone. Urgency made me hit the wrong buttons twice, but I finally reached my mom. I asked if she could watch the kids a few more hours, trying to keep my voice breezy. Both Jon and Anne got on the line.

"I love you, kiddo-beans." My throat went all thick, and I fought to hide the tears so I wouldn't alarm them.

"We got bored with Crazy Eights and Go Fish," Anne chirped.

"And Anne cheated," Jon complained.

My heart swelled. Their bickering was the sweetest sound in the world.

"So grandma's gonna teach us poker." Anne smacked some carefree kisses through the phone. "Bye, Mommie. Love ya."

"I love you, too." Poker? I stared at the phone before setting it down, and shook my head slowly as I headed back to the hall.

Mark came from the bedroom, back in his Braide Wood clothes, sword once again at his side.

"We'd better hurry," I told him. "Jon and Anne need rescuing, too."

I made one more call, to Karen's friend Amanda. Amanda's mom said they had gone to a movie, and asked if Karen could spend the night. That taken care of, I followed Mark back up the stairs.

For a moment a voice as subtle and dangerous as a Rhusican's spoke into my mind. "It's not fair. You just got back. You've done enough. You shouldn't have another problem to face." I pushed the thoughts aside and ducked under the eaves long enough to pry the lid off the dress-up bin. I grabbed my cloak and the plastic sword.

Mark held out his hand to me, strength and trust drawn in hard-earned layers on his strong features.

My own faith swelled. I took a deep breath and stepped toward him and the portal.

Any road, Lord.

etc.

bonus content includes:

Reader's Guide

1. Few of us will have an experience like Susan Mitchell's fantastical journey into a different reality. Yet many people find themselves pulled into worlds they didn't expect: a diagnosis of cancer, a friend's death, a parent's Alzheimer's, a child's illness, divorce, addiction, or unemployment. Have you had to struggle through a "foreign world" that you wouldn't have chosen to explore? What "portal" pulled you into the experience? Can you relate to Susan's early emotions of shock, numbness, fear, and denial?

2. Susan was challenged to fill a role for which she felt unequipped and inadequate. When do you struggle with feelings of inadequacy in your daily life? What roles feel overwhelming to you?

3. Friendships helped Susan survive her first weeks in the new world. Who were some of your favorite characters in *The Restorer* and what did they offer Susan? In your real life, who are your allies and how do you support each other?

4. The People of the Verses lived among many dangers. The Rhusicans were a particularly troubling enemy.

What made them difficult to fight? What parallels can you draw in your own current life-battles? If you had to identify a thread of mind poison that has affected your thoughts, what would it be?

5. Each major character in *The Restorer* has a unique relationship with the One, from intimate closeness, reverence, and profound trust, to confusion and frustration, to outright scoffing and refusal to believe in His existence or benevolence. Which character has a spiritual framework closest to your own? Why?

6. In the Old Testament book of Judges, the twelve tribes of Israel are threatened on every side, and God raised up a series of leaders who delivered the people. *The Restorer* is loosely inspired by the story of Deborah, one of the Judges. What parallels did you notice between this novel and the Old Testament accounts? What differences?

7. Do you think Susan's experiences as the Restorer changed her? Why and in what ways? How do you think this might affect her attitudes and choices when she returns to her normal life?

8. Do you ever see your life as an epic adventure? The Bible says we are pilgrims in a world where we no longer belong. Did anything in Susan's story inspire you in facing your own daily battles?

Glossary

bitum tree: Tree with broad, shiny leaves far overhead and a smooth black trunk coated with runnels of glossy sap, which is used to make roads

caradoc: Docile herd animal with soft hair that is used for creating fibers

clans: The People of the Verses comprise twelve original clans; however, two have separated from the others and are now known as the lost clans. Excluding these two, the clans are Lyric, Braide Wood, Rendor, Shamgar, Corros Fields, Blue Knoll, Ferntwine, Terramin, Sandor, and Taborn.

clavo: Spicy tea with a rich flavor and near-healing properties; favorite hot beverage of the clans; usually brewed in a wide wooden bowl over a heat trivet and ladled into mugs

Council: Governing body of the People of the Verses, comprising chosen representatives from each tribe; meets in Lyric and makes decisions that affect all the tribes

Council Guard: Elite group of guardians with the specific role of serving and protecting councilmembers

Gray Hills: Area where Shamgar clan once prospered, near the clay-fields and the border of Hazor; named for the rolling hills covered with gray-green moss; full day's journey from Braide Wood

guardian: Member of any clan who trains for a military/ protector role, which includes serving the Council and the people, training for and engaging in battle, and patroling the borders

Hazor: Nation across the mountain border of the People's clans. Hazorites worship the hill-gods and sacrifice their children to those gods. Zarek is the current king and rules from the capitol, Sidian. He plans expansion and the destruction of nations in his way.

healer: A person skilled in treating illness and injuries with electronic diagnostic devices as well as herbal remedies. Most villages have their own healers, but near Braide Wood there is a lodge where especially difficult cases from all the clans are handled.

heat trivet: Flat panels or tiles that glow with heat or light. Various sizes are used to provide surfaces for cooking and illumination. They are a smaller version of the technology used to create the light walls common in homes.

Kahlarea: Nation across the river that borders one side of the People's lands. Kahlareans are pale, with bulbous eyes, and their assassins are feared everywhere for their stealth and ability to hide and appear from nowhere.

lehkan: Animals used for riding. They look similar to elk, with fierce antlers and soft llama-like fur. They are ridden under saddle and guided by leg commands.

Lyric: Central city of the clans. The Lyric tower is the place where the One meets with the People in an especially tangible way. Lyric's walls are white and form a scalloped pattern as they encircle the city.

magchip: Renewable energy source for a variety of technologies

messenger: Because the clans and the surrounding nations don't have a written language, messengers memorize information to take from place to place. Messengers are often young, agile, and fast.

orberry: A tart juice made from small orange berries that grow on low-lying shrubs along the edge of Morsal Plains. Sometimes fermented to create an intoxicating version of the drink, which is especially popular in Hazor.

People of the Verses: The collection of clans who worship the One. They pass down the Verses to their children through daily recitations.

portal stones: Fist-sized, round, smooth objects with hidden technology. When three are aligned correctly and activated, they create a portal between the world of the People of the Verses and ours.

Records: A sacred recording of the Verses in their original form, spoken by the One. Each clan has one, which the clan's eldest songkeeper plays on end-of-season Feast days.

Rendor: Markkel's tribe along the river

Restorer: A leader sent by the One to save His people, traditionally a guardian. Once called by the One for this role, the Restorer develops heightened senses and strengths of various kinds, and heals rapidly from most injuries.

Rhusican: A person from Rhus, a nearby nation; usually attractive, with reddish-gold hair and vibrant aqua or green eyes. Rhusicans have the ability to read and affect minds and to plant poison in people's thoughts that can influence their behavior and even cause death.

rizzid: Lizard-shaped creature, muddy red in color and

covered with fur; climbs walls and has rows of sharp, venomous teeth

season: The time it takes grain to go through one full cycle of planting, growth, and harvest. There are six seasons each year.

songkeeper: A person who leads worship, composes songs, encourages people, and promotes the faith life of the People

syncbeam: Long-range, focused energy beam used as a weapon

three-peg: A weaving technique where yarn is wrapped in patterns around a small, three-pegged loom to create a variety of textiles, including sweaters and bedcovers

transtech: A person skilled in designing and repairing the wide variety of technology used by the clans

transport: Automated vehicles of various sizes that follow programmed routes between and within cities; long, sleek, and silver, with curved doors that slide up into the roof

venblade: Small dagger used by Kahlarean assassins; reservoir in the handle injects poison into the blade to cause paralysis in the victim

Verses: Holy account of the People's history, laws, and promises about Restorers and the coming Deliverer, given directly by the One. The Records contain an audible version of the original directives from the One. However, the Verses are still a living tradition and the One guides each generation of songkeepers in adding the next section of history. These additional sections of the Verses are not in the Records, but are equally unchanging and sacred, and passed down by vigilant oral tradition.

Song of First Light

Words by Sharon Hinck
Music by Joel Hinck

Coming Soon

The Restorer's Son

Chapter One

"HILLS OF HAZOR TAKE YOU," I swore for at least the tenth time since first light. My sword hacked at thick underbrush, but when I shouldered my way forward, a twig snapped back to hit my face. I cursed the day I'd met the last Restorer. It was because of her that I was battling through this forsaken forest below Cauldron Falls. My blade deserved a more substantial enemy.

A squint-eyed badger rambled out from a thorn bush and paused to sniff the air. It bristled and ducked back under cover. Wise plan. I was hungry. Stinging beetles landed on me from the low-hanging branches overhead. I swatted them away and stalked onward.

Why hadn't I convinced Tristan to leave her in Shamgar when she first turned up? A witness to his crime, and he had brought her to our refuge in the deserted city. Typical. He was a naïve idiot sometimes.

She hadn't looked very threatening that day—rain-soaked, bloody, and unconscious. If only I'd known then how much trouble she was capable of causing. What was that old saying? Don't judge a rizzid's menace until you see its teeth.

The trouble had started when a deep scrape on her face healed. Instantly. Hairs on my neck pricked as if I'd touched a misaligned magchip. I'd heard the old stories, but I'd never seen it happen. It had been years since our people had chased after a mythic Restorer, but I knew the signs.

Exactly the kind of problem we hadn't needed. We would have been in enough danger if she were just a Council spy or some other enemy. But as I had watched her wounds vanish, I knew: If she also had Restorer powers, things were going to get very complicated.

And they did. I circled the trunk of a large spice tree and stopped. My hearing had grown unnaturally keen in the past days—keen enough, I hoped, to warn me if there were any Kahlareans nearby. Cauldron Falls roared in the distance, and a few animals rustled in the damp leaves of the forest floor. Guardians from our clans patrolled the river below the falls. I should be able to hear or see some sign of them.

I frowned. Nothing.

I pulled another beetle off my arm and ground it under my heel, then pushed through a clump of bracken and caught a glimpse of the river. Water crashed from the hundred-foot falls and swirled in an angry mass at the base. Over the years, the rocks had worn into a rounded bowl, earning the name Cauldron Falls. I hiked along the river's edge, picking my way over the boulders and scanning the opposite bank. The river surged, wide and rough, a natural barrier to protect our lands. Unhappily, upstream from the falls the river narrowed, and a gap cut between steep rock cliffs. The pass provided a natural pathway into our lands.

The trail to the top of the falls rose steeply. I sheathed my sword and grabbed the rocks to pull myself up. A few stones dislodged beneath my boots and crashed down behind me. I climbed faster. This was a bad spot to be caught by an enemy.

The river border used to be easy to guard, but lately our patrols were in danger from syncbeams—long-range weapons the Kahlareans used from cover on their side of the river. Tristan was worried about an invasion, so I agreed to check things out. He probably figured my trip here would follow some historic precedent because a past Restorer gave his life fighting off two hundred Kahlareans at Cauldron Falls. Tristan liked traditions.

When I reached the top of the falls, I settled on a boulder, pulled out my gourd of orberry juice, and savored the loneliness. At my feet, the water rushed by, violent and unpredictable, and I knew an instant kinship with the river.

The past few days had honed my irritation to a fine edge. After Susan and Markkel disappeared, Tristan begged me to present myself to the Council and inform them that I was the Restorer. I refused. He nagged. I snarled. Then he fought dirty. He sent my sister, Kendra, to talk to me. They'd been wearing me down. When I overheard Tristan talking about his concerns for the River Borders, I jumped at the excuse to leave. I couldn't stand any more of their earnest trust in me. The look of hope in their faces. The expectations I could never fulfill. Spare me from Braide Wood's overgrown reverence for the old myths. I wasn't the Restorer they looked for. It was a cosmic joke—a worse joke than the last Restorer had been. Susan of Ridgeview Drive, she called herself. No clan I'd ever heard of.

I pushed myself back to my feet and headed upstream. With luck I'd reach the outpost before the afternoon rains. The sky pressed low in the flat gray tones of midday. The air was warmer than in Braide Wood, and my tunic soon clung to the sweat on my skin. I knelt by the river's edge to splash cold water on my face, rub dirt from the stubble on my jaw, and rake some sticks and leaves from my hair. My black hair had always marked my status as an outsider. Even as a child I'd refused to hide my Hazorite blood. Instead, I made the folk of Braide Wood even more uncomfortable by cropping my hair short, like the enemy Hazorites. It would have been impossible to hide anyway. Both Kendra and I took after our mother and had the thin frames and angled cheekbones of her heritage.

I straightened up and inhaled deeply, taking in the smell of pine and the tangy bite of the golden spice trees. The non-stop roar of rushing water muted my chafing thoughts, and some of the knots in my back loosened. I rubbed the back of my neck. The cave where I slept last night had an uneven rock floor. I could have stayed in Rendor's central city but decided I'd rather take my chances with the scavengers and bears than make conversation.

I adjusted my pack, shifting the weight to a more comfortable spot on my shoulders, and scanned the opposite shoreline for any sign of movement. With a little concentration, I could see small details from miles away, one of the few advantages to being the Restorer. A red-furred rizzid sunned on the rocks of the far bank, but I didn't spot any human enemies. I made a point to study the tree line closely. Kahlarean assassins were notorious for being nearly invisible in their hooded masks and mottled gray clothes. They would be a far greater danger than an average Kahlarean soldier, even one armed with a syncbeam.

I'd fought their assassins twice now and hadn't come off well either time. I suppose simply surviving an encounter with them should be considered a success—though I'm not sure my last experience counted as surviving. They were swift and silent, and even a scratch from their venblades caused fatal paralysis. And—my stomach knotted like a three-peg weaving at the thought—the Kahlareans were obsessed with killing the Restorer. I wasn't eager for *anyone* to find out I was the new Restorer, least of all the people who still held a grudge against Mikkel, the Restorer who saved our people from Kahlarean attack a generation ago.

With a deep breath and another scan of the area, I continued upriver at a quicker pace.

The foul smell in the air was my first warning that something very bad had happened. I edged my way toward the outpost, waiting to be challenged by one of the handful of guardians assigned this patrol. Although some were young, the guardians tended to be fairly well trained and should have been watching their perimeter. A droning sound buzzed through the air as I drew closer to the clearing near the pass. Using a large tree for cover, I peered into the open area. Three men sprawled on the ground in front of the outpost's hut. The low hum was caused by swarms of insects feasting on their dead bodies.

I ran forward and crouched by one of the still forms. No need to look for signs of life. They'd been dead several days. All three showed the charred marks of syncbeam blasts. One boy hadn't even had a chance to draw his sword.

Kahlareans. How many had slipped through the pass after

killing the guardians? Was this the first wave of a full-fledged invasion, or were they clearing the way for another small group of assassins to make their way toward Lyric, hunting the Restorer?

Crunching footsteps startled me. I stood and swiveled my head, but too late. Three Kahlarean soldiers entered the clearing. I took a few slow steps back, thinking fast.

"You're late," one of the men growled. Like most Kahlareans, his huge black eyes and sunken chin reminded me of a cave insect. His skin was the unnatural white of a corpse. These soldiers weren't hooded or masked, and they'd stopped long enough to talk, so they weren't assassins. So far, so good.

I shrugged. "Look's like there's been some trouble."

The soldier laughed. "No trouble at all, thanks to your syncbeams. So where is the next delivery?"

I rubbed my jaw. The Kahlareans had gotten their syncbeams from Hazor—from Hazorites with short black hair and angled features. I could work with that.

"Well, there's been a problem." I stalled, scrambling for inspiration. I could pretend to be from Hazor, but I couldn't produce a non-existent delivery of syncbeams.

The soldier drew his sword and stepped closer. My hand tightened over my hilt, but I didn't draw.

"We don't have time for games." He kicked one of the bodies. "They could be sending reinforcements any time."

Show no fear. Show no repulsion. I decided to try for irritation. "Don't you get any news out here? Our armies took a beating at Morsal Plains. Hundreds of our own syncbeams were destroyed. We don't have any to spare right now."

The soldier tilted his head and rolled his bulbous eyes in my direction. "Then what are you doing here?"

"Just making a friendly visit to let you know we're working on it. I can set up a new delivery time and bring word back to Sidian in Hazor."

The Kahlarean shook his head. "Too risky. We're across now. Who knows how many more guardians will be sent here in a few days' time?"

I shrugged. Not my problem.

The Kahlarean stepped closer and grabbed the front of my tunic, his sword close enough to my belt to force me to suck in my stomach. It had just become my problem.

I lifted my hands away from my sword. "Relax. I'm sure we can work something out."

"I'll tell you what we'll work out," said the soldier. "You'll escort a group of us back to Sidian right now to collect the delivery."

I laughed, but regretted it when he twisted the fistful of tunic under my neck, all but cutting off my air.

"You can't travel through the clans," I said. "You'd be spotted the first time we tried to use a transport. And if we cut cross-country, it would take half a season."

"Not us," he said. "Them." He let go of me, and I stumbled back. Three figures had melted into the clearing. They wore gray hoods, and their faces were covered with cloth masks. Assassins.

Caradung, I cursed silently.

"Them?" I said. "Why would they want to go on a trade mission?" Even a weapons trader from Hazor would know that Kahlarean assassins were an elite group. They were the villains in the tales told around glowing heat trivets on cold nights—with good reason.

The soldier grinned. "They have a few things to take care

of on the way, but that doesn't need to concern you. They'll have no trouble blending in. You"—he jabbed a fat finger into my chest—"get them to Sidian."

This would be a great time for some special Restorer vision to give me a plan. I wasted a few seconds waiting. Nothing. I shifted my gaze from the assassins back to the soldier.

I could draw my sword. I might have a chance against the three soldiers, but how many heartbeats would it take for an assassin's dagger to fly through the air and lodge in my chest? I'd recover, but that would be even worse. Then they'd know exactly what I was. I shrugged and willed my coiled muscles to relax.

"All right. If they can keep up. I don't have time to waste in the clan territories."

The tallest of the three assassins walked toward me on feet that didn't make a sound. His large eyes looked into mine.

I hoped that with all their other talents they couldn't read minds.

Finally, he nodded once.

I started breathing again while sweat ran down my back. "When do you want to leave?"

The two other assassins looked at each other. The tall one in front of me gestured with his arm toward the edge of the clearing. I caught a glimpse of metal strapped to his wrist when his sleeve moved. A venblade. One of a host of silent and hidden weapons I knew he carried.

I needed to get word to Tristan about the outpost attack. I needed to get as far from these assassins as I could. I needed a drink—something stronger than orberry juice.

Instead, I turned and led the way into the woods, my skin crawling at the thought of the three silent figures following me.

About the Author

SHARON HINCK is a wife and mother who has had many adventures on her road with God, though none have involved an alternate universe (thus far). She earned an M.A. in Communication from Regent University in 1986 and spent ten years as the artistic director of a Christian performing arts group, CrossCurrent. That ministry included three short-term mission trips to Hong Kong. At various times she has been a church youth worker, a choreographer and ballet teacher, a homeschool mom, a church organist, and a freelance writer. She is the author of *The Secret Life of Becky Miller* (Bethany House, 2006) and *Renovating Becky Miller* (Bethany House, 2007) as well as numerous non-fiction articles, devotions, and essays. She loves to hear from readers, so send a message through the portal into her writing attic on the "contact Sharon" page of her website: www.sharonhinck .com.

MORE INTRIGUING BOOKS FROM THE NAVPRESS FICTION LINE.

Demon

Tosca Lee ISBN-13: 978-1-60006-123-3
       ISBN-10: 1-60006-123-0

Clayton, a book editor, has just been hired to author a once-in-a-lifetime memoir. The subject is Lucian, a demon with an extraordinary story to share. As he begins to find eerie similarities between Lucian's otherworldly life and his own, Clay reaches a devastating conclusion: He is writing his own life story. After stumbling onto the revelation that his life is nearing its end, Clay will be forced to make a choice.

The Return

Austin Boyd ISBN-13: 978-1-57683-946-1
       ISBN-10: 1-57683-946-X

While John begins to uncover a web of lies on Mars, his wife and daughter are struggling for survival on earth. Now John must survive his dangerous mission and find a way back home, even as a shocking plan begins to unfold millions of miles away on earth.

Chateau of Echoes

Siri Mitchell ISBN-13: 978-1-57683-914-0
       ISBN-10: 1-57683-914-1

When an extensive, painstaking restoration of the chateau reveals an ancient treasure, Frédérique Farmer kisses her reclusive life good-bye. She opens an exclusive bed-and-breakfast, hires a capricious graduate student, and gets talked into hosting a handsome American for an extended stay. Little does the gourmand know, she's unwittingly concocted a recipe for intrigue, romance, and possibly disaster.

To order copies, visit your local Christian bookstore, call NavPress at 1-800-366-7788, or log on to www.navpress.com.
To locate a Christian bookstore near you, call 1-800-991-7747.

NAVPRESS®
BRINGING TRUTH TO LIFE
www.navpress.com